An Orphan's
Song

BOOKS BY LIZZIE PAGE

Lizzie Page

An Orphan's Song

bookouture

Published by Bookouture in 2022

An imprint of Storyfire Ltd.
Carmelite House
50 Victoria Embankment
London EC4Y 0DZ

www.bookouture.com

ISBN: 978-1-80314-536-5
eBook ISBN: 978-1-80314-535-8

This book is a work of fiction. Whilst some characters and circumstances portrayed by the author are based on real people and historical fact, references to real people, events, establishments, organizations or locales are intended only to provide a sense of authenticity and are used fictitiously. All other characters and all incidents and dialogue are drawn from the author's imagination and are not to be construed as real.

To Charlie and Oliver

Who ran to help me when I fell,
    And would some pretty story tell,
    Or kiss the place to make it well?
    My Mother.

Ann Taylor

Something jolly... something to give Britain a lift.

Herbert Morrison

1

JANUARY 1951

Suffolk

They were lucky with the weather on the day of the wedding. The week before it had been typical January: grey skies and a never-ending drizzle; but that Saturday from early in the morning the sky was Royal Air Force blue and the sun was beating down. It felt like a sign.

It meant that Clara, housemother of the Michael Adams Children's Home, could go back to her original plans and wear the tweed twin-piece, and the children could wear their dresses or shirts and trousers. And she needn't worry about raincoats and umbrellas, which were the last thing you wanted to worry about at a wedding (especially at a wedding you had mixed feelings about).

Sister Grace came by to watch the children in the morning. Clara wouldn't usually have called on her, since between them the two oldest children, Peter, sixteen, and Maureen, fifteen, could keep an eye out, but thirteen-year-old Clifford had only been at the Home for a few weeks, and it didn't seem fair to leave them unsupervised, so Sister Grace it was. And Sister Grace insisted Clara go to Beryl's Brushes to get her hair done.

Everything about the wedding was last-minute. The invitations had only gone out at Christmas. They had only one week to RSVP. Clara had said yes on behalf of Joyce, but Joyce had gone to live with her new adoptive family in Letchworth; and Clara hadn't said yes on behalf of Peter – she thought Peter would have gone to start his job in London – but Peter was not off until next Tuesday. She hadn't accepted on behalf of Clifford either, but the bride-to-be, Miss Bridges, said, 'Goodness gracious, Clara, I would always find a place for you and the children.'

Miss Bridges was less forthcoming when Clara asked her what the rush was to get married. Was it Clara's fault there was no way of phrasing this that didn't sound like a dig?

'I've waited most of my life for this,' Miss Bridges said. 'I don't see why I should wait any longer.' Miss Bridges worked at the council – she was part-time children's officer and part-time cemeteries. Clara had been at the council-run Home for two and a half years, and while at first reluctant, she was now proud of the fact that her home was regarded as the best-run in Suffolk. She was also very fond of Miss Bridges, who had helped her so much – although she was rather less fond of the groom, Mr Horton, children's care inspector.

At the church, the sun streamed through the stained-glass windows. Clara had gazed up at the Last Supper in its brilliant colours and thought of the thousands, perhaps hundreds of thousands, of people who had sat here before her. Today, for the wedding, there were several of Miss Bridges' colleagues from the council, people from Mr Horton's bowls club, and Mr Horton's elderly mother and her friends. And there was Miss Cooper wearing one of her fantastic trouser suits and as ever, looking more like Ingrid Bergman than a full-time children's officer. Miss Cooper greeted her, and Clara was glad to sit next to her on the pew because, even if Miss Cooper did outshine everyone, most of the guests were in comforting twos and she wasn't. The children took up most of the pew in front. Clifford immediately started fiddling with his Bible and his velvet cushion, but the other children sat nicely, which was a relief, because in those two and a half years Clara had been in Suffolk she had only brought the children to church a handful of times. Her own father would be horrified if he knew.

'Clifford,' she whispered, poking the back of his neck. 'Stop it.' To his credit he did.

Clara looked around for her neighbour Ivor but couldn't see him anywhere. She knew he'd had an invitation because Maureen had told her he was *definitely* coming, and Rita somehow knew that he had a new tie for the occasion and Peg said (or rather, wrote, for Peg didn't speak) he was going to give Miss Bridges and Mr Horton an eiderdown as a wedding gift and that it was beautiful.

It wasn't like Ivor to be late, and Clara felt impatient for him to arrive. The last few months had been awkward. It felt like a wall had gone up between them. Last summer, Ivor had taken on his ex-wife's baby. Clara was – hard to put a finger on it – jealous but not jealous exactly, hurt but not hurt; confused maybe, so she had concentrated on her own thing. It wasn't like she didn't have lots of things to do running the Children's Home. Just as Ivor was dashing around, getting used to baby Patricia, getting baby Patricia used to him, Clara was doing much the same with the children in her care.

Then Stella the cat had got sick – too much tripe? The children would drop it from the table when they thought Clara wasn't looking – and because Clara was running around with the cat (three vet appointments in one week – not cheap!), Clara hadn't caught on quickly enough that Peter was sick too, or that it was chickenpox. And just when he was looking better, Rita came down with it, then just as they were out of the water with Rita, it was Peg's turn and Peg was scratchy all over and laid up for two whole weeks with it. And of course, Clara didn't want any of them to give it to baby Patricia. Ivor would have hit the roof. So that was November and most of December gone. Clara, Ivor and Miss Bridges had spent Christmas Day together, which would have been glorious, had not baby Patricia cried virtually the entire time, and once the crackers had been pulled, there was simply no consoling her, confirming Clara's opinion that she and babies did not mix.

And after that, Clifford had arrived, and she had been busy settling him in, and on his second day, the poor boy went down with chickenpox too, and he had only just recovered really, and since then Clara hadn't spent any time with Ivor at all. She had seen him put out the rubbish, bring in the milk, and she had once handed him a parcel, but she hadn't seen him *properly*. Had it only been three weeks? It felt like much longer.

Recently, Clara had read an article in *Woman's Own* with the usual bad news statistics, but even these were more depressing than the usual. Something about how, since the war, there were twice as many women of marriageable age as men in Britain. You were more likely to find a needle in a haystack – no, a needle in a haystack in darkest Peru – than you were to get an eligible bachelor interested in you. Despite those terrible odds, Clara had been daydreaming about Miss Bridges' wedding, quite possibly as much as Miss Bridges herself. Things *happened* at weddings. Everyone knew that. People got a bit dizzy, a bit romantic – magic in the air, love in the diary. As *Woman's Own* resident Agony Aunt said: *'There is no better opportunity to throw your cap at someone than a wedding...'*

Ivor would be wearing his Sunday best. Clara didn't need to daydream about that! She knew he looked fine in it. He'd probably be holding baby Patricia in the crook of his good arm. Patricia would be smiling, for once – she really was not a smiley baby – and Ivor would have that half-shy, half-humorous expression she liked so much. He'd meet her eyes and she would say, 'Oh, hello, Ivor,' in a surprised tone like she hadn't been expecting him. And then when Miss Bridges and Mr Horton took their vows, Ivor would take her hand between his, look her in the eyes and say—

'Is anyone sitting here?' It was Mr and Mrs Garrard, the local florists, both of them done up to the nines. He with his fancy waistcoat stretching over his paunch and his pocket watch shining, her in a pleated dress and hat and lipstick. Clara reluctantly gave up the seat she had mentally reserved for Ivor and shoved up even closer to Miss Cooper.

'No Bertie today?' Clara asked to be friendly; she wasn't actually interested in their yappy dog.

'Chewing the banisters at home probably,' Mrs Garrard said. 'He hates being alone.'

Et tu, Bertie?, thought Clara. Although she herself would never stoop to banister-chewing.

And then Miss Bridges arrived, and the church door was slammed shut behind her. No latecomers, they'd said that on the invitation. Perhaps it was a good thing that Ivor hadn't turned up, Clara decided, since her hair was still rather pungent and probably highly flammable after her appointment. Beryl at Beryl's Brushes always said it took time for a do to relax. *I also need to relax*, Clara told herself. What was the matter with her today? Her first friend in Lavenham, her *best* friend, getting married should be a simple happy affair, yet she was feeling horribly antsy. *It's not about you*, she told herself crossly. But her heart was beating faster than it should be. Everyone knew romance was contagious as chickenpox. Where *was* Ivor?

Miss Bridges, who had worried so much about walking down the aisle on her own – *should she, shouldn't she?* – now walked down the centre of the church by herself, looking carefree and glorious. She was wearing a calf-length beige dress – at fifty-four she claimed she was too old for white – and she was radiant. In a pillbox hat – also beige, with a veil to the nose – she peered into each of the rows and smiled, waving at the children. She was holding a bunch of healthy-looking hyacinths (Mrs Garrard whispered proudly that she had supplied them), and she didn't look nervous any more, even though when Clara had seen her on the high road yesterday, darting between errands, she said she was having palpitations and organising a wedding was 'worse than arranging an adoption. Honestly, Clara, the details!'

She gave Clara such a warm smile that Clara felt tears prick her eyes. What was it about weddings that made you cry more than funerals? Perhaps it was hope that made the difference.

Here was Miss Bridges full of hope.

Clara gazed at the back door again.

Nothing. Nada.

They went to the nearby Cloth Hall afterwards and Ivor wasn't there either. Should Clara go over and check everything was all right, or perhaps send one of the children to find out?

Or was that none of her business?

It was a proper sit-down affair. The Hortons had made the hall so pretty some of the arriving guests gasped when they saw it. There were tablecloths (from Ivor!) and bunting (provided by the postmistress) and shiny glasses and gleaming plates. There was one long line of seats, about six tables joined together, down the length of the room, and then another table going across, making a T-shape. And then there was a table for the five children from the Home at the back. Miss Bridges believed firmly that children should know their place. These seating arrangements were both good and bad. Good because they meant Clara could enjoy the company of adults without her charges' interference, bad because you never quite knew what the children would get up to by themselves. Indeed, before long, Peg and Rita were giggling over something unwelcome on Peg's plate, and Clara could see Maureen, who hated being with 'the little ones', had a face like thunder. Clifford, the new boy, was working at his head – was it nits now? – and then he was scratching his scabs too. 'Stop scratching,' she mouthed at him, and he mouthed back something like, 'I'm not.' Or perhaps 'I can't help it.' Peter was just tucking into his food, getting on with it like Peter always did.

Clara was seated next to Miss Cooper again, and some other women from Suffolk Council. Clara saw there were no other housemothers or foster carers there. A children's officer's close friendship with a housemother was quite the anomaly and Clara was proud of that. A woman at the table with straight mousy hair and a big flowery hairclip leaned forward and said, 'We're the unmarried table,' and the rest of them laughed. 'The unmarriageable, more like!' said another woman and they laughed again. Gazing around, Clara realised that the other tables were indeed mostly made up of couples. She wondered where Ivor would have sat if he had come. Well, he was too late now.

She and Miss Cooper didn't have an awful lot in common, and once they'd discussed the service, the radiance of the bride and the decor, there wasn't much to talk about, but she asked Miss Cooper if she'd been to any Labour Party meetings lately (she had) and Miss Cooper did ask after the children.

'How's the new boy getting on?'

Clara glanced over at Clifford, who had stuck his serviette on his head and his tongue out. He seemed to be peeling back his eyelids.

'CLIFFORD!' hissed Clara.

Clifford ignored her.

'PETER!' She gestured to Clifford and Peter obligingly

nudged him. Clifford thumped his head down on the table, then pretended to go to sleep.

Clara returned her attention to Miss Cooper. 'He's a character!' she said.

Patience. Tolerance. Affection. Consistency. Some children took longer to settle in than others, but Clara was sure it wouldn't take too long. They were all nice kids, underneath.

'He certainly is,' Miss Cooper said.

'I do need his files though,' Clara added, trying to make her voice sound light even though this had been weighing on her for some time. 'It's been weeks now, Miss Cooper. It's essential to have background information. I've asked several times.'

'Fine,' Miss Cooper said, turning her attention back to the more important question of the sandwiches. 'Is it margarine or have they got butter?'

Clara loved just about any food that she had not prepared herself, but even so the sandwiches were delicious. She downed a second glass of sherry and then dug into the trifle, also sherry and delicious. Mr Horton's elderly mother and friends had collated their coupons to provide a truly bumper feast.

Mr Sommersby, head of children's services, tapped his glass with a teaspoon for quiet. Clara whispered, 'What's he giving a speech for?' but Miss Cooper scowled. She didn't answer but made her expression full of rapt attention. Mr Sommersby tried to make it sound like love was always blossoming in the workplace at Suffolk Council, but this was the first Clara had heard of it. He said the Hortons were two of the finest staff members there ever were and if they worked as hard at their marriage as they did in children's services, they'd make a formidable job of it. Then he looked across the tables and chuckled.

'I'm not saying that marriage is hard work. No, not at all – Mrs Sommersby will vouch for that!'

And everyone's eyes, naturally, went to Mr Sommersby's wife, who was wearing a sunflower coloured dress, which was pretty but clashed with her desperately scarlet cheeks. Clara had never met Mrs Sommersby and had on occasion doubted she even existed. But she looked a thoroughly nice and normal woman, which surprised Clara. She nudged Miss Cooper. 'I had no idea he had such good taste.'

Again, Miss Cooper ignored her.

Then Mr Sommersby said, 'Seriously now,' and everyone quietened. He said the children in Suffolk had been lucky to be in their safe hands. He said he hoped the new Mrs Horton would consider continuing at the council post-marriage. She was always welcome. This made Clara squirm, for she was certain her friend had no intention of giving up her post. It was misjudged of him to suggest publicly she might. Was this Mr Horton's idea? She wouldn't put it past him.

Then the groom himself, Mr Horton, stood up while the new Mrs Horton fanned her collarbone. Mr Horton's mother, Ada, was the other side of him, sipping from a teacup. Mrs Horton had told Clara that she had a face that could sour milk, but that was putting it kindly. Over the last few weeks, the new Mrs Horton had talked to Clara about Mr Horton: Mr Horton was not a bad man. He was not a drunk, he was not unfaithful, he was not a bully. He was not lazy and he was not violent. *What is he?*, Clara wondered. Well, she was about to find out.

As he spoke, Clara tried not to warm to him, but it was hard. He was truly besotted – he was glowing, dizzy, he was a man in love. He said that Mrs Horton – 'My dear Emily' – had changed his life. He said he would do anything to make her happy. At this, Mr Horton's mother slammed down her cup, rose trembling to her feet and left the room noisily. Mr Horton pulled a face and then said, 'On that note, let the dancing begin,' which Clara was surprised at – she had hoped Mrs Horton was going to speak. It was normal of course that she didn't – brides hardly ever did – but it felt funny too, because Mrs Horton was usually such a chatterbox, and it was unlike her to allow convention to muzzle her.

The band were the ones Clara and her ex-fiancé Julian White had had many moons ago, for their engagement party. Back then they were called Harry and Swingtime. Now they were the Beats. The chairs and the tables were pushed to the side of the room to create a dancing space and Clara was proud that the children joined in to help without being asked.

As soon as the band struck up, Julian came weaselling over, eyebrows going up and down, and asked her to dance. When Clara had asked Mrs Horton why she was inviting Julian, with whom she had an awkward relationship, Mrs Horton had grimaced and said she hadn't. It was Mr Horton's doing. He was inviting everyone from his club, which included Mr Julian White as well as his partners in his law firm, Robinson, Browne and White. At least the other two were nowhere to be seen. Young Maureen had been involved with the married Mr Browne only a few months previously, and it had taken a lot of guile for Clara to detangle them.

'Only a dance,' Clara said to Julian and then felt embarrassed when he laughed. 'Good Lord, Clara, I wasn't planning on eating you.'

'I know,' she said. He always made her so clumsy with her words, and it was annoying because he assumed it was because she still had designs on him. 'I'm just making sure you don't get the wrong idea.'

This amused him too.

She didn't particularly want to dance with Julian. But the children were watching, and it was important to let them know that adults can have good times too, otherwise they would think growing up was a hundred per cent chores (which it did feel like sometimes). And dancing was one of Julian's many talents and somehow, he turned you into a better dancer than you usually were. He guided Clara around the floor so that she had no choice, where to put her feet. He twirled her firmly, once to 'In the Mood' and then to 'The Way You Look Tonight'.

She was reminded of dancing with her Michael, long ago. That *was* their thing. That was how they'd got to know each other: got to understand each other's bodies, the way they moved, their scent. Michael had been her first love. He was an American pilot based in Suffolk, she was in essential war work at Harris & Sons in London. Even when lifestyle, culture or accents differed, out there on the dance floor they were the same.

With Julian, it was more a matter of fending him off. He was tipsy and when he was tipsy, he got frisky.

Peter and his friend Mabel were doing some modern dance, which involved making duck signs with their hands. Clara wondered where young people picked these things up, then laughed quietly. Oof, she was sounding old even to herself. It was always lovely to see Peter looking exuberant, especially after the time he'd had over the last few years.

If Ivor did turn up, Clara decided she would generously offer to hold baby Patricia so that he could dance with someone, preferably someone very old like Mrs Horton senior or very young, like Peg, and just hope that would inspire someone else to offer to hold the baby – and then she and Ivor could dance together. Clara had never danced with Ivor before and this suddenly seemed very important to her – in fact, another sign, although not a good one in this case. The fact that he didn't have an arm didn't have to be a problem, she thought, Ivor was well adjusted, but would he feel awkward?

Maureen had Peg perched on one knee and was playing a clapping game with Rita when Joe Matthews, Maureen's ex-beau, came along. Maureen had dumped Joe last year and Clara had heard Joe was seeing another girl, but tonight he made a beeline for Maureen. *Maybe not any more*, pondered Clara. Even from across the room, Clara saw Maureen's little face light up at the sight of him, and Clara wanted to warn her, 'Hey, don't make your feelings too obvious.' Not that she could talk! *Where on earth was Ivor?* Not getting dizzy or romantic, that was for sure. Clara felt snubbed. She reminded herself that it wasn't she who Ivor had snubbed but the Hortons, but she still felt as if he had snubbed her. He must surely have some idea how much she wanted him to be there?

Maureen and Joe danced together, a faster dance, and the older couples backed off and clapped, although some of the friends of Mrs Horton looked disapproving, because hadn't their coupons paid for this?

When the Beats said, 'Ten minutes to rest your weary feet, ladies and gents', Clara went out the back for some air. Standing outside under the fire escape, there was not much of a moon and the dark sky was full of darker cloud. The Beats' trumpeter came out and offered her a cigarette. She accepted, almost knocking the hat off his head as she leaned in for the light. He was a nice-looking man, not a patch on Ivor, of course, but the suit with the bow tie looked good. The sherry had made her head spin a little. They'd only been small glasses, but the trifle had been pretty lethal too and she wasn't a drinker usually. And Ivor had snubbed her, no doubt about it.

In England, there are twice as many women of marriageable age as there are men...

'I remember you,' the trumpeter said as he blew impressive smoke rings. 'We played your engagement party here, two years ago, right? You didn't want us for your wedding, then?'

Clara smiled at him. 'Oh, we would have... only, we split up.'

He grinned like a fox. He had good teeth and he knew it. 'You were too good for him, I bet.' He moved closer to her. The rest of the world became smaller as he grew larger.

The back door was opening. The lead singer of the Beats –
Harry? – poked his head around it.

'Your missus is wondering where you are,' he said sternly to
the trumpeter.

The trumpeter shrugged and then followed the lead singer
inside. Clara waited a few minutes, then threw down her
cigarette and went back inside too. Sometimes she was so lonely
that she near forgot herself, although she never quite did. The
short exchange had made her uneasy. Both men seemed to have
formed an impression of her that didn't feel right.

The children were still dancing. Peg had lifted up her petticoat
and was whirling around, making Rita laugh. Maureen and Joe
were holding on to each other. The groom's mother had been
carted off home apparently – a touch of the vapours. Mr Horton
didn't look worried though; he was clutching Mrs Horton
amorously in the middle of the room. The way he looked at his
bride made Clara feel wistful. She told herself there was a time
for everything – she just had to wait.

'Thank goodness I found you!' Clara's friend Anita interrupted her thoughts. 'We need to talk.'

No one there looked as put-together as Anita Cardew, not
even Miss Cooper. Anita was in a slim-fitting skirt suit, royal
blue, with a crisp white blouse. Everything about her was
impeccable and she made Clara feel like a scarecrow with her
flushed cheeks and flyaway hair. Why had Clara had so much
trifle? It swilled around her stomach. Anita hadn't been at the
church service; she had just popped in to give her best wishes to
the Hortons while Dr Cardew and their adopted daughter
Evelyn were looking after baby Howard. Evelyn used to be one
of Clara's girls at the Home and was practical, resourceful and
kind. Clara thought it a shame that Evelyn hadn't come with
Anita, but Evelyn tended to prefer to stay at home.

'What do we need to talk about, Anita?' Clara ventured nervously because she suspected what it was about.

'The Festival!' Anita had to shout to be heard over the Beats' upbeat version of 'Galway Bay' but she didn't have to shout *that* loud.

'We're at a wedding, Anita,' Clara responded irritably. 'Can't it wait?'

The Festival of Britain was a national celebration happening in May – it was mostly going to be in London, but other areas including Suffolk were participating too. Anita wanted the children to sing – and Rita to play the piano – at one of the Festival shows and she had written the music herself. She had signed them up months ago and had paid the small entrance fee. If they got through the audition – only four weeks away – they would go on to perform at the Hippodrome in Ipswich in April as part of Suffolk's contribution.

Apparently, it couldn't wait. As Anita went on about the Festival and 'time was running out' and 'we all need to step up', Clara bristled with annoyance. First of all, the whole scheme irked her. What was the nation supposed to be celebrating exactly? The fact they hadn't died in the war? Well, yes, but so many had. Clara thought it was an indecent waste of time and money. They still had hardly enough to eat – they were down to one egg per person per week these days – everything was grey and grotty and now they were expected to pretend everything was *la-di-da*. To what end?

And the other thing that annoyed her was Anita's attitude. She seemed to think Clara should simply get in line. *We* need to step up? Anita didn't understand the work things like this entailed. There would be so much more running around to do, and who would that fall to? Not Anita – with her devoted husband, inexhaustible nanny and pliant adopted daughter – but she, Clara. It was like taking on a whole extra child. Perhaps if Anita hadn't been quite so absorbed by the Festival, Clara might also have been caught up in the excitement, but it was as though there was only room for one of them and Anita had taken that spot.

'We could really do with more bodies. I mean, it's supposed to be "the Children of Shilling Grange Orphanage" – that's what I put down—'

'The children from the *Michael Adams Children's Home*, you mean,' corrected Clara.

Anita ignored her.

'Now that Peter's going, we'll be down to four, and Evelyn doesn't even live there any more and Peg doesn't sing, so...'

'Well?' Clara shrugged, thinking Peter was making a lucky escape. 'What do you propose? I can't just pull extra children out of a hat.'

But there is Clifford, she thought. She watched him now, leaning against the wall, his cap pulled low. He probably wouldn't be what Anita would want and he probably wouldn't want to do it either.

'How about you?' Anita said. 'It would be sweet, the house-mother joining in.'

'No!' said Clara firmly. 'Good grief, Anita. Even if I wanted to – and I don't – I have an awful voice, we don't want to scare anyone off.'

Anita laughed. 'After a few sessions with me, even toads sound like angels.'

'Not this toad... and if you don't stop going on about it, I won't let the children do the audition at all.'

It was a false threat. Rita would be absolutely crushed if it didn't happen. Like Anita, she spoke of little else.

'Galway Bay' came to a gentle end and Anita clapped loudly. 'Bravo!' Then she turned to Clara and grimaced. 'Rita plays better than the lot of them.'

Clara laughed and hoped no one else heard. Just as Clara

thought she had got away with it, Anita started up again. She was obsessed.

'The other thing is, what were you thinking they would wear?'

'School uniforms?' Clara answered lamely. She hadn't thought much further than the council's refusal to budget for clothes as it was, never mind *costumes*.

'You don't mind asking Ivor, do you, if he would do something for it? It's his kind of thing, after all.'

Clara didn't respond. On the one hand, she didn't want to impose on her favourite neighbour. And she was not Anita's festival lapdog, thank you very much. On the other, wouldn't it be a great excuse to talk to him?

At eight o'clock the happy couple made to leave and everyone gathered at the front steps of the Cloth Hall to see them off. The Hortons bounced ahead to the car, which was done out in tin cans, bows, ribbons and crêpe paper. They were driving to the station and taking the train to stay in a hotel in London that night, before going north tomorrow. Mrs Horton was so proud of Mr Horton's planning: 'He doesn't leave anything to chance.'

At the car, Mrs Horton turned back, smiling shyly. At first, Clara thought she was finally going to make a speech, but instead she brandished her flower bouquet in front of her like a weapon, and everyone cheered. Then, underarm, she threw it right towards Clara.

Clara caught it. She didn't have much choice. It wasn't deliberate, it was an instinct, like cupping your hands when a child was throwing up or sneezing at Stella, or even like racing out to the garden to unpeg the washing when a particularly ominous cloud was hovering over.

All the guests turned to look at her. It felt like everyone was laughing and shouting at once. Within eyeshot, Maureen was sniggering and Peter and his friend Mabel were kissing (yes, they *were* more than friends!).

Mrs Garrard sidled closer. 'Why doesn't that surprise me?'

Of course, Rita had to spell it out for everyone. 'Miss Newton, you'll be the next person married!' she yelled.

'Ha ha,' said Clara and then, 'Ho!'

The bouquet in her hands wasn't like a child's sick, it was so pretty, it was little stalks and tiny leaves, and tiny little prickles. It smelled of morning in the garden. Tears came to her eyes. *Sentimental old fool.* That moment was the only time that day when she was really glad Ivor wasn't there. She couldn't have borne it if he'd looked at her pityingly.

'Still making sure I don't get the wrong idea?' Julian had sidled up to her. 'Just say the word, sweetheart.'

'Ha.'

That night, the children were as slippery as Julian. One moment they were in front of Clara, pleading for more orange squash, the next they were gone. They were playing hide-and-seek and annoying both the bowls crowd and Mrs Horton senior's friends.

'Of course, the Hortons have got a thing about helping disaffected youth,' Clara heard one say. 'But still – letting them run riot at your own wedding?'

By ten o'clock, Clara was weary of socialising, and apologising. It had been a long day and as the sherry wore off, her head was beginning to thrum. Had Ivor snubbed her or not? It was difficult to tell. The Beats trumpeter kept winking at her and then making regretful *what-can-I-do?* faces. By contrast, the lead singer was scowling at her, and she wanted to go over to him and say, *I've done nothing wrong,* but he clearly had her marked down as a scarlet lady. Mr and Mrs Horton would be in London by now, presumably, ensconced in the three-star hotel that Mr Horton had picked because it was only five minutes from the station and 'who wants to travel on their wedding night?' Clara shook her head, appalled. She did not want to think about that.

Everyone had reverted to their own easy-to-be-with groups: council folk, bowls folk, Mr Horton's mother's folk. Clara didn't have her own group – unless you counted the children. She tried again to collect them up. She found Clifford by the back door with a gaggle of local boys. Clara recognised only one – Martin Browne, the local solicitor's son – in the shadows, surly lips, hands in pockets. Out of all the boys, she hoped Clifford wouldn't make friends with him.

Inside, the band were off on a rousing version of 'Chattanooga Choo-Choo'.

'Time to go home, Clifford.'

Dark looks passed between them.

'Party's still happening,' said Martin Browne.

'Not for us,' she said. Many moons ago, Clara had been advised to be firm with children from day one – a piece of advice she had dismissed. She had thought she knew better. She regretted that now although Clifford looked at the boys apologetically and then back at Clara: 'I've had enough anyway.'

As she herded the children back, Clara saw the lights to Ivor's workshop were shining. So, he *was* home.

'You go ahead,' she told Maureen abruptly, giving her the key. 'I'll only be a minute.'

She had an excuse now too, if she needed it.

Ivor let her in. He was wearing just a white vest and his trousers – she had rarely seen him without a shirt on and she had this ridiculous impulse to slip her fingers inside the hem of the vest, where it sat between shoulder and chest. She pulled her eyes away from him and realised the workshop was a shell of its former self. She had loved his workshop before. It had been cosy and colourful. Now there was just one sewing machine on an entirely bare bench. The floor, which used to be full of rolls of material and piles of fabrics, was completely naked. Lots of wooden crates were stacked up to the sides. It felt like she was late to another thing changing.

'Where *is* everything?'

Ivor led her to the back, to the seating area she loved, near the telescope she had once looked up at the stars with. Fortunately, that was all still there. He asked if she wanted a drink and she would have liked one, nothing she'd have liked more, but it wasn't fair to leave Maureen with the children for long, not when Clifford was, as Mrs Horton liked to say, 'an unknown quantity'.

'I wanted to make the workshop safer for Patricia.'

'Oh, of course.'

The baby who spent most of the day horizontal? These changes seemed premature, excessive even, thought Clara, but what did she know? If those who cared for small children seemed to inhabit a different country to her, sometimes it felt as though those who cared for young babies belonged to a different universe.

'It was a wonderful wedding,' she said. 'You couldn't make it along?' She had to know.

'I had planned to come,' he said, then puffed out his cheeks. 'But I was waylaid.'

Ruby's back, Clara thought suddenly. *It must be that.* Ruby – mother of baby Patricia. Ivor's ex-wife. Beautiful, fashionable Ruby. Back without warning, dropping in and destroying like a V_2 rocket.

'The thing is... Patricia's growing out of her bed.'

Oh. Ruby *hadn't* returned, Clara realised, relieved, yet annoyed with herself for jumping to her fears first. The spectre of Ruby's reappearance always haunted her.

Clara looked over at Patricia. Now seven months old, she slept in a massive drawer – one of the largest Clara had ever seen – amid Ivor's best blankets. No child could have asked for better bedding.

Patricia had dark hair and eyebrows. Clara didn't like to think who she'd inherited her looks from. Ivor had told her the baby wasn't his but... but. Clara still found it hard to understand why – if she wasn't – he had taken her on.

'So, I made her a cot.'

He pointed behind a curtain. Clara got up and saw the most exquisite cot, with shapely spindles. Above it hung a sort of drape of lace curtains like a bride's veil, or something from *Sleeping Beauty*.

'Oh, it's so lovely,' breathed Clara. It was a work of art. Ivor was so clever.

He sighed. 'I couldn't get her out.'

'Huh?'

'I managed to get her into the cot, but I couldn't lift her out, not for ages. You know, with my arm. So that was why I didn't come today.'

The image of him trying and trying broke Clara's heart.

'It's easily solved, I just have to make the side drop down. I don't know why I didn't do that in the first place. I was just so pleased it was done, I thought she could try it and...'

'Yes.'

'But...' He paused. 'I felt so useless.'

'You're not useless. Ivor, you're doing brilliantly. Your circumstances are unusual, but we're all here for you.' She wanted to say *I'm* here for you. 'Let me know if there's anything we can do.'

'A new one of these would be nice.' He stroked his upper arm, just above the stump.

'I'm afraid that's something I can't help with. Is it hurting?'

He had never complained about his arm before. Never

mentioned it, and she avoided referring to it too. He always let his sleeve hang over it like a Fireworks Night guy. She wished it didn't, but it still made her tongue-tied. Other people were so easy around these things. It was a fault in her.

'A bit.'

'Can I look?' she asked. He looked horrified. 'Just to see if it's infected, Ivor.'

'No.' He said it so sharply, she backed off. Ivor didn't lose his temper often, but when he did...

'I'm only trying to—'

'—Help. I know, Clara. That's all you ever want to do.'

Clara stood uselessly. That wasn't all she ever wanted to do, but she wasn't going to tell him that.

'I don't want anyone's help,' he continued as though he was talking to himself. 'Especially not yours. I can do this.'

He went to his bench and sat behind his machine. 'I'd better get on with some orders before Madam wakes up for her next feed. I'm just feeling sorry for myself, Clara. Forget it.'

'It's going to be fine, Ivor...' She still hadn't asked him about the children's audition outfits. She couldn't bring herself to.

'I know.'

Sundays were much quieter these days without the twins Billy and Barry bashing each other around the head or Alex reciting Shelley's 'Ozymandias'. Billy and Barry had gone to live with their Uncle Stan and Aunt Ruth in Highbury. They played football in the streets there, and in the fields and the stadium, seven days a week. Alex was enjoying a rather more sedate existence with his best friend Bernard and Bernard's father Victor and Victor's sister in Oxford. (Clara and Victor had had a short-lived relationship last year before Victor had decided that they would be better off as friends.)

Peg sat at the kitchen table and wrote a long letter to her new teacher, Miss Fisher. Rita practised piano in the shed for most of the day. Clara didn't even realise Clifford had gone out until he appeared late afternoon, his hair mysteriously damp and his trousers mysteriously covered in mud. It was good he was making friends, thought Clara, but she hoped it wasn't Martin Browne again. Peter was out with Mabel – he was leaving on Tuesday to start his new job creating comics at a magazine publishing company in London, so he and Mabel were spending every last moment together.

On Sundays the children expected more food at lunchtime, so in the evening they had less. Clara prepared a vegetable stew with mash. Like everything, cooking took confidence and practice. Nowadays, she had the confidence and the practice, but she still did not love it and she tried to shrink food preparation to take up as little a part of her day as possible (and even that was too much). Peg, Maureen and Peter usually helped with chopping vegetables. Clifford and Rita did too, if they were there.

Anita loved cooking for others, and sometimes she sent Evelyn over with a pot of left-over cassoulet. And Mrs Horton enjoyed baking, although now that she had Mr Horton to cater for, Clara doubted there would be as many cakes as before.

Clara didn't like doing the laundry much either, but it was the putting away that irked her most. The children were meant to do theirs themselves, but somehow, left to them, the clothes never found their way into the right cupboards or drawers.

Clara liked filing, building and updating the children's records – Maureen's was now over six pages long, while Peg's was a *War and Peace*. She told herself she must remember to call the council on Monday about Clifford's missing file. Partly these records were for the council and for future families – but partly they were for herself. There was something about putting information about the children on the page that felt like wrapping them up in cotton wool. If cooking made Clara feel like she was failing at her job, keeping records made her feel like she was doing brilliantly. She kept all the children's files locked up in a safe. When Maureen had got hold of hers last year and read it, it had been a disaster – Clara often wondered if Maureen would ever forget some of the shocking things she had read there. Clara never would.

. . .

That Sunday afternoon, Clara took Peg and Rita for a walk – and while they were out, they saw Maureen and ex-boyfriend Joe ahead of them on the high road, their hands not quite but almost touching.

'Hello, Joe!' Clara called gaily, for she was fond of the young man and had been sad when they split up. Rita and Peg gaped at them both, open-mouthed.

Joe coloured, touched his cap. 'Hello, Miss Newton, girls.' He looked even more shifty than he usually did.

Maureen was holding Clara's picnic basket, the basket that she had *not* asked to borrow. Clara didn't want to show her up in front of Joe, but she bristled. Maureen had no respect for her property.

'Does she love Joe again?' Rita asked, once they'd moved off. Peg nodded and puckered up her lips.

'I don't know,' mused Clara, thinking of her borrowed basket. 'Stop kissing the air, Peg.'

'They're on and off, aren't they?' Rita said. She sometimes spoke like a grown woman, other times like a small child. 'Like you and Ivor.'

'Not like Ivor and me at all,' said Clara haughtily. 'And this is adult stuff, Rita, not for you, thank you. I think we'll turn back for home now.'

She and Ivor had never been *on*, Clara thought later that evening as she fed the children, cleaned up after the children, told the children to go to bed; yet her mind leapt to him all the time – she didn't *want* to think about him, he just sort of drifted into her consciousness like rain clouds on a sunny day. She could be bleaching tea towels and there he would appear in the dishwater, wearing that vest. She might be swinging her hips to 'In the Mood' and there were his words, 'God knows, I'm crazy about you.' She might be sweeping up the upstairs bedrooms and there he would be, that delicious sensation of his hand on her back.

They had established a détente – a non-combatant pact – but she didn't want just to not fight, she wanted to love him. She had to tread carefully now though. He didn't want her help, that was clear. And so, she would wait until he didn't need it. It didn't suit her nature to wait, but then what was it they said? Madness was trying the same thing over again and expecting change.

One part of her could never understand why Ivor had put himself in this situation. Why had he turned over his life for Ruby's baby? Her head thought more of him because of it: *a good man, a kind responsible man*; but a resentment gnawed at her too. She didn't resent baby Patricia, but she resented Ivor's choice. Everything had changed since Patricia's arrival: he had chosen someone else's baby over them.

Peter was leaving on Tuesday so the next day, Monday, Clara made his favourite leek and potato pie. There weren't enough leeks, but it still went down well. Clara felt quite hollow at the prospect of Peter's departure. Although his move had been planned for a long while, it still felt like things were changing at a dizzying speed. It was an integral part of her job, to support the children and then to let them go, to love them but to not get attached, but still she worried, still she hurt.

After tea, they played Newmarket. Four court cards from another pack of cards were laid down and then another hand was dealt out. The children put matches (instead of money) on one each of the court cards, and one in the kitty (or the 'Lily', as Rita called it). The person who got rid of their cards first was the winner. Clifford was cheating – he didn't declare his cards, and sometimes he dropped them in his lap. Clara said it when she saw it, but she didn't catch him at it again. Anyway, it was

Peter's last night, everyone seemed content, and she didn't want to make a scene. By the end, Clifford had collected all the matches.

Then Peter went out to say goodbye to Mabel, and as the others tidied up the kitchen, Clifford began crowing, 'You're all useless.'

'Clifford, it's only a game.' Clara kept her voice measured, although she was feeling quite cross. This was a side to Clifford she hadn't noticed before.

'And I won it,' he said. 'And everyone else lost.'

Just as the younger children were going to bed, there was a knock on the front door and Ivor was there, in a shirt this time, with braces, holding Patricia in the crook of his arm. Clara's spirits lifted at the sight of him – they always did.

'I came to say goodbye to Peter. It *is* tomorrow, isn't it?'

She thanked him, and while they waited in the kitchen for Peter's return, she screwed up her courage. 'Shall we go for a walk sometime? You can bring Patricia and I'll borrow baby Howard.'

He looked at her, but Clara couldn't read his expression. 'She's teething.'

'Have you tried a bit of whisky?'

'I've tried everything,' Ivor snapped and then apologised, rubbing his cheek. 'Sleepless nights...'

Clara didn't want to ask favours of him, not now. He seemed so downhearted; he had lost his spark, but Anita was on tenterhooks about the Festival – and Anita was her friend too.

'I've got something to ask – well, Anita has. Would you mind making clothes for the children – for their audition? It's for the Festival of Britain thing.'

Ivor knew about the audition, of course. Rita talked of nothing else these days.

He grimaced. 'I'd love to, but I can barely keep up as it is. I just don't have the time anymore – and my arm isn't so great. You do understand, Clara?'

'Absolutely.' She hated to make him feel bad and she could see that it did. 'I'm sorry to have—'

'No, *I'm* sorry. I wish things were different.'

Clara thought for a moment. She knew he'd refuse help from her, but he needed help from someone.

'What about Maureen?' Maureen needed a part-time job since she had left Robinson, Browne and White under a black cloud over the Browne affair, and very soon she would need a full-time job. Clara was certain she'd jump at the chance. 'She could look after the baby after school while you work – not on the costumes, I mean, but on your other stuff?'

'Send her over,' Ivor said, but he looked unconvinced.

And then Peter came home for the last time. He seemed bright and cheerful, although Clara thought his face was slightly puffy. He and Ivor chatted for a bit. Ivor asked about National Service, and Peter said not for another two years, thank goodness, and then Ivor asked about his position with the comic company, and Peter gave his pat answers.

'Yes, they provide accommodation. No, I can't do my own stuff immediately. Yes, I'm really excited.'

Ivor peeled a pound note from his wallet and then hugged an astonished Peter hard.

'You know where I am,' he said, thumping the boy's back. 'Don't be a stranger.' And Peter, who had been so stoical up until now, started to cry.

In bed that evening, Clara read a *Good Housekeeping* story about a woman who had a baby out of wedlock during the war and then after the war an old friend fell in love with her and helped bring up the baby with her.

Would it work the other way round?

The differences: Ruby was not dead. Clara and Ivor weren't old friends. Clara was definitely not some distinguished, aloof gentleman with a country pile. And Ivor had made it abundantly clear that she was the last person he wanted help from.

Clara sighed and put the magazine down. Just as she was drifting to sleep, Peg came in needing fresh sheets, and then later Rita appeared, upset from a bad dream where she had been at the audition for the Festival and forgotten all her notes. 'My fingers were like sausages!'

'That won't happen, will it?' she whispered, wide-eyed as Clara tucked her back in.

'That's not going to happen.' Clara yawned. *Damn Anita and the blooming Festival.*

Clara had found a battered suitcase at the market the week before. In the morning, Peter half-filled it – he didn't have a lot – and stood it downstairs by the front door. Although he was a whole foot taller than Clara, he still seemed to look up to her.

'Now, no putting me in the comic strips, Peter, but if you must, I want to appear rich and glamorous.'

He laughed. 'For the first few months, we're creating a really naughty boy: Maurice the Menace. He's going to be brilliant to work on.'

'I like that. I think he should have a naughty pet too.'

'I was thinking a cat just like Stella.'

Clara laughed. 'You'll be wonderful, but don't forget to keep in touch.' She had told Peter this a dozen times, but she had to make sure it went in.

And then Peter said goodbye to the others, and he had done a cartoon drawing each for Peg, Rita and Maureen. In her picture Maureen was baking, in an apron, her hair askew, cheeks flushed. Rita was playing the piano with her neat plaits in ribbons, while in hers, Peg was holding on to one of her precious seashells and grinning a gummy grin.

He apologised he hadn't had time to do one for Clifford, but he shook his hand solemnly. 'You'll be fine here,' he said, and 'Look after Miss Newton. You're the man of the house now!' He winked. 'And no cheating at Newmarket either. Don't think I didn't see.'

Clifford's expression was icy.

Dr Cardew had offered to take Peter. He was driving to London anyway, he said, for a conference, this time on tuberculosis.

'You have all the fun,' said Clara on the doorstep.

And he replied wearily, 'Believe me, if I could stay home all day with Anita and the baby, I would.'

Peter miaowed a goodbye to Stella, and then carried his suitcase out to the car, where Dr Cardew was now discreetly doing the crossword. As Peter waved out the passenger seat window, Clara's eyes filled with tears.

'Peter, you will—'

'Call? I will, every month.'

Every month?! despaired Clara. That was *nowhere* near often enough.

That tall skinny boy who had played fielder in cricket, who built wagons, who played a mean game of charades, who smoked too many cigarettes, who loved cheese on toast; he was leaving home. He was still under her care, but not. Unlike all the other children she had let go, he was not finding a new family. He wouldn't be looked after by new parents. She was not handing him over to a new carer, she was unlocking the cage and letting him out. He was her first child to launch out into the world. And it felt wrong. She was his parachute – but did he know that? Would he fly, or smack to the floor?

3

Peter had only been gone an hour or so when the high school called and asked Clara to come in. It was a twenty-minute walk, but it was good to abandon the chores and blow the cobwebs away, for she was feeling wobbly.

She sat in the headmaster's office while Clifford glowered next to her. He'd been pulled from his metalwork class. Clara knew that was the only lesson he really enjoyed, and he would be furious at missing it. It was a new headmaster; he'd only been in place since September, but already he came across as jaded and gloomy, as if he'd been working there for a thousand years.

'Clifford locked a child into the store cupboard.'

Clara looked at the boy, astonished. 'What on earth did you do that for, Clifford?' She thought it was a reasonable question, but the headmaster shook his head at her, then wrote something down in the enormous book he had on the green leather surface of his desk.

'I dunno,' Clifford said.

'Was he... was he a bad child, this one you locked in?' she asked. Sometimes, the local children were cruel to the children from the orphanage. Clara had been up to the school several times when the 'you've got fleas' and the 'nobody loves you' chants had become too much.

'The child is half his size and an excellent student,' snapped the headmaster. 'Not that it should make a difference.'

'Oh,' Clara said.

Perhaps Clifford himself was once locked in a cupboard, thought Clara. Poor boy.

The headmaster was staring at her like she was something he couldn't quite work out. Clara realised a stronger response was expected.

'Can you imagine how that must have felt?' she asked him.

Clifford stared out the window, his hands tucked under his thighs. Clara couldn't help glancing towards the light too. In the playground, some children were queuing up for their milk. She wondered if she might catch a glimpse of Rita or Evelyn – who had also started at this school in September – or Maureen, who was in her final year now.

The headmaster cleared his throat. Clara thought she could have handled this so much better if he were not there.

'Well?' she said.

'I dunno.'

'Horrible?' Clara suggested. 'It must have been frightening.'

She couldn't get a reaction from him. This was yet another side to Clifford she hadn't seen before. He had more sides than a dodecahedron.

'And he threw a screwdriver in woodwork,' added the head-teacher, still scratching on the paper. 'Fortunately, it didn't hit anyone. This time,' he added ominously.

'That's awful,' Clara said. 'Clifford – what do you have to say for yourself?'

He shrugged.

The headmaster said he had smacked Clifford every single day since he had been at school. 'It's important that you know what is going on here, Miss Newton.'

'Absolutely,' Clara said smoothly. She'd had no idea. 'And Clifford is going to try to put things right, aren't you?'

Clifford turned his flinty eyes to her. He nodded his chin slowly up and down like it was being pulled by strings. It was like he was mocking her. Clara's heart fell.

A couple of days later, she was asked up to the school again. This time Clifford had thrown a chair in science class. The headmaster said, 'You know we've always treated the children from Shilling Grange Orphanage the same as everyone else.'

The Michael Adams Children's Home, Clara thought, but she didn't say anything. That morning, she had given Clifford some marbles she had got half-price at the market. They were beauties, like shiny glass eyeballs. She had wanted him to feel special. If he felt special, she thought, he might behave differently.

'Our patience is being stretched. He's had the slipper. He's had the belt. None of it has the slightest effect on him. What are you going to do about it?'

Clara hesitated, but that was a mistake. The headmaster jumped in.

'Oh, so your plan is to leave the discipline to us?'

'Of course not!' said Clara defensively.

She wondered why the headmaster was a headmaster, given his clear antipathy towards children. But then, she thought, she could talk. It wasn't like she was crazy about them either sometimes.

'I will discuss it with the council and the children's officers, and decide on an appropriate course of action.'

He tsked. 'The course of action you should take is corporal punishment.' He said the word punishment slowly, as though savouring it.

Clara always got muddled up between corporal and capital punishment. *This was definitely corporal, the body, yes? He wouldn't be proposing hanging, would he?*

'I see...' she said vaguely.

'They wouldn't have a name for it if it didn't work.'

What a bizarre theory, Clara thought. *It didn't make—*

'You need to make the boy *afraid*.'

When in the history of fostering and adopting had that ever worked? Clara wondered. Yet she had to acknowledge she was hardly an expert. She'd never really had to deal with a naughty boy before. Maybe it *did* work – if you could do it properly? She doubted if she could make Clifford afraid. Not least because he was taller and stronger than she was. If she tried, he might well turn round and whack her back.

Yet something needed to be done, obviously.

'Thank you,' she said to the headmaster. 'You've been very helpful.'

'Waste of space,' he replied, and Clara wasn't sure if he meant Clifford or her.

That afternoon, Anita came round with baby Howard. Howard slept as much as Patricia howled. His hair reminded Clara of a medieval monk in a tapestry, and he had the same kind of vacant expression. It didn't help that he always wore strange hats too.

Even though it was cooler in the parlour than the rest of the building, they always sat in there because Clara assumed Anita preferred it. Clara brought out a tray with the teapot and the good china. She also brought out the fresh serviettes and the nicest teaspoons. They were good friends now, but with Anita, that didn't mean you could drop standards. During the war, Anita had been sent to a place called Dachau – Clara didn't know much more than that, but she knew Anita had suffered enormously there. The only time she ever mentioned it was to say that having a good life was her way of getting revenge.

At first, Clara was thrilled that Anita had come over; she was feeling low about Peter's absence, even lower about Clifford's behaviour at school. And Anita had brought along fresh macaroons. But then Anita insisted on asking how Victor was, then how Julian was, then how Ivor was, and her phrasing, whether inadvertent or not, made it seem like there was a constant stream of men in Clara's life.

Pouring tea, Clara scowled. Victor was fine so far as she was aware. And Anita probably saw Julian as much as she did, which was sometimes a lot and sometimes not at all; the same with Ivor – and there was *not* a stream of men. Indeed, only two men had ever made indentations on her heart. But by the time she was ready to tell Anita this, the other woman had moved on once again to her other favourite subject: the annoying Festival of Britain – and could Ivor help with the costumes? Had Clara asked?

Clara explained that Ivor was overwhelmed. She said his arm was causing him pain. Terrible pain. She expected Anita to be irritated at this – not only did Anita have a one-track mind, but she was not a terribly empathetic person – yet for once she was surprisingly kind.

'Not surprised. Looking after a baby is hard for a man,' she clucked. 'Never mind a man with only one arm. I don't know how he does it, he really is something.'

Clara knew that. She nodded.

'I have my Benjamin – Dr Cardew – to lean on but for Ivor, he must be very lonely.'

'I offer to—'

'But it's not the same, Clara, really it isn't.'

Clara wondered if Anita was trying to say that she, Clara, had no idea what parenting was like. She hoped Anita *wasn't* trying to say that. She sipped her tea thoughtfully.

Anita had moved on. To the Festival again, of course – and the auditions. 'And don't forget, Rita has a whole-day rehearsal on Saturday. The other children are to attend for two hours in the morning and one in the evening. Make sure you bring them.'

'I'm not sure—'

'They must!'

Clara considered. They didn't have anything else on this Saturday, she probably could take them back and forth, but Anita didn't understand: Clara also had files to keep, a house to run, Clifford who was behaving awfully at school; Maureen had decisions to make about her future and didn't seem inclined to make them, Peg had to learn to speak. Rita was practising with the group *and* she still did hours and hours of her own practice too. And Clara still hadn't heard from Peter – should she send a telegram, or was that melodramatic? No, it *was* melodramatic. Sister Grace was helpful – more than helpful; Sister Grace was wonderful, but she was only employed by the council to cover for Clara once every other Sunday, on her day off. The rest she did out of the goodness of her heart. Recently, it was only when Sister Grace was there that Clara felt she could relax. It felt to Clara like she was staggering under a heavy bag most of the time.

Anita went on obliviously. She was still desperate for more children to join the group.

'What about the new boy?' she pressed. 'Clifton?'

'Clifford. And I don't think so,' said Clara, thinking of the meetings at the school, and his reaction. 'He's... difficult.'

'Well, he needs to learn right from wrong. That's what he's here for.'

Anita was always teaching Clara how to suck eggs.

'I know that,' Clara began. 'I just don't think Clifford is your answer.'

He locked a child in a cupboard! He threw a chair in science.

Anita laughed. 'I'm used to rebellious ones.'

But she wasn't really, thought Clara. Anita's adopted daughter Evelyn was a sweetheart, who would rather die than disobey or hurt anyone's feelings. And Howard was a serene baby and Dr Cardew was as involved as any father could be and they also paid handsomely for extra help.

Just then a car squealed up outside, its door slammed and there were quick footsteps on the path. Clara excused herself to Anita and hurried out.

Mrs Horton – formerly Miss Bridges – was at the door.

'Hey! Why aren't you on honeymoon?'

The car still had tin cans and ribbons attached and this time Clara noticed the handwritten sign, 'Just Married'.

Some part, some tiny evil part of Clara, hoped the Hortons had had a row and split up. The honeymoon had proved to be awful, Miss Bridges had run away, and Clara could play the role of the hero friend. She imagined hiding Miss Bridges behind the sofa in the parlour and shouting at Mr Horton, 'She's not here, and even if she were, I wouldn't let you in!'

Mrs Horton said, 'We're only back one day early.'

'And?' The 'we' was not an auspicious sign.

'A child needs a place to stay.'

'What about the emergency carers?'

Mrs Horton was always raving about the emergency carers, the Beasleys who lived in Dedham. *Wonderful family.* They took in the urgent cases: babies left in bus shelters or on train platforms, or children who'd run away. They went over and above the call of duty; children thrived so well with them that sometimes Mrs Horton could hardly bring herself to prise them away.

Mrs Horton made a face.

'It turns out they were... thieves.'

The emergency carers were thieves? 'What?'

'Mr Beasley lost his job, they didn't tell us, and when a child arrived with a trust fund, they dipped into his savings...'

'Oh no!'

'The police are involved. Anyhow, it leaves us in a sticky situation. The child who needs a place to stay is in the car outside. There was an accident this morning.'

'This morning?!'

Clara looked out at Mrs Horton's Ford Anglia. She saw now what she had missed before – a small, silhouetted figure sitting in the back.

'You've brought a child straight here? From the hospital?'

'A boy, yes, but as Peter's gone, you have the space and—'

'Peter's only just left.'

'I can't imagine anyone better equipped to manage this emergency than you, Clara. I know it's not ideal.'

Nothing was ideal in children's services, but Clara supposed that if everything were ideal, children's services wouldn't need to exist.

Since she already had Clifford to worry about, another boy would be quite a strain. But maybe it would be better if there were two young lads – they could help each other out? Maybe Clifford just needed a good friend.

Mrs Horton went out and then came back in with a child with a large plaster on his cheek. Both knees were bandaged, and his arm was in a sling. He had big tombstone teeth, long eyelashes and thick blond eyebrows.

'This is Denny Reed.'

Whatever terrible thing had happened to him had only happened hours before.

Clara knelt by the little boy's side. He had golden hair, plenty of it, in that style that made you want to tousle it although Clara managed to resist.

'Is Denny your real name?'

'It's Dennis,' he said softly. 'I'm named after my dad.'

He swallowed and his pretty eyes swam with tears. She

couldn't read him, she didn't know him, but she could see recent and powerful heartache shot through him.

'Dennis is a beautiful name,' she said, 'and so is Denny.' She looked over his head to Mrs Horton and mouthed, 'Of course we'll have him.'

Clara hurried into the parlour, where Anita was stacking the teacups on to the tray. When she turned around and saw them, her face was rapturous.

'Anita, you'd better go—'

'But this is wonderful news!' Anita's eyes were shining. 'For the audition! He couldn't be more per—'

'No,' Clara said.

4

Denny would have Peter's old bed. It would just be him and Clifford in the boys' dorm. It was a shame that sensible Peter wasn't here to settle him in, but Clara hoped that it might encourage Clifford to step up and take some responsibility. Maybe this would be the making of him?

Late in the afternoon, Clara had some whale meat delivered – Mr Dowsett the local librarian had told her, 'It's a delicacy in some cultures, Clara!' – but it was grey, rubbery and shiny. It looked like dirty snow. Clara tried to disguise it first with leek and onion, then with her last rasher of bacon, but nothing seemed to help. At teatime, she dolloped it with some mash onto the plates.

It was Denny's first meal at the Home.

His face crumpled.

'The food is usually better than this,' Clara admitted.

'Is it though?' said Maureen, picking at it with her fork. Peg had begun to do the sniffing she always did before her full-blown crying. Rita tucked into the mash, Clifford poked it and said, 'Bloody Nora, is this human flesh?' After a few more cannibal references, Clara warned she would send him upstairs if he couldn't keep quiet. 'And I mean it,' she said, shaking her serving spoon at him.

Denny put one bite in his mouth and then made choking noises. Clara dug for her handkerchief, threw it at him, and he spluttered lumps into it, tears pouring down his cheeks.

'Oh, Denny,' she said.

Cliff nudged him hard. 'Cry-baby blue.'

'No!' said Clara firmly and this time she sent Clifford upstairs. He laughed loudly all the way to the dorm. The rest of them chewed and made terrible faces.

Maureen got up and emptied the left-over meat into the food caddy.

'The mash was nice,' she said cheerfully. The girl was exasperating but efficient. Peg had got out some old scrap paper and was scribbling pictures of the sea at the table. Rita disappeared off to her piano in the shed. Denny gazed around him, looking petrified, probably wondering what disgusting thing would be put his way next.

That night, Clara put a hot-water bottle in Denny's bed, and then, because she didn't want to show favouritism, put one in Clifford's too. Some children took equality very seriously. Clifford looked surprised, then he handed it back to her like it was something vile.

'I don't want this.'

During the night, Denny cried, and Clara went in and soothed him back to sleep twice. The third time she heard him, she hoped that if she ignored him he would fall asleep, but about midnight, Clifford hammered on her bedroom door, shouting, 'He won't bleeding shut up.'

She went back into the room, patted Denny's scrawny shoulder, told him it was going to be all right, until he stopped sobbing and fell into a deep sleep. Poor darling. By then, it was past two o'clock.

. . .

Clara had to shake the boys awake in the morning. Clifford seemed more furious than ever, but she told herself to ignore him. *He's tired and he needs to feel loved.* She gave him extra honey on bread to cheer him up, asked about his marbles. Fortunately, the girls had slept through it all.

She was stirring the porridge when Denny pulled her arm.

'Can I go to the hospital today?'

'Wha-why, Denny?'

'To see my mummy.'

She knelt to him. 'Denny, Mummy is not at the hospital.'

'What about Daddy?'

The porridge was burning the bottom of the pan. It was more watery than usual because they'd run out of milk.

Clifford looked up from polishing his shoes. 'They're dead. Both dead. Like everyone else's here. Get used to it.'

Before Clara could say anything, Maureen had jumped in. 'Shut up, Clifford. You don't know anything.'

Clifford shouted back, 'I know all about it!'

'Enough!' Clara cried. 'Everyone, get ready for school.' She looked at Denny's astonished face. 'It's okay, not you, Denny...' but he was crying again.

~

The council were deciding that morning whether Denny would stay with Clara or if he would be moved to another home. Poor child. His fate depended on Miss Cooper, Mr and Mrs Horton and Mr Sommersby. Once the other children had left, Denny helped with the washing and with cleaning the sinks. He also paid attention to Stella. It was nice to have someone else in the house who remembered her.

'I used to help Mummy,' he said. He was a little shadow with his forlorn face.

While they were hanging out the clothes in the garden, they saw a magpie making itself at home. It kept its beady orange eye on them and strutted across the lawn.

'Salute it,' Clara said, before adding thoughtlessly, 'One for sorrow.'

Denny looked at her.

'I bet there's another one somewhere...' Clara found herself hunting around for two for joy, but there wasn't. Stella came out to scare it away, then Denny stroked Stella, tears in his eyes again.

Later, Denny asked, 'What is going to happen to me?'

'The council are looking for your relatives.'

Denny said his grandparents were dead. Two of them were killed in the Blitz and two of them died from 'being old'. He talked of a great-aunt who maybe lived in the West Country, but they hadn't been able to find her yet, and even if they did, would she be too elderly or too unsuitable for Denny?

He said he had an uncle in Northumbria, but he had been in a home since the war.

'What kind of home?' Clara asked. *Perhaps this could be a solution?*

'A home for people with... with strange minds.'

'I see.'

'Mummy used to say, you can turn friends into family.'

'She sounds very sensible, Denny.'

He munched his crusts. 'She has lots of friends.'

He had an afternoon nap, woke up when the others came home, and burst into tears again. The council did not return Clara's calls – the deciding was taking a long while.

That night, Denny sleepwalked right out of the house. Ivor brought him back before Clara had even realised he'd gone. Ivor had one arm looped around Patricia, the other hooking Denny upright; the boy was wide-eyed yet fast asleep. Clara averted her eyes from Ivor's chest in his crisp white vest and tried not to notice the way it showed off the shape of his shoulders.

'I think this is one of yours,' he said.

She apologised and he laughed. 'There's no need, Clara, don't worry about us.' He gave her a helpless look. 'Patricia never sleeps anyway.'

Denny must have got out the back. Clara put him in her bed and lay on blankets on the floor next to him so she could keep an eye on him. She cringed at how she had opened the door to Ivor in her nightdress. It wasn't an attractive look – it was like a huge white tent. She couldn't even call it matronly; was *tently* a word? What must he have thought of her? She would use her coupons on a new one soon.

She telephoned the council first thing the next morning.

'Have you come to a decision?'

Miss Cooper yawned. Clara could imagine her taking aspirin and sipping water at her desk after some party or other last night. 'On what?'

Clara inhaled loudly. *How could she be like this?* 'Dennis Reed, of course!'

At this, Miss Cooper sounded none the wiser.

'The... the emergency boy,' Clara whispered into the telephone, for the walls at the Home had ears – or rather, you couldn't hide anything from Rita. 'The one whose parents were in the car accident.'

'Oh, do you think you can manage?'

'Uh, yes, I suppose...'

'Then he can stay with you,' Miss Cooper said blithely. 'Would you contact the school and open a file on him?'

Just like that? thought Clara. Just like that, Denny's little world has been upturned. Just like that, he will be living with her. But she didn't really know a better way of dealing with it either. She told him and he didn't seem to be listening and, instead, fiddled with his wristwatch. She asked if everything was okay, and he said, 'Mummy gave it to me for my birthday,' and burst into tears.

She called a locksmith and got an extra lock put on the back door.

CHILDREN'S REPORT 11
Dennis 'Denny' Patrick Reed

Date of Birth:

16 March 1941

Family Background:

Denny is an only child, who appears to come from a happy loving family. They were on their way to a trip to a museum when a lorry drove into the back of them, pushing them into another vehicle. His parents died instantly.

Health/Appearance:

He has the face of an angel. Some bruising, sprains and soreness from the accident. Bedwetter and sleepwalker. See Dr Cardew for more information.

Food:

Good appetite. Fond of peas. Dislikes whale meat. Jelly reminds him of home.

Hobbies:

He says he likes sports, but doesn't seem motivated. He used to collect coins. He likes Stella the cat very much.

Other:

Perhaps Denny is in shock.

5

Peg wasn't quite as jolly as usual, thought Clara that evening. It couldn't have been because of Clifford or Denny; Clifford left her alone, thankfully, preferring to have his spats with Maureen or Rita, and Denny was a sweetheart who wouldn't hurt a fly. Clara guessed what it was: Peg had been blossoming with her speech therapy and although she still never spoke, Clara had felt that the day she did couldn't be too far away. But now Peg's speech therapist had got married and left, and there was no one else to fulfil the role. Clara was used to disappointments and dead ends but this one hit hard. Why did these young women have to disappear off the face of the earth? She remembered all the teachers who had left, and Mrs Harrington, one of the children's officers (who she hadn't liked, but still). Wasn't there a way to marry and stay in the world of work? It raised Clara's hackles, although she couldn't quite put her finger on why. Perhaps it was that each woman who left felt like a rebuke, as if she should leave too – like a game of penny shove while she was a penny clinging on.

Clara dreamed about Peg sometimes. She dreamed about all the children, but the Peg ones she remembered vividly when she woke up. They would be walking in a field and see a fire. Clara would shout but no sound would come out, but then Peg would shout. Her voice would ring out clear and sweet and everyone would come and rescue her, but not Clara. In another dream, they were at the Festival of Britain on a stage with all the children and Clara was locked in a cupboard and Peg knew but couldn't tell anyone.

That evening, Peg drew more pictures of her teacher from school. She had pages and pages of them. In the drawings, Miss Fisher had a large head with a tiny little neck that could never have supported it. Her smile was frightening and in her three-fingered hands she was holding... tennis balls?

'What are these?'

Peg scowled, then wrote down 'shells' and underlined it several times. Clara now saw that she had drawn a series of love hearts around the teacher. She was quite surprised: she was used to being Peg's number one.

No need to be jealous, Clara thought. And she wasn't quite jealous; it was something else. Something felt off with Peg recently.

~

The first time Maureen came back from helping at Ivor's workshop, she was over the moon.

'I rocked her to sleep. Ivor said no one else makes Patricia feel as comfortable as I do.'

Since then Maureen had gone over three times, and Ivor was pleased, for he had managed to get lots of work done.

Maureen was one of those people about whom Clara's father would have said, 'Devil makes work for idle hands,' so Clara was especially grateful that she was well occupied, and she was also happy to help ease Ivor's load. And if Ivor could find some equilibrium, you never knew, he might even have more time for her too...

Clara also tried to find out what was happening with Maureen and Joe since that time she had seen them nearly holding hands on the high road. Sometimes, she thought Maureen and Joe had got back together. Other times, she thought they were just good friends. One thing was indisputable: Maureen never missed an opportunity to mention his name. Clara wished Maureen devoted even a fraction of the time she spent on her love life to thinking about work. She would be out of education and out of Clara's care soon.

The day after Maureen's third trip to Ivor's to help with the baby, she and Clara were pegging up the sheets when she said, 'Joe says I sing really well.'

'You do.'

'Not as good as the others though.'

Then she said, 'I don't like Clifford.'

'He's still settling in,' Clara said defensively. Everyone seemed annoyed with the boy and yes, he did stupid, reckless things, especially at school, but maybe he had good reason. She wasn't going to join the braying mob (even if she had nearly slipped on the marbles he'd left on the bathroom floor that morning).

'Joe doesn't like him either. He says he's bad news.'

'In what way?'

Maureen shrugged. The children could never say anything specific.

Later that day, Maureen was gloomy. 'Joe can't see me tonight. He's got work.'

'The petrol station is open in the evening?'

'Whatever.'

~

On Denny's second weekend, Clara took him to join the library with Rita and Peg. She wanted Clifford to come too, but he politely said he preferred to stay home, which Clara thought was fine; that was his choice. On the way there, though, Clifford whipped past them on a bicycle, pedalling like mad, with his arms in the air and whooping. Maybe it would have been a good sport, a wholesome pastime, only Clifford did not own a bicycle. Clara had asked the council for bicycles for the children at Christmas, but they had replied that bicycles belonged in the 'extraneous items' category and so could not be provided with current funding. Clifford was ringing the bell with abandon. People jumped out of his way.

Rita was holding Clara's hand. 'Everyone at school is scared of him,' she said brightly.

'How about you?' Clara asked. She had a tense feeling in the pit of her stomach.

'He doesn't bother me.'

Clara tried not to let this sighting spoil the library trip. Denny was surprisingly keen to get his library card, Rita wanted to exchange sheet music and Peg was working her way through the *Secret Seven* books. Clara was glad Mr Dowsett the gentle librarian was free to show them around – he always talked to the children as if they were grown-ups. Last year, Mr Dowsett had been a fantastic support when the children were going to be sent to Australia. He had burrowed and burrowed – in fact, he did remind her a little of a mole, with his round glasses and his squinty eyes – and he had uncovered all sorts. He was telling them about his love of detective stories and memoirs when Rita interrupted to tell him about the audition. Mr Dowsett didn't mind though, he said it sounded marvellous and what an opportunity for 'impressionable brains'.

Clara nodded. Her impressionable brain was darting all over the place. *Whose bicycle was Clifford on?*

'A friend's,' said Clifford later at home. 'Obviously.'

Clara tried to stay cool. 'What's this friend's name?'

'Why?'

'I want to know.'

'Jimmy,' said Clifford, quick as a flash, but she knew he was lying.

'I want to help you, Clifford. I want you to be happy here.'

'I am happy,' he sneered. 'Can I go now?'

6

A few days later, Maureen was supposed to have gone to Ivor's straight after school to take care of Patricia – it would be her fourth time – but instead Ivor came to the door of the Home with the baby to ask where she was: she hadn't turned up. Clara was more annoyed than Ivor; he seemed resigned to it. Maureen must be out having a good time with Joe, Clara supposed. The thought of the pair of them canoodling obliviously on some park bench while Ivor suffered made her blood boil – it was time Maureen grew up.

'She has no sense of responsibility,' Clara said apologetically. Just when she thought Maureen was maturing, she went and did something like this. She hated to see Ivor let down.

'I need to do some work.' Ivor looked exhausted. 'Patricia cried all night and morning – I got nothing done.' *No wonder he didn't have time for them, for her, right now.* Clara knew she had to take a back seat – but she could also offer to help.

'Let me take Patricia for a couple of hours then, I may as well.'

Ivor looked doubtful and that made Clara's heart ache.

What must he think of her that he couldn't trust his daughter with her?

'Honestly, Ivor. I can manage.'

'I know you can. It's just... I feel bad imposing on you.' He gestured towards the house. 'You have a lot on too.'

She took the handle end of the pram and gestured at him to help her push it inside.

'She's no trouble, look.'

He chuckled darkly. 'You wait until she wakes up.'

Patricia clutched a wooden ring in her sleep. She smelled of milk. It was strange to look at his child. Not his blood, but his child anyway. The child who had stolen his heart.

If it weren't for this child...

No, she wouldn't let herself think that way.

Clara's ex-boss, Mr Harris, had visited the Home once before, not long after she'd started there. That time, also, he hadn't let her know he was coming. Today, Ivor had only been gone thirty minutes and Patricia was sleeping in the parlour. The children – except for the missing Maureen – were outside. Denny and Clifford were kicking a ball around with some other children in the street, Rita was in the shed and Peg was playing hopscotch. Clara laughed with astonishment as she opened the door to Mr Harris. 'Well, this is a surprise!'

He handed over a box of pencils, 'for the orphans'. Clara suspected they were the first thing he'd found in the office supplies cupboard.

'To what do I owe the pleasure?'

'It's been a while, that's all,' he said, but she thought there was more to it than that.

She had nothing sweet to offer him, but he said that was fine. Just tea would be fine. And no, he didn't need milk, he was watching his weight. And no sugar? That was fine too.

She drank her tea self-consciously. They used to have a lot in common: common enemies – Nazis and petty bureaucracies – but she wondered what they had in common now.

'Sorry to hear about Judy,' he said gruffly. 'Lovely woman.'

Clara remembered that Mr Harris had sent a commiseration card at the time. It was nice of him to mention her best friend – no one else knew her. Clara thought about her time at Harris & Sons and how the lovely Judy had taken her under her wing and how much she missed her. If she had known Judy would be gone so soon, she would have done so many things differently. And how much easier things would be if she had Judy by her side now.

Mr Harris moved on from Judy quickly though. He was another one who wanted to talk about the Festival of Britain. It seemed to Clara that the whole world was obsessed. The newspaper devoted pages to it: 'will it kick-start a new Britain?' and 'why I will be going/not be going to Festival of Britain events'. Even *Good Housekeeping* had run a picture feature: '*Putting your best foot forwards: What we'll be wearing to the Festival of Britain.*' (Dresses with sailor collars, and tweeds, apparently.)

It was a distraction, decided Clara. Like the way Maureen made cake when she was angry or the way people talked about films and books rather than face up to real-life losses. The whole country was unable to face the horror of the last few years – the grief, the debt, the austerity, the drab – and their way of dealing with it was to focus on small, ridiculous things – country dancing and pageants – in order to forget. But how could you forget running for shelter, a soldier jumping in front of a tram on your way to work, a small shoe in the rubble, those photos from the concentration camps...?

Clara was about to say this when Mr Harris suddenly said: 'I made a bid for a section in The Dome of Discovery. Spent a week preparing. Didn't even get shortlisted! They've got all sorts of foreigners involved.'

'Ah,' said Clara. She couldn't imagine her old company involved in something so cutting-edge, but that was probably unfair. They had moved with the times plenty during the war, they were as resilient and responsive as anyone.

Mr Harris said they had a tea lady again now. And they had upgraded their typewriters. He and Clara reminisced about the good old days of typewriting mistakes. When she'd left, the rule was that if there were more than three errors on a page, they had to start the whole page again. But when Clara first started, it had been only one error. It was a strange thing to have successfully campaigned to let more errors get through – Clara wasn't sure that was a legacy she quite liked.

And then Mr Harris couldn't help himself; it was as though he was magnetically pulled back to the subject of the Festival. 'They went for some bizarre ideas in the end, didn't they?'

There was no avoiding it, thought Clara wearily. The Festival of Britain obliterated all other subjects, took over all other concerns. It was a shame Mr Harris hadn't called round when Anita was over. The two of them would have had a grand old time dissecting it.

'You know what they say about the Skylon?'

She had read about this. The Skylon was a thing suspended in the air, made from aluminium apparently, looked like a rocket. It was the centrepiece of the whole stupid fandango.

'What do they say?'

'Like the British economy, the Skylon had no visible means to support itself.'

Clara laughed at that.

'Do you know how the Skylon got its name?'

Clara did not.

'It's a mixture of pylon, sky and nylon.'

The children came in, wanting tea. Peg and the boys were red and sweaty, their fingernails grubby. Rita said she needed to get a haircut before the audition. 'And not by you, Miss Newton,' she said firmly. 'I want a pro-fes-sional, please.'

'Well, that costs money, Rita,' Clara said wearily, avoiding Mr Harris's eye. There was still no sign of Maureen and Clara was still furious with her.

The previous time Mr Harris had come, Clara had dished up watery soup. This time it was creamy pumpkin. She hoped he noted the improvement. The children tucked in hungrily. Clifford declared it delicious, and Clara felt grateful to him. You could say that about Clifford: he had a good appetite and he appreciated his food.

'And will you be going to the Festival of Britain in London, children?' Mr Harris asked.

Rita and Peg stared at each other as though he'd just invited them.

'*Can't* we go, Miss Newton?'

Peg scribbled down, 'please!!'

Now Clara felt irritated with Mr Harris for bringing it up in front of them. How *could* they be expected to go? Didn't he know most of their shoes had holes in? They were barely scraping by. Even if they could afford the entrance fee, they would never be able to afford the train fares. And even if they did go, doubtless someone would see them there and complain about them being there: '*My taxes going on children's holidays.*'

'We'll see,' said Clara distractedly. She wiped around the kitchen surfaces. She remembered when Harris & Sons was her whole life. She still didn't know what Mr Harris was doing here. What was the point of this visit? She was certain there *was* a point.

Rita was telling Mr Harris about the audition and how marvellous she was when Patricia woke up. Clara sent the children off to do their chores, left her guest downstairs and took Patricia upstairs, where she changed her nappy. She was uncertain at first how to go about it, but it wasn't too complicated.

Patricia blinked at her with disdain, but at least she wasn't howling and she did lie still. Sometimes Clara had this absurd idea that inside Patricia, a rather cantankerous old lady was struggling to get out. Clara did 'round and round the garden' on her tiny palms, 'like a teddy bear, one step, two step... tickly under there!' She got one smile out of her then, and it felt special since it was so hard-won.

Patricia was getting used to her, which was a positive thing, Clara supposed. She looked forward to reporting to Ivor how good the baby had been. She hoped he would understand that as how good she was with her. She carried Patricia back into the kitchen and was disconcerted when, even though it was growing dark out, Mr Harris asked if he might have another cuppa: if it wasn't an inconvenience.

'It's not an inconvenience,' she lied. Both Patricia and Mr Harris had stopped her getting her usual things done – she might as well accept the fact.

Finally, Mr Harris got to his point.

'Mrs H and I... well, we're thinking of adopting a baby.'

'Adopting?'

'As long as it is under two. We wouldn't want anyone older.'

They didn't want anyone older. And sometimes Clara understood this, and sometimes she did not.

'What about her?' He pointed at Patricia, who eyed him suspiciously.

Clara laughed before she realised that he was being serious.

'Oh no! This one is not up for adoption. She's a friend's baby, I'm just sitting her for the day.'

'Pity, she's beautiful. Dark eyes. I bet the mother was a knockout.'

Clara gulped.

'One like her then? We'd want one that speaks though,' he said, then lowered his eyes. 'No offence.'

'That's not how it works. You'll have to have an interview with the childcare team in London – see if you're appropriate.'

'How difficult is that, compared to the Skylon?'

After Mr Harris left, Clara wondered whether to tell Ivor about the conversation and decided not to. *I bet the mother was a knockout* was painful enough to hear without sharing it with anyone else. Ruby *was* a knockout, she thought glumly. Which perhaps explained Ivor's attachment to Ruby *and* her daughter.

She had told Ivor she'd have Patricia until eight, but he came over earlier. It didn't escape her attention that his face was flaming. He didn't greet her but stormed over to the pram, checked Patricia was in it, then growled, 'How can I trust you if you go about telling half the town my business?'

'Wha-at?'

'For weeks it's been going on. Anita's been round, Mrs Horton's been round, Mr Dowsett... every bloody person in this town has been round offering to help with Patricia. I thought it was just coincidence, but today was the final straw – Dr Cardew has been round, telling me to see him at the surgery!'

'It wasn't like that, it was only Anita. I simply told her—'

'That I'm in terrible pain and hardly coping – humiliating!' He was roaring now. 'Utterly humiliating. And she told everyone. I know you have this this urge to fix everyone but I'm not one of your children. I'm perfectly capable of making my own mistakes.'

At this, Patricia let out a little yelp and he bent to soothe her, his face softer. When he straightened up, though, his face was as hard and as angry as it had ever been.

Quickly, Clara said, 'I *don't* think of you in that way.'

But he was already at the door. 'Yes, you do. Enough now. How many times do I have to tell you? I don't want your help, leave us alone.'

. . .

It was gone nine when Maureen came swinging into the kitchen, singing 'Shine on Harvest Moon'. After nine o'clock! On a school night. She *must* have been out with Joe.

'You forgot Patricia,' snapped Clara. She felt horribly bruised by Ivor's words. 'You were supposed to look after her today.'

'Oh, Lordy!' squealed Maureen, slapping her palm over her mouth. 'I'll go over and apologise.'

'It's too late now, it's just... it's too late.'

Ivor had been so angry; Clara didn't know what to do. It was true she'd said those things, but only to Anita, and she hadn't meant them the way he seemed to think. He seemed to think Clara thought he was useless. Helpless. Childlike. But she didn't think that. In fact, she felt quite the opposite about him – she couldn't stop thinking about him. The knot in her stomach tightened. She was just contemplating her next steps – try to explain herself? Apologise? – when Rita shouted to come quickly, Denny was being sick.

Clara found him in the boys' lavatory, white-faced and weeping. There was sick all round the bowl. The last thing they needed. She gave him some water and then hauled him up to bed. He fell in, holding on to Molly Mouse, Rita's old cuddly, that she had let him have on weekdays.

'I want my mummy,' he murmured into his pillow.

Clifford was grinning behind her.

'What are you smirking at?' she asked curtly.

'Him,' he said scornfully. Clara could have hit him then. She was already raging, and there was something callous about Clifford's cheer in the face of the little boy's illness. 'Don't worry, he's not poorly,' Clifford added, chewing his lip. 'He'll be fine.'

Denny raised his head. 'I didn't like the cigarettes, Miss Newton!'

Clara spun round. The frustration she felt towards Ivor was now directed towards Clifford. And she had been warming to him recently too, despite his behaviour outside the Home. Every time he said something like, 'Miss Newton, thank you for my tea,' she thought they were having a breakthrough.

'Did you do this?'

He stared at her. 'Must have been my mate... Jimmy,' he said.

'You do not EVER give the children cigarettes again, do you hear me?'

'I didn't.'

In a surge of temper, she stormed over to his bedside table and pulled at the sticky drawer. Clifford let out a half-hearted, 'Don't.' There were loose cigarettes rolling around. Some had been started. A box of Swan Vesta matches and a Swiss army knife. She snatched at them furiously.

'Where did you get all this?'

'Found them.'

She was not used to such stunts. She was not used to being strict. The children were largely cooperative and if they weren't, there was usually good reason and she could usually get to the bottom of why. This... this was something else.

Back in her room, she studied the matches and the knife. The blade swivelled out and then tucked back in. It looked innocuous and then it came out to cut you – a bit like Clifford himself, she thought. Then told herself not to. He was only a boy, an abandoned boy. She would win him over, she had to. She lit one of the matches, enjoying the friction the stick made against the side of the box, and the sudden flame, then, when her fingers grew hot and she panicked, blew it out.

And now Ivor hated her too.

. . .

The next morning, Clara was walking away from the high road when she saw the postman wheeling his bike. Was it her imagination or did he have quite the turn when he saw her? He nearly dropped his cycle to the ground; he stopped but the wheels kept on spinning.

'Is anything wrong?' she asked. Her hair was untidy – she'd had a terrible night's sleep, up and down with Denny sleepwalking and crying out, and with fretting about Ivor – and her coat had seen better days but really, was she that much of a fright?

'Miss Newton! I thought you were dead.'

'What?'

'In a terrible accident.'

'No.' She wondered if this was a premonition. It seemed such a bizarre thing to say.

'Blood coming out your mouth and all sorts.'

'What on earth makes you think that?'

'The boy who lives in your house told me.' He hesitated. 'Big fella with the surly face.'

'I see. I'm feeling quite well, thank you for your concern.'

On returning to the house, Clara called Miss Cooper. 'Please can I have the notes on Clifford?' and when Miss Cooper hesitated, she tapped her fingers on the wall. 'The boy who came in November...'

Clara could hear Miss Cooper place the receiver down, then filing cabinets opening and shutting in her tiny office.

Finally, shoes clip-clopping on the floor, she returned. 'You must have them there, Clara.'

'I don't!'

'Well, they're not here.'

'I don't know what to do with him,' she said softly.

'Rewards and punishments?' said Miss Cooper in an uninterested voice. 'Isn't that what they say?'

· · ·

Clara didn't have a leather belt or any kind of belt except for the woollen one from her dressing gown, but she did have slippers. They were ones she'd had since her days at Harris & Sons. She'd bought them in a department store near work, before the Blitz. They were good slippers – good enough to run out in the street in, in the early days of the air sirens. Furry on the top, the bottoms of the slippers were leather and hard. She wasn't even sure what she was meant to do with them.

He needs to be afraid.

She had a ruler too; she didn't use it for much – underlining the subheadings of her files or occasionally measuring things around the house. She still hadn't seen Clifford's file, so there was nothing to underline there. Where was it – and what was within it, and would that make any difference? Her inexperience with children now stared her in the face. How had she coped before? She had coped because the other children's naughtiness was explicable. Clifford's didn't seem to be. He made a mockery of everything. Why did she ever think she could do this? She had ideas above herself, that's what.

What would Mrs Horton do? What would Judy say?

Take control of the situation. Tell him who's boss. Show him right from wrong – and if he refused to see that, show him again. Consistency. Fairness. Carrots and sticks. She'd tried carrots. Corporal punishment was popular for a reason, wasn't it?

She thwacked the side of her arm with the ruler as a test. It hurt. It would hurt more on her palm. She wouldn't try that. *Deep breaths.* It would hurt more when it was done by someone else, obviously.

She took the slipper and the ruler downstairs – she'd decide when he was in front of her – then called the boy into the parlour. Stella the cat ran out, perhaps sensing something was amiss. Clara's voice was horribly shaky and she knew she didn't sound like someone with authority. Rita and Peg were out in the shed, Denny was reading a copy of *White Fang* from the library, Maureen was in the kitchen mooning about Joe.

Big fella with the surly face. Clifford was that all right.

He slunk in and she saw his shocked expression as he took in what was in her hand. That gave her a surge of power. He respected that, huh?

'Why did you tell the postman that I was dead?'

As soon as she said it, she thought it was a ridiculous crime. Certainly, a ridiculous thing to be slippered for. Already she felt sorry for him, and she hadn't even done anything yet. Maybe the boy was just overimaginative – and that wasn't a crime, was it? Otherwise every artist and writer would have belt marks all over their legs.

'I didn't,' he said automatically. His face white, his eyes suspicious.

'If you don't tell me, I'll have to... I will...'

He licked his lips.

She couldn't let it go. It wasn't just the lies, it was... she listed in her head – the bicycle, the bullying, the rudeness, and oh God, the boy in the cupboard at school.

'Hold out your hand then.'

He did, he knew the deal, and his eyes were squeezed shut in preparation. The things he'd done whirred in her head. She hesitated. Which was best? Ruler or slipper? What was she trying to achieve?

She remembered how she had had to sit straight in church and not fidget. Fidgeting was her father's bête noire. She never knew how well she'd done until afterwards, once she'd got home. The verdict would be conveyed through her mother. 'He's not pleased with you' wasn't too bad. 'You're a disappointment' was normal. 'He can't believe you let him down like that' was terrible.

Her father used to take her up to his bedroom and draw the curtains closed. Now she realised it was so that no one would be able to see in from the street. The backs of the legs and palms of the hands were his preferred locations. *The stinging bloody indignity of it.*

'It hurts your father more than it hurts you,' her mother would say afterwards as though that was going to help. 'He hates doing it.'

Clara looked at the boy in front of her. He was around the same age as she had been back then. He was trying to look like he didn't care but he did, he must. How could he not? The anticipation, the act of violence itself, the aftermath – which was the worst? It was all horrible.

'If you do anything like that again,' she said weakly, 'I will punish you.'

Rewards and punishments. Corporal punishments. Make him afraid.

He didn't even seem grateful as he walked out. He seemed to think he'd won.

Clara sank into the sofa. Well, that was *awful.*

Anita remained desperate to try out both Denny and Clifford for the audition; where verbal persuasion hadn't worked, she had sent Evelyn over, firstly with rock cakes and then later with a lace tablecloth that Clara had once admired when they were out together.

After school on Monday, Clara finally acquiesced. She took the boys up to the Cardews' residence, over the surgery. Bless him, Denny looked petrified. 'Do I have to?' he kept asking. Clifford was scornful. Anita was going to be disappointed, Clara thought. She could have told her that it wouldn't work and saved her some time.

At the front door, Evelyn ignored the boys and spoke only to Clara. She told her she had learned to knit, and she showed Clara the pattern she was working from, and she demonstrated, needles clacking together.

The boys gaped at the Cardews' living room. Clara supposed that to Clifford, certainly, and maybe to Denny also, it was the poshest place they'd ever been in. They both took in the imposing grandfather clock with its loud tick-tock, the drawers with their elegant handles, the glass cabinet with the pretty plates on display and the centrepiece: the grand piano.

Anita was so delighted they'd come that Clara almost, but not quite, felt bad for withholding them for so long. Anita apologised for her outfit, although there was no need – despite running around after baby Howard, Anita always looked fabulous – then put her hands on Denny's narrow shoulders.

'This one certainly *looks* the part.' Then she whispered to Clara, 'I know you're not keen but it's always good to be part of something bigger than ourselves, isn't it?'

Clara nodded grumpily. *Wasn't it enough that she had submitted? – she didn't have to like it.*

'Boys!' Anita winked at Clara. 'Let's get this show on the street.'

'Road,' mumbled Clara.

Denny went first. On the piano, Anita asked him to repeat the notes after her. Clara did it too, in her head. *La, Lah, LA, LAHHHH...* She would never sing aloud though. Hadn't done for nearly fifteen years. She even managed to avoid singing 'Happy Birthday' – she mouthed it or pretended to be busy with the candles.

As soon as he did it, it was obvious that Denny had the most unremarkable voice. It wasn't terrible, but it was meek and weak – it certainly didn't match his choirboy features.

'Can you, by any chance, play a musical instrument?' Anita asked. Her tone was neutral but Clara knew this wasn't what she wanted.

He shook his head nervously.

'We'll probably start you off on percussion,' Anita decided. She didn't ask if he wanted to or not. Denny looked worn out again. The effort of putting one foot after the other was clearly taking its toll.

'I'll show Denny the fish tank in the waiting room,' Clara suggested. She doubted Clifford and Anita would be together very long.

Clara and Denny stayed out in the waiting area for a bit, watching the fish. The water was a dark gloomy green and the tank now had a stony floor and hair-like seaweed. Dr Cardew had told Clara that this was the fourth Billy and the fifth Barry, which had come as quite a shock. She had thought they were Billy and Barry 2; it had never occurred to her that the fish her former wards Billy and Barry had won at the fair were not these same fish. Evelyn oversaw the care of the tank; Anita was fond of saying she had 'taken to it like a fish to the sea'.

When Anita called them back in the living room, she was beaming.

'Why didn't you say?' she said to Clara, clutching Clifford's elbow, where his jumper was badly patched.

'Say what?'

'That this one was born to perform!'

Clifford shrugged modestly.

'You never told me!' Clara was surprised. When Clifford had first arrived, she'd asked what he liked to do. He'd winked: 'Smoking, drinking and taking out ladies.'

'This is going to transform our little group,' Anita said. 'Two new members. Aren't we lucky?'

Lucky? thought Clara as Denny looked up at her, pained. She put her hand soothingly on his back. Two weeks ago today the child had been in a car going out for a day to a stately home: toffees and knights with swords and priests and cubbyholes on his mind. Now he found himself without parents and pressed into playing triangle in an orphanage choir. And as for Clifford, he was still behaving poorly at school – and getting worse at home. She wanted to say to Anita – *go slowly, caution* – but Anita was already setting them homework.

Maureen's Joe stepped in to make the costumes. He could use the old Singer sewing machine that had been left in the shed and if they could supply the material, he'd have it done 'in a jiffy'. Was his goal to impress Maureen?

'You don't have to, Joe,' Clara told him. She still felt terrible about pressuring Ivor, and she was slightly aggrieved at the way Joe sometimes took Maureen away from her chores, but he insisted he would be delighted to.

'It's the least I can do,' he said gruffly.

It was lovely having Joe in the house again. Some people make a place a home somehow, and Joe was one of them. His big black boots stood by the back door and he sat at the kitchen table while Maureen fussed over him, delivering tea and Anita's bread pudding that Clara had been saving for Sunday. Maureen had pencilled in her eyebrows and her face was powdery too, but she was subtler about it than she used to be when she worked at Robinson, Browne and White, which Clara thought was wise.

Joe worked hard. The sewing machine worked harder. And Clifford didn't disrespect anyone when Joe was in the room. Clifford seemed to look up to the older boy. That made Clara hopeful that change was in the air.

The girls were going to wear simple smock dresses. Obviously, they couldn't look too glamorous, even if they had the wherewithal for that. The boys were going to be in matching checked shorts and their white school shirts. Maybe hats and ties too. Clara was alarmed they might end up looking a little like Nazi Youth, but she couldn't say this to Anita, and anyway, Anita thought they were adorable.

Anita also wanted the girls to curl their hair and put it in ribbons like little Shirley Temples but the girls said this was a step too far and refused. Secretly, Clara was impressed – they resisted Anita's demands better than she did.

While Joe and the sewing machine whirled, Maureen helped Clara change the bedsheets.

'Are you and Joe back together then?' Clara asked, tucking in the corners. Maybe she shouldn't ask, but Maureen wouldn't tell you anything unless you did.

Maureen flushed. 'I don't think so, not yet,' she said.

'But you'd like that, would you?' Clara asked. Maureen was sneaking off again, and this time it wasn't to Mr Browne. Clara thought she must be with Joe. It wouldn't be a bad thing if she was, but she hoped – good God, she hoped – precautions were on Maureen's mind this time.

She did more than hope; painful as it was, awkward as it was, she had a duty of care here. Palms down, they smoothed the wrinkles in the sheet until it was flat as a pancake.

'Maureen, you and Joe simply must be more careful this time round.'

'I don't know what you mean—'

'I mean – you're too young for all that.'

Maureen knew damn well what she meant. She fed the pillow into its case and smirked. 'Are *you* being careful, Miss Newton?'

Much as she disliked everything to do with the Festival of Britain, Clara had to admit that there were upsides to the rehearsals at Anita's. Now the auditions were approaching – they had only two weeks to go – the children were kept busy all day Saturday, half the day Sunday, then Tuesday and Thursday evenings. This *had* to be good for them, and it was, Clara reflected, quite good for her too. With the children out such a lot, Clara found she had less to do, fewer fights to referee and certainly fewer clothes to pick up off the floor. This free time would have been an opportunity to help Ivor, but they were still not talking – and Clara was determined not to say sorry... well, not first anyway. Ivor had ignored her for the first few days after their altercation. He was now giving her tight-lipped smiles across the road, which wasn't much of an improvement.

As the big day drew nearer, Anita said Clara should come along and listen to them rehearse, but Clara didn't like going out in the evening in case Peter called. She would always worry about Peter. The boy had been abused by his uncle in the past and Clara lived in fear of the man getting back in touch with him. This was unlikely because he had been in a traffic collision (with Evelyn's mother) last year and was due to appear in court, but you never knew. Clara would fight with her bare hands anyone who upset her Peter. He had called only once since he'd left – and that had been gone eight o'clock one night. She had given him a somewhat frenzied report of all the children's activities while he tended to answer in the monosyllabic. Everything was good and/or busy. He was eating, yes.

Towards the end of that call, she had asked him: 'Do you stay in touch with Mabel?'

'I call her every week,' he said proudly.

Every week!

8

There was some toing and froing about the arrangements for the Festival of Britain audition. First, Dr Cardew was going to hire a van to drive them to Ipswich, but then there was baby Howard to worry about, and Anita said she would rather *not* have him to worry about, so they decided Dr Cardew and Howard would stay at home. Clara, Anita and the children would take the train. Anita studied the timetables as though they were a matter of life and death.

'If we do get through to the next round, Dr Cardew can drive us then!'

And then it will be all over, thought Clara, and she would have done her part – got Clifford and Denny involved, supported the girls, indulged Rita's dreams...

'And maybe they'll do more than one performance,' added Anita hopefully.

'No,' said Clara. 'One is quite enough, thank you.'

One is too much.

. . .

The day before, though, Rita caught a cold and spent the evening under a towel at the sink, breathing in camphor.

'What if I'm not well enough?' she kept saying before diving back under.

'If you're not well, you're not well,' said Clara before adding guiltily, 'there will be other shows, I'm sure.'

She let Anita know that Rita was poorly. Perhaps they wouldn't be able to go after all? She couldn't help it: the prospect of cancellation filled Clara with joy. Oh, to get out of this damn thing! She wondered what she would say to comfort Rita if they didn't go; she could suggest next year, or another event. She would be encouraging, of course, but it was all so tiresome. There were so many other worries, this was just another unnecessary worry planted on her back. Putting themselves out there, what if everyone laughed, what if the council got angry? What if they failed? She had always wanted the children to pursue their interests, but performance was a different thing – performance was vulnerability, performance depended on other people. Having lost their parents, some of the children were desperate for validation, and Clara thought it was not helpful to feed that need. And she was concerned Clifford would do something to spoil it. Anita never stopped telling her how marvellous he was, a born performer, and yet he was so unpredictable...

Rita being poorly might be the best news yet. Clara went to bed feeling lighter than she had for ages.

Rita woke the next morning feeling much better: 'I'm one hundred and twenty per cent today, Miss Newton!' she said as she ran to do her plaits. (Clara suddenly missed Alex, who would have enjoyed the mathematical hyperbole.)

'We'll be the best there!' Rita diligently added her matching ribbons and put her costume on, clutching Peg with glee. 'We're going to perform at the Hippodrome!'

'They might not choose you.' Clara knew that was dour, but she couldn't help herself. She had that heavy feeling back in her stomach.

'Why wouldn't they?' Rita looked bemused.

Denny was so nervous he couldn't eat. Clifford tucked into his left-over porridge and then spent a long time staring in the mirror.

Clara had thought the boys might resist the costumes, but the thrill of clothes that weren't hand-me-downs had won them over. Clifford was delighted: 'I didn't know clothes could feel so soft.'

They met Anita and Evelyn at the station and Anita gave Clara the up and down and said, 'You're wearing that?'

Obviously.

'Yes, why?' *I took off my apron*, thought Clara, *what more do you want?*

And she was wearing a nice jumper, actually, with cuffed sleeves, that made her look like she had a shape, and not a rectangle. It was the jumper she had worn to the auction last year, that time when Ivor had said, 'God knows I'm absolutely...' And the skirt was only three or four years old, definitely post-war.

Anita pursed her lips. 'There might be some eligible chaps there.'

Eligible chaps are the last thing I need, thought Clara, but she offered brightly, 'I can run home and get changed if you like?' It was safe to say that since Anita was very worried about missing the train.

Evelyn and Rita were holding hands as they walked from Ipswich station. Remarkable how much better they got on now they didn't live together. Evelyn was taller and broader than ever, making Rita look even more slight and skinny than she really was. Peg and Maureen followed, then Clifford and Denny, both looking like they were pretending they weren't there. Clifford's hands were deep in his pockets. Denny had his usual air of uncertainty and bewilderment. Clara took Denny's hand, but he kept his limp and unresponsive, so she went back to walk with Anita.

The audition was in a hall so tucked away, so inconspicuous, that they would have walked straight past it if Rita hadn't spied the small handwritten notice:

AUDITIONS   TODAY   FOR   SUFFOLKS   OWN FESTIVAL OF BRITAIN

All capitals and not an apostrophe in sight, thought Clara pedantically. *Not a good sign.*

But the children responded differently: they were building themselves up to a state of frenzied excitement. Peg jumped up and down.

Rita squealed. 'Will there be any famous people here today?'

'Most definitely,' Anita promised.

Clara looked around her and snorted. 'I doubt it.'

At the door they were met by a tall, young woman with a clipboard and an expression like a prison guard.

'Have you a pencil?' she greeted them.

'Uh no, sorry,' said Clara. She patted her coat pockets and then trawled through her carpet bag just to appear helpful. Anita was looking horrified. Clara wondered if perhaps this was all going to be a big let-down for her. Anita had been looking forward to it for so long. Maybe in pre-war Poland, festivals were a big and wonderful thing, but she might be going to find out that in post-war Britain, they weren't up to much.

'Oh well.' The woman gave up and peered at her list. 'Who are you then?'

'We're from the Michael Adams Children's Home.' Clara enunciated clearly. Already Denny was jiggling up and down like he needed the lav.

Anita cleared her throat and then grimaced.

Clipboard lady looked up, confused. 'There's no one here by that name.'

Clara leaned over and looked down the list.

'Oh, you've got us down as the Children of Shilling Grange Orphanage. It will need to be changed.'

'Well, I haven't got a pencil,' Clipboard lady said.

'But it's not... we're not called that anymore.'

Anita made an embarrassed expression. 'I might have put that on the entry form – but it was before everything.'

For goodness' sake!

'It's fine to change it though, isn't it?' said Clara.

But Anita wasn't having it. 'Children of Shilling Grange Orphanage sounds better.'

'I think so too!' Maureen jumped in. 'Even my Joe thinks so.'

Anita was determined. 'And this is about giving the children as good a chance as possible.'

'But,' Clara began. 'But...' She had promised to send Michael's mother Marilyn the programme. She had been looking forward to that. How would it look if they weren't listed as the Michael Adams Children's Home? She pictured Marilyn's expectant face as she rifled through the pages – and then her disappointment.

So here was yet another reason for Clara to hope they wouldn't proceed to the next stage.

.   .   .

Once they were in, Clara went on a wild goose chase to find the lavatory for Denny. Then she stood outside the men's, awkwardly waiting for him. When eventually Denny came out, he said, 'My tummy hurts.'

'It's just nerves,' she told him, crossing her fingers behind her back.

They were shown to a room to wait and Clara was pleased to find it was large and bright. Clipboard lady had told them they were expecting nineteen acts and that they would be number twelve. She didn't know how many would get through the audition, though. As they had some time to kill, Anita took out some playing cards. Clara was impressed that she had had the foresight to bring something to do, but at the same time, she was nervous. *Cards.* Clifford was bound to start a fight; there'd be crowing or loud accusations of cheating. However, for once – maybe it was the change of scene or Anita's beady eye – everyone looked delighted and played rummy nicely in a circle.

At a small hatch in another room, they were charging two shillings for a cup of pale grey tea. Clara remembered her father complaining that tea was 'exorbitant' wherever he went, and hoped she was not turning into him. The two women were chatting as they brewed, and ignored her.

'Did you see the crowd of orphans? I swear one of them spoke like the Artful Dodger.'

'They're all like that. I'm surprised they're allowed out.'

'Make sure you keep an eye on your bag.'

'I hid it soon as I heard they were here.'

Reaching across the sopping-wet counter for the cups, Clara lied tartly: 'They're actually the favourites to win.'

Awful people.

They started calling up the candidates. Number one was two girls in ballet tutus. Both had their hair pulled back so tightly, it must have been painful. They did a ballet routine that was sweet but nothing special, Clara decided, but it got a big encouraging cheer, so what did she know? Next up, number two, was a one-man band. 'The acoustics aren't bad,' said Anita. Clara nodded agreeably. Acoustics were something to do with sound, but they were another thing she didn't know much about. Treading the boards and greasepaint weren't her world – never had been – and it felt uncomfortable to be leading the children into the unknown. Bored by the acts, she kept going over Ivor's bad temper with her. Had it been that bad to tell Anita that Ivor was struggling? She knew he was a private person, but there was private and there was shutting yourself away from the world. Anyway, she hadn't said anything that wasn't true.

The puppet theatre – number three – looked lovely, European somehow, but the story itself, of a woman who lost her goose, was disappointing. Clara yawned. She had seen better, years ago with Judy.

When Clifford thumped down next to her on the floor, Clara braced herself. He always seemed to want a fight.

'I've decided I'm calling myself Cliff from now on. It's more modern,' he said. 'You don't mind?'

Clara thought there was hardly any difference, but she saw from his expression this was important to him. Perhaps this was a chance to reach out to him. 'I don't mind.'

His face broke into a rare smile. 'I thought you'd tell me I mustn't.'

'No, Clifford – Cliff,' she said correcting herself quickly. 'Why not?' It was nice to be encouraging for once. 'I'd love to change my name,' she added, although it had never actually occurred to her.

'What would you change it to?'

'Something sophisticated like... Ingrid. Or Diane?' She couldn't imagine her mother's reaction, had she come home saying that: 'What will your father think?' probably.

He nodded.

She realised it was the first conversation they'd had in a while that didn't involve her telling him off. Perhaps things were improving? Perhaps all it had taken was a passion?

Number four fell off a unicycle. The audience were kind and didn't laugh the first time, but when he did it the second time there were a few sniggers, and the third time a man sitting near them shouted out, 'Learn to ride!' The poor chap picked up his unicycle and stomped off the stage, shouting, 'I bet you couldn't do any better.' The shouty man shrugged at Clara and said, 'That's one hour I'll never get back.'

Clara thought you could never get back hours, but she smiled because she found him intimidating and she didn't want him to turn on them too. He was drinking out of a hip flask and his nose glowed red.

Number five didn't turn up. While number six, a small boy on the piano played 'Keep the Home Fires Burning', Anita told the children to gather round, and Clara watched, impressed, as even Clifford joined the Anita-huddle obediently.

'We're up twelfth,' said Anita. 'As I always say: lucky number twelve.'

Clara made her face. She had never heard Anita say any such thing. To her mind, few people were less superstitious than Anita. Clara had to yell at her about putting up umbrellas in the house.

Clara wondered what the children were thinking about it all. This was really Rita and Anita's circus. The rest of them were the monkeys. Anita hissed advice at them – apparently, they were to lower their heads for three seconds at the end.

'These people have your future in your hands. Make it easy for them to say yes. Be likeable people—'

'Anita!' interrupted Clara. She was filling their heads with rubbish. 'It's not that important.'

'Shhh,' said Anita cheerfully. 'This is my – how you say? – prep talk.'

'Pep,' muttered Clara.

And then they did their warming-up and their loosening-up exercises, and Clara wanted to laugh at Clifford pulling his mouth into all sorts of shapes, and Denny touching his toes, Rita's finger stretches and Maureen sticking her tongue out and curling it up at the sides like a cigar.

Number seven played the flute beautifully. Clara watched a couple in the audience – presumably his parents – brimming over with pride and it made her heart ache that her children, the children of the Michael Adams Children's Home, didn't have that.

Anita made a face at her, then whispered, 'Derivative.'

On the other side of her, Maureen whispered, 'Did you know Joe can play whistle?'

Number eight were violin-playing twins. The 'Bow Sisters' were talented and beautiful but, Clara thought, and she wasn't being biased here, they belonged in an Edwardian sitting room; they just didn't seem to be crowd-pleasers. She remembered suddenly that years ago, she and Michael had gone to a variety show, and it had been mostly ladies with feathers over their privates, blowing kisses at servicemen. She remembered sniffing, 'Where's the variety?' and Michael laughing.

Number nine was an impersonator – Clara didn't pay much attention so she wasn't sure who he was impersonating, but the audience clapped and laughed. Ten was a band who said they were the next big thing. After their tuneless set, Anita leaned to Clara: 'If they're the next big thing, God help all of us.'

Anita was in great spirits, and Clara wondered if it was just that Anita loved this kind of thing or if she really was sure the children were that remarkable. She was acting like the results were a fait accompli.

Number eleven was another clown with a terribly sad face. The hip-flask man was here to support him, Clara realised, for he howled at his not-funny jokes – and he was the only one who stood up to clap. And then it was the children's turn and Clara realised she was very nervous indeed. This *had* to go well.

None of the audience looked up when the children trooped up to take their positions. *It'll be fine*, Clara told herself. *If they make fools of themselves, it doesn't matter*. The whole thing was a disappointment waiting to happen and yes, if that made her a misery-guts then so be it.

Denny stood with Clifford, both leaning over the piano. Clara was confused. Wasn't he meant to be on percussion? Please let him get through it without wetting himself. Even more confusing was Peg. She was sitting at a set of drums, her hair clipped back, her face screwed up in concentration. *What's going on*, thought Clara. Peg couldn't play the drums. She wondered if they were for number thirteen instead. But there were Maureen and Evelyn too, giggling and nudging each other; Evelyn searched the crowd for a familiar face and, bewildered as she was, Clara gave her a thumbs-up.

Rita rearranged her plaits and then her papers. She knew the set by memory, but she needed the score for reassurance. She never played without it – 'It's like a coat of armour!' Anita had explained to Clara. Now Clara watched as Rita deliberately placed her fingers on the keys, counted to herself, then began. Clara breathed a sigh of relief. It was a lovely serene, sweeping introduction, which you were led to believe – tricked into thinking – was the beginning of a very serene classical piece. But just as you were nestling down to that, it segued into a *doo-wop, doo-wop* bit, with Clifford and Denny singing and clicking their fingers.

It was an upbeat arrangement of 'Twinkle, Twinkle, Little Star', realised Clara suddenly. *Clever Anita*, she thought, annoyed that she hadn't recognised it straight away. Well, what an idea; this was Anita trying to win over the locals. How could they say no?

Anybody would have thought Denny was sweet – impossible not to – but Clifford— Cliff, he was a revelation. If usually he was shifty or sly, he was the opposite on stage – so confident and charming, it was hard to take your eyes off him. He loved the spotlight and the spotlight loved him. Clara had never seen him like this before and she could hardly believe it.

Maureen was also a little star, she and Evelyn swaying and singing alongside each other, joyous and heartfelt; and Peg? She really could play the drums. She looked wonderful there: a wild little thing, giggling as she smacked the life out of them. *How? What?* Clara wondered. The girl who never kept still for long had found her hobby. Peg was always a happy little girl, but behind the drum kit she looked like a queen.

It was Rita's event though, of course it was. First, she played the piano and then she sang, with the others backing her. She had an unusual voice – it was very grown-up especially for one so small – and you could sense the audience react warmly to it. It was wonderful but still, Clara couldn't relax, she remained nervous of what Clifford might do. Once he winked across at her, and she wondered, *is he going to jump off the stage or set light to it or smash it up?*

He didn't ruin it. At the end of the song, the group did their three-second head bow, then impeccably walked offstage. Two elderly women in the audience struggled up to stand and clap. The drunken hip-flask man also stumbled to his feet and shouted, 'Bravo!', and the twin ballet dancers hopped up and down.

Anita was the first to find Clara, her face wreathed in smiles.

'What did you think then?'

'Well!' Clara said. 'You didn't tell me about Peg!'

'I invited you to watch,' Anita said coolly. 'You never wanted to come.'

'I had no idea...' Clara said.

'She made a couple of mistakes,' Anita said, 'but she's not bad.'

The children raced over to them. Denny and Peg were laughing. Clara hadn't seen Denny so happy since he'd arrived. She had thought that Anita had included him and Peg out of sympathy or a sense of duty, but now she saw it was more than that – they added spirit and fun to the group, they kept them together.

Clara hugged the children who would be hugged and smiled at those who wouldn't.

'You missed a bit in the third section.' Anita nudged Rita.

'I know,' Rita said, downhearted. 'I forgot the change of key in the second verse.'

'It was still wonderful,' said Clara quickly. *Why did Anita have to be so strict with Rita?* 'And you had a cold yesterday, didn't you?'

But the children didn't seem to mind. Anita said to Clara, 'And Clifford sounds like Sinatra, doesn't he?'

'Kind of,' admitted Clara, watching the boy strut around the room. He would make a peacock feel inadequate. Today he hadn't been half so difficult as she imagined. Perhaps it was all in her head.

Rita's piano playing was exceptional, Clara had always known that. And Anita had been rehearsing Maureen, Evelyn and Peg for a while. But Clifford and Denny were new and in just a short space of time, Anita had whipped them all together into something remarkable.

'Goodness, you sounded like a real group!' Clara said. She still couldn't quite believe it. Even Denny, even *Clifford*! He was a rare talent, it was true. She would never have guessed. And the way they gelled together was really something.

'We *are* a real group!' Maureen snapped at her, while Anita smiled proudly.

'Aren't we just! I told you it was worth it, Clara. We're going to upset a few expectations.'

And then there were more acts on stage. Number thirteen was the unicycle man again, only this time he was *sans* unicycle and with puppets: one was a dog perhaps, the other was a horse. The shouty man from before didn't like this one bit and shouted, 'That's not a real dog!'

'How long until we know?' Clara whispered. Now they'd performed, the knot in her guts had unravelled. And she wanted to know. They *were* in with a chance, she realised; and what's more, she thought they *deserved* one. Despite herself, Clara found she was rooting for them – although it would be fine if it ended here, of course.

'Just four more. There's Mr and Mrs Scallywag next – they're clowns, I think.'

More clowns? Clara sighed. She had never understood the point of clowns.

A juggler came on. He was young and spotty and when he dropped his rubber balls, he ran off, while the balls wobbled poignantly there.

Peg didn't like the ventriloquist, Bartholomew Parsons – or rather she didn't like Nathan the dummy's waxy face – and sat on Clara's lap, covering her eyes. Clara thought it wasn't bad at all. And then they were finished. They waited half an hour or so for the announcements, and then a young man hobbled out with a walking stick (the war?) and said, 'Sorry, folks, the judges can't agree – we're going to take some more time.' A few people hissed and he raised his hands in surrender: 'The standard is so high!'

Clara felt restless. It had taken a whole day! She thought of her washing still out on the line. She thought of dinner that she had only half-prepared and food deliveries she was expecting and how busy she would be tomorrow, catching up. *Anita didn't realise that*, she thought ruefully, no one did.

The children were back on the floor, playing cards. Clara wished she had brought a magazine or a book for herself. Then she noticed Clifford was trying to chat up one of the violinist sisters. She was squirming away from him, pulling at the cuffs of her sweater and wagging her bow. Clara hurried over.

'I'm sorry, I'm not allowed out,' the girl was telling him uneasily. She was looking around for support.

'And nor are you, Clifford.'

'I'm Cliff,' he snapped, 'remember?'

'Whoever you are.' Clara steered him away, apologising to the girl as she did so.

'I was only—'

'No,' she snapped. 'Please. Not now.'

You couldn't take your eyes off him for a second.

Finally, a spotlight on the stage floor – all eyes turned to it – and then a different man, an older man with a double chin, came and stood in the centre of it. For a moment Clara thought he might be beamed up to Mars like the spacemen in one of Peter's comics. She was holding her breath.

'Ladies and gentlemen, we are so proud that Suffolk is taking part in the Festival of Britain, a celebration of our nation's resilience and courage. This festival is to mark the start of our progressing to a brighter and more prosperous future.'

Rolling her eyes, Clara looked around for kindred spirits. No one believed this propaganda, surely? No one seriously thought things were suddenly going to turn around because of a series of concerts and variety shows? But everyone else was nodding along, so she kept her cynicism to herself.

'We will be sending three acts to perform in the Hippo-drome in Ipswich, and it will showcase our county's contribution and talent. And the show will be compèred by none other than star of stage, screen and wireless, Donald Button.'

Donald Button? At this the audience gasped – everyone, that is, except for Anita, who merely shrugged like she had known this all along. Clara's stomach – already wobbly – went disconcertingly swirly. Everyone loved Donald Button.

'Without further ado, I am going to name the winning entrants. In no particular order...'

Denny tugged Clara's hand. 'I really need the toilet.'

'Just a moment... shhh.'

'Mr and Mrs Scallywag, the clowns.'

They were a popular choice, Clara saw, incredulously. Hip-flask man stood up to clap.

'It's too late,' whispered Denny.

'Bartholomew Parsons and Nathan the dummy.'

The ventriloquist? thought Clara. Oof. Two places gone. It was looking more and more unlikely that it would be the children, then.

The man on the stage was drawing it out, enjoying himself. 'And finally, a very special entrant, with a very Suffolk flavour...'

And Clara knew.

'We're sure you'll agree they were *exactly* what the Festival of Britain is all about: The Children of Shilling Grange Orphanage.'

9

The Children of Shilling Grange Orphanage, who would be part of Suffolk's Very Own Festival of Britain celebrations, had the train carriage to themselves on the way home. They spread themselves out, luxuriating in their victory, lying around with their feet on the seats, and for once, Clara didn't tell them off. How could she? They were beside themselves. Clifford yanked down the window and leaned out, 'We won!' then cursed as the wind blew his Brylcreemed hair all over his face.

'Told you we'd do it,' Rita said matter-of-factly.

'Now the hard work really begins,' Anita kept saying but no one was listening, or rather no one was taking it in.

'Joe is going to be so excited to see us at the Hippodrome,' squealed Maureen.

Joe is not invited, thought Clara, but she'd tackle that one later. She had to get her head around this first. It wasn't over, they were going forwards and she had to support them all the way. She forced herself to smile. Rita and Evelyn were virtually bouncing on their seats and even little Denny, now he was in the clean trousers and pants Clara carried everywhere 'for accidents', was smiling fit to burst.

Now Peg scribbled a note: 'Who is Donald Button?' it said.

'Donald Button,' Clara explained, 'was *Good Housekeeping* magazine's Man of the Year in 1942, 1946 and 1949.'

Peg frowned.

'I hope he wants to meet us,' said Rita.

'He's like a movie idol!' Maureen said authoritatively. 'He's handsome. Even my Joe says so.'

Clara lost her smile. Much as she adored Joe, hearing what he thought about every single thing made her want to kick things.

Anita was mulling over a schedule. 'Three evenings a week, two days at the weekend,' she said. 'We can do this.'

And Clara couldn't help thinking guiltily, *well, that's a lot of free time for me!*

Dr Cardew met them at the station exit with a bouquet of chrysanthemums. Howard was napping in the pram behind him, one socked foot peeping out of his blanket like a tail. They were both a vision of tranquillity and Clara couldn't help but feel relieved to see them there.

'How did you get on then?'

When they told him, he kissed Anita's cheek: 'I knew it! I'm proud of you, darling.' And then he flicked Evelyn's chin. 'Well done, my lovely girl! Well done, EVERYONE!'

It was sweet to see.

He leaned to Clara's ear and whispered, 'I bet you're delighted.' Dr Cardew was one of the few people who knew how Clara really felt about the Festival.

'Hmm,' she said, raising her eyebrows. 'Once this one is over with, I'll be happy.'

.   .   .

Of course, Rita wanted to go straight over to Ivor's workshop to tell him the news. Clara said no. She and Ivor hadn't spoken for two whole weeks now, since he'd told her off. Since he'd told her he didn't want her in his life. He'd gone way too far. She supposed they would make up soon, but he would have to come to her first. No way was she going to crawl to him.

Rita looked sulkily around her, then said, 'Well, *I* like Ivor.'

'So do I,' snapped Clara, 'but we've got lots to do at home, chop-chop.'

But they hadn't been home for long when Ivor appeared at the front door, Patricia nestled in his arm. She was wearing a shiny pair of baby shoes. Clara had never seen her in shoes before and it was a jolt. She was growing up quickly.

'She's walking now?'

'Not quite,' he said. He puffed out his cheeks and made an awkward popping sound. 'I was told she had to have them so I went and got them.'

Clara laughed. She knew *that* feeling.

He looked at her intently. 'I'm really sorry about the other day,' he said as he jogged Patricia up and down. 'It was unkind of me. I've just been so exhausted, Clara. It wasn't fair to take it out on you, though. I'm sorry, I was wrong. I know you mean well.'

Clara was still struggling to find the right words to say to him when the children ran downstairs and threw their arms around him and then there was no need to say anything. He knew she'd forgiven him anyway, she supposed. He accepted Rita's shouted offer of tea. Clara had to tell him she had no cake, no biscuits, nothing to offer him with it, and he said that was fine – in fact, he'd had some Victoria sponge earlier – and she squinted at him. *Where was he getting cake from?* She didn't like that.

Despite the lack of refreshments, it turned out to be a lovely evening. The children were still brimming over with their success; even Clifford was full of it, and for a while Clara could forget how naughty he had been recently. He had been brilliant; he *did* sing like Sinatra and he was so generous with his praise: 'Lovely cuppa, Missus,' he said as she passed him a cup, and 'Miss Newton really looked after us today.'

Ivor raised his eyebrows at Clara as if to say, *and what have you done with Clifford?*

Clara lit the fire in the parlour without getting too sooty and they relived the day. The children were aghast that Mr and Mrs Scallywag, the clowns, had got through too.

'It's an insult,' Rita said.

Clara stifled a laugh.

'My Joe gets scared by clowns,' Maureen said, 'I'm not joking. Clowns and policemen.'

Denny's peaky little face was lit up as he laughed just a touch later than everyone else. Sometimes his eyes filled with tears. Peg rested her head in his lap and he stroked her soft hair. Clara liked seeing them together.

Rita was showing off. If it weren't for her, she announced, they'd have got nowhere. They'd have been like the awful fella on his unicycle. This was harsh, Clara thought, although it was probably true: Rita had carried the show. The other children didn't seem to mind hearing it though; it probably wasn't the first time they had.

And Clifford – she kept forgetting to call him Cliff, but he was being all right about it – was better at impersonations than number nine, the man who had done impersonations at the auditions had been. Who knew? Cliff's Churchill, Lord Haw-Haw, and Chamberlain and his White Paper had them all in fits. Denny laughed so much, it turned to hiccups. Ivor said, 'It was genius,' and Clifford kept saying, 'I thank you.' He did a great impersonation of the King stuttering and then of Edward VIII getting amorous with Mrs Simpson until Clara told him that was quite enough, thank you.

Clifford was like the girl with the curl from the nursery rhyme. *When he was good, he was very, very good, but when he was bad, he was horrid...*

'Now, Miss Newton,' Ivor said in the formal tone he sometimes used with her in front of the children. 'I need to know your middle name.'

The children loved a guessing game. They made some wild guesses – *Cleopatra? Really? What about Boudicca?* Clara was chuckling too. 'Okay, I'll give you a clue. It begins with A.'

They guessed again. *Ann. Ann with an E. Anna. Annabella.*

Peg wrote down some guesses. At the bottom of her list was 'Agnes?'

'Peg got it!' yelped Clara. Everyone fell about laughing, Ivor the loudest of the lot.

'Agnes? I'd never have put you down for an Agnes.'

'Well, I am!' Clara pretended to be offended, but she loved it when Ivor was playful. This was how he used to be before Ruby came back, before everything. 'Named for a great-aunt. And very happy with it, I am too.'

Ivor laughed so hard, then straightened up. 'Well, for my purposes, it couldn't be better.'

Then Patricia woke up and put her all into those high-pitched wails again, and the old, carefree Ivor disappeared, replaced by the new, clenched-tight father Ivor.

'Right, boss,' he said to the baby. 'Let's get you home. Sorry, Clara.'

Clara walked Ivor to the door. Everything felt brighter now. The effect he had on her mood was tremendous – she didn't *like* that he had that power, but he did. The world looked different when Ivor was on her side.

'I'll look after Patricia again tomorrow if you like – me and Maureen perhaps? You'll be able to get some work done. And she's a lovely little thing.'

Clara knew that the more sweet things she said about the baby, the more she would come to mean them.

He was already half into the street. Patricia was screaming to wake the dead. Her mouth was a wide-open black tunnel of rage.

'Don't worry, it's fine.'

'It's fine for me too!' Clara had to wait until Patricia took a breath to say it.

'No, honestly, I... er... might be getting a proper babysitter.'

'Oh!' Clara was flabbergasted by this. She reminded herself she had no right to be; she and Maureen weren't the only capable women in the world, or in Lavenham. But still it felt like a rejection.

'Maureen could have still helped.' *Damn Maureen. If she hadn't let him down that time...*

'I know, but I needed someone in the day when Maureen is at school.'

She was glad he didn't say out loud that Maureen was unreliable but Clara guessed that was what it was.

'Or I could help?'

'Clara...' Ivor laughed gently at her as Patricia howled for England. 'Don't you have enough on your plate with five orphans and now the Hippodrome?'

'I suppose,' she said uselessly. 'Excellent.' Patricia quietened down, probably building up to one of her grand finales.

'And Dr Cardew and I are having some discussions about my arm, thanks to you.'

'Oh.' She found herself tongue-tied again. 'That's good too.'

She would never tell him that sometimes she had silly fantasies of tending it herself, like a nurse in the films. Not that she knew anything about caring for an amputated arm, but in her daydream, she did. She would tell him his arm didn't matter or that she'd never let it come between them. She would say it didn't make her feel differently about him one iota – but then he probably never suspected that it would (or cared very much either way).

Once he'd left, she couldn't help thinking of the way he looked at her when he said, '*for my purposes*' about her middle name.

What did that mean?

It was a look of affection – or was it one of conspiracy?

His smile, even when exhausted, and the outline of him… These were very shallow thoughts, Clara knew that, but the shape of him made her breathless. The more she tried not to think about him in that way, the more she did. *Don't even think about him in his white vest…*

She hoped that one day it would go away, this infernal *thing* she had for him. It got in the way of their friendship. It was untidy. It would disappear, she was sure of it. No one could live in this heightened state for ever, not if they were married – *imagine if they were married?*

NO. They were friends now. He knew how she felt about him, she might know how he felt… Did she, though? But between them they had a vast army of commitments, one of whom was only eight months old. Well, to do anything about silly feelings at such a precarious time would be selfish and irresponsible and downright wrong.

And yet now he had a 'babysitter'?

She shoo-shooed the children to bed. They were still radiant; success had set them off. As she was tucking her in, Rita suddenly covered her mouth.

'We didn't ask Ivor his middle name!'

'No, we didn't,' Clara said guiltily. What an oversight.

She watched out of the window until she saw Ivor's lights go out, and then for a little longer so if anyone had happened to see, it wouldn't look too obvious that was what she was doing.

10

Clara had some invoices to take to the council and while she was there, she went to see glamorous Miss Cooper in her messy little office. There was a photo of Clement Attlee behind her chair, peeling in the bottom left corner. Other women liked film stars, Miss Cooper liked Labour politicians.

'Denny is settling in well,' Clara began. She thought of his growing attachment to Peg and Rita. His schoolteacher said he was 'a credit but quiet'. He was *very* quiet, but he didn't cry as much as he had when he first arrived, and he got on with things. He had found a banana box and filled it with bits for Stella. On the side, it said, '*Stella's space. Only cats and Denny aloud*'. If it wasn't for his wetting and occasional sleepwalking you mightn't know that he was grieving – and even those could be down to other reasons too.

Miss Cooper massaged her feet. She said she had been dancing too much lately. Clara didn't know how to respond.

'Have you?' she finally asked and Miss Cooper looked up at her with narrowed eyes, saying, yes, yes, she had, before putting her feet away.

'And the other new one?'

'Cliff is not easy,' Clara confessed. Just when she thought he was behaving himself, she got a report from someone – the postman, the headmaster, Mr Browne – that he wasn't. At home, he joined in, did his chores and was, if not pleasant, then quite okay. It was when he was out of the house that he couldn't seem to resist getting into trouble. The other evening, Clara had quietly asked Ivor if he had any jobs for the boy and he had sucked in his breath and said he hadn't. But he said Clifford could come over any time, perhaps they could chat? Clifford, of course, wouldn't go. *Why would I want to go over there and sew like a girl?*

'That's all right,' said Miss Cooper breezily, her chin resting on her fist. 'Can I help you with anything else?'

'I don't know if it is all right,' mused Clara. She wished she still had Mrs Horton as her childcare officer. Clara had asked to see her, only to be told she was too busy with cemeteries. Mrs Horton would tell her what to do. Mrs Horton would have an A–Z plan. Miss Cooper just wafted around dreamily – the only thing that got her animated was elections.

'Have you found the file on him yet?' Clara asked.

'I don't have his files, Clara,' Miss Cooper said, 'You'll just have to start your own.'

'I don't know how to get him to behave...'

'You could take away his pudding?'

'Pudding?' They only had pudding once a week.

'Or his crackers,' Miss Cooper said impatiently. 'Or give him less breakfast?'

As Clara was leaving the first floor, Mr Horton followed her out. She hadn't seen him since his wedding. He did, she had to admit, look very well as a newly-wed. His shirt was ironed, his hair was flattened, and his skin had a healthier pallor. They greeted each other, and Clara tried not to imagine Mr and Mrs Horton leading their idyllic married lives together. She thought again of how she missed Mrs Horton.

In the somewhat gloomy stairwell, he turned to her.

'About the boy... Clifford, is it?'

'Yes.'

'I thought so.' He crinkled up his newly-wed face. 'Do you want me to take him out? I could take him to the bowling green.'

Mr Horton take him out? 'Sorry?'

'Good for young chaps to get some fresh air.'

She could just about imagine Clifford's expression if she suggested that. Surely bowls with Mr Horton was worse than sewing with Ivor?

'It's worth a try,' she said. Better than a belt or a slipper, that was for sure. If she couldn't use punishments, well, maybe it was time to focus on rewards.

Marilyn Adams – Clara's late fiancé's mother, great friend and now landlady from a distance – was much better at telephoning than Peter. She called Clara every two weeks or so and she also wrote long letters and sent funny postcards. She loved travelling and told Clara she was shortly setting off to Central America. Clara didn't know what to say to this – Central America felt as remote to her as the moon. Possibly, Clara could have asked for some financial help from Maureen, but she didn't. Although Marilyn was helpful, immensely helpful, she wasn't very interested in the practical side of things. She liked hearing about people and relationships, not burst drains and rotten windows.

She telephoned that evening, and it was a relief to hear that warm, encouraging voice down the line.

'How are my babies?'

If anyone else said 'my babies' Clara would find it annoying. Or as if they were staking a claim. Not Marilyn, though – Marilyn was too big-hearted for that.

'Did you get through to the next round of the Festival thingy?'

'We did...' Clara said cautiously. Would she mind that for this the children were still using the old name of Shilling Grange? Marilyn was a woman who didn't mind anything until she did, and then she really did. She had a hot temper if one of her own was wounded.

'So, I'll see the Michael Adams Children's Home up in lights soon?'

'Something like that,' mumbled Clara, watching Stella claw at the washing basket.

∾

Peg wet the bed that night.

'You can come in mine,' said Clara as usual. 'I'll tell you a story about a...' She racked her brains. What would Peg like? '...about a... travelling band of children.'

Peg shook her head.

Clara felt a little hurt. Peg had never refused a story or Clara's bed before.

'Everything okay, Peg?' she whispered as she pulled the damp sheet off the mattress.

Peg nodded.

'Is it... are you happy performing?'

Peg winced, then nodded vigorously. Moving quietly, Clara placed the clean sheet down. Rita and Maureen were both still asleep.

'You know you don't have to do it, no one does.'

Peg climbed into bed and squeezed shut her eyes. It was like she was trying to get Clara to stop. Clara pulled the blanket over her, whispering, 'Night, Peg.'

Clara blamed herself. She had taken her eye off Peg lately – you did with the quiet ones, the ones who just got on with things. Peg was always off skipping or dancing in the garden or playing hopscotch or jacks. She had written down once that she pretended that she was the mummy looking after her children. She could be alone for hours and hours. If she wasn't outside, she would be rearranging her collection of seashells or drawing. No one entertained themselves as well as Peg did. And Clara had had no idea she played the drums so well. That had been a shock to her, and it shouldn't have been.

But maybe something else was going on now.

A few days after Clara's trip to the council, Mr Horton picked up Clifford and they went off together. It was lovely, Clifford being out, yet Clara knowing where he was. She hoped it was the start of something positive. She had thought singing in the group would be that, and yes, it had been, but it was not quite enough. The previous morning, the school had called to say that Clifford was no longer to eat in the canteen because of an incident with another boy over a sherbet lemon.

When they came back, Clifford thumped upstairs two at a time, and Mr Horton stood uneasily in the kitchen, fiddling with the paper of scores.

'He's very good at bowls actually. Great hand-eye coordination.'

Clifford was that rare type who was good at everything he put his mind to.

'So, you'll take him again?'

'Don't think so.' Mr Horton admitted. 'He is a... difficult boy.'

On Monday morning, Mr Browne was at the doorway of the Home, blocking the way, just as the children were about to set out for school. Maureen flushed scarlet and backed away from the door like a bear was there.

'Hello, Maureen,' he said in his pompous voice. 'Long time no see.'

'Go out the back door, everyone,' Clara told the children, and approached Mr Browne nervously. She wasn't going to invite him in. She loathed the man and the ground he walked on.

He touched the brim of his hat. 'I need to talk about one of your charges.'

It wasn't about Maureen, Clara quickly realised. But there was no time for relief – she could guess who it was about and that wasn't going to be any better.

'Your boy hit my Martin.'

Martin was a mean-spirited, mean-faced youth. Out of all the people Clifford could hit, she would get the least agitated about him hitting Martin Browne.

'I see.'

Mr Browne grabbed Clara's arm. 'What are you going to do about him then?'

Clara shook him off. *Hateful man.*

'I will talk to him,' she snapped. 'Now, if you'll excuse us, we have to get to school.'

He tipped his hat at her, but sneered, 'Talking is not enough.'

No, talking was not enough, but talking was all she had right now. She'd been able to understand the children's bad behaviour, seen its roots, seen the conditions that had made it grow. Clifford was different. He'd shut the child in the cupboard at school, he had weapons, he was overfamiliar with girls, and now he was beating up Martin Browne.

She was not going to go down the violent route though; she would not. Neither the slipper nor the ruler was for her.

~

Later, the children had finished tea and were about to go to Anita's for their rehearsal. Clara called Clifford back.

'No singing practice for you, Cliff!' She was relieved she'd got his name right. He seemed delighted when she got it wrong these days. 'Not until you apologise to Martin Browne.'

He sank down on his chair, quiet for a moment. And then he burst out, 'Mrs Cardew said I had to come.'

'Well, you can't.'

'I have to.'

'No.'

'He's a fat pig,' he said.

'That's two rehearsals you're going to miss.'

'I'll squash him.'

'Three...'

Clifford stared mutinously at her, but finally, he submitted. 'I'll say sorry then. Can I go now?'

She told him that wasn't good enough – he had lost his chance and would still miss three rehearsals. He went to sulk in his room. Clara had doubts, but she felt she had to send a message. If he wanted to perform, then it was imperative that he learned how to behave.

She realised that, at last, she had some leverage. He didn't care about much, but it seemed he cared about this. This was a result. Clifford responded to strictness and boundaries. Not all children liked Clara's softly, softly approach and that was why it was difficult, but now she could identify their individual needs, Clara knew she had cracked it.

As she walked up the road to the Cardews' later to fetch the other children, Clara felt quite happy. *Finally. This would make a difference.* Unfortunately, Anita didn't share her positivity. She was annoyed with her.

'Clifford is my main male voice.'

'Cliff,' said Clara automatically, but it seemed Anita didn't feel obliged to call him his new nickname.

'It's important he comes.'

'Well sometimes,' Clara said, '*other* things are more important.'

Anita looked mystified. Other things? Dr Cardew, who had popped in with a red-faced Howard, laughed: 'Anita, it's just one rehearsal.'

Clara cleared her throat, she decided now was not a good time to say it was three.

11

It was Mrs Harrington who was Patricia's new babysitter. Bloody Mrs Harrington – ex-council worker, enemy of Clara. Clara knew this because she had seen her come out of the workshop, tall and red-haired, with her pram, two babies sitting up in it, babbling away in bonnets. And then she had turned round and in her cloying sweet voice said to Ivor, 'Oh, we'll be good, I promise!'

Clara couldn't see if she winked, but she could well imagine she did. She felt sick.

Mrs Harrington?

Clara didn't see her come back that afternoon – Clara couldn't stare out all day, she had things to attend to – but later, when her car had gone, she told herself not to go over there: *none of your business, remember?* But Denny had already worn out the knees in his school trousers, so she had the perfect excuse.

'Hi, Ivor!' Now she sounded overenthusiastic. 'How are you?'

Of all the people in the world to look after Patricia, Ivor had to choose Mrs Harrington. What did that woman used to call

Ivor? 'Your dishy neighbour'! And she used to make eyes at him like no one's business. Even Mrs Horton, who pretended to be above observing such things, used to say it was possible Mrs Harrington had an 'infatuation'.

He was sewing by hand, a cushion cover or a pillowcase maybe. Patricia was on the rug, clutching a ball and then pressing it to her mouth.

'How's the new babysitter working out?'

Ivor smiled wryly. 'You saw who it was then?'

'Uh-huh.'

'I bumped into her at the library last week. She's bored, it's a pity she gave up work – she misses it and this way, Patricia gets company. It's a good arrangement. And it's not expensive. She's going to look after Patricia three times a week!'

Clara had a sinking feeling. It was not just that Mrs Harrington liked Ivor, it was that Mrs Harrington was so *slinky* somehow. She reminded Clara of a certain type of girl at school – the understudy always waiting to get the main role. Waiting, waiting and wishing bad things on everyone until she took her turn. And then everyone said she was marvellous.

Mrs Harrington had been cruel to Rita too, shattering the girl's dreams about her mother returning.

'She brought round cakes,' Ivor continued obliviously.

Oh yes, that would be right, thought Clara furiously. Mrs Harrington always had cake on her person – Anita often did too, and Mrs Horton, but Mrs Harrington always made such a song and dance about hers – and hers were always chocolate. Lord knew how she did it when no one could get chocolate. Clara suspected Mrs Harrington didn't even really like baking, she just did it for the power.

And there they were now, small rounds of chocolate fairy cakes. Clara's mouth watered. She hadn't seen cakes as beautiful as this since Mrs Horton's wedding.

'Take one.'

'No, thank you. Is she still married?'

Ivor looked at her strangely, for this was by any measure a strange question. 'I assume so.'

'Of course.'

Clara stared at the cakes. She remembered the May fête at the school and how the twins had slipped chocolate sponge cake onto the May Queen's seat. She wished someone would slip chocolate cakes under Mrs Harrington's bottom.

Clara had just been getting used to Ivor and their new fumbling way of getting along. Flirtatious Mrs Harrington felt like the worst kind of complication.

A few days later, Clara saw Mrs Harrington in the street, bumping the pram along the cobblestones. Clara tried to slip past her, pretend she was on an urgent mission, but Mrs Harrington was too wily for that and called out loudly: 'Miss Newton, I wondered when I'd bang into you.'

'Ah!' Clara performed a smile.

'Look at us, you're the old hand and I'm the young mother.'

Clara scowled. Mrs Harrington always managed to phrase a situation in the best possible way for her, and the worst possible way for Clara. It was quite a talent.

'I bet you're thinking about babies now. You must be what – thirty?'

'I'm not yet, actually.'

'Oh, well then.' Clara wasn't sure if she was listening or not. 'There are fewer eligible men now, aren't there, because of the war? I heard there were two times...'

'As many women as there are men. Yes, we're all aware of that,' Clara said, this time not bothering to be polite.

Mrs Harrington had the good grace to blush. 'Sorry.' She lowered her eyelashes. 'I forgot you know all about that.'

Clara muttered that she did indeed.

Mrs Harrington soon cheered up. 'I heard about the Suffolk show. I didn't think you were, you know... musical? At all. What about the one who doesn't speak? Peggy?'

'Peg.'

'What on earth does she do?'

What business was it of hers?

'She does very well.'

'I can't believe it. When Ivor told me the children were performing at the Hippodrome, I thought it was a joke.'

'We're thrilled,' lied Clara. *A joke? What did she mean?* 'It's a massive opportunity. It's part of the Festival of Britain. We will be showcasing this county's contribution and talent,' she said, copying the words of the presenter at the audition. 'Such an honour,' she added. Mrs Harrington was pushing her to it.

'Oh yes, hubby and I are going to that in London. We're going to stay in a hotel. A five-star. With a television set in the lounge.'

She always was fiercely competitive too.

Clara knew she was socially obliged to admire Mrs Harrington's baby, and after all he was a sweet, wide-eyed thing with a flat nose and shiny cheeks. It was not his fault that Clara was not mad about his mother.

'This is Leslie, Leslie with an I not a Y,' Mrs Harrington explained, as though there were something terrible about Y's. 'He's gifted.'

Of course he is, thought Clara to herself. She wasn't going to ask in what way, she wasn't.

'In what way?' she said finally. She couldn't stop herself. All she could see was a round baby, with chubby wrists like they had elastic bands round them – nice, but not half as nice as

Howie or Patricia. It made Clara pause to think how loyal she had become to her friends' babies.

'His milestones? He reached them way before anyone else. And Patricia, she's a darling, but hopefully, she's got more of whoever the father is than Ruby. Ruby wasn't the brightest sandwich in the picnic, was she?'

'I don't know, I never met her properly,' said Clara vaguely.

'I would have thought *you* of all people had,' said Mrs Harrington incredulously.

She seemed as pleased as if Clara had just outright admitted, *I don't know Ivor as well as you do.*

12

There was a dead mouse in the hall. It was the first thing Clara saw when she came down the stairs in the morning, and she let out a squeal. Poor little thing. Its tail was longer than its body. There were no signs of violence. It must have died of shock.

'STELLA!'

'She's only trying to be nice,' said Rita, lavishing love on the culprit. 'She's saying thank you.'

'I hope you all find other ways of thanking me.'

In fact, sighed Clara, the children did very little to thank her ever. One could say her entire day was a series of thankless tasks.

Peg was upset about the mouse and drew pictures of it. Clara thought one would be enough, but Peg did a whole dozen. Then she told Clara with signs and expressions that she was very angry with Stella, she was a bad cat.

'Stella does what cats do,' said Clara philosophically.

'Peg says that is stupid,' Rita jumped in.

Usually Peg accepted these pronouncements made on her behalf, wearily but with equanimity, but this time she got up and slapped her hand over Rita's mouth. Rita pushed her off and Peg pushed her back. Then Rita grabbed her hair.

Clara jumped in. 'What *is* going on?'

Both sat back at the table. Denny put his arm protectively around Peg. Maureen put her hands on Rita's shoulders.

Peg scribbled, 'Go away, Rita.'

Rita shrugged. In day-to-day life, she had amazingly thick skin. 'I didn't do anything.'

That evening, they went to Anita's for rehearsal, but Cliff wasn't allowed to go. He went up to his room and sulked. When Maureen got back, she said the rehearsal was rubbish. They *needed* Clifford. Clara wondered if she had been put up to say this by Anita, but Maureen seemed to mean it.

'He's being punished,' Clara explained again.

'For hitting Martin Browne?'

There was no point lying about it. Not to Maureen, who could smell an untruth several miles away.

'It may have been that, yes.'

Maureen gripped her arm. Her intensity took Clara by surprise. 'Martin was being horrible about me again – he calls me the Orphan-whore, he tells everyone my father is in jail for murder, he calls me a witch too. That's why Clifford hit him.'

'I see,' said Clara, though she realised she hadn't seen it at all.

She went up and told Clifford that he could go back to the rehearsals next time. He muttered that his name was Cliff not Clifford. She apologised. She waited for his reaction to the change in punishment, but he just grunted. She added violence was never the answer. He still said nothing, he was still angry with her. A mouse on the floor would have been an improvement.

13

Clara hadn't missed a Jane Taylor society meeting since her first one two years earlier. Now, this was something she loved, she only wished they were held more often. She enjoyed being in the library too – she had many happy memories of visiting with previous Home children: Joyce, Terry, Alex. Plus, the library was always cool and shadowy, whether it was freezing or humid outside.

Since she was early, she leafed through some magazines. She did the quick quiz in *Woman's Own*: 'Which Brontë sister are you most like?' and it turned out she was most like Anne. She sighed. What had she expected? she reprimanded herself. And Anne was brilliant! (Yet, she had hoped for Emily. Who wouldn't?)

She hadn't expected Ivor to come, because of Patricia, and he hadn't been for a while, but she had still hoped. Anita wasn't there either. Mr Dowsett took his place at the lectern. Sometimes Clara wondered if he would run out of things to say about Jane Taylor, but he never seemed to. He talked about how when Jane wrote, the country was struggling with the aftermath of the Napoleonic Wars. It was a time of great poverty and discontent, there were strikes and anti-government action. Mr Dowsett asked if anyone had questions, and Clara had one, but it seemed both obvious and rather obscure, and she didn't want to ask in front of everyone – the Garrards, the postmistress, Mr Robinson.

Over the tea trolley though, Clara had her opportunity: 'Do you think that the time we live in now is a bit like it was back then?'

'There are many similarities, yes,' Mr Dowsett said, he never made her feel silly. 'That was a generation recovering from great hardship; they were changed by these things: scarred but optimistic. War is terrible – but the response is often a powerful generation who endure and go on to do great things.'

'Do you think the next few years will be like that too?' She was only half-serious. 'We'll go on to do great things?'

'I sincerely believe the 1950s are going to be brilliant.'

Clara smiled at him fondly, this forward-looking, old mole-like man with his white beard – he must have some stories – and then he said, 'The Festival of Britain is going to kick-start a new golden age.'

Startled, Clara gulped. 'Maybe,' she said, before adding, 'or maybe it's just a big old fuss about nothing?'

It was Mr Dowsett's turn to look surprised. 'Oh? But I thought you and the children were involved.'

'The children are,' she said. She shook her head and one of her hair grips fell into her teacup. 'Not me. And well, it's only Suffolk not London. The Hippodrome in Ipswich.'

'Only Suffolk?!' he repeated incredulously. 'There's nothing *only* about Suffolk!'

As she fished out the grip, that at least made her laugh.

Before she left, Mr Dowsett thrust an old book of poems into her hands. 'I've been saving this for you,' he said. 'Poems by Jane's sister. There's one there I think you might like: "My Mother".'

~

March came in like a lion. It was cold and then searingly hot, sometimes in the same day. The mornings were brisk, coat weather; in the afternoons they were sweltering in short sleeves.

There was not long to go until the performance at the Hippodrome in Ipswich – and sometimes it felt as though the children were at the Cardews' more than they were at home. Rita talked about little else – would there be hippos at the Hippodrome? Or horses, what about them? What is a drome? Why isn't it a dome? Would Donald Button want to put them on the wireless? Why was he called Button? Did he collect buttons?

'Rita! Hush!'

~

Clara was in the kitchen heating up what Rita had decided was 'the most boringest soup in the world' when Maureen crashed in.

'Joe doesn't want to see me again!' she howled, then ran upstairs, almost knocking Peg out of the way. Clara followed and watched as Maureen threw herself dramatically on the bed. She was still wearing her muddy boots. Clara decided not to mention them.

'Joe said that? Why?'

'Because...' She was sobbing now '...he doesn't.'

'He must have given you a reason.'

Sudden turnarounds were often suspicious. And it *was* sudden. The last she'd known, the two of them were looking forward to going to an Easter egg hunt on Farmer Buckle's land. You wouldn't plan that if you were going to break it off.

'He won't say...'

Clara shouted downstairs to someone to please turn down the heat on the soup.

That night, for the first time in a long time, Maureen slept in Clara's bed, and Clara stroked her hair. Peg slept on her other side and kicked her in the throat. Rita joined and chatted until the cows came home.

Clara felt so sorry for Maureen. Her face was blotchy from the tears. The situation was none of her doing.

'You've got so much to look forward to, Maureen.'

'Like what?'

Clara startled. 'Well, the Festival of Britain for a start. The performance at the Hippodrome, remember? It's only next week.'

'No,' Maureen said firmly. 'I'm never going to sing again.'

14

At first, Clara wasn't too worried about Maureen's declaration. But as the days went by and Maureen still didn't budge, and she stopped going to rehearsals, she began to fear that the girl was being serious. Surprisingly, Anita wasn't alarmed though. She smoothed her lips with a finger and said, 'Maureen will come round.'

'I'm not sure she will,' Clara said. Maureen had seemed pretty adamant. That morning, Clara had thought it best to avoid the subject, but over the porridge Maureen had said, 'And you can tell Anita to stuff the stupid Hippodrome.'

'Oh, she will do it,' said Anita airily now. 'I'll make her.'

Anita's confidence in her persuasive talents was unwavering.

Miss Cooper was typing in her office. She wasn't a good typist, she was a one-finger-at-a-time typist. And something about this pleased Clara, for typing was something Clara could do better than anyone, and there was something so funny about people who had to stare at the keys. Clara would have liked to be able to cycle, to bake better and to knit well – but her special skill of typing, no, she wouldn't swap it for the world.

Miss Cooper wasn't very good with children either. She had no rapport with them. She treated them like little adults – which did work for some – but with no humour or gentleness. Clara sometimes wondered what she was doing in children's services at the council – she had her convictions, Clara supposed, and then what else was there to do? She'd make a worse shop assistant, nurse or teacher. Women who were allergic to children were well placed in the council.

Miss Cooper's office was boiling and the windows wouldn't open. Clara almost felt sorry for her until she asked her about Clifford's files – and was again told they had nothing.

What annoyed Clara even more than the nothing was Miss Cooper's reluctance to do anything about it.

'He has a history that I don't know anything about.'

Clara had been going to apologise to Cliff again about the whole Martin Browne affair when he came back from his next rehearsal. However, when the boys were out, she had made their beds and found scorch marks in his sheets. What had he been doing in there? Anita said he was very good again, 'more than good, wonderful', but increasingly, Clara found it hard to meet the boy's shifty eyes.

'You could open a file yourself?' Miss Cooper suggested again.

'I already have but there are thirteen years of blanks.'

'I will continue looking.'

Clara gazed around the office in despair. *How could Miss Cooper be so lackadaisical?*

'I could help you tidy up, Miss Cooper – or Maureen could.'

At this, Miss Cooper looked aghast. Her hand flew to her mouth. 'Our files are highly confidential.'

And *lost*, thought Clara. What was the point of them being

highly confidential if you couldn't find them? 'I'm just worried about what Clifford, Cliff will do – he's highly unpredictable.'

Miss Cooper gave up her one-finger typing and instead took a fly biscuit off the plate next to it. She dabbed at her lips, then raised her palms.

'I'd offer you one, but it was the last.'

Clara was already at the door when Miss Cooper called out, 'Good luck at the Hippodrome!'

'Will you be coming?' Clara asked.

Miss Cooper laughed and then looked serious again. 'Oh sorry, Labour Party meetings, you know.'

On the day of the all-important dress rehearsal – *the last chance to get it right!* – Maureen came back from school and went straight up to bed. Anita and Evelyn called in for her, but Maureen refused to see them.

Even then, Anita didn't seem overly worried. 'It's the Hippodrome!' she purred. 'Who'd want to miss that? They'd have to be mad, wouldn't they, Evelyn?'

Evelyn chuckled in her non-committal way.

While the other children rehearsed, Clara stayed home with Maureen. She could hear baby Patricia howling from across the road. She wondered if she should go over there to offer a hand, then decided not to. Although they'd made up, the things he'd said still burned. And she had enough problems of her own.

Maureen's broken heart was making the girl even more unpredictable. Would she really not go tomorrow? Would she really miss out on all the fun? Clara didn't have the stomach for a fight. She wasn't only worried about Maureen, she also worried about Joe. Joe was a good lad, not usually impulsive, nor did he have tantrums. He mightn't be her remit, never had been

– but still. If you didn't worry about young people, remit or not, there was something wrong with you.

Clara worried about the other children too: Poor Denny. And poor Peg. Cliff was still getting punished daily at school – what was she going to do with him? Rita was devoted to her piano and nothing else – did she have poor social skills? (Yes, she probably did.) Peter hadn't called again. Clara had tried calling him and there was no answer. She hadn't expected letters, but drawings or postcards, was that too much for him? Didn't he know how scary it was for her to have handed him over to... no one?

Sometimes, it felt like things were crumbling again. She just got things in her castle straight and firm and just-so, and along came a kid with a big spade and knocked everything down.

And elsewhere, the nation was gearing up to a big party! A big hurrah to say farewell to the lean times, adieu to bad luck – wasn't this all a bit premature when they were still having to ration eggs?

Clara thought of when she had first arrived in Lavenham off an early train from London, dragging her suitcase along. She wasn't yet thirty and yet she sometimes felt she had so much behind her, there couldn't be much room to go forward.

Recently, she found herself thinking about the war years more and more often, and that felt out of step because everyone else seemed to think those years were old news and they'd moved on. It was over now. But she couldn't forget sights she had seen – children mostly, things she hadn't thought about at the time: a child screaming in a subway, a baby. There had been a squeeze, the mother thought the baby was dead; it turned out it wasn't dead, then the mother's face. Did these memories come back to everyone – when they least expected it – or was there something wrong with her?

It was like she had been woken up to injustice against children, more even than when she was going through it. She thought about the war children a lot: where were they now? She added up their ages too – if that child was two in 1940, then he'd be twelve now. Would he be a good boy, or would he be a Clifford with his shifty ways? Would that little girl she'd seen skipping in a bombed-out church be eight now? Did she still speak or had she, like Peg, lost her voice to trauma?

Clara would have liked to talk about it to someone, but her best confidante, Judy, was gone. She couldn't talk to Anita because Anita would rather die than go back there even in her memory; Mrs Horton was wrapped up in married life, and Ivor? Well, things with Ivor were still complicated.

At eight o'clock, the other children came back home from rehearsal, exhilarated – 'We're going to be brilliant!' Peg clacked her drumsticks together. Even Denny was bright-eyed and laughing. And Clifford, troublesome Cliff, turned his dark eyes on her when she asked him how it was, and said, 'Yeah, it went well, I reckon.'

'We've rejigged it,' Rita explained. Gripping her papers, she insisted on going out to practise in the shed. 'Just one more hour, it needs to be...' – she kissed the tips of her fingers in a strange gesture she must have copied from Anita – 'just so.'

'Ri-ta...' began Clara. It was already late, but then Rita was that rare child who understood the correlation between hard work and success.

Clara went back up to stroke the broken-hearted Maureen's hair.

'The rehearsal went well apparently. They're all ready for tomorrow.'

'I don't care, I'm not going.'

∼

Something half-woke Clara. A smell maybe, or an instinctive 'something's not right'. She sniffed in her half-sleep. Nothing to see out the front window. She left her room and looked out of a back window. She saw smoke first and then flames. The shed was on fire. She ran down the first-floor landing and banged into a pyjamaed Denny, yawning and stretching.

'What is it?' he asked. 'I couldn't sleep.'

She raced into the girls' room. 'Up, up, everyone and outside. Maureen, call the fire brigade.'

Maureen's hair was standing up. 'Is this a joke?'

'No, it bloody isn't!' yelped Clara. 'Tell them to be quick. The shed is burning down.' She was still shouting while she ran into the boys' room. 'Cliff! Up! Now!' Incredibly, the boy was still fast asleep.

She clattered downstairs. 'Out, out…' She was petrified the fire would reach the house – catch the place alight. *Dear God, what would Marilyn say?*

One whole half of Rita's piano shed was alight with flames. Clara ran to the tin bucket next to the tap, filled it up and threw it over the shed. It was a pathetic attempt and much of the water went over her bare legs. Flames were lapping up the far end, where it was dry and warm. She had to keep that piano safe.

All the children were in the garden now, in shock at the shed, and possibly also shocked at seeing Clara so dishevelled.

'They're coming,' Maureen said, flushed and important.

Rita was next to Clara in her nightie. She was spellbound. In that moment, in her expression, Clara remembered the Blitz and knew Rita was remembering it too. After Rita's house was bombed, she never saw her family again. The bright, bold orange was licking the wooden sides of the shed. *Better the shed than the house*, thought Clara.

'My songs. I need my SONGS! They're in there.'

'The fire brigade will get them,' Clara promised. She didn't know they would, but the girl was trembling and shivering and mouthing, 'Mama.'

Clara ran off with her tin bucket. She noticed the hose, lying like a dormant snake: 'You do that,' she yelled to Cliff, pointing at it. She thought she saw him grinning.

It was only ten metres from tap to shed. She stumbled back, the full bucket knocking against her shins. In the time that took, Rita had dashed to the shed door.

'My music!' she shrieked. 'I need it!'

The horror when she realised Rita was about to go in.

Cliff yelled, 'I'll go!'

'No!' Clara threw off her dressing gown and pushed Rita aside.

'I'll go.'

She gripped the hem of her nightgown and yanked open the door. *The heat, the heat...* Clara's cheeks felt like they were on fire. Inside, it wasn't dark, it was lit with flames. She saw the piano – the blessed piano – wasn't affected yet, it was the cardboard boxes that were burning so merrily. Oof, and the smoke.

Clara was coughing. She felt her way to the piano – so hot to the touch – there were no papers there. Where were the damn sheets of music?

The roof was on fire; the beams, the reinforced beams, were burning. The smoke was black. 'Where the hell are they?' she coughed. Rita was behind her, yelling, 'They're on the floor.'

On the floor? What kind of stupid place was that? Clara looked down and saw, just near where the flames were missing, white paper rectangles. She reached for them and, just as she did so, a beam broke off and collapsed inches from her head. She had the papers now and as she backed out, the fire engine's clanging bells told her that help was arriving.

She lay on the grass panting and Rita stood over her, then gripped those damn music sheets out of her hands and embraced them like long-lost loves.

The firemen stormed into the garden. Four, maybe five of them. She remembered them in the war. Gathering around their ladders. Accepting tea. She remembered kissing a fireman once, an older man with a bristly moustache that gave her a rash. He'd just rescued a woman and a baby trapped in a car. Strange the way unwanted memories popped up like this. Still coughing, Clara took in their black shiny boots, their trousered legs. The hose began, and it felt like rain on her face and, with the shock of it all, she began to laugh.

~

Clara couldn't speak for a while. She wanted to just breathe. They had put the fire out in minutes, although they warned it would smell for days. The firemen wanted to take her to the hospital, but Clara resisted. 'I can't... It's the Hippodrome tomorrow.'

'Course it is, love,' one said, like she was unhinged.

'The... the children are performing,' she told him. 'It's part of the Festival of Britain.'

For the first time she felt a surge of pride.

'Oh well, if it's the Festival of Britain...' he said and she didn't know if he was being sarcastic or not.

They agreed she didn't have to go to hospital, but only if she got herself checked over by a doctor in the next day or two. She told them Anita's husband would see her; she found herself laughing: 'He is a doctor!'

While she was explaining, she saw out the corner of her eye that Ivor, Patricia squirming in his arm, a panicked look on his face, was rushing towards her.

'Clara! Are you okay? And the children?'

'Yes,' she whimpered. 'We're all fine.' She would have loved to throw herself at his broad chest and nestle into him, just for one sweet moment – he was like an oak tree, something solid and durable – but instead she coughed again, and noticed Patricia's shocked little face bright white in the darkness. If Ivor was a great tree, then she was his bud.

'Take her home, Ivor.' She swallowed a grateful sob that he had come – he always did. 'We're fine. Nothing to worry about.'

He kissed her forehead and she sucked in her teeth with longing, and he said, 'Are you hurt?' And she said, 'No, please go... Patricia,' and he went.

She invited the firemen in for tea – she had muffins, 'Mrs Cardew made them,' she added to convince them, 'she's a wonderful baker' – but they said they had to go, which was a relief, as Clara felt suddenly engulfed by a huge wave of tiredness. She could have slept standing. She sent the children up to their rooms: 'Try and sleep, children. Up early tomorrow, remember!' Then she walked out to where the fire engine stood in the road so red and bright and perfect like a child's crayon drawing, she almost couldn't believe it was parked here, had come here for them. That they were the centre of attention.

They were usually so careful. She asked one of the firemen how he thought this could have happened and he recited his reply like he said it regularly: 'Straw bales, wiring, candles.' He didn't seem interested. 'Lucky it didn't spread.'

Lucky, she thought. He seemed to think it was 'only' a shed too.

Denny had been awake, she recalled. What had he been doing up? But Clifford hadn't been. Cliff had been deep asleep, snoring under the covers.

Back in her room, it felt suddenly too big, or was it that she was too small? Alone again, she pulled at the drawers of her unit. They were still locked; her key was still in its special secret place.

She kept her files in the large safe, which had the larger key. And then in a small metal safe, for money really, was a tiny key, more fitting for fairies and toadstools. Could Cliff have found the key and opened it while she was outside? She didn't feel like anything had been disturbed; it didn't feel like anyone had been in. She turned the key and it opened with a satisfying click.

Cliff's matches and the penknife were still there *and* they were in the exact same position she had carefully placed them in, the matches pressed against the side, the penknife at a 45-degree angle to it. Whatever had happened, he hadn't been in here. But then, how hard was it to get matches?

Clara didn't sleep well and when she got up, she felt terrible. *Why did it have to be today of all days?* She made toast, but the smell of it made her feel worse. She felt nervous about seeing the children, couldn't contemplate dealing with one of their dramas. Then Maureen came in the back door. Clara hadn't even known she wasn't in bed. Before Clara could say anything, she said: 'I've decided – I'm going to go today.'

'What happened?' Clara got up to make tea. How *had* Anita persuaded her?

'I went to see Ivor.'

Ivor? Of course. Clara wanted to smile. She remembered his panic-stricken face in the garden. He must feel *something* for her, surely?

Maureen chewed Clara's left-over toast. 'He wasn't there, but that woman was. The lady who looks after the baby now?'

'Oh...' *Mrs Harrington*, Clara thought, depressed, the woman got everywhere. *And at this time of day too?* Her heart sank. It was only five to seven. Mrs Harrington didn't stay there overnight, did she? Maureen however was beautifully impervious. She went on: 'We had a talk, and she explained that sometimes the time is not right to be with someone—'

'She said that?'

'But if you are patient then maybe they'll learn to appreciate your value and come back to you... Why are you looking at me like that?' Maureen continued. 'She also said that it would be silly to give up on something I enjoy just because I'm upset with Joe.'

'Correct,' said Clara, thinking, why didn't Maureen listen when she had said *exactly the same?*

'I have to go and get changed.' Maureen left the room.

Anita and Evelyn arrived in great spirits. Somehow, Dr Cardew, Anita, Evelyn and even baby Howard had slept through the commotion. The look of disappointment on Evelyn's face when she realised she had missed out on a happening!

Rita was shouting about it. 'And then Miss Newton saved the songs!'

'You really shouldn't have risked yourself for the music,' cautioned Anita, looking at Clara pointedly. 'But I'm glad you did. That's the only copy we've got, I should have done something about that. And Clara,' she said resolutely. 'I'll get a man over to fix the shed. As soon as possible. There's no point waiting...' she meant for Ivor, Clara knew she did. 'It'll be good as new.' Clara couldn't bring herself to talk about it. They were acting as though it was a jolly bonfire – that was what the children were making it sound like – and Clara couldn't convey either the fear, the heat, the smell, or the worst thing: her suspicions about how it had started.

'Maureen is just getting ready to go,' she said. *Could they all still smell smoke or was it just her?*

'I never doubted she would,' said Anita, tickling the back of Evelyn's neck. 'Did I, Evelyn?'

Evelyn sniggered.

When Clifford whirled in in his suit. Anita called out, 'Here he is!' Clifford was the one she always gushed over. 'My Sinatra.'

Clara couldn't bear to look at him. He wouldn't look at her either but instead went to ask Anita to help with his bow tie. Clara realised belatedly she had to hurry and get ready too. She was going to wear the dress she had worn to the Hortons' wedding – Anita's idea. She left the kitchen just as Anita was starting another *prep* talk.

'This is a big occasion, a very special occasion. This, children,' she said, 'is the Festival of Britain in Suffolk.'

Clara had one foot on the stairs, but she paused to listen.

'I've been waiting so long for this,' sighed Rita. 'It's going to be the best day of my life.'

Dr Cardew had borrowed a Morris Oxford van from a friend. It was brown with wooden panels, more like a cupboard than a motorcar. A discussion ensued about who should sit up front with him, even though to Clara it was obvious it should be Anita and baby Howard.

Clara, who was already feeling exhausted, was glad that Evelyn sat next to her in the row at the back. Evelyn was delightful company and she didn't demand anything from Clara, which was refreshing. She rambled on about helping in the surgery, about the fish, darling Howard and her favourite sweet, gobstoppers. Clara had been planning to ask outright if she was happy living with the Cardews, but she didn't need to – the girl was almost popping with contentment. Even when she showed Clara a gold locket with a photo of her late mother in it, and her voice became shaky, her eyes were bright and lively. She was a different girl and Clara was reminded that a permanent home – the *right* permanent home – could do wonders for a child.

Rita was engrossed in her sheets of music. They were slightly charred on the edges, but she said it only made them more precious. Cliff stared at his shoes. Peg was drawing in her notepad and Denny was laughing at whatever it was. Maureen tapped her fingers on the window pane.

You could really feel the van going over every single bump, every single pothole in the road. The children went 'woah!', and when it went round corners, they all swung into each other and shrieked. And then suddenly, Denny stopped chuckling and began to cry. Clara realised – it hadn't occurred to her – that this might be his first time in a car since... She saw his checked shorts darken – oh no! – and Cliff yelped, 'That stinks!' And Denny sobbed some more.

'What's going on back there?' Anita called out.

'It's okay,' Clara said to everyone. Denny clambered onto her lap and sobbed into her shoulder.

'It's all right,' she whispered to him. She had spare clothes for him, but her dress was going to be ruined. Never mind – she was getting used to small disasters now.

Clara didn't know Ipswich very well. Alex had gone to school there, and she had been for a harvest assembly and then onto the seafront with Victor Braithwaite – but she had never been to the Hippodrome. Dr Cardew drove down a back street where a bright-eyed fox ran out in the road and confronted them, and then down another wrong road and another. Finally, they pulled up in front of an old pink building, the Hippodrome. Built 1893. Clara couldn't begin to imagine Anita's disappointment. It looked gloomy, deserted. The sort of place they'd put in horror films. It was far worse than the venue for the audition and that had been neglected enough.

Dr Cardew reversed all the way down the street. He was muttering to himself, 'I don't get it – have we got the day wrong?'

He and Anita started arguing. Clara had never heard the Cardews argue before and she could feel herself growing panicky – she didn't care about finding the right place, *only please, please don't row*. It made her feel like a child. And she didn't want anything to set off poor Denny again.

Dr Cardew rolled down the window and said he would ask the next person he saw.

Anita laughed and said to Clara, 'He hates asking for help.'

Clara nodded, *just like Ivor*, she thought. There was a lot of it about.

The next person they saw was a toothless old man smoking tobacco roll-ups, and he said he'd only answer for a shilling, and then when they'd patted their pockets and found one, he said, 'Which Hippodrome?'

There was a bit more back and forth and then they were away, laughing. Who would have thought there were two Hippodromes in one town? Anita and Dr Cardew were incredulous. And Clara felt she could melt as the atmosphere turned sweet once again.

Their Hippodrome was big and impressive, an art deco building not ten minutes away. And outside there were queues and queues of people – some waving Union Jacks, some sitting on their coats on the kerb. 'They'll get piles,' said Evelyn disapprovingly.

Denny changed in the back of the car and Clara sprayed her dress with Anita's perfume. It would have to do. Denny wouldn't let go of Clara's hand as they walked up to the right Hippodrome and Anita asked for the performers' entrance. They were pointed through and as they walked past the queues, incredibly, some of the people started clapping.

'What if I wet these too?' whispered Denny.

'You're not going to.'

'Cliff makes me nervous.'

Clara felt like saying, 'me too,' but she said, 'There's no need to be nervous, darling, I'm here to look after you.' After a pause, she added, 'You will tell me if he does anything though, yes?'

They were sent upstairs. Having debonair Dr Cardew with them meant people assisted them quickly.

On the way up, she glimpsed the crowds queueing outside from the windows. Then they were backstage in a room filled with people and piles of clothes and a hum of excitement.

Cliff was loud. *He's nervous*, Clara thought, and overcompensating. She wouldn't have thought he'd be the one to have stage fright. If anything, the stage was more likely to be frightened of him!

Tall, dark and not un-handsome, presenter Donald Button was walking amid the performers. You wouldn't have thought he would do that. He had an air of Cary Grant. He was wearing an Anthony Eden hat, tweed jacket and flannels. And then, before Clara had time to be anxious, he strode over to them, introduced himself and vigorously shook hands, even with the children.

'I know who you are,' said Rita. 'I'd recognise your voice anywhere. You're the fella off the wireless.'

He laughed. He had a distinctive deep voice; the sound he produced seemed to come from way down in his chest.

'*And* stage and screen,' he said.

'What?' said Rita.

'Star of stage, screen and wireless,' he told her.

Rita stared at him, undecided. Clara fanned herself. It was the lights, she told herself.

He paused and looked Clara up and down. It was so intense, it felt like he was touching her.

'You must be the Three Rays of Sunshine from Clacton?'

Rita blinked at him, stern-faced. It was hard to believe anyone thought she was a Ray of Sunshine.

'We're from the...' Clara wouldn't say Shilling Grange, whatever Anita, Maureen (and Joe) thought. 'The children's home in Lavenham.'

She could tell Donald Button didn't know what she was

talking about, but he covered it up marvellously – of course he did, that's what stars of stage, screen and wireless did.

'My, my, how wonderful! How modern! How lucky we are!'

He looked around. Evelyn was fussing over baby Howard.

'And you've brought along a little brown girl too! Marvellous.'

Clara looked at him, confused. *What on earth was he trying to say?*

He went on, to Clara, 'Are you singing?' And his eyes were blue like cornflowers.

'No, I am the children's, um...'

Chaperone. That's what the word was.

'Oh, you look after these?'

'Ye...'

'You're a nun, then?'

'Housemother,' Clara corrected nervously.

'You once were a nun?'

'Er...' He seemed convinced that she had been. 'Not... no.' He turned to the man standing quietly next to him, who Clara had hardly noticed. 'You know what they say about nuns once they've left the monastery...?'

'The nunnery,' the man corrected him. 'What do they say?'

Donald Button didn't say but he slapped the man on the back and winked.

Clara wanted to say something about how his wireless documentary last year had caused an upsurge of interest in adoption but he was looking at her intently again. 'Yves Saint Laurent?'

'Anita Cardew?' she said and pointed to where Anita was in a heated exchange with one of the organisers.

'I meant your perfume.' He laughed and after a beat, the man next to him laughed too. Clara blushed. She suspected she smelled like the perfume counter at Selfridges.

'It might be...'

'If you do well, you'll go on the London stage, you know. I bet you would love that.'

'I don't think so,' Clara told him. 'This is it.'

He winked at her. 'Don't hold your breath!'

The man next to him smiled ruefully, then followed him away.

Anita had returned and was now talking intently to Evelyn about Howard's schedule – 'He must be put down for a nap at eleven.' Clara waited, but then when it looked like there would be no end soon, she interrupted.

'You didn't tell me about any London thing,' she said, appalled. 'You said it was going to be all over today.'

'Did I?' Anita said nonchalantly.

'She told *me!*' said Maureen brightly. 'Did she not tell you about the show on television?' She pinched a piece of fudge from one of Anita's many paper bags, then walked off.

Television?

'Anita,' Clara said. She felt miserable and the perfume was giving her a headache. 'I'm not sure I want all that.'

'It's good for the children,' Anita said firmly.

'Oh, for goodness' sake! This is enough, they're not performing monkeys.'

'All I'm saying is, give it a chance. Success, performance, is life.'

Clara looked around her. Peg was watching Rita hold forth about the Festival of Britain: 'It's called the Skylon because it's in the sky and it's long.' Denny was jiggling – he must need the loo again – and Cliff had done his usual disappearing act. Maureen was gazing into the dressing-room mirror, squinting and probably trying to make herself seem older.

'*Anita,*' Clara said in a hushed voice. 'I have a lot of trauma-tised children here. I don't want things spiralling—'

'Pfft,' said Anita. 'Spiralling! And girls, come, take these sweets. They're good for the throat.'

'What? One recently bereaved, one still believes her mother is alive, one never speaks, one needs to think about her future, one is very difficult... These things bubble up. '

'You can't hide them away for ever.'

'Goodness, I'm not talking about *hiding them away* at all. You're talking about exposing them to far too much!'

Last year, Clara had taken the children to the fairground. And there had been a newspaper article about it, saying that it was a waste of money for orphanage children. From then on, Clara had understood how important it was to keep a low profile.

'The council would say no to London or... or to being on television, anyway.'

The council had better say no! she thought.

But Anita was unpacking her case and only half listening. 'Anyway, Clara, it's extremely unlikely they'll be selected. Have you seen the other performers? Just relax and enjoy the show.'

The auditorium was packed. Two thousand people? They made a terrific din and it felt like there were even more than that. Clara couldn't believe how calm Anita and the children were – she was so nervous, she could hardly speak.

Was it more nail-biting for the onlookers? Surely not?

There were seats reserved for them. She asked Dr Cardew if he was going to come with, but he said he was going to stay backstage with Howard.

'I'm off to sit down,' Clara said as the children gathered around Anita.

'Best of luck.'

No one looked at her.

'Won't you at least pretend to listen to me?' she added rather desperately.

Rita turned, looking surprised. 'Mama!' She grabbed hold of one of Clara's hands. Peg squeezed the other. Clara swallowed. Now it was time for *her* 'prep' talk.

'Don't worry if it goes badly. The Shilling Grange kids stick together. I mean, the Michael Adams Children's Home kids always...' she lost track. When Ivor said this, they always whooped and high-fived him.

'What if it goes well?' asked Rita.

Clara hadn't thought of that. She supposed it wasn't the most inspirational speech she could have delivered. She just didn't want them to get hurt. Or humiliated. Or sent to London.

'Well, if it goes well then... then... see you after for the cele-bration.'

She bade them farewell – they hardly noticed – and got a seat in the row reserved for family members, between a woman who said she was the wife of a clown and a man who was the father of a flautist. *Three hours to go.* The chair arms were scratchy.

Why did she always prepare them for the worst? But preparing for the best wasn't her nature.

She sat through several acts, including Bartholomew Parsons and his dummy Nathan, who was better than last time, and the clowns, Mr and Mrs Scallywag, who were worse. She found it hard to concentrate and told herself she was there for the chil-dren, that was all. She missed Peter suddenly – she used to enjoy sitting next to him in the cinema watching his reactions, laughing with him. He hadn't been in touch for ages, she remembered again. And she missed Ivor too. His appearance last night – was it only last night? – had made her heart soar – and yet, Patricia was there, always there, and Ivor didn't seem able to find a way that could include her.

And then finally, *finally!* it was the children's turn. Like the man himself, Donald Button's introductions were smooth. He said that traditionally, Suffolk wasn't famous for its orphans but this afternoon that may be all set to change. It surprised Clara to see that he was reading from a poster someone was holding up beneath the stage. She felt awkward, like she'd seen him do something private. He spoke so fluently, you'd think it was all his own words.

'A big hand for the children from the Shilling Grange Orphanage.'

Still Shilling Grange! Scowling to herself, Clara clapped. The woman next to her also clapped, but the father of the flautist folded his arms, which Clara thought wasn't in the spirit.

And then the curtains went back. Denny peeked out desperately – *oh God, he's not going to pee himself again, is he?* – and she made her expression as encouraging as she could. Before the show, Maureen and Cliff had been arguing. Now they were all best-buddy smiles as they walked across the stage together. Rita took her time, and Clara, who hated the limelight, wondered how she could do that. She looked cool and collected. Then Evelyn, Denny and Peg walked on hand in hand and some people in the audience said, 'Aww.' Their outfits were perfect.

First up was Rita's introduction on the piano. For a moment Clara wondered if the wistfulness of the piece was on purpose, then she realised: of course it was, Anita was no fool. And then there was this mellifluous sound – Clara almost didn't know what it was at first, but it was the children of course, singing not words but beautiful eerie sounds, and that tish, tish, tish beat was Peg joining in on the drums.

Then it was on to a jazzier segment, a showpiece for Cliff really, but this time he was paired with Maureen and they did a skit – will-they, won't-they? – back and forth, Peg really rocking the drums and Rita playing exquisitely too. She could play light as well as heavy. And Cliff was such an endearing showman, he could win the coldest heart over! Which Clara reflected was why it was impossible to understand why on earth he might have set the shed on fire... *It can't have been him*, she told herself. Not that boy thrilling the audience right now, no way! Then it was Denny and Evelyn's turn and they were a great pairing too, for where Denny's voice was weak, Evelyn's was strong and seemed to match his. Funnily enough, his was higher while hers was deeper. They were ably supported by the others.

Then it was the four of them singing at the front of the stage – Rita also singing and on the piano – this was what Anita referred to as the schmaltzy segment, and it was. How little they all looked, quite tiny amid the grandeur, but how clearly their voices rang out. They were performing 'Twinkle, Twinkle' again, but it was even better than last time.

'How I wonder what you are,' came the surprisingly breathy final line from Evelyn – that made tears come to Clara's eyes. Good grief! And then everyone stood up and clapped, Clara too although the man next to her didn't. He was muttering to himself, 'Load of rotters.'

'Pardon?'

'That one there' – he pointed to Cliff – 'told my son that he would break his legs if he so much as looked at him.'

Clara excused herself and got up.

15

The show had finished, but they'd been told to wait backstage. Clara kept her eye on the clock. It had gone faultlessly but she still wanted to get the children back home. They would be needing their tea. And she wanted to have a look at the shed again. No doubt the council would have heard by now. She could probably expect a few questions, and she would have to answer without really knowing the answers. Cliff was showing the other children some tricks with a coin. He flicked his fingers and then produced it from Rita's and then Peg's ear. Why didn't they realise it was just up his sleeve?

He threatened to break the legs of the flautist. Clara had only the father's word for it. But then, why would he lie? Whatever it was, it had put quite a dampener on her already damp day.

Donald Button, star of stage, screen and wireless, raced over to them theatrically, his cape flapping behind him.

'You are such little superstars,' he said. His tie was so bright, his face was dazzling panstick. 'I had no idea.'

Clara wondered if he could talk normally or if he only spoke in the superlative. Everything that came out of his mouth seemed designed for show. Would he even exist if other people weren't there to admire him?

He grabbed Clara. 'Well, well, well. What a troupe! You and the children belong in London.'

'Sorry? What?'

'On the circuit. The entertainment circuit. I could help, I'm friends with an awful lot of people.'

Clara heard *awful people*. He kept both hands on her elbows. Close up, Donald Button's face was as waxy as Nathan the ventriloquist's dummy but his teeth were very even, very white and unlike any she'd seen before.

'I don't think so.'

'There's money to be had.' He snorted, then in a lower voice, he said, 'You are a beautiful woman, and the fact that you don't know that makes you all the more alluring to me.'

Clara flushed scarlet. Thank goodness for Anita; with excellent timing, she appeared next to them, and Donald Button turned his attention to her.

'Mrs Cardew, I presume,' he yelped. 'The musical director extraordinaire. I have some wonderful news. We want you to perform in London. In the brand-new Royal Festival Hall!'

'The Royal Festival Hall? Wow!' Cliff's mouth was wide-open astonishment. Then he whispered hotly in Clara's ear, 'What *is* the Royal Festival Hall?'

'It's where the King has his royal festivals,' said Rita.

Clara interrupted. 'Not quite. It's a new venue in London.'

'It is the centrepiece of the Festival of Britain,' Donald Button said in his impressive baritone. He finally relaxed his grip on Clara. 'As for you, young lady, I will be in touch *very* soon.'

There was a long queue for the ladies' and as Clara waited, she didn't know how she felt. Today was supposed to be the end of it, but she realised now that it wasn't – was that a bad thing? And Donald Button – star of stage, screen and wireless – telling her she was beautiful? That was a turn-up for the books or was it? Her reflection stared back at her, wondering what he saw that she couldn't.

The two women ahead of Clara were chatting. 'Those orphans were wonderful, weren't they? I couldn't stop crying,' said one, which was nice, and the other one said, 'You wouldn't think they were orphans, would you?' which was mixed. (*Why wouldn't you?*)

When Clara came back from the ladies', the children weren't where she had left them. She sighed. The day had been long, and she had started out tired. Now she was so exhausted, it was hard to think. She wished she could transport herself home to her little room with a cup of cocoa and a magazine quiz: *What variety act are you: Singing troupe, clown, ventriloquist or puppets? Mostly Es. None of the above.*

She thought how different it would be if Ivor were here— No, it was too painful to think like that.

She went to look for the children. They'd be being silly somewhere, no doubt. She didn't find them but instead found Anita draped over a chair, looking very pleased with herself, with her nose in the programme. Dr Cardew was feeding Howard his milk just beyond. A couple of women were staring admiringly at him.

'We did it!' Anita said. 'They're already saying we were the best act there.'

'Where have the children gone?' Clara asked starkly. 'We're supposed to go home.'

'In there.' Anita pointed to a door with a red light above it. 'Being interviewed for the BBC. It's live,' she added.

Oh goodness, thought Clara. *This way calamity lies.* She ran over to the door even as Anita said, 'No, Clara. They don't want us—'

Inside the room, the children were lined up in a row and in front of them was a woman holding a great black microphone, furry as a bear. Opposite them, at a table loaded with equipment, a man wearing headphones was dialling buttons on a box, rapt in concentration. With relief, Clara realised it was for wireless rather than television, but the relief didn't last long. What on earth would the children say?

'This is so exciting,' the woman said into the microphone, although her expression suggested the opposite. She was wearing a long navy skirt and white lace-up shoes. The outfit was oddly girlish, yet beneath the caked-on powder she seemed a woman of steel. Clara wondered what it must be like for her, to assert her voice in front of thousands of people every day.

'Many of the children at Shilling Grange Orphanage lost their parents in the war and have lived in terrible hardship. And yet what a harmonious sound they make – so sweet – and now I'm going to interview them. What's your name?'

'Maureen.'

'And you're an orphan?'

'Only my mother is dead,' Maureen said proudly. She looked over at Clara.

Don't ask, begged Clara.

'And your father?'

'He's in prison. In Holloway. London.'

Too late.

'Oh... oh.'

The woman moved down the line to Cliff, who had his arm up and, for some reason, had decided now was the time for a chimpanzee-with-fleas impression.

Oh no, thought Clara. *Here we go.*

'Mine are both dead, Missus.'

'I'm sorry.'

'It's fine, it wasn't your fault, was it?'

'I'm just... well, I don't know what to say.' The woman seemed lost for words. 'My condolences.'

'It's all right. They weren't very nice. Not that I wanted them dead or anything.'

'I see.' She was already edging away. 'Thank you.'

'You're bloody pretty though.' Cliff pulled a cigarette from his pocket. 'Want a smoke? We can go outside.'

'How about you?' the woman asked Peg, who shrank back, shaking her head.

Rita spoke up. 'She doesn't speak.'

The woman looked around her desperately. Rita continued: 'Peg's a foundling. Do you know what that means?'

'I do. I'm... sorry. And how about you then, dear?'

'My mum's not dead,' Rita said loudly. She put her thumb in her mouth, then took it out again. 'Mama.'

Evelyn piped up. 'My mother died last year. My dad is from America. He doesn't even know I exist. They used to call us "the brown babies".'

'Very...' said the presenter, gulping loudly, 'interesting. Thank you.'

Finally, she got to Denny. He was stood straight, such a good boy, with his hands tidy and his hair swept to one side.

'My parents died in a car accident only three months ago. I miss them.'

The woman raised her eyebrows and the man looked up from his control panel and Clara could feel the emotion sweep over them both. This was more like it. A child they could properly feel sorry for. Not a child with a monstrous family, or wounds or trauma or neglect. Denny was a poster boy.

'Oh, that's so sad, I'm so sorry. And that's it from Suffolk and the Festival of Britain, and the children from the Shilling Grange Orphanage, ladies and gentlemen.'

The woman strutted away without looking at anyone. The

man turned a few more twirly buttons, then said, 'Well done, kids.' He grinned at Clara as she approached. 'Ten thousand listeners on average. Won't be a dry eye in the house after that.'

'Don't blow it, Clara,' warned Anita as they waited in the street for Dr Cardew to bring the car round. It was dark out and the flies were buzzing around the orange streetlights. They were not far from the stage exit, where a few teenage girls and a couple of older, more glamorous women were still queueing up with autograph books, waiting for Donald Button to come out.

'By hook or by crook, he'll be first in my book,' one of them said and another said, 'He'll be first in my *nook*,' and everyone roared.

Cliff was smirking in the shadows and Clara felt herself shrink away from him every time she remembered last night's fire. She knew it could have been so much worse – but it shouldn't have happened at all. And if he had anything to do with it— well, she didn't know what she'd do.

Denny and Peg had their arms round each other again – they seemed to give each other a great deal of solace – and Rita, Evelyn and Maureen were playing slapsies – that game where two of you held out your hands, palms together, then slapped the other's hand unless they managed to pull it away in time.

'How do you mean, "don't blow it"?'

'Don't spoil it for them. The children need something in their lives.'

A car pulled up at the kerb next to them, but it wasn't Dr Cardew. Anita checked her watch impatiently.

'They have plenty of things in their lives...' said Clara. *Good grief, Anita.*

'You know what I mean. The Royal Festival Hall!'

'And we're going to be on television!' Maureen called out.

Slap. 'Ow!' yelled Rita. 'Not so hard!'

'This was supposed to be the end of it,' Clara replied uselessly but Anita wasn't listening. She ran out into the road and waved at the oncoming vehicle.

The council will say no, Clara thought to herself. *I won't have to. I'm not going to have to be the killjoy here.*

Dear Miss Newton,

Salutations, Congratulations and Felicitations.

Uncle Victor, Aunt Elsie, Bernard and I gathered round the wireless to listen to the *Variety! It's the Spice of Life* show on BBC Suffolk. Aunt Elsie has been a huge fan of Donald Button since his days in *How Do You Do, Miss*, and she spent the segment complaining how hot the room was (but the windows were open!).

Everyone was brilliant. Rita really is a genius at the piano. Do you know 10,000 hours of practice turn you into a master? I imagine you are a genius at nit-removal or burning cakes. (Joke!) I miss your burnt cakes very much! You would put King Alfred to shame. (Joke! I'm disappointed to admit I'm no funnier than I was. Victor says my sense of humour is 'unique'.)

I have to say, I'm glad I'm no longer resident at Shilling Grange. What would Mrs Cardew have made me do? Do you remember I was always bottom in the form for music? Ivor used to say it was a heroic kindness and that someone has to be. I struggle to differentiate between quavers and semiquavers. As for singing, Bernard says it's lucky I'm tone deaf otherwise I'd drive myself to despair. (He is learning the oboe. Frankly, I really can't tell if he plays well or not.)

Once again, thank you, I hope we can meet up soon.

Yours faithfully,

Alex

_____

16

'Why on earth would we say no to the Royal Festival Hall?' said Miss Cooper in her fug-filled office the next day as she lit up another cigarette. 'Or being on television?'

Clara sighed. She hadn't wanted to go to the council but she'd felt she had to. She thought Miss Cooper might mention the shed-fire but it seemed she was unaware – or, if she was aware, she didn't think anything of it. Had the firemen thought it too trivial to report? Clara had tried to telephone Marilyn, but she had moved on from the hotel where she had been staying in Mexico and the receptionist said she was now going on a trek to see ancient civilisations. Clara wondered if her risk assessment was askew or even if she was going mad – should she bring up the fire?

Leaning back (dangerously) in her chair, Miss Cooper put her feet up on the desk. She was wearing a slim black skirt, real stockings and a white blouse. She looked incredible, not a crease in sight, while Clara had on her crumpled apron, which was like a second and wrinkly skin. Miss Cooper seemed very relaxed too, Clara thought, even more so than usual. She said she'd just come back from a 'long liquid lunch', whatever that was.

'Because... because putting a group of orphans on a bigger stage, a *London* stage, doesn't seem a sensible idea to me.'

'Oh no. We trust you, Clara.'

'It's not about trust.' Clara's stomach had shrivelled up. 'It's just too much spotlight on them, don't you think?'

'Don't the children want to do it?'

Clara considered. The children were desperate to go. All the way home they'd been chanting, 'We're going to London, cha, cha, cha!' and 'Royal Festival Hall – here we come!' She didn't know what they imagined it would be like.

'They do but—'

'Well then.'

She had a vague memory: Michael persuading her to go out one more time; he was on leave – they'd been gallivanting for three nights in a row and when she hadn't wanted to, he'd called her a 'party pooper'. She'd never heard that phrase before and it had made her laugh. (And of course, she'd agreed to go out in the end.)

Mr Sommersby came in without knocking and Clara was relieved. At last the grown-ups were here, someone who would understand that the Royal Festival Hall idea was highly unorthodox. Mr Sommersby would put his foot down – he always did.

He tugged at his shirt collar. He seemed unusually focused on Miss Cooper, who retracted her legs from on high, but slowly, as if she was in no hurry to do so.

'Good afternoon, Mr Sommersby,' Clara said, for he hadn't yet acknowledged she existed.

'Ha, oh yes, good afternoon, Miss Newton,' he said, and his words sounded thick and slurry. There was nowhere for him to sit, so he stood behind Clara. He smelled of whisky, or it might have been wine. Miss Cooper told him that the children had done the Hippodrome show and they were a success and he said, 'Good to see one of our orphanages in a positive story for once.'

Clara was glad he couldn't see her expression.

'The children are going to perform at the Royal Festival Hall,' Miss Cooper said.

'Maybe. And on television,' Clara interrupted; he might as well have the whole sorry tale at once.

'Miss Newton was concerned that we'd object, but I told her there was nothing to worry about. Isn't that right, Mr Sommersby?'

Clara waited. Mr Sommersby usually objected to anything out of the ordinary.

'That is right, Miss Cooper,' he said.

Clara couldn't believe her ears. 'You don't object?'

He looked uncertain. 'Should we?' he said to Miss Cooper.

'No,' she said firmly. 'We've been inundated with enquiries from the wireless broadcast too.'

'Enquiries?' said Clara. 'What kind of enquiries?'

'About the children. Adoption enquiries.'

'Excellent,' said Mr Sommersby, his shoes were creaking behind her. 'That's what it's all about. Good work, ladies.'

Clara remembered that this had happened last year too, after *The Joys of Adoption* was on the wireless. She should have expected it, but she hadn't.

'Really? Who? What people?'

Miss Cooper flushed. She licked her finger and then turned the pages of her notebook. Clara felt Mr Sommersby react somehow. *Why hadn't he left?* 'Well, they are for Denny mostly. He made quite the impression. Maureen and Clifford are probably too old, no one likes a teenager.'

Clara stared at her nails. While she knew this, it was always painful to hear.

'We'll be meeting some and registering them this week...'

She paused. 'Of course, a fair few are the usual nutters and will be ruled out – but it only takes one, yes?'

'It only takes one' was something Mrs Horton had liked to say. In love and in adoptive parents. But Mrs Horton would never have said 'nutters'.

Mr Sommersby leaned across the desk and shook Miss Cooper's hand. He told her she was doing a fantastic job. *Fantast-tic*. Clara thought suddenly of his demure wife blushing in her belted dress at the wedding and she felt sorry for her. Then he said, 'Goodbye, Miss Newton, nice to see you again.'

Once the door was shut, Miss Cooper lit another cigarette and put her long legs back on the desk. She seemed even more pleased with herself than usual. 'And Clara, this will surprise you. We've finally got some interest in Peg.'

'Peg?!'

'I know!' Miss Cooper got up. 'They've already met her and they adore her.'

'What? Who have?'

Miss Cooper went to her filing cabinet. To get there she had to step over a stack of yellowing folders, her own handbag, a box of Labour Party leaflets and a teddy bear that said, 'Love from Weston-super-Mare' on a ribbon round its neck.

'Mr and Mrs Hurley.'

Clara racked her brains – the name was familiar, but she couldn't quite...

Miss Cooper had managed to find the handwritten file. She read: 'The Hurleys live in Colchester. He is twenty-six years old, she is thirty-two.' She gave Clara a look of caution. 'Unusual age gap. No issue with that. They work in show business. Their stage name is Mr and Mrs Scallywag.'

'They're the clowns!' burst out Clara.

'Entertainers. And there's nothing wrong with that either, Clara,' Miss Cooper said firmly. 'Looking for a sweet little girl to complete their fun-loving family.'

Clara rolled her eyes.

'And they know Peg is sweet. She loves dancing and being on the stage.'

'Yes, but...'

What did that have to do with clowns? And actually, Peg didn't love being on the stage. She got shy. It was only behind the drums that she felt safe.

'What about her speech?'

'They think it's fine.' She gave Clara piercing look. 'You know clowns don't say a lot.'

Clara hadn't thought recently about the children moving on, which was strange because last year, it had been pretty much *all* she could think about. Back then, the threat of the Child Migrant Scheme and Australia had been hanging over her like the blade of a guillotine and she had woken up nightly in a sweat, terrified that all would be lost. Once she had solved that problem, she had settled into complacency – this was her mistake. Recently, she had started to think that they were all a family. She had been so focused on keeping everything level for them that she had failed to remember she wasn't in charge of *keeping* them.

She had forgotten that she was the place of transition, a mere pit stop. She was simply another shelter, not the *ultimate* shelter. The Home was a place of transience, not permanence. She should have remembered that.

It made her burn with embarrassment that she had forgotten.

Clara had a few coupons to use, and she still had time before the children got back from school, so she decided to go shopping. Miss Cooper looked so groomed, maybe she should work a little harder on her appearance too.

There was a new British Home Stores just opposite the council building. Places were coming back to life; they were seeing more colour in the street recently, after the drab of the war years and the austerity: less khaki and less blue, more reds and yellows. It had been gradually changing and now – it had changed. She remembered how during the war they used to talk about how euphoric they'd be when it was all over – and yes, for a day or two they had been. But actually, the end had been fuzzier than they had anticipated. They couldn't seem to rope it off – and the men who came home did so at different times and as different versions of themselves, and the ration continued, and it still rained. And they hadn't realised they would all be so exhausted and jaded. For while the relief was tremendous, there was also the trauma. For six years, they had kept on going, kept on running, so when they did slow down... Well, it was an adjustment.

In the department store, Clara spritzed perfume on her wrist. She tried a powder puff. The woman at the beauty counter told her she had lovely skin and maybe she should try a little more make-up?

She thought about dresses. Maybe if the children were going to perform on a London stage... and how the heck could she stop them? 'The Children of Shilling Grange Orphanage' were like a tank, she couldn't stand in their way. So then maybe she should think about trying to roll with it, for once. And she could try to shine. Maybe she *did* look dowdy compared to Miss Cooper, Mrs Harrington and Anita. There was always something appealing about trying on different lives, different looks for herself; these dresses represented possibilities.

There was one dress that stood out from the others. It was midnight-blue crêpe and it was simple and probably the sort of thing she might have worn before the war or if there hadn't have been a war. She tried it on in the changing cubicle behind a blackout curtain but couldn't do up the zip at the back. And then she could and she got it on, but she didn't like it. It didn't look anything like it did on the hanger – who was she kidding? – and worse, she now couldn't undo it. She strained and reached and hoped and thought, *dear God, what have I got myself into?* That's what getting ideas above your station did to you – it got you stuck in shops. She would have asked the woman waiting outside the cubicle to help, but she was chatting loudly to her friend in another. 'He's a married man,' she was saying, 'that doesn't mean he's a saint.'

Finally, the sweet release of it. The zip went down and she climbed out of the dress, with all the dignity of a peeled banana, and returned hurriedly to the oblivious shopgirl, who was reading a Penguin book under the counter. No sign of damage, thankfully.

'Any good?'

'Not today.'

Nor any day, she decided. Who was she kidding? A new dress was the last thing she needed.

That afternoon when she got back to Lavenham, Clara thought she'd go and see Ivor. Usually when the impulse occurred to her – which it often did – she quickly dismissed it. Ivor was being as elusive as ever. Friendly when she saw him but no more than that. 'I don't need help' was still his mantra – as if help was something heinous, something shameful. She felt they had paused everything between them, unspoken but frozen. That was fine – they could wait. Every time she thought they might have something more than a friendship was like a false start. The needle went over, and skated across the record; they had never quite managed to get into their own groove, she thought. She wondered if he spent any time at all thinking about her. *Probably not*, she thought. Men didn't. But that afternoon, bolstered by the subtle scent of lavender – *he must like laven-*

der, everyone likes lavender! – Clara knocked at the workshop door.

But it was Mrs Harrington who answered it. Mrs Harrington didn't say anything, she merely walked back in and took Ivor's own chair, at the back of his workshop. She was the very image of domesticity in her seersucker blouse, her circle skirt, her pink cheeks. Clara stayed in the doorway. She hadn't been invited in, and anyway, she felt glued to the spot. Sitting in Ivor's chair, Mrs Harrington seemed to be performing an incredible act of ownership.

'Oh, is Ivor not about?'

'He's out delivering.' Mrs Harrington paused, got up and went to a workbench. 'Can I help? You know I do his books too.'

Clara did not know. How would she know?

'Books?' she repeated.

Mrs Harrington was looking at her as if she were strange. 'His accounts. And his diary. You used to do secretarial, didn't you?'

It was a question, but it wasn't. Mrs Harrington pulled an album-sized book towards her, then turned the page, her proprietorship spilling out from her.

'Well, you know Ivor. He needs help – not that he'd ever ask for it. He's a very proud man.' She ran her finger down a column. 'I see he's in Manningtree today. Can I help you with anything else?'

'No – I just, if Ivor...' She paused. *If Ivor what?* 'Just let him know I...' She felt like water was running through her cupped hands.

'I will,' Mrs Harrington said and slammed the pages shut.

When the telephone rang that evening, Clara went running for
it. *Peter?* But her slippers slowed her down and Rita got there
first. 'Shilling Grange, no, I mean this is the Michael Adams
Children's Home. 557209? This is Rita Ann Withers speaking
now – how may I help?'

Rita loved answering the telephone. She listened carefully
and then said, 'I see, please wait.' Covering up the receiver as
Clara had instructed her, she hissed, 'It's a strange man.'

Mr Harris? Mr Sommersby?

Rita's eyes were tennis balls: 'He *says* he's Donald Button,
star of stage, screen and wireless!'

'What?' *Donald Button was on the telephone?* 'It can't be,'
Clara hissed to Rita. Cliff, gliding past, did a low wolf whistle.
Clara was grateful the receiver was covered. 'Shhh, give that to
me! Now go away, everyone.'

Possibly it was a prank call.

'That's what he said.' Rita thrust the phone at Clara and
stood waiting for more.

'He-lllooo?' said Clara in her best telephone voice. 'Clara
Newton speaking.'

Rita hadn't gone away and was standing at her elbow smirking. They always laughed at her phone voice. Clara put her finger to her lips.

It really was Donald Button, and he had a wonderful unruffled telephone voice, just as you'd expect. He said he wanted to take her out in London. Clara dabbed her forehead with her apron. She *was* ruffled. She couldn't understand why he would want to do that. Should she just come out and ask?

'What's... what exactly is the purpose?' she stammered, and he laughed so hard down the wires, he must have woken up the operator.

'It's to talk through the performance. I understand how daunting this might be for you – coming from the country.'

The country? Lavenham was hardly Outer Mongolia.

'I thought I might be able to help you prepare.'

'Really?'

Stella came and rubbed herself against Clara's legs. She was always hungry lately.

'And a little champagne wouldn't go amiss.' He laughed as though he'd said something hilarious.

When she'd put down the receiver, Rita was still behind her. She pulled at Clara's arm. 'Do you think he wears that toupee to bed?'

'Ri-ta!' Clara said. There was a lot to wonder about.

Peter did call, a couple of evenings later, and Clara felt her mood lift exponentially. Once a month wasn't enough for her, but she had to accept it, of course. Peter didn't owe her anything. He talked about the comic strip he was working on; they'd changed the boy's name from Maurice to Dennis. Clara wasn't sure about that; she had liked the idea of Maurice. And they had given him a dog rather than a cat. They hadn't settled on a distinctive look for him yet though. Clara racked her brains.

'When I first arrived, you used to wear a stripy sweater. When you outgrew it, I gave it to Alex and now Denny wears it sometimes.'

'Great!' he said, and she felt a thrill that she was still useful, still relevant.

∼

After lunch the next day, Clara went and sat with her book on a park bench because it was good to get some distance between her and the house now and again. The house was run-down and Clara felt awkward asking Marilyn, who had done so much – or the council, who tried to do as little as possible. The wardrobe in the girls' room had broken and the back step was crumbling, perilously, and the windows still needed doing. Clara sighed. There was so much to worry about. She seemed to exchange one worry for another these days. When Mrs Garrard stopped for a chat, Clara pretended that all was well, and when Bertie peed up the leg of the bench, Mrs Garrard said it meant he liked her.

If Clara told Mrs Garrard that Donald Button, star of stage, screen and wireless, had asked her out for a date in London half the town would know in seconds. No, the *whole* town would. Mrs Garrard was what *Good Housekeeping* would call a blabbermouth.

When Clara took the 'Are you good at keeping secrets?' quizzes she got mostly Cs – *it depends. You keep the secrets that need to be kept, but you will let go of those that need to be out in the wild.*

∼

Without their wigs, facepaint and baggy trousers, Mr and Mrs Scallywag – or Mr and Mrs Hurley – looked extraordinarily normal. You wouldn't look twice at them in the street, although they were laughing very loudly, so perhaps you might.

Clara offered them the left-over strudel Anita had brought over, and Mr Hurley said, 'I've brought you a custard pie!'

'Oh, lovely!' Clara responded, but they were making a joke: there was no custard pie.

Usually when prospective adopters came, Clara liked them to arrive at about three o'clock so she could chat with them for half an hour or so without the children present, and then when the children returned from school, they could spend some time getting to know each other. Today, by ten past three Clara was desperate for the children to return. It wasn't that the Hurleys weren't pleasant, but they weren't her kind of people. She had an instinct that Peg wouldn't be impressed either.

'Miss Cooper is a bit of all right, isn't she?' Mr Hurley said.

'She's a good childcare officer,' said Clara loyally. *Except when it came to files.* 'She takes great care that each child is placed in the right home for them. We all do.'

Mrs Hurley said she wasn't sure about the strudel. Wasn't it Nazi food?

'I haven't heard that,' said Clara, wondering what the punishment would be if you pushed a clown's face into a strudel. *Surely no jury in the land would convict?*

The children came in, Rita was exclaiming loudly about a dog chasing a chicken in the street and Peg was laughing. Denny was holding Stella, who was wriggling to get away, and Maureen was complaining about one of the teachers, who'd had the temerity to give her another detention for not doing her work. Fortunately, Cliff was out playing with friends, so that was one less person to worry about.

'Children!' Clara announced seriously. 'We have guests. These are the Hurleys.'

'The clowns?' asked Rita. Clara had no idea how she knew. The Hurleys liked that, though. Mr Hurley got up, stood on the armchair seat, then its arm, and then pretended to collapse into it. Mrs Hurley clapped and said, 'Children love him!'

The children looked at Clara. Peg had folded her arms and looked very tiny and very fierce. 'You can go and get on with your chores,' Clara said and, for once, they ran off without complaint.

'It's that little one we're interested in.'

'Does she bounce?' said Mr Hurley. 'Kidding!'

'She will speak though, won't she, eventually?' Mrs Hurley asked, suddenly worried.

'We don't know.'

'She was so good on the drums. She's a talent. And they told us she likes dancing too.'

Mrs Hurley said. 'I think we've struck lucky.'

'We've hit the bullseye,' Mr Hurley shouted and then fell to the floor.

'Mr Hurley!' yelped Clara, but he was joking again. 'Geronimo!' he shouted and held his arm to be pulled up. Mrs Hurley obliged, creased over with laughter. 'He. Does. Not. Stop,' she said, and Clara wondered if that was perhaps a cry for help.

Just before they left, Mr Hurley asked Clara to sniff the flower in his buttonhole. Clara blinked at him.

'Oh no, Edwin, no,' squealed his wife.

Clara would do anything to get them out. She leaned in. Squirt! It was a fake flower and he had sprayed her in the face with water.

'Hilarious,' Clara said, and they clapped her on the back, told her she was a good sort and congratulated her on her fantastic sense of humour.

. . .

As soon as they had gone, Clara ran up the stairs to the sanity of her files and put down her thoughts about the Hurleys.

She heard the doorbell go, and feared they were back with more clown humour, but when she ran down, she found Ivor at the door, smiling. Crisp white shirt, braces; just as she always pictured him, only better. Goodness knows how he would react if he knew just how much he occupied her mind.

'Cake?' He was holding out a tin like a peace offering.

The children jumped up from the table. Even Cliff did. Peg got to him first. Firmly, she led him to the table.

'Ivor,' said Clara, less keen. The cake was one of Mrs Harrington's creations; it had to be. 'Who made this?'

'Does it matter?' Ivor said slightly impatiently. 'I've cut it into slices. Everyone?'

The children tucked in. Even Denny nibbled at a bit.

'How does she do it?' hissed Clara from behind a tea towel. He got up, holding a piece for her. 'Mrs Harrington, I mean. What about the rations?'

He shrugged. 'Her husband works at the Ministry of Food.'

'What? Really?'

The children already had chocolate cake in their hands and crumbs around their mouths. They were saying it was delicious, and Cliff was going in for another slice. 'Or four.'

'He's breaking the law then,' Clara said pompously. 'I won't have any, thank you, Ivor.'

'She's a good help, Clara. I feel like I can get back to work now. It's really turned things round.'

How happy he looked again. A vision of contentment.

'I would have helped.'

'I didn't want your help.'

They stood facing each other.

'Thank you.'

'Oh, I don't mean it like that. I don't want to be reliant on you. I don't want you ever to feel you have to look after me.'

She had a lump in her throat. She told herself she would not cry, she mustn't.

'Because you think I'm useless?'

'No. Because it makes *me* feel useless.'

Clara nodded slowly. She could almost understand this in her head, but in her heart it wasn't enough.

'But you let Mrs Harrington help?' She didn't even know what Mrs Harrington's first name was. Always at an arm's-length with her.

'That's different.'

'How though?'

He smiled at her, that old cheeky smile of his. 'It just is. You're going to have to take my word for it.'

Maybe he would have said more but just then Peg ran out to the hall, gave Ivor a big hug and handed Clara a folded note.

'I'd better go,' Ivor said. 'See you later, Alligator,' he said to Peg. She said goodbye but Clara felt as though something was unsaid or unfinished between them. She looked at the paper in her hand.

I do not like those clown people. I do not want to live with them.

As Clara lay in bed that night, her stomach growling for cake, she was furious at Mrs Harrington. She tried to feel furious at Ivor as well but she could never manage that, which was aggravating. As for Peg and the prospective adopters, she was determined: Peg was *not* going to live with the Hurleys. She didn't save Peg from Australia, from Sister Eunice and from the Home for Disabled Children in Walthamstow to send her to a couple of clowns, thank you very much.

18

Joe must have waited until the children had left for school, because they'd only been gone seconds when there was a faint tap on the back door.

He was sweating on his upper lip. She remembered the first time she ever met Joe Matthews, whistling 'Shine on Harvest Moon' in the girls' bedroom, cap pulled over his eyes. Then the second time, in the back garden, tending to Maureen as she was miscarrying and in great pain. And hadn't she supported him when he was squatting, as they called it nowadays, in Ivor's workshop?

'Joe,' she said curtly as he handed her a parcel that had been left on the steps. 'I didn't expect to see you again.'

Joe stared at his shoes. What *was* that he smelled of? She sniffed. Of course – petrol.

'I know,' he said faintly.

'Maureen is heartbroken. I never thought you – of all people – would mess her around.'

Unlike Cliff, Joe was someone you could effortlessly scold. At the same time, this made Clara feel sorry for him. It didn't seem fair that because of his gentle nature, he was an easier target.

'I didn't mean to hurt her, Miss Newton.'

'You blow hot and cold.' She thought: *the same as Ivor. What is it with men?*

Joe burst into tears. He sobbed into his hands, tears running over his fingers.

Of course, Clara couldn't maintain her *froideur* any longer. Not with sweet Joe. The boy who diligently delivered papers and had started up the Shilling Grange newsletter. She had stood up for him and he had repaid her multifold. She invited him in, told him to sit, pulled a handkerchief from her sleeve and gave it to him.

'Oh, Joe, love, what is it?'

He was shaking his head and crying. His plain features were screwed up in angst, his cheeks wet with tears. 'I'm marrying Janet,' he said from behind the handkerchief. Clara moved closer; she could hardly believe her ears. *Joe was getting married?*

'I've got to, Miss Newton, I don't know what else to do.'

It was a shock. As a housemother, Clara was used to pretending that she wasn't shocked; although it wasn't part of the job description, perhaps it should have been. Nevertheless, it took some doing this time. Janet was pregnant. *Good grief, Joe! Had he learned nothing from last time?*

'Oh!' she finally managed to say. 'That's... awkward. No, you keep it, Joe.'

He was holding up the handkerchief.

'I didn't two-time Maureen,' he said. 'I wouldn't do that.'

As if that was what Clara was thinking.

'No, I didn't think that.'

Tea was the answer. Filling the kettle had never felt noisier.

Clara lit the hob. Where were the matches? Cliff? No, they were here. Silently, they waited for the kettle to boil. Stella was under the table in Denny's box, fast asleep, curled up in that disarming way she had. The morning sun sent shafts of light over the plants on the windowsill and a couple of shells that Peg had placed there. It was a peaceful scene and yet Clara's mind was in turmoil. Poor Joe...

Loud gulping, burn-your-tongue tea. Joe said he'd love sugar if she had any – not to worry...

'It's okay, Joe.'

He had stopped weeping and tidied himself up a little, but still he sniffed.

'So, I have something to ask you...'

Everything felt less frightening after a cup of tea.

'Ye-es?' Clara said. *What now?*

'Will you come to the wedding?

Janet came from a large, well-known Suffolk family. Clara realised now that she had met some of them. The aunt was a waitress at the pub and the grandfather was a friend of the stationmaster and was often there, rolling cigarettes, chatting to anyone who would stop. They had lived in Lavenham for so long they were in the Domesday Book, apparently.

Joe had no one. His parents weren't dead, but they had cut contact with him.

'All right,' Clara said. And his tears came again, and she said quickly, afraid she'd misled him, 'I mean, we'll see.'

Then Joe asked her to tell Maureen for him. Clara knew this was a step too far. She told him, 'That's your job, Joe, but please, do it soon – and be gentle.'

Her heart went out to him. Maybe it shouldn't have, maybe Maureen would say she was disloyal, but it did. 'Another cup?'

19

The junior school called her in the following morning. Despite a frosty start, the receptionist and Clara were quite friendly with each other these days. Clara presumed Denny had wet himself again or had a crying fit. She was surprised when the receptionist said it was about Peg.

Peg? Clara started jamming her heels into her shoes. In hospital, or an accident? She *knew* that balancing bar in the playground was dangerous. Or had Peg choked on a biscuit? Yes, she had probably choked.

'Nothing to worry about, just... if you could come in – Miss Fisher would like a word.'

When she got to the school, Clara was told to make her way to Miss Fisher's classroom. Peg wouldn't be there, she had her exercises in the hall. On the way, Clara saw groups of seven- and eight-year-olds in vests and shorts, listening to the instructions, flapping their arms around as though they were planes landing. She thought she picked out Peg, but there were so many, she wasn't quite sure.

Miss Fisher's classroom was as plain as ever. Other teachers filled their walls with drawings. Miss Fisher's only decoration was a command on the blackboard: I WILL LISTEN TO MY TEACHER. Clara eyed the desks with their lids nervously. She remembered catching a finger in one of those on more than one occasion.

Miss Fisher offered Clara a seat, but Clara said she was fine. It seemed to her that Miss Fisher was more conciliatory than usual. She took off her thick glasses and rubbed her tiny eyes. She looked softer, fuzzier without them.

'What I am about to say is – well, it's awkward.'

'Oh,' said Clara, racking her brain at what it could be. *Peg and her friends? Peg and her drawings? Peg and…?*

'You see, Peg has some strange ideas.'

Clara didn't think Peg had particularly strange ideas. Or rather *all* the children did. Perhaps all adults did too.

'I'll just say it, Miss Newton. Peg seems to have decided that I am… her mother.'

'Oh!' Clara considered. To be fair, that *was* strange. There couldn't have been a less likely candidate for Peg's mother than Miss Fisher. She was past sixty and made no pretence or effort at appearing younger. She had a careworn, wrinkled face, glasses thick as jam-jar bottoms and an old-fashioned hairstyle. She was the strictest teacher at Lavenham Primary by a long shot. Her favourite saying was 'Hold out your hand', and it wasn't for a sweet.

'There must be some mistake,' said Clara.

'Well, obviously it's a mistake,' said Miss Fisher, her lips tight and pale. 'I think it may have something to do with this.'

She led Clara over to a display of shells and stones. They were mostly pale and pearly and curled like snails. Clara picked up a pink one. It was smooth and spherical, and it fitted perfectly into her hand. She couldn't resist pressing it to her ear. Disappointingly, she couldn't hear anything.

'It seems, as a baby, she was left with a shell and she decided that her mother would also collects shells. When she found out that I did, Peg thought that it had special significance – she put two and two together and came up with... me.'

'How ridiculous—' Clara began.

But Miss Fisher had turned away from her, and it seemed she was trying not to cry.

'I... I'm so sorry, Miss Fisher. I will speak to Peg.'

Miss Fisher gathered herself. She always wore very old-fashioned clothes, and a large cross hung from her throat. She was an unlikely candidate for the woman who had abandoned baby Peg at the doorway of a Lincolnshire church about eight years earlier.

'There is no need to apologise.' She took the shell out of Clara's hand. 'I thought it was advisable that you know, that's all. It seemed a spurious connection at first, but then I understood that it was her heart yearning.'

'I see.' Clara thought this was very poetic.

'Oh, and I've explained I'm not her mother but it seems to go in one ear and out the other.'

'She... yes.'

'She is rather worried about these clowns. I don't suppose... you see, I really am very fond of her, I don't imagine it would be a... I could apply to adopt her instead?'

Clara swallowed. Miss Fisher was too old. *And too single.* Clara suddenly felt choked up. Peg was loved. Miss Fisher was very fond of her. But she knew exactly what the council would say: 'Rules are rules.'

Miss Fisher, who had a lifetime of nurturing, caring and elevating young people, wouldn't be eligible. Clara couldn't bring herself to spell it out though. Instead, she said, 'I'll see what I can do.'

Clara watched Peg carefully after school, and she watched her over tea. Rita, Maureen and Cliff went for a rehearsal, but Peg and Denny weren't needed, so they stayed home and played marbles in the parlour. Nothing seemed different and yet Clara felt like a tide was rushing in.

In the girls' dorm, the shells were on the shelf. The one from Peg's mother and others too. There were white shapes and curves and surprises, flat stones that looked polished, and crystal jagged ones. Such pretty things to hold in the palm of your hand. Like many children, Peg liked possessing something beautiful. Clara put the one from her mother to her ear and this time she could hear that swishing sea sound.

20

Joe kept his word. A couple of days later, he intercepted Maureen on the way home from school and broke her heart again. She stormed in the back door. Clara braced herself.

'I thought he was *my* Joe,' she said repeatedly, tears trickling down her cheeks until Clara thought her heart might break too. 'I thought he'd come back to me.' Her voice shook. 'And now he's marrying someone else!'

If Clara had hoped the worse was over, she was wrong. Maureen was devastated. Clara did what she could to cheer her up. She let Maureen listen to a funny show on the wireless even though it was past bedtime and the newspaper advised it was for adults only. She told Maureen she absolutely must have a cake – didn't baking always cheer her up? – and she let her use the flour and sugar she'd been saving. She found a story in the newspaper about a sheep who had lived in the wild for over fifteen years and amassed 78 kilograms of wool.

'Look at this poor sheep, he looks like a shrub or a tree.'

Maureen did look up at that. She said it did not look like a tree at all. What on earth *was* Miss Newton going on about?

When Mrs Harrington wasn't at the workshop (for once),

Clara told Ivor about Joe and Maureen and he said, 'Oh no, what a horrible thing to happen,' and Clara blushed, thinking yes, it is horrible when the one you love chose someone else over you, didn't she know all about that? He said he had some lovely silk left over from some work he had done, he'd turn it into a pretty headscarf for Maureen.

This time round, though, Maureen kept up with her rehearsals at Anita's. She was excited about performing at the Royal Festival Hall and on television. But she also said, 'It's the only good thing in my life – the rest is rotten.'

Julian also had a new girlfriend. Peg and Rita told Clara. They had seen them sitting on a bench when they were walking back from Anita's.

'She looks just like you!' Rita said. Peg nodded fiercely.

Clara sniffed. She didn't know how to react to this news. Of course Julian was a free agent, but his continued affection for her had been rather flattering. He liked to say to her: *You had your chance*, but she had never actually thought she no longer had a chance with him (if she'd wanted) – not until now.

She didn't for one moment believe that the woman, whoever she was, looked like her. That was just the kind of thing Rita said about older women: to her, they all looked the same.

Maureen asked what Clara was wondering. 'How do you know they were together?' Rita put her arm round Maureen and squeezed. 'Because they were sitting like this.'

'Oh, rubbish,' said Clara.

But then Clara saw Julian in the post office one lunchtime. He was leaving with a bundle of unposted parcels – Julian did not like a queue – and he said, 'Sod this. Darling Clara, come for a drink, I've missed you,' and she said no, no, but he insisted he'd bring Bandit along – and how could she resist her favourite dog? He told her all about it then. The pub was dark even though it was sunny outside, and despite it being the middle of the day, it felt quite intimate sitting in the corner, under the wooden beams and oak panelling.

'Her name's Margot,' Julian said, 'and she looks a bit like you.'

Bandit licked Clara's fingers and she felt like he was trying to tell her that he missed her.

'I've missed you too,' she whispered. Bandit hadn't been enough to keep her and Julian together – but he very nearly was.

Julian even passed Clara a photo of Margot he kept in his wallet – *had he ever kept a photo of Clara in his wallet? She didn't think so.* She looked at it, and there was a similarity – if Clara were only a little taller, slimmer, and better dressed. Margot looked like a wealthier, more upper-class version of herself. *Now* Clara felt a little jealous.

'Her personality is nothing like yours though.' He laughed to himself.

'How do you mean?' Clara wondered what aspects of her personality Julian was referring to. Embarrassingly, she wasn't sure what her personality was – which was one reason she enjoyed the quizzes in *Good Housekeeping* so much, she supposed. To Ivor, she was a petty bureaucrat, to Michael, the quintessential bright-eyed English girl, to Victor, she was a woman of action, to Mrs Horton, she was a maverick, to Miss Cooper, she was a conservative – she sometimes felt like a hollow Earth without a real core, everyone imposing their own opinions on her.

Julian went to fetch another round of drinks. He took ages, his booming laugh echoing through the bar. He was at home everywhere. He liked chatting with the landlord; he prided himself on getting on with the working classes. She tickled

Bandit's belly and wondered if Margot loved him as much as she herself did – she hoped Bandit preferred her to Margot.

Finally, Julian came back, exuberant, a drink in each hand.

'Well, how are we not alike, Julian?' Clara asked impatiently.

'Oh, she's bossy,' he told her happily. 'She's always telling me what to do. If she were here now, she'd be telling me to drink up, wrong drink, do this, do that.' He wiped his mouth and roared with laughter. 'For example, she hates it when I do that.'

Clara knew she wasn't bossy – in fact, her lack of bossiness dogged her constantly. She wouldn't be having such trouble with the children if she could rule them with an iron fist.

'And you like that, the bossiness?' she asked querulously.

'Very much,' he said, winking at her. 'Most men do, you know. She says exactly what she thinks.'

Does Ivor like that? Clara wondered. She doubted it. The couple of times she had tried to gently steer him over the smallest of things, he hadn't taken it well.

When Julian said that *actually* Margot was divorced, Clara nearly spluttered into her gin. *Divorced*! She didn't know any women who were divorced. She herself used to have all sorts of preconceptions about divorcees – strange that she would have, especially since she had encouraged Judy to divorce, but she did. A left-over from her childhood. She was, she supposed, her mother's daughter. Instantly, in her mind Margot became even more fascinating, but also flighty. She imagined the other woman wore coats with fasteners instead of buttons and mules in the house; definitely mules, with a fluff.

'And that's all right with you?'

Julian could be very traditional over some things. He himself had travelled a very straight path, like a line on a graph going up, up, up: boarding school, university, law – and he didn't usually empathise with those who deviated.

'Oh, I don't mind,' he said magnanimously. 'You reach our

age and everyone you meet has a history of some sort, don't they?'

Less of the 'our age', thought Clara, but she didn't say it, because unlike Margot, she did *not* say everything she thought. She couldn't imagine the small disasters that would ensue if she did. Julian picked and chose his morals according to whichever served him best at the time. At least he never hid it.

They drank and Julian crunched the peanuts (with his mouth open) and kept pushing the bag towards her. Clara declined, wondering if Margot was a peanut-eater or not. And if that was another thing that she hadn't known that men like in a woman.

He scrunched up the bag. 'Actually, the other thing – she's not half as kind-hearted as you.'

'Really?' Clara tried not to sound grateful. *What did Julian's opinion of her matter, really?* But it did.

'She thinks the orphanage should be turned into a workhouse!'

Clara spluttered with laughter before realising Julian was being serious.

'Well, I hope you told her we're here to stay,' she said proudly.

'I did.' He laughed too but it was probably at her reaction. 'She can't wait to meet you.'

Time for another politeness. 'Likewise.'

~

To whom it may concern,

I am writing to you concerning the child, Peg, who is currently resident at Michael Adams Children's Home (formerly Shilling Grange Orphanage). I would like to make an application to adopt.

I am sixty-two years old. I am a teacher and have been working at Lavenham Primary since I graduated from Walpole College, Oxford, in 1921. Many of my students have gone on to do great things. I live alone in Dedham. My hobbies include reading, fossil-hunting, listening to classical music. I also play piano (level 6) and flute (level 4) and I am a regular church attender.

I have been teaching Peg since September and we have covered a variety of topics, including changing landscapes, the Plimsoll line and Florence Nightingale.

Peg is mute and needs a home with someone understanding and patient. I believe I could be that person.

I was advised by Miss Newton to approach you directly. The vicar of All Saints and the headmistress of Lavenham Primary will supply references on request. I look forward to your response.

Yours sincerely,

Claudette Fisher Bachelor of Science.

21

Clara hadn't heard from Peter for a month again. No, it was more than one month now; the last day he had called, she remembered, she had run in from the garden and only picked up on the tenth ring, and she had left Anita and baby Howard out there for ages. That had been five weeks ago. And the time before that was around four weeks too.

There was a telephone at his lodgings, and she had the number, but no one answered it much – and when occasionally they did, they didn't take messages. There was a telephone in Peter's office too, but when she rang there, to wish him a happy first day of spring (yes, that was a spurious reason), he had sounded surprised and then cautious. She asked what was wrong and he grumbled, 'I'm working,' and she had promised not to ring there again. She couldn't help but worry. He wasn't her business any more, but so what? She had a moral responsibility, she told herself.

She knew where his office was. Would it be a bad idea to drop by? Maybe she could take him a jumper, or a... something. Just to check.

. . .

Once the children had left for school, Clara hurried to the train station, waving to the postmistress and Mr Dowsett on the way. At the ticket office she ran slap bang into Ivor, which wasn't such a bad thing because she hadn't been so dolled up for a while and she was becoming afraid that he might think she only ever wore frumpy aprons or that hideous nightdress (which she still hadn't replaced). Today, she was wearing a tweed skirt and a fitted jacket, and Anita had bequeathed her a red lipstick, probably only because she wanted her to wear it to the Royal Festival Hall.

One of the issues Clara had with Ivor (and there were many, when she thought about it, which she did often) was that he never asked where you were going. In fact, he never asked anything. He hated other people 'prying', and in turn, he hated to pry – you just had to volunteer information. When you did, though, it did stick with him; he often brought things up months later.

'I'm going to Soho.'

She saw the shadow of surprise on his face, which he covered quickly to turn into disinterest.

'Have a good day then.'

Was he jealous? Hopefully, he was jealous. Hopefully, he realised she was a woman of interest.

What would never make sense was why he had blocked her out of his life and let in Mrs Harrington instead. That was the worst of it. That was such an unreasonable thing to do. She could have helped more than anyone. It was so illogical of him to refuse her.

Clara arrived in London at half past ten and was immediately engulfed in the busyness of the city. Funny how she felt less equipped to deal with it than she used to. Everything felt too loud: the double-decker buses, the reversing delivery trucks, the ringing church bells, the construction workers shouting, throwing bricks down into the road. The air was dusty. Where it was not dusty, it was smoky. She had to cross the road in front of a horse and then a motorbike with a sidecar and then a police car. And watch out for the trams. Nevertheless, she got that excitement in the pit of her stomach that she sometimes got in the capital – yes, she was at the epicentre of things here. Here, things would happen.

She would have liked a cup of tea before she went in, to steady her nerves, but she was saving room for when she met Peter. She didn't want to get caught short either. Bracing herself, she made her way to his office and knocked, and when no one answered, she opened the door. The first time she went there with Peter, people had dashed over to greet them, but this time no one dashed; they were all in a meeting in another room, poring over large sheets of paper. The door to the meeting room was open, so she could see Peter's bright copper head where he was sitting at the large table, like a dining table. He clocked her, rapidly spoke to the person next to him, who looked up also concerned, then Peter rushed out.

'What's wrong, Miss Newton?' he asked breathlessly.

'Nothing!'

This was a bad idea.

Peter's limbs went soft and easy. He steadied himself on the table next to him. 'Oh God, okay. I just thought something must have happened.'

Clara gulped. *What might have happened?*

'I thought we could sit outside for lunch?'

It was eleven o'clock! He wouldn't be wanting lunch!

Peter tugged his tie – he wore a tie! And not a school tie but a grown man's tie – and looked awkward.

'I usually work through,' but he looked at her sympathetically like she was an elderly person who needed special treatment, then added, 'Of course. I'll just ask my boss.'

They sat outside. Peter jiggled his long legs and said he wasn't hungry, then wolfed down the sandwiches she had brought with her. *Did he eat enough?* They were her ration egg and cress, his favourite, and she had made them with (uncustomary) care. He still had all those lovely freckles – well, of course he did! But there was something different about his face too. Something older, more man than boy now, in shape and complexion. His hands were covered in different colour inks. There was a lot of yellow. It looked like he had jaundice— *he didn't have jaundice, did he?*

'Aren't you eating?' He was a boy who noticed things.

'I'll eat tonight,' she said. 'Do you always have to work through?' she went on. *Had she sold him into slavery?*

'To be honest, I'm usually so busy I don't notice lunch. I eat at dinnertime though,' he said 'and I make myself porridge every morning. The others laugh, but that habit's stuck.'

He was fine. He had moved on.

She told him about the clowns who wanted to adopt Peg and how unsuitable they were. He looked incredulous and worried – 'Won't the council insist?'– and she said, more bravely than she felt, 'I'll make sure they don't!' She told him that Clifford, no, Cliff had finally settled in, and he raised an eyebrow in surprise. She said that he was good at singing and he didn't dare defy Anita and he said, 'Ah, yes, I get that.' And she told him about Denny and his sleepwalking and he said, 'That's weird,' yet she could feel he was making an internal note perhaps for his own stories. He had told her once, 'Orphans are the superheroes in comics.'

Peter said he would show her his accommodation if she

liked. He lived in an old block behind the office. It looked like a prison with the tiny windows. He said it was a conversion from a factory or a warehouse and they were 'all the rage'. She didn't want to put him out, but she agreed to see it since she was eager to know how he lived – it would be easier not to worry about him if she could picture his life better.

'As I'm here,' she said.

'Might as well,' he said.

Wooden bunks and unmade beds and a shared kitchen and a tin bath. It was basic, she thought, but she didn't say that. Peter obviously thought the world of it, and why wouldn't he? It was his first home of his own.

She felt guilty though; she didn't know what she was doing here. Perhaps she shouldn't have come. She was nothing to him now. She wasn't his real mother, or his blood sister. She wasn't an aunt or any kind of relative and their history, two years – which at the time had seemed like for ever – wasn't long after all. She saw that now. Maybe she was a reminder of things he'd rather forget. She felt tearful suddenly.

But Peter was kind, and he needed reassurance too.

'It's a bit messy, isn't it?'

On his bed, lots of clothes and papers and of course, comics.

'It's fine.'

He excused himself – 'The only downside is the lav; it's the end of the block,' and she laughed because she thought there were lots of downsides but how lovely that he didn't think of it like that.

While he was gone, she thought about tidying up for him – she would have done at home. She picked up the jacket and the shirt from the bed and looked for somewhere to put them. There wasn't anywhere obvious, so she folded them and laid them back on his blanket like they were tender, fragile things. She picked up a comic. Was it wrong to be nosy or was it still her job to be nosy?

There was a postcard from Alex of boats, with on the other side his usual verbose yet affectionate storytelling, and a note from Maureen, all in capital letters –

> *YOU MUST COME TO THE ROYALL FESTEVAL HALL AND SEE US SINGING OR I WILL NEVER SPECK TO YOU AGIN.*

Clara laughed. Maureen didn't beat around the bush. And then underneath those was a newspaper cutting from the *Suffolk Gazette,* 14 January 1951.

RECKLESS DRIVER GETS FOUR YEARS IN JAIL.

Lavenham man, James Clarke, a small businessman (35), pleaded Guilty to reckless driving on the Lavenham High Road last summer. In court, Clarke of Elgin Road was described as an aggressive man with several motoring convictions, who had driven into a pedestrian at speed. The victim Susan Smith, a nurse (26) from Scotland, died on impact. Clarke apparently got out of the vehicle and ran. He attempted to commit suicide in a police cell by tying a handkerchief round his throat. Mr Justice David described at Suffolk Crown Court that by his cavalier attitude and arrogance, James Clarke had destroyed a young woman's life and that he had no option but to put him away from the public for the maximum length of time.

Before Clara could take it in, she heard Peter's footsteps echo along the corridor. They were so loud, it sounded like there were four of him. Panicked, she threw the comics and clothes back on top of the cutting. Her mind was whirring. *Who could have sent it?* James Clarke – Peter's uncle – had tried to kill himself? Well, Peter wouldn't be sorry about that – although he might be sorry that he'd failed.

Peter was back, looking sheepish. 'Sorry for the wait.'

'What are the others who live here like?'

At this, he brightened. He talked for a while about his room-mates' escapades: Jack always forgot his key and locked himself out – and Tony never tidied up, but was a nice chap, and Nat was a good cook – had Clara heard of spaghetti? Clara said she had, but she wasn't sure if she had really.

'It's Italian and very tasty,' he said, all knowledgeable. She agreed she would try it. She wanted to ask the right questions, she didn't want to come across as a country bumpkin. He told her he had been taken to a Chinese restaurant too. Did she know what that was?

'I used to live in London, you know,' she eventually blurted out and he reddened and said, 'Oh, yeah,' and she felt like she had been harsh, so added, 'but I expect it has changed a lot since then.'

'What do they do?' she went on, 'the other boys? For a living?'

'All cartoonists here,' he said. 'Like me.' It made him proud to say that too, she could tell. He was a cartoonist, his friends were cartoonists. She kind of felt that way about the word 'housemother' (only nine times out of ten she had to explain what that was – at least everyone knew what a cartoonist was).

And at the same time as they were chatting about this and that, she was trying to get her head around the idea that his uncle, James Clarke, was in jail – *good*, her head said. She wondered if Julian knew? Of course he knew – Julian knew everything. It looked like he hadn't defended the man, this time at least.

'Let me show you around the office too,' Peter said, flushing to his freckles. 'Before you head off? The meeting should have finished by now.'

There were strings criss-crossing the main office and posters pegged to them like washing on a summer's day. Clara saw pictures of horses rearing up and cowering rats in the Underground and squirrels guarding their nuts. Most of the desks were covered with papers too; some drawings had not been coloured in yet, others were a riot of colour. And then there was a paper guillotine and rulers, and some people were shouting about Daisy losing her handbag something – she didn't know if it was a person or someone in a cartoon, but she'd lost it last month too apparently – and all the excitement. And she saw a lovely place to work.

The young fella who had shown Peter and herself around that first time and who had suggested taking Clara on a date was there. This time he did not suggest a date, but his eyes widened appreciatively when he saw Clara, and she was glad that she had made an effort with her outfit. She wasn't *too* out of place in London. She wasn't entirely provincial; she could still hold her own. The young fella seemed to have grown a moustache since they last met (the Clark Gable look was popular now), and he was less flirty and more like a teacher reporting to a parent.

'*Dennis the Menace* has exploded,' he said after they had been reintroduced.

'What?!' Clara squinted at him.

'In popularity, I mean,' he said awkwardly.

'Oh, good! I thought you meant literally...' She trailed off.

'And this chap here is a big part of that.' He slapped Peter on the back, and Peter, who was unused to such manly appreciation, jolted forward.

The young chap asked if Clara wanted tea. Clara looked at the filthy cups with their filmy, transparent lines cluttering up most of the desks and said, 'Thank you but I'd better be off. The children, you see.'

Peter walked her to the door.

'Thank you for coming,' he said.

'Thank you for having me.'

Even though it was something she'd always instructed the children to say, between them, it sounded oddly formal. It marked a separation

'Right then.' Clara handed over her last bribe. A paper bag of Anita's strudel cut into slices. They were meagre things compared to Mrs Harrington's chocolate ration-busting monstrosities, but Clara thought they were perfect and Peter's expression said he did too.

'I will share them with everyone,' he promised.

She said, 'I'm sorry to have taken you by surprise,' and he gave her his biggest smile and said, 'There's nothing to be sorry for. I'm fine, it's fine. I didn't expect you, but it is lovely to see you, Miss Newton, honestly.'

She nodded. She still felt silly and unnecessary somehow, like he was the grown-up and she was the irritating child, waiting for something more.

'I'll call you next week, shall I?' he said.

'Whenever suits,' she said, knowing he wouldn't call.

On the train, she had a foolish little cry, then dabbed her tears with a handkerchief. She felt a little ashamed of herself that she had looked to a very young man for reassurance. She had to trust Peter was all grown up now. And that bad news travels fast, and all the other sayings like that: the sayings that parents whose children have left home say to comfort each other. And although she hadn't given him much thought for some time, she was glad that Peter's uncle was in jail, even if it was not for what he did to Peter; at least he was suffering, at least he was being punished. And that chapter of Peter's life had closed now, although hopefully, he had not closed *all* the chapters of his past.

The man opposite her, in a three-piece suit and a bowler

hat, tentatively asked, 'Can I be of assistance?' He looked like a conventional man – she could imagine him as one of Julian's club members maybe, or at least on a similar trajectory, if it hadn't been for the pink scar down one cheek and his soft eyes.

'Everything is fine,' she told him and he looked so relieved, like he could have kissed her.

22

Miss Cooper was at the front door when she got home, and instead of her usual uninterested expression, she was wearing a furious one. Clara strained to remember if she had been expecting her, but she was sure she wasn't. Miss Cooper was holding out a pink paper file – one of the prospective-parent ones – and she was jiggling it like she was frying an egg.

'I got your assessment of the Hurleys,' she said. 'No, I'm not coming in.'

'Ah.'

'You can't turn people down, Miss Newton. I don't know where you got the idea that this is some kind of beauty parade where you select a winner—'

'That is the last thing—'

'You don't get to pick and choose,' she insisted. She really was in a deathly mood. 'As for the Fisher woman, she doesn't fit *any* of the criteria. I mean, not even the basics.'

'That's a bit harsh.' Clara took off her coat and hung up her bag. Miss Cooper stayed in the doorway.

'I got her letter. Level-four flute? Shells? Church? I hope you haven't given Peg false hope.'

'Of course, I haven't.'

Clara thought of Miss Fisher's tired face and pictured a chalked blackboard of her own: I MUST NOT GIVE FALSE HOPE.

'She should adopt a kitten or something.'

This struck Clara as especially unkind. To hear this long-standing advocate for children dismissed outright was painful. She thought of Miss Fisher's darting eyes and the way she pushed her spectacles up her nose. If she and Peg had formed a lovely bond, well, that was something to be embraced, not thrown away.

And why was Miss Cooper so agitated? Was this the same Miss Cooper who had stood by her last year?

'Well, Mr Sommersby and I have been discussing it in depth. It's the *principle* of the thing.'

'The principle has always been that I can offer my assessment.'

'We'll see,' Miss Cooper said ominously, stuffing the folder into her bag. 'We need to have some successful adoptions soon, Miss Newton, you know that.

Now Clara remembered that Miss Cooper, Mr Sommersby – all of them were under pressure to get the children out from council care and into private homes again.

'I agree,' she said coolly. 'And the key word there is success-ful. It is not good to have children going into unsuitable homes and then returning – or worse.'

Miss Cooper stormed away.

That evening, Clara narrowly beat Rita to the telephone. She had decided what to say to Donald Button if he called again. Annoyed, Rita slumped down by the wall and played with the hems of her knee-high socks. Her shoes were scuffed, and Clara realised with a sinking feeling that it had been a while since she'd had new ones. She would put in an invoice to the council. She would send it by post. (After today, she didn't fancy seeing Miss Cooper for a while.)

But it wasn't Donald Button: it was Alex. 'There's a... *shdkhsd.*'

'I can't hear you, the line's bad. Stop shrieking, Rita – your music is there in the shed, where you left it. An awards ceremony? Of course I'll try to come.'

'And will you ask Ivor too? I'd love him there.'

Ivor. Clara baulked.

'I don't know, Alex, he's so busy with the baby and...' All she could think was *Mrs Harrington.* 'And his cakes.'

'What? Please... It would mean such a lot to me.'

There was nothing Clara would like more than having Ivor to herself for a few hours – no children, no babies to take their attention away. But there was nothing she liked less than giving Mrs Harrington the opportunity to inveigle her way further into Ivor's life – for if she was out with Ivor, then Mrs Harrington would surely be spending even more time with Patricia, and that was not pleasing.

Perhaps I could suggest Maureen as a babysitter instead, Clara thought, but it was a school day and Maureen's results were already below average. The Head said she was sixteenth of seventeen in the class. Because of this, Clara was trying to steer Maureen towards a future in domestic work, or in a bakery perhaps. Unfortunately, Maureen barely looked further than her own nose.

She went over to Ivor's. *Strike while the iron's hot,* she told herself; if she didn't do it now, she wouldn't do it – and she *did* want to go to see Alex and she did want Ivor to come too.

'Did you have a nice day in London?' Ivor said as he greeted her. He never looked surprised to see her, she thought – although why should he?

'I went to meet Peter,' she said and was she being ridiculous, or did he look relieved? He asked questions about Peter's well-being, and she told him, neglecting to mention either that she had gone there uninvited or Peter's evident shock. She asked Ivor if Peter had been in touch with him lately, and he stood still like he'd been found out and said, 'Yes, I write occasionally – not as often as I should.'

'Do you ever send him anything?'

'Anything?'

'Oh, you know, newspaper cuttings or...'

'I might have,' he said cautiously.

'Good,' she said to tell him she knew and that she approved.

'Is that what you...?'

'No, I...' Clara told him about Alex's event and what Alex had asked.

'When is it?' Ivor said.

'It's next Tuesday.'

'And Alex wants me there?'

'Absolutely,' she said nervously. 'You were always...' she coughed, '*his* favourite.'

She was still certain he'd say no.

He rubbed the nub of his arm – he looked so weary nowadays.

'To tell the truth,' he said, 'I *could* do with an afternoon off. And now I've got Mrs Harrington... let's go, Clara, why not?'

Clara wouldn't have dreamed of asking Anita for help with an outfit in the past, but Anita was always so enthusiastic and so generous with her clothes that Clara had almost overcome her fear of being the poor relative.

Anita suggested the dress she had worn for Miss Bridges' wedding, but Clara said that was too much, she wanted something casual yet special, 'if you know what I mean'. Anita didn't really agree with casual, she thought it was falling standards, but she agreed.

As they looked at the clothes hanging in the wardrobe, baby Howard was toddling, cruising around the floor. Every so often Anita chased after him with a feather duster, which he seemed to adore. Then Evelyn appeared and took Howard's hand and led him downstairs. Evelyn seemed so grown-up suddenly. She had grown taller and at the same time slimmed down; she seemed happy in her skin. Her hair was in one of her pretty bows and she was not half as shy as she used to be.

'She's brilliant with Howard,' Clara said to Anita.

'She's brilliant in every way,' said Anita. 'We're lucky.'

And then Anita talked about the TV event, which was only three weeks away and the London performance, which was longer away, but Clara found she didn't mind so much about either of them any more – the Royal Festival Hall would be the end of it, and it did keep the children occupied and happy. Denny was the only one she had reservations about, but he loved the rehearsals, and she would deal with it when it came to it. It certainly kept Clifford from under her feet. She was still getting calls to go to the school but much less than before. Sometimes she went three or four days without hearing from them and his misdemeanours didn't seem as bad as before.

Clara went away with two choices – Anita had insisted – one was a box-pleated skirt, which was in vogue, and the other a dress that was more cosmopolitan. Clara nodded at the words, but she didn't know what Anita was talking about. *Vogue or cosmopolitan*, Clara didn't know which one she was. She suspected she was neither.

Although she and Ivor were going to a busy awards ceremony, there was still the train journey and plenty of standing-around time when it would be just the two of them. It made her heart leap to think of it. She hadn't had a moment with him without children or babies for... it felt like for ever. They hadn't shared intimacies or confided stories for months. She told herself not to get too excited; something was bound to go wrong – something Patricia -related – and he'd have to let her down or something. Even so, Clara managed to fit in an appointment to Beryl's Brushes, although she spent most of the visit getting told off by Beryl for not coming more often: 'Children are no excuse,' Beryl said indignantly, 'I've had eight of my own and I still take care of meself.'

On the morning of the prize-giving though, it was Clara who nearly changed her mind. Denny had had another series of bad nights. Cliff, an unusually heavy sleeper, mostly slept through the sleepwalking and the crying out, but that night he'd woken and had thrown socks at Denny to get him to shut up. Denny had appeared at Clara's door at 2 a.m then 4 a.m., weeping. She thought about putting him in the girls' room, but it wouldn't be fair on the girls. Then she thought about putting herself in the girls' room and Denny in hers, but that wouldn't work long-term either.

But she didn't want to disappoint Alex and of course she wanted to spend time with Ivor and when she saw Mrs Harrington swan into the workshop without a care in the world, she thought why not? She told the children where she was going and Rita, Peg and Maureen gave her messages to give Alex, while Cliff said, 'He managed to get away from here, did he?' while Denny got confused and asked, 'Have I ever met him?'

'No, honey, he was before you came here.'

Perhaps it was the mention of before-you-came here, Clara wasn't sure, but Denny burst into tears. Peg comforted him though, and soon they had all left for school.

∼

The train was too crowded for anything but the smallest of small talk: the weather, Ivor's work and Patricia's (improving) sleeping habits. Ivor sat opposite her by the window and three men in suits surrounded them. Ivor winked at her though, which she loved. She couldn't help it; she felt giddy as a school-girl. Of course, the men were talking about the Festival of Britain. Interestingly, only one of them was for it, the other two were against. Clara tried not to look as though she was listening to their arguments, and pretended to be engrossed by the galloping telegraph poles and fields coming in and out of view through the window. When one of them said, 'Do you know how the Skylon got its name?' she had to stop herself from yelling out the answer.

'It's our stop,' Ivor said.

Once out of the confines of the carriage, he said, 'I bet you wanted to join in,' and she couldn't meet his eye when she said, 'You know me so well.'

At the station steps, he stopped to help a woman with her baby in a pram. He strode off ahead with it and the woman said to Clara, 'Thank your husband for me. He's too kind.' And Clara didn't correct her.

If she had thought the Ipswich grammar school was posh then this, the venue for the prize-giving, was tremendous, and Clara could see why Alex had wanted to invite them. It was an impressive place, with oil paintings of podgy aristocrats on the walls and dark wood, uncomfortable-looking chairs. She understood it was a place you'd want to show off. Men were walking around in robes and mortar boards, women were in frocks and pearls, and there was an atmosphere of hush but not like in a church, more like in a cinema. Ivor became po-faced and quietly respectful, and then he went to look for the gents'.

It was while she was waiting for him that Victor Braithwaite found her. He wasn't in a robe, and he was no better dressed than he had been before, but something about him had changed. He certainly looked happier than when Clara had known him. His walk was jaunty, his shoulders were back, and his Beethoven-esque hair was tidy and brushed. After he thanked her for coming, he said, 'Alex is doing so well. He never stops talking about you, you know.'

'I know he never stops talking.' She laughed.

'And I'm enjoying family life very much, thanks to you.'

Clara bowed her head. 'You were the one who made it happen, Victor.'

'And finally, you are with Mr Delaney?' He smiled encouragingly. 'I'm happy for you.'

'What?'

'You aren't together? You make such an attractive couple. A bit Spencer Tracy and Katharine Hepburn.'

'No, Victor.' This was mortifying, but also quite elating. 'Why do you think that?'

'I always thought he was a bit in love with you,' Victor said in a low voice, pushing his hair away. 'That time I met him in his workshop – he couldn't keep his eyes off you.' Then he grimaced. 'Sorry, Clara, maybe I got it wrong. As you know, I'm no expert on affairs of the heart!'

Clara coughed. 'How about you, Victor? Do you have any special lady friends?' He'd told her last year that he was still mourning his late wife, Iris.

'I'm working on it,' he said with that embarrassed look he had, and Clara had a pang – not of regret but of wistfulness perhaps. It was for the best nothing had developed between them, but it was a shame you couldn't get a shot at an alternative life.

Alex got a prize for contribution to science and history. Clara thought of how far he'd come in just a very short space of time. She remembered his awful father and the time he had got Alex horribly drunk. Now look at him! She wanted to stand on a table and shout it to the world. *These children just need the right conditions*, she wanted to say, *before you write them off!* Alex waved his trophy around him and opened his mouth wide in a pretend roar. On the outside he was the gleaming towers of Oxford, but inside he was still her boy, the little professor, from Shilling Grange.

Clara thought they'd all go out together after the ceremony, but Victor and Alex looked uneasily at each other and apologised; they had a prior arrangement. Clara could see this was already a source of some tension between them and she didn't want to add to it.

'I'm awfully sorry for the confusion,' Alex said, but she told him it didn't matter – and it didn't matter. She had had a view into his world today and that was priceless. And now she had extra time alone with Ivor.

On the return train, Ivor said, 'I told Mrs Harrington I'd be back at three.'

Clara's first reaction was, *bloody Mrs Harrington*, until she realised what he was saying.

'I have until around then too.'

They looked at each other.

'How about tea at the Shilling Arms – to celebrate the success of one of your chicks?'

'Perfect,' she said. And then, thinking 'perfect' was too much, she said, 'Nice idea.'

She hadn't been to the Shilling Arms Hotel before. Although it was very popular in Lavenham, she associated it with people with money and had concluded it wasn't a place for her. It had those revolving doors that the children would adore. She stepped into one of the doors' sections and when Ivor joined her, she could feel herself growing scarlet at the proximity; she was sure she could hear a heart beating, but wasn't sure if it was his or hers.

'Shall we go again?' He laughed, and she laughed too, and they revolved again. And Clara felt herself grow less shy with each revolution. What was the point of being shy?

They slipped out after four revolutions although she could have kept revolving forever. She was feeling more and more frivolous. And reckless. And hopeful. *This is it. This is the time.* They were away from their burdens, their responsibilities. Childcare is not an aphrodisiac. Eyes meet across crowded rooms, not over grizzling babies' heads.

The windows of the lounge were misted up, which somehow made even that look more romantic. Clara popped to the ladies', was surprised at her overexcited face in the mirror and had to tell herself to calm down. She and Ivor were neighbours, old friends, having a quick cup of tea without the children, that was all.

Ivor was good-looking enough to double-take at, and indeed Clara noticed the waitresses looking at him as if he were a delicious desert. *Spencer Tracy and Katharine Hepburn*, she thought. No one had ever said anything like that before – and she doubted anyone ever would again – but what a nice thing to hear. She was glad she had gone for the 'cosmopolitan' outfit. She might feel out of place, but thanks to Anita, she didn't look it.

She told Ivor about Peg and the prospective adopters, clowns, hanging over her, and he said, 'They wouldn't, would they?'

'I don't know any more.' And it was true – she never knew about the council these days. They did make strange decisions, and sometimes they didn't make decisions, and she thought if she told someone who didn't know the council, everything – from Australia, to Peg, to her – she would find it hard to believe too. There were many things she loved about her work but being a pawn in an indecipherable chess game was not one of them. And everyone said that the childcare department of Suffolk Council was far better than most!

'And Denny? I see him playing out with a ball, sometimes.'

'Oh, he's lovely,' she said, smiling at the thought of Denny's cherubic face, 'apart from his sleep, which is dire,' she went on. 'Well, you know all about that. Apart from that, he's probably the easiest of the lot.'

'And Clifford?'

'We have to call him Cliff,' she said. She tried so hard to get it right and he got so angry at her when she didn't.

'Okay, has... he settled in?'

'He's settled in all right.' Clara didn't feel inclined to air her concerns about Cliff that afternoon. Not when she and Ivor had two hours – *two hours!* – to themselves, and the tables were clean and the cushions on the seats were plump and everything was luxury. She might have been in a different universe to the Home. Who wanted to rake up the shed-fire? She had almost forgotten it herself.

They ordered tea from a waitress who fluttered her eyelashes at Ivor, then took a step back when she clocked his arm. Ivor's expression didn't change though, not one iota; he must have been used to it.

He told her more about Patricia. He said he sometimes wondered if she were special, then chuckled self-consciously. 'I suppose all parents think that...'

Clara didn't know what all parents thought. 'You've adjusted so well to it all. I imagine Ruby is hugely grateful.'

There, she had done it: she had brought Ruby up without thinking. Ivor looked startled to hear her name too. His shoulders went back, his expression was tight as he folded his napkin.

'Maybe,' he said and Clara was glad that the waitress brought over the teapot and the china just then. Ivor, who liked it weak, poured his tea almost instantly; Clara, who liked hers strong, waited and then stirred. The waitress hovered; it was like she wanted to hear a codeword before departing.

'Very good, thank you,' Clara said finally and she backed away.

Clara decided she wouldn't be put off now. 'Do you... do you hear from Ruby at all?' She had to know.

'She doesn't want any contact,' he said shortly. 'That was the agreement.'

'Oh, I'm sorry, Ivor. About...' He looked up at her with narrowed eyes. 'Everything.'

He suddenly let his shoulders slump.

'I'm sorry I've been so difficult. It's... I feel like I'm going mad. The whole rhythm of my days has changed – there are these great moments of calm, and then there are storms. It's without doubt the hardest thing I've ever done.' He gulped back his tea. 'Things are improving now, I hope. I know you don't like Mrs Harrington much, but she does help.'

'I'd like the chance to help too,' Clara said throatily. His admission had taken her by surprise.

'I really don't want that,' he said quietly. He was almost pleading. 'Can't you understand?'

Clara said she was trying and that made him smile. 'I like your honesty,' he said.

As they walked away from the Shilling Arms and up the high road, Clara felt like, at last, Ivor might take her hand; it had been such a magical few hours. Once they had navigated past the elephants in the room – Ruby and Mrs Harrington – they had laughed and talked and ordered more tea. She was sure he must have felt something too – but she was on the wrong side for hand-holding. Should she manoeuvre to his other side? Just as she was about to negotiate that, she saw in the distance a small crowd gathered in the street outside the Home.

'What the...?'

As they drew closer, she could see Mrs Harrington, and the Silver Cross pram, gleaming like a motor vehicle, Mr and Mrs Garrard. Mr Sommersby, Miss Cooper and Mrs Horton – who she hadn't seen for some time – in a fat huddle.

Clara's mouth went completely dry.

'Something's happened,' said Ivor and he charged off towards them. 'Patricia?'

Clara gulped. Then she too ran, wobbling in her heels. She saw Mrs Harrington catch Ivor by his lapel and guide him to the pram, where the two babies were sitting upright. *She touches him*, Clara thought, even as she was telling herself that wasn't the point. *She puts her hands on him and he lets her.*

Mrs Horton galloped up to meet her and even amid her fear, Clara thought, *I've never seen her move so quickly*. It was Cliff, she knew it. *What the hell had he done now?*

'Denny is missing,' Mrs Horton said when she reached Clara, her eyes pained. 'Don't panic, Clara, but he didn't go to school today.'

'Denny?'

Clara couldn't think. *Denny? Denny hadn't got to school?* She felt hot and cold and then like her legs might give way. 'Where is he then?' she asked in a tiny voice and Mrs Horton said in a gentler tone than usual, 'We don't know... do you have any ideas where he might have gone?'

They were still standing in the street as the other children arrived home. They all looked worried, even Cliff, who was pulling at his ragged jumper sleeves. Peg was crying and Rita slung a comforting arm round her, but she shook it off. Maureen was as white as a sheet. 'I said goodbye at the crossroads as usual. I didn't think anything was different.'

'It's not your fault.'

She should have taken them to school. Why had Clara ever let them walk on their own? All the other schoolchildren did – but hers were different, she should have realised that. She felt a thickness in her throat, like she couldn't swallow. She would have to find Denny and put this right – it was all on her.

Mr Sommersby said there was nothing they could do, they should just wait. Miss Cooper made sympathetic noises and then she and Mr Sommersby went off together in his car, which made Clara pause for a moment, then Mrs Horton shepherded the children and Clara inside. Sister Grace was on her way, apparently. Ivor promised to take his bicycle out to look for Denny too. 'It will be all right, Clara,' he told her but she could barely think.

In the kitchen, Clara made each child relate the last time they'd seen Denny and what had happened. Clifford's expression was guilty, but then it always was. She cross-examined him – he'd last seen Denny when they left the house, he was fine at breakfast, no, nothing different about him, no, they didn't argue – until she felt confident that for once this had nothing to do with him; Clifford was innocent.

'Where do you think he will have gone, children? Think, think...' she asked again.

'He talked about his old school sometimes?' Peg wrote down.

'He didn't like it much,' said Rita.

'He used to like his grandparents' house,' Cliff said before adding, 'They're dead though.'

'Where did they live?' Clara pressed.

'They lived in Westcliff – he said his parents used to take him to Southend Pier,' Maureen said.

'Yes,' chimed in Rita. 'The longest pleasure pier in the world. He told me about that.'

And Peg scribbled down, 'He won five shillings in the amusement arcades there.'

'Well done.' Clara stood up. 'Let's see if that's where he's gone.'

Sister Grace would feed the children – there was barley soup left over from yesterday – and Ivor would check on them.

'Go-go,' Maureen insisted so within minutes of leaving the Shilling Arms, Clara was out again, this time sat in Mrs Horton's car holding a map and willing the car to get them to Southend faster. *Denny, poor Denny.* She hadn't noticed anything was wrong – no, she hadn't noticed anything *especially* wrong. It was impossible to keep all the children in her head all the time. It would be impossible for anyone, wouldn't it? Or did some people manage it? She seemed to go from worrying about one to the next, and in the meantime, the one she was not worrying about was going wrong. Denny. Sweet, heartbroken Denny.

'Do you think you can manage?' they'd asked and she'd said she supposed so. And there she was exactly *not* managing him, going into a posh hotel instead, playing at revolving in the doors. Maybe Denny had gone because he hated them all. Maybe Denny had gone because he hated Cliff?

You're a disappointment, the voice in her head said, clear as a bell. I *can't believe you let him down like that.*

'Clara?' Mrs Horton was asking, her hands ten to two on the wheel. 'Which way now?'

Mrs Horton was still mithering around locking up the car when Clara spied a couple sitting on a bench. The woman was warming her hands on a Thermos flask and the man had a Scotch egg on a paper bag in his lap. The clouds were grey, the landscape was too, and everything about him was grey except for that golden egg.

'Have you seen anyone go past?' she asked. She told herself not to sound so panicky, but she couldn't help it.

They looked up at her in surprise. The man had a mouthful of egg, but he said, 'What?'

'A boy? Ten – looks younger? Blond, small...' *He looks like a choirboy*, she thought, but didn't say.

The woman perked up. 'A youngster went that way, didn't he, Alfie?'

Clara didn't wait for Alfie's response. She marched off that way, towards the pier.

She had nearly lost children before. That cold fear, that prickling, that kick in the guts was familiar.

Denny, Where are you?

The light was fading quickly. They were running out of time. Red, pink, purple bruising streaks across the sky. It was eight o'clock now. If she'd had time, she would have told Sister Grace to make sure they polished their boots for tomorrow, that it was Peg's turn to sweep the fireplace, and that Rita needed to eat her greens. They'd have a story, if they could concentrate; Sister Grace loved reading... They were safe. She just had to concentrate on Denny for now.

The pier. What a wind there was. Too cold for him, he wouldn't like it here.

Halfway down, in a shelter, there was something, no, someone, huddled up on a bench. It looked like a tramp, a very small tramp. A dark outline, more animal than human. That lump in her throat solidified. A sudden memory: her parents had been kind to homeless people. She struggled to remember good things about them, but there was that.

It was Denny. She went over to him and he opened his eyes and then closed them again. She sat down by his head and patted his shoulder. She could sense her body shedding its fears, letting go of the adrenaline of the hunt: Denny was safe.

Take your time, she told herself.

'Denny,' she whispered. 'I'm here.'

'I want to go back.'

Back? Where did he mean? The Home? No.

'I understand.'

'I hate it, I hate everything.'

He had smashed his watch, she saw. His pretty little watch, his birthday present. She wondered if he'd done it on purpose.

'Take me back to my mum and dad, please.'

He wanted to go back in time.

'Denny, I'm sorry.'

'It's not fair, it's not fair.'

She took his tiny hand and it was frozen. She repeated his words back to him: 'It isn't fair.'

That stopped him crying. He sat up and looked at her, eyes widened in amazement, and then he said, 'I thought you'd say something else.'

'It's not fair and it's not right, and it's not fair.' She was about to add, '*but it is what it is*', or '*but you can't let this define you*,' but she didn't – he didn't want platitudes.

Mrs Horton had caught up with them. 'Here you are. We've been looking—' she said in a sing-songy voice, but Clara put her finger to her lips, and Mrs Horton knew when to hush and she came and sat herself next to them. She felt very warm. Clara put her arm round Denny and he leaned into her.

It was still light enough to see – barely – and they could see across to the other side of the water, and they could see the mud, the endless plains of mud. Mud like a battlefield. In just a few hours, the mud would be covered. You wouldn't know it was there; the sea would be swirling above it. The waves, the pull of the sea. But for now, it was exposed, it was sandworms and broken crabs. It was glass bottles too and rocks covered in slime. In twelve hours, it would be revealed again. And again and again and again. *Exposed. Covered up. Exposed.*

'What is that land out there?' Clara asked.

'France, I think?' said Mrs Horton.

That made Denny chortle. 'It's Kent,' he said. 'And that bit is the Isle of Grain.'

'Well, aren't you the clever boy?' Mrs Horton said. 'You'll have to take us there one day. What say you, Miss Newton?'

Clara found the enforced jollity difficult, but she agreed. 'Count me in, Mrs Horton!'

There was an attendant at the pier head, and he said, 'Shame you haven't seen it at its best,' and 'Hope you come back when the tide's in,' but Clara thought she liked it ugly like this, the authenticity of it; you could walk for miles out there, in a small window between the tides when you could kid yourself that you controlled the world. And then in a matter of hours, everything would change again.

Nothing will ever be smooth, she thought in the car as Mrs Horton drove them home. She drove fast whether it was an emergency or not – Clara wondered if Mr Horton ever mentioned it. She would take Denny's watch to be fixed tomorrow. Now, she watched him sleeping in the back under her coat, his fingers clenched. Occasionally he let out a moan.

23

Denny cried a lot that week. Maybe he needed to cry. It had to come out somewhere. He cried in the kitchen, he cried in his room. He cried when Clara showed him the blossoms in the garden. (Spring was his mother's favourite season.) He cried that nothing was wrong. He cried that everything was wrong.

There was another emergency meeting at the council. Clara sat nervously in Mr Sommersby's office, with Mr Sommersby, Miss Cooper and Mr Horton. Mrs Horton wasn't there, which was a shame since Clara could have done with her support. They didn't seem to blame her as much as she blamed herself though.

Clara was surprised that Miss Cooper got up to make everyone tea but of course she didn't remark on it – no one would thank her if she did.

'How did he get all the way to the Essex coast?' pondered Mr Sommersby as he stared at Miss Cooper's legs, today in a smart trouser suit.

'Well, at least you found him,' said Mr Horton encouragingly.

They decided Denny would stay with Clara until...

'Until when exactly?' Clara asked. *Until someone claims him like an umbrella at lost property?*

'There's no point moving the little chap now,' Mr Horton said. 'Until we find him an appropriate permanent home, Miss Newton is his best chance. Nowhere is better than Shilling Grange for him at present.'

He smiled warmly at her, and she didn't even think to correct him and say it was the Michael Adams Children's Home. She let his words wash over her. *She* was Denny's best chance, the Home was the best place, she felt this, but from him this was a big compliment. She wondered how much of it was what he thought and how much was Mrs Horton's influence. Then she told herself off for overanalysing it. They had concluded that Denny should stay with her even though she'd nearly lost him – that's what mattered.

She took Denny to see Dr Cardew and, whispering, Denny told him he sometimes felt like he was broken. Clara wanted to gasp.

'He's been through a trauma and he's obviously a very sensitive young chap,' Dr Cardew said to Clara while writing in his notepad.

'And that can be a wonderful quality,' said Clara.

'Absolutely,' agreed Dr Cardew.

That morning, as she was getting ready to leave for the council, Cliff's school had called again. This time Cliff had punched another boy in the face, made the boy's nose bleed for the entirety of science class, and it was a particularly foolish move, for the boy was the headmaster's nephew. No one could call Cliff a very sensitive young chap. Still, on the whole, he was getting better – and Clara was sure it was because of the singing.

She tousled Denny's hair. 'No running away again, please. I

cannot survive another long journey with Mrs Horton at the wheel,' she said and was grateful he let out a laugh.

'She does drive very fast.'

'Fast is one word.' Clara sniffed. 'Erratic is another.'

'And she thought Kent was France!' Denny added delightedly.

'Silly thing!' And then Clara had another thought: 'Denny, you don't mind performing, do you? Is that worrying you?'

Denny looked up, surprised. He chewed his lip with his big white teeth. Dr Cardew laid down his pen carefully, in line with his book and his desk. Clara met his eyes. Would he tell Anita that she had asked? Anita might think she had steered him. 'I just don't want Denny to feel under any pressure, with the rehearsals or the television or Royal Festival Hall or...'

Dr Cardew nodded. 'How do you feel about it, Denny?'

'I don't love it,' Denny admitted. 'But I don't mind. Can I see the goldfish now?'

Ivor knocked later, when the children were rehearsing, and Clara was delighted to see him, had been waiting to see him. After their afternoon together the other day, she felt she understood him better, and she felt closer to him than ever. He said he couldn't come in; he just wanted to say how pleased he was that Denny was home safe and if she needed help with him, she knew where he was. He seemed uneasy with her though, especially compared to how he had been at the hotel. He said he had to get going – Mrs Harrington – and Clara's heart sank and she said, and it just came from nowhere, 'What's really going on, Ivor?' He was blowing hot and cold; she was sure it wasn't her imagination.

He put his hand over his eye, rubbed it, breathed out. He said he needed more time with Patricia.

'Of course you do,' Clara said, feeling light-headed. *Did he imagine she didn't think he did?* She understood he needed time with his daughter. Of course she'd never want to take him away from that.

He paused. 'And I don't want to ruin anything – between us, I mean. Our relationship is precious, Clara, and I want to keep it that way.'

Clara blinked at him. Why was he saying this? 'Ruin' made her think of the war. 'Precious' made her think of stones or jewels – things being wrapped away in muslin and put in darkness, sheltered from the real world.

She gaped at him slightly and he stammered, 'Anyway, I just... well done and give my love to the children.'

But why would it ruin anything? She went over and over it all evening and all night. It made no sense. And it wasn't as if she'd demanded anything of him – why did he think she would? She tried to work out his reasoning. She had no doubt it was sincere; it just didn't seem to add up.

She would try to forget about thinking of Ivor 'like that'. Think about him as a friend, as a neighbour, as someone concerned. Don't think of him as... a man. But it wasn't easy and she had tried before, many times. He was stuck in her heart like a needle in a groove. It embarrassed her how much she desired him – for she did, she could no longer pretend she didn't. *Good Housekeeping* gave advice on how to endure your husband's ardour, but it never advised on decreasing your own. She had the sense that her passion for him was unfeminine, unladylike. She should have designs on sweet words, poems and flowers, not physical intimacy, not – the look of him when he smiled in his vest and braces, nor the smell of him when he had stood behind her once to look at the stars. There had to be a way to stop craving someone. If only she could give him up, like sweets or chocolate.

She suddenly remembered *The Best Years of Our Lives*. She had wanted to see the film for ages but newly-married Judy was always busy and finally, Clara had secretly gone without her, sitting alone in the cinema eating penny chews. Then Judy was free, and full of apologies, and Clara went again with her. She gasped at the gasp-worthy moments and laughed loudly at all the jokes as if she'd never seen or heard them before but actually, she loved that film, she was happy to see it twice, would have been happy to see it again too.

One of the main characters in *The Best Years of Our Lives*, Homer, like Ivor, had lost an arm in the war. She remembered Homer pushed away his love because he hated himself and he didn't want her to have to help him.

She wondered why she'd never made the connection before.

Maureen was also still wandering around, broken-hearted.

The next evening, over rhubarb for pudding, in front of everyone she said, 'She's also pregnant, did you know that? Janet Morgan, Joe's girlfriend – that's why they have to get married, of course. It's a shotgun wedding.'

She scraped the bowl, then put down her spoon triumphantly.

Rita and Peg's mouths were wide open.

'A shotgun wedding!' repeated Rita, already committing the phrase to memory; no doubt most of the first-years at the high school would know all about it tomorrow. Peg took aim and fired an imaginary gun and Denny pretended to fall to the floor dead. Clifford said the B-word and Clara sent him to his room. She'd had enough of his cheek.

'She's having a baby.' Maureen wouldn't stop. It was like she couldn't believe it herself.

'How did the baby get in her stomach?' enquired Denny, and Clara sent him and Peg to bring in the washing from the garden. Good grief. She had enough on her hands without a human biology lesson.

And Clara realised that for Maureen, it wasn't just the loss of Joe. It was the loss in the past. It was fear of the future – oh, it was lots of things wrapped up in this.

That Saturday's cinema trip came as a very welcome distraction. Sir Alfred, a local artist, arranged for the children to go monthly in his chauffeur-driven car, and for once, he came along too. It was a joy to see the old man engaging with the children before and after the film. Clara had thought about not letting Cliff come, as a punishment for fighting, but he behaved better on Friday and even mopped the kitchen floor and remembered to feed Stella and when Clara got his name wrong *again*, he didn't bark at her but didn't seem to notice.

The film was *Tarzan*, always a favourite. Maureen and Sir Alfred were talking earnestly about it all the way home. Clara was glad to see the sparkle back in her eyes.

That evening, Rita answered the telephone, and whoever it was must have been teasing her, for she giggled, then explained, 'It's a difficult opener, and the others aren't as good as me, but Anita says we can't all be extraordinary.'

Was it Donald Button?

Clara grabbed the telephone.

It was Peter, lovely Peter, but just as Clara settled in for a nice chat – it had been less than a month too! – he asked if he could have his file. He sounded nervous. His voice went up and down like Denny's sometimes did.

Clara's first reaction was to say no. And her second reaction was no, too.

'Why do you want to see it?' instead she asked cautiously.

'I just want to know all the stuff in it.'

She thought of Cliff's file. There was something about having this information kept from you that she understood; and yet... Peter's file was a torturous affair. And after he'd told her about the abuse, there was a lot of drawing of lines, lots of analysis and speculation, observation and assignment. He *couldn't* see it. It wouldn't be right.

'After all, it's about me, isn't it?'

'I'll think about it,' she promised. He didn't want to talk about anything else and she put down the receiver uneasily. Another dilemma to solve.

24

Mrs Horton now lived with her husband in a 1920s red-brick house in a cul-de-sac in the small Suffolk town of Hadleigh. The houses in the street had uniform doors and bay windows. They were pretty, thought Clara. She had never been to Mrs Horton's old house though, so she didn't know how it compared.

Mrs Horton answered the door wearing a housecoat and slippers, the front of her hair in a curler. Clara had never seen her look so domesticated. She didn't look pleased to see Clara, although she invited her in immediately.

'I didn't think you were stopping work.' Clara couldn't believe it. Miss Cooper had been the one to tell her, too, which was upsetting.

'Mr Horton's mother had a fall and became poorly, and it just seemed easier if one of us was home. It was shortly after you took in Denny.'

Clara wondered if there had been any discussion or if caring for her husband's mother had just fallen to Mrs Horton, like overripe fruits dropping to the ground. The idea annoyed her. Like seeing an animal in a cage.

'And how is Mrs Horton senior now?'

'She'll never be the same, unfortunately. They deteriorate quickly at that age, you know.'

At all ages, thought Clara. Her mouth was dry. So, Mr Sommersby's insinuation was right: Mrs Horton wasn't continuing at the council now she was married. Women marry and their careers are over. Mrs Horton didn't even like Mr Horton's mother!

In the kitchen, Mrs Horton got some teacakes out of the enamel breadbin and put them under the grill. Clara took in the decorative brass hanging saucepans and frying pans. It was a kitchen large enough for three. She could *almost* see the appeal.

'They were making it more and more difficult for me,' Mrs Horton said.

'The council were?' Clara had thought it was a good place to work, especially for women.

'Kind of,' she said, and it felt as though she didn't want to give too much away. 'It was all right at first, but as time went on it became impossible. The split jobs. Cemeteries and children. I didn't know if I was coming or going. I'm not saying it doesn't work for anyone, but...'

It was a cautionary tale, thought Clara. If she wanted to be her own person, to be independent and to have a good life, it would be best to stay on her own.

When she went to the loo, she saw there was a furry cover on the toilet and one over the toilet roll holder. She had never seen this before. The toilet paper was also a far cry from the cuttings of discarded newspaper they still used at the Home. On the way back to the kitchen, she peeked into the front room, where the old lady was sitting with a blanket over her knees. She was asleep and her mouth lolled open. Clara felt a sudden despair about it – the wedding was only six months ago, how could she have gone downhill so quickly?

Mrs Horton buttered the teacakes and then shoved the

plate at Clara, who made a polite show of reluctance before tucking in.

'So, how are the children?'

'That's what I wanted to talk to you about,' Clara said although she felt guilty now. Mrs Horton clearly had a lot on her hands. 'Peter wants to see his file.'

'Why?'

'I think he feels it would explain things.'

'But you don't?'

'I think it might complicate things.' Clara inhaled the burnt raisin and buttery smell – delicious. 'He thinks it will answer questions, but I think it will raise more.'

Mrs Horton agreed. She suggested Clara proceed with caution. She felt Peter wouldn't benefit from reading the content of his files – in fact, he might be harmed.

'The other thing is... I still haven't got Clifford's files.' Clara was feeling more nervous about him in the house. He had sworn at Maureen and had been sullen towards Clara. Rita told her he had been fighting in the streets. In the evenings, she double-locked the doors so that Denny wouldn't go sleepwalking into the darkness, but it had the effect of making her feel trapped. What if Cliff did something stupid? It didn't bear thinking about.

'Well, that's not good,' Mrs Horton said solidly. 'Really, it isn't. He's been in care for a long time, hasn't he?'

'Yes, and...' Clara sighed. She thought of the long stream of offences, some trivial, some larger – she was beginning to find it hard to detect the difference. 'He's up and down, it's difficult,' she admitted finally.

'What would you say about a cabbage that doesn't grow?' Mrs Horton responded, collecting the empty plates. Clara, who hadn't been hungry when she arrived, had somehow found space for two teacakes and plenty of butter.

Clara thought. She had never been good at gardening. One

of the children who used to live at the Home, Terry, was. Terry would have told her what to do.

'I don't know. What *do* you say about a cabbage that doesn't grow?' Clara repeated it like it was a joke.

Mrs Horton did not laugh. 'Do you blame the cabbage?' she asked in a serious voice.

'Not really.'

'Do you look for the reasons?'

'What like – sun, soil, water...?'

'Yes?'

'YES,' said Clara warming to the theme. 'You can't blame the cabbage – you have to change the conditions.'

'Exactly,' said Mrs Horton, a big smile on her face. And then she spelled it out, in case Clara were still in any doubt. 'Clifford is a cabbage.'

When she laid her hand on the table, Clara noticed the wedding ring. She couldn't avoid it; it was a big diamond sticking out on the pink of her finger, but it was more than that: it gave Mrs Horton authority.

'I know you see me as a career woman, Clara.'

Clara nodded. She did; she had. She liked to see women working – she'd got used to that in the war. They couldn't just go back to the kitchen now, could they?

'But I always wanted just what I have now.'

Clara gulped, nodded. She looked through to the living room and took in the pretty floral curtains with the pink rope tying them back. The electric fire with its cream marble surround. The carpets with plenty of spring. No wonder Mrs Horton felt a debt to Mrs Horton senior.

Mrs Horton talked about the Festival of Britain – she was another one who couldn't wait – and how well the children had done. Clara nodded along patiently, trying to hide her lack of interest, and then Mrs Horton said, 'Oh, I forgot! I do have something exciting to tell you. We're going to apply to become foster carers.'

Clara grabbed her friend's hand. This. *This* was so right. At last, she thought to herself, something made sense. She couldn't find the words at first and then she added, 'I can't think of a lovelier home – or a lovelier person for children to come to.'

On the way back to the Home, Clara's positivity wore off when she saw Mrs Harrington pushing the pram up the road. She crossed to avoid her, but Mrs Harrington crossed after her and cut off her route.

The two babies were sitting opposite each other like they were in a bath. Mrs Harrington's usual expression was serious, but looking at Clara now, she forced her mouth into a huge smile.

'Where *have* you been?' she said as though she had been waiting for her and, although it was none of her business, Clara felt it was important to say: 'I went to see Mrs Horton.'

She hoped that spelled out clearly: *We're still friends. Unlike you. You didn't even go to her wedding!*

'You know she's going to foster?' Mrs Harrington responded, quick as a whip.

Clara faltered. *How had she already heard?*

'Ivor and I think she'll do a wonderful job.'

What did this have to do with either of them?

'Look what Patricia's learned to do now!'

Clara looked at the sweet-faced girl sticking out her tongue and blowing raspberries. Both children were holding crusts and dropping breadcrumbs. It made her think of Hansel and Gretel – which would make Mrs Harrington the witch. Clara knew she was being ridiculous. She tried to compensate for her evil thoughts by being nice.

'They are such sweet babies,' she said.

'I love Patricia almost as much as I love Leslie,' Mrs Harrington said, earnestly and, to Clara's mind, somewhat out of the blue. Mrs Harrington stared at Clara intently as she stroked Patricia's hair. Clara caught a strong whiff of her perfume. It smelt of oily late nights and spice. 'I understand now how you can love them even if they're not your own. And Ivor is so devoted a father. It's important that nothing comes between him and his daughter, you know that.'

She went off swinging her hips, her red hair glistening in the sun. With a sinking feeling, Clara remembered the soppy look on Ivor's face when anyone mentioned Rita Hayworth.

Mrs Horton had advised Clara to contact Mrs McCarthy over the file issues. Clara felt it was too small an issue to take to the brilliant yet intimidating woman who oversaw Suffolk County Council, but Mrs Horton convinced her it was a procedural issue and reminded Clara that hadn't she once been invited to send in ideas? And hadn't Clara been the one to say that all files should arrive before the children – a measure the council had acted on too?

It took a couple of days, and a few deep breaths, before Clara felt able to make the telephone call but when she did, Mrs McCarthy's tone was kindly. She said how nice it was to hear from her and went on, 'I wish housemothers got in touch more often! We should share information.'

Clara explained her predicament: 'I think Peter is right about wanting to see his files, but I'm also right about not wanting to show him these ones.'

'That makes perfect sense.'

The response surprised her. She went on, 'So, I think the style they are now is not appropriate, but I think if we look at refashioning the files – we could have a version for the children and one for the adults?'

'Two versions?' said Mrs McCarthy.

'Yes,' admitted Clara. She understood not everyone was as file-crazy as she was.

But Mrs McCarthy said, 'You've identified a problem and come up with an excellent solution, Miss Newton.'

Clara flushed with pleasure. She would do that, for Peter, create an abridged or edited version of his files – and in the future she would make sure these were available to all the children. It was easy to say they were *just files* but these were the stories of people's lives here. And who should be able to read those stories? – the people *in them*, of course. It was a simple modification, but it felt like her suggestion was being taken seriously. *She* was someone to be taken seriously.

'And Miss Newton,' Mrs McCarthy said at what felt like the end of the call. 'How is life at the Michael Adams Children's Home?'

Clara broke into a smile at her use of their new name. Mrs McCarthy approved!

'It's challenging, but I love it.'

'And the lovely little one who doesn't speak? Still with you?'

'Peg is very well... She still doesn't speak but we live in hope.'

'And I hear exciting things about the group?'

Clara found she could almost talk about it now without wincing. She told Mrs McCarthy the children were practising regularly, and it had been the making of them. She also told her about the TV show they would appear on: *The Great British Songbook!* 'How wonderful,' Mrs McCarthy said and she sounded sincere. She mentioned that she had friends who worked in TV, they were the brains behind *Muffin the Mule*. Clara said they were not quite up to *Muffin the Mule*'s dizzy heights yet, but never say never.

'And your lovely neighbour?' Mrs McCarthy went on. 'The one who galloped to the rescue.'

Clara gulped. When Clara had been at the tribunal, about to lose her job, and all seemed over, it was Ivor who had made the difference. Sometimes, she forgot that. And also that Mrs McCarthy had once said that Ivor adored her.

'Ah, Ivor...' What else could she say? He had stopped rescuing her, and rather needed rescuing himself. 'So far as I know, he's very well, thank you.'

～

A few days later, Peter called. And while a call from Peter usually filled Clara with joy, this time she felt anxious because she anticipated what it was about, and she knew what she had to tell him was not what he wanted to hear.

'What did you decide about my files?'

'I'm afraid it's difficult. We're going to change the way we do things in future though,' she said brightly, proud of her simple modification. 'It's going to make things better.'

The line went silent. And then Peter said, 'So how will that help me?'

Clara scratched the wall where the join in the wallpaper was. One of the strips was coming free from the wall slightly. It would only take a little tug.

'I don't suppose it will, Peter, I'm sorry.'

It was agonising. She had never said no to him before. Not since the moment he revealed what was happening with his uncle. Everything had changed then. She had learnt to tiptoe around him and to always try to smooth his way. She did everything she could to avoid hurting him for anyone to avoid hurting him. It was only now she could see that, and how her hands had been tied because of it. It hadn't been a normal housemother–orphaned child relationship since then – she hadn't let it be.

'I really am,' she said limply. 'And I am going to send you a file but it's not... it's not everything you want.' *It's a watered-down version.*

It was so quiet down the line, she wondered if he had gone or had put his hand over the receiver. He might hate her now. He might never want to see her again.

'Peter,' she said, 'you're coming to the performance at the Royal Festival Hall, aren't you? I have tickets for you.'

She heard him clear his throat. 'I've got work then.'

'How do you know the date?'

He cleared his throat. 'I mean, I'm working all the time.'

Was he being serious? Did they make him work that hard?

Just when she was beginning to despair, he said, 'But you know that bank holiday weekend in August – when the children go on their Lyme Regis trip? I'll come and see you then.'

'Perfect,' she breathed. She hadn't lost him entirely. Those strange imperceptible strings that bound them together were still intact. 'Thank you.'

25

Clara had forgotten Joe's wedding – or rather, she hadn't
forgotten he was getting married but she didn't know the actual
date. It was Mrs Garrard who told her –exactly four months
after the Hortons' wedding. Mrs Garrard was doing the
bouquet for Janet Morgan.

'She's chosen pink roses,' Mrs Garrard said conspiratorially.
Clara couldn't tell if she approved or not. Probably not. 'Are you
going? I thought you and Joe Matthews were close.'

Fortunately, Bertie the dog began making noises like he was
about to throw up, so Clara was able to make her excuses.

Clara couldn't go to the wedding; she had belatedly realised
that. And she felt stupid, terrible that she had ever agreed she
would. Broken-hearted Maureen would never forgive her. But
she had to tell Joe that she wouldn't go, at least. The thought of
him expecting to see her in the church, under that sombre
stained glass of The Last Supper, was too painful. It felt odd as
well that Joe was marrying in the same church as the Hortons –
that church seemed too grand, too grown-up for *children*, as she
saw them. It was like they were dressing up in oversized clothes.

And to think – she remembered Mrs Horton's bouquet that

she had caught – *she* was supposed to have been the person to marry next, not Joe...

Clara hoped she would run into him in the street or the park, but she didn't. She suspected he kept himself well out of the way on purpose. Eventually, one morning, she knew she should wait no longer, and she walked up to the petrol station where he worked. It was rainy, cold too, and there were puddles all over the road. He was sat in a little hut reading a newspaper. He didn't look up when she came into the forecourt and she was about to walk over when a Rover 16 pulled out in front of her. She had to jump out of the way to avoid getting splashed. The driver wound down the window and yelped, 'Sorry, old girl!' Clara flapped her hands as if to say it doesn't matter.

As Joe was filling up the tank, he finally saw her and waved uncertainly with one gloved hand. Clara inhaled that petrol smell that she wasn't supposed to like, but mm, it was lovely.

'I can't come to the wedding.'

'I knew you'd say that.' He sighed.

He invited her into his little hut. There was a small heater, a three-legged stool, a bowl full of coppers and that smell again. She shivered.

'How is Janet?'

'Worried about the weather.'

'I can imagine.' It seemed very dark for ten o'clock in the morning. It certainly wasn't promising. 'Well anyway, I thought I'd give you your wedding gift in advance.'

What do you get the boy who has nothing? Clara had racked her brains for a while and come up with blanks. The usual gifts all seemed wrong. She handed him a pen and a pot of ink. She remembered he had dreams of journalist college although those dreams must have seemed more unlikely than ever now.

He hardly looked at it and instead hurriedly put the gift in his drawer. She thought she'd made a mistake – she was like

Stella with her dead mice – but his eyes had filled with tears. He said ruefully, 'It's too good to use.'

'No, you must— for when you get writing.'

He sucked in his teeth. 'I'll be off for National Service soon anyway. At least it's two years now.'

She thought what a contrast he made to Peter, who was dreading it, although Peter had recently wrote to Maureen saying he hoped to apply for a language section so that he could come back and create comics in French and German.

'I hope they send me to Korea.'

Joe was just saying it, she hoped. It was bravado. Surely he didn't really want to be sent so far from home?

She would have hugged him but he seemed to have gone into himself. She stood over him. The stool made him short.

'It's going to be all right. You're going to be a terrific dad.'

'You've always been so generous to me,' he said finally. 'I don't deserve it.'

He pulled his collar up and his cap low. The space where his face was became shrunken and shadowed. He couldn't even say goodbye.

As she walked home, she thought of the rhyme her mother used to say:

> *Change the name and not the letter,*
> *change for worse and not for better.*

Janet Morgan becoming Janet Matthews was not a good omen. But hey, an old wives' tale was the least of Joe's worries.

Maureen didn't go to school on the day of the wedding. It was 19 April. The night before, Denny had been sleepwalking and Clara had to steer him from the parlour back up the stairs, maybe three or four times – she'd lost count. She was exhausted. The children came home for lunch but Maureen wasn't with them. Nobody had seen her. Clara was petrified that she would go and make a scene at the church, like in a film they'd once seen at Saturday club; but she didn't really think it was Maureen's style. She was not a dramatic girl. It was Clifford who kicked outwards; Maureen suffered everything inwardly.

Or perhaps she was just going to spy? To watch him walk in, whistling, 'Shine on Harvest Moon' maybe, and then to watch them walk out 'man and wife'. Perhaps she would go, but wouldn't show herself.

Clara tried getting on with her normal routine that afternoon, but it was difficult to knuckle down as thoughts of the wedding intruded. She imagined Joe in an ill-fitting suit, his hair newly brushed and his shaky hands. She pictured him trembling as he tried to put the wedding ring on the girl's outstretched finger. And what of Janet? Did the poor girl have any idea of Joe's state of mind? She couldn't realise that his heart was elsewhere, could she?

In the end, the weather was *one* thing that was kind to them. It was overcast all morning, but the rain held off until after the ceremony. When it did come down, about four, it was torrential. The sky even threw in thunderclaps and some lightning for good measure. The children squealed. They leant out of the windows, counting the seconds between lightning and thunder to work out how far away the eye of the storm was. By that time though, the wedding party should have been safely ensconced in the knees-up at the Shilling Arms or at least whirring around in the revolving doors. The happy couple were going to Brighton for their honeymoon but not until the next day apparently. Clara wondered who had caught the bouquet.

It was hard to imagine Joe married. *It mightn't be too bad*, Clara told herself. Janet's big exuberant family, the Morgans, would welcome him. And he liked to be part of something, did

Joe. Some people suit company. Maybe with them, he'd finally find himself a home.

Maureen didn't arrive back until after tea. The others were out rehearsing at Anita's – Maureen was too late to go. She was a drowned rat, hair drenched and clothes dripping. Upstairs, Clara helped her out of everything; she really was wet through and her movements were slow and sluggish. She stood shivering in the girls' room in her bra and slip. Clara couldn't tell if it was tears or rain running down her nose – it was probably both. Maureen let Clara wrap a towel around her like she was a much younger child but she refused a bath.

'Are you going to tell me where you've been?'

Maureen looked away. She cried some more. Her skin was a raggedy red and her lips blueish.

'Maureen, please. I only want to help.'

If only Maureen would talk to her more. It was impossible to know what was on her mind. She rubbed the girl's shoulders as her teeth chattered. It was more than cold; it was shock perhaps.

'Maureen, I didn't go to the wedding. You know that, don't you?'

'I know you didn't. I know you wouldn't do that to me,' Maureen said and Clara thought, *thank goodness she doesn't know how close I came to going, nor about the gift.*

Maureen came down to the kitchen later and thumped around looking to bake, so Clara delicately kept out of her way. She made some bread-and-butter pudding – slammed it into the oven, then spun round to face Clara. It was as though making the food had cleared her head.

'I took the train, Miss Newton.'

Clara imagined Maureen in the carriage, her stockinged legs curled around each other. Men staring at her. She was so naive!

'By yourself?'

'Yes...'

'Where did you go?'

'Can't you guess?' Maureen said, her eyes lowered.

This was one of Clara's worst fears. She refused to guess but she had feared it for a long time; that she would want to find her father, the man who had beaten Maureen's mother to death. She imagined Maureen on her mission, pent-up and full of hope to find one man who wouldn't desert her.

'I went to London. To the prison.'

Oh God.

'I wasn't allowed to see him.'

Good, thought Clara. She could have thrown up her arms: *Thank you, God.*

'Visiting day is Wednesday. I'll go then.'

26

Miss Cooper drew up in the new car that her parents had bought her for her twenty-fifth birthday; when she saw it, Clara had a sinking feeling. It was hard enough not having parents for the emotional support, but the material support came in handy too. The absence of that was another thing she had in common with the children, she supposed. They were all alone in the world. It hit you in subtle ways; you didn't have a box to jump on when you wanted to reach something. Instead, you had hurdles, locks and dark looks.

'It's lovely,' Clara said admiringly about the car although Miss Cooper looked lovely too – a vision of privilege. She was wearing her immaculately fitting trouser suit again, but this time with bright shoes, and her hair fell to her shoulders in glossy waves, looking both beautiful and effortless.

'Oh, don't be fooled, my parents are frightful!' She shook her head exasperated. 'They really are the pits!'

Clara was shocked. She had imagined the Cooper family home to be a cocoon of wonderfulness. *Frightful? The pits?* Were they not the country-dwelling, *Good Housekeeping* ideal family she had imagined? This was interesting.

'In what way?'

'My father thinks I can't do any wrong. Literally. Have you heard the saying: he thinks the sun shines out of your bottom? That's my father and me.'

Clara cleared her throat. 'Awful.'

'Isn't it! And my mother, well, she seems to think I am ten years old. She worries so much.' She sighed, and her wavy hair shook with her. Clara readjusted her headscarf, feeling like a slug.

'Now, about Denny. We've had a nibble. Someone who used to know him, apparently.'

'Oh, wow!' This was good news. 'And Peg – the cl— the Hurleys?'

Miss Cooper scowled. 'I gave it a lot of consideration and – I've sent them to Norwich.'

'Really?' All nonsense forgiven; Clara could have thrown her arms round Miss Cooper.

'Yes, I've found them someone else. I'm sure it will work.' Her face said, *no thanks to you.*

'A child who likes clowns?' asked Clara, keeping her voice neutral.

'A child who will be grateful to have a warm and loving home with two...' Miss Cooper paused, 'entertainers. It will be a successful adoption; I don't doubt it. And one off our lists. Everyone is very pleased with me.'

That told Clara.

'What about the teacher, Miss Fisher?'

Miss Cooper shook her pretty head. 'Utterly unsuitable. I don't know what you were thinking.'

Clara didn't know what she had been thinking either. It was hard to say why Miss Fisher had struck such a chord with her: perhaps it was just that she had all this love and nowhere for it to go. And to see someone who *wanted* to do a kindness be sat upon and suppressed made Clara's heart ache. Let her do good, for heaven's sake.

Miss Cooper stroked her hair. 'Will she be awfully upset?'

'Mm, I think so.'

'Perhaps as a compromise, she'd like to be an adoptive aunt or a godparent or something to Peg?'

'How do you mean?'

'She could see her at the weekends, take her to church if she wants— what is it, Miss Newton?'

This time Clara really did hug her. 'That's a great idea, thank you.'

Clara went to see Miss Fisher after school. The message on the blackboard was GOOD MANNERS COST NOTHING and there was a little boy at a desk writing this slowly into an exercise book. When Clara arrived, Miss Fisher told him he could go now and he gathered his things and then, with tear-filled eyes, whispered, 'I won't do it again, Miss Fisher.'

Clara told Miss Fisher what Miss Cooper had suggested about seeing Peg at the weekends, taking an active role. And the teacher said, 'Oh! That probably would work better, wouldn't it? Rather than being a mother. It seems I'm not up to that job.' She blew her nose loudly. And suddenly it dawned on Clara that this was why she had such compassion for this awkward big-hearted fierce woman. It was because she saw so much of herself in her. It felt so obvious – Miss Fisher was her in forty years' time – Clara was shocked that she hadn't realised it before.

When Miss Fisher looked up again, though, she was smiling and she had chalk in her hair.

'I've got some wonderful shells to show her.'

∾

On Wednesday morning, Clara felt so full of dread that Maureen would attempt to see her father in prison, she could hardly bring herself to knock on the dorm door.

'Rise and shine!' she called out. She had to act positive whatever she felt. 'Everyone, time to get up.'

'We know!' Maureen yelled back.

Why did men like Maureen's father always get so lucky? He was a murderer – yet still she loved him. Mrs Horton said it came with the territory. They had been talking about Alex once and Mrs Horton sighed and said, 'Sometimes the worse they are, the more their children love them. It makes no sense.'

Clara felt like a crow as she beadily watched the children over breakfast. Rita was pretending to play the piano as she absent-mindedly ate her porridge, Denny and Peg were sniggering over something in Peg's notebook. Cliff was stabbing his toast with the butter knife. Maureen ate and then dressed in her school uniform, but that didn't mean anything. She checked her bag was packed and ran back upstairs for her maths book, but that didn't mean anything either. But when she was at the back door, she blew a kiss at Clara and said, 'See you lunchtime,' and Clara said, 'Will I?' and Maureen had a big smirk on her face when she said, 'You surely will.'

Clara was so relieved that she couldn't even clear away the breakfast things for ages. She just sat stroking Stella on her lap, going over and over it again: Maureen was *not* going to see her father. Maureen was safe.

~

That night, Maureen said she couldn't sleep. 'Can I come in your room, Miss Newton?'

'Of course.'

The poor girl smelled of breadcrumbs and coffee. 'I miss Joe so much. Why doesn't anything ever work out for me?' She asked Clara to tell her some memories to distract her.

'It's a funny thing,' Clara mused. 'I feel like I have only old tired memories, I could do with some new ones.'

Maureen looked confused.

'I mean, I go over the same ones all the time – I wish I remembered different ones.'

Maureen looked at her doubtfully, as though this wasn't what she had in mind.

They sat side by side in Clara's bed, drinking cocoa. It was lovely. Clara knew she had no memories of ever doing this with anyone, not even Judy, and she decided that this was one memory that she wanted to keep. They talked a little about the rehearsals and *The Great British Songbook*. Maureen was looking forward to it – but it was clear she had other things on her mind.

'Miss Newton, what was your father like?' she asked shyly.

What was Clara's father like? Mr Newton didn't seem to age as fast as most men, or maybe he'd got his ageing over when he was young. It seemed to Clara that he had just always been around sixty. He had short white hair and wire spectacles. He was smart, but not too smart. He liked to give the impression that he was not interested in material things. He found a lot of things 'trivial'. Not just fashion or music but things like sport and food although she reconsidered, he did like planes. He loved plane-spotting almost as much as he loved church. He carried the New Testament in the inside pocket of his blazer. If Clara was unlucky, he'd get it out and quote from it. If she was really unlucky, she'd be made to repeat it.

'He...' Clara found it difficult to put into words. *He didn't like me much*, she thought suddenly. *That's how it felt*. But all she said to Maureen was, 'He is religious.'

'Have you got any stories about him?' Maureen was keen to hear more.

'Well, I remember a time we were singing in the church choir – my father insisted I attend, but after a while, I didn't hate it.' Clara paused. The memory was now as vivid and clear as the pillow she was leaning on. 'I remember I grew to really enjoy it, and the choirmaster told me I was doing well.' The smell of the place came back to her: the dripping candles and the smoky incense and the bulk of the church organ and its rows of pedals.

'That's lovely.' Maureen pulled the blanket up to her shoulders.

'Unfortunately, the choirmaster also told my father how well I was doing. And do you know what he said to me? He said, "It's a team effort, Clara, we want to hear everyone's voices, not just yours." He said I had ideas above my station, that I was a disappointment and—' Clara found she couldn't go on. She was back there, watching the anger lines on her father's face, waiting for her punishment.

Turning to Maureen, Clara was surprised how shocked the girl looked.

'That's a really nasty thing to say,' Maureen said.

'Mm.' Clara didn't add that maybe the reason she remembered it now, word for word, was because it wasn't only awful at the time; her father used it to chastise and humiliate her for months, even years, afterwards. She was a nail that stuck out – he said – and his duty as a father, as a *good* father, was to hammer her down.

She had never told this story to anyone, not even Michael, and she had told him a lot. Maureen's simple and honest reaction had moved her.

'It was difficult – no, it was nothing like what happened with your father of course, but I am here to help you whatever you decide to do,' Clara said, 'about seeing him.'

'I know you are.' Maureen spoke lightly. Her toes stuck out the end of the bed and she wriggled them. 'I wish he was a nice man, but I know he's not. I've wished that so many times.'

Clara held her hand. The boundaries that she was having to hold were so tough for a young girl.

'He will never be the dad I want, so there's no point... I need to accept that I'm on my own.'

Clara felt in awe of the young girl's judgement and her resilience. She was a lot further along than Clara was at the same age – perhaps even than Clara was now.

'You've got me...' Clara added.

'And you,' Maureen said.

'And the other children – and Ivor, Anita, Mr Dowsett and everyone around here. We're a community,' Clara said.

'Thank you.'

It was midnight; Denny would probably start his moonlit wandering soon. They drained their cups of cocoa, then Maureen went off to her own bed.

27

If you stood on tiptoes and looked out of the boys' bedroom window you could see Farmer Buckle's fields quite far away; and if you squinted, or your eyes were good, better than Clara's possibly, you could see the little shepherd's hut further away still. It looked like there was just a small cluster of trees, but Clara knew it was there because the children had told her once.

They came running home from school the next day, shrieking that the hut was on fire. Cliff came back five minutes later and then disappeared to the lav. *Did he wash his hands for longer than usual?* She asked him.

'Don't be daft,' he said, sticking his tongue out. 'Are you the hand-wash police?'

From the upstairs windows, you could see smoke – not great plumes, but definitely something, hanging in the air even though it was windy.

'What happened?' Clara asked the children but no one knew. She looked at their excited grubby faces – Rita, Denny, Peg, Cliff. Not Maureen – she had ignored them and started making some dumplings to add to tonight's stew – but all the others leaning out of the window to get a better view. She watched Clifford, laughing, his eyes shining like a fox.

It's nothing, nothing, nothing. Nothing to do with him.

Denny said the fire engine was on its way there. Rita wondered if it would be the same one that had come to them when the shed caught fire. Clifford laughed, 'Keep 'em busy, won't it?' Clara couldn't bring herself to ask him what he meant.

It's nothing, she told herself as she cleared up some milk that had been spilled. *It's nothing*, she told herself as she told off Stella for sitting in the clothes basket.

As Clara peeled potatoes, Maureen rabbited on about a teacher who had run out of the class, crying. (Maureen's teachers seemed to do this a lot.) Peg tugged at her sleeve and handed her a message: 'Will the sheep be okay?'

'Yes, Peg, they'll be fine.'

After dinner, Denny and Peg went to the parlour to play marbles. Cliff washed up his plate, and said he was a little bit tired. Clara waited for someone to come and shout at them, Farmer Buckle or the fire officers maybe, but no one did. *It's nothing.*

She was just overly anxious, that was all. She checked the safe in her room, and everything there was in order, everything in there was unmoved – which was more than she was.

∽

Another night of poor sleep. She saw Ivor collecting his milk bottles early the next morning and he waved.

'Heard about the fire? Poor Farmer Buckle – after the year he's had.'

Farmer Buckle's fields had frozen in the winter, and some of his animals had contracted a mystery illness.

'Yes.' Clara wanted to close this conversation down. She didn't know why – she just wanted to shut the book on it.

'There've been a few lately.'

'Mm.'

'Clara,' he said. He was trying to look her in the eye, but she couldn't, wouldn't. 'If you know anything... you will go to the police, won't you?'

She looked at the ground. *What had it got to do with him?* 'I don't know anything.'

Later that afternoon, Clara went to see Anita in her lovely garden, to sit by the beautiful pond. Howard was playing on the blanket with an abacus and seemed intent on putting the beads to his mouth. It seemed like a different world here, a world of tranquillity, music and peace. It occurred to Clara – perhaps for the first time – what a huge adjustment it must have been for Evelyn to come and live at the Cardews'.

Anita was in a playful mood. 'And how are your men?' she asked.

The stream of them.

'Ivor is just a friend now. Victor has several women on the go, and Julian has Margot.'

And Michael is dead, she thought and it felt like she was engulfed in a wave of sadness.

Whereas the grass at the Home was tufty and muddy, the grass here was bright green and well-watered, and the trees were flourishing. It was genteel. Marilyn would say it was 'little England'. There was a slender crab-apple tree, but Anita always complained that maggots got to most of the apples before they were ripe. Clara watched a ladybird land on the wooden arm of her deckchair and thought back to the house and the garden in London where she had lived as a child. She used to make little homes out of twigs for insects: they never seemed to be that interested in them.

There was that burning smell again – or was she imagining

it? Was she becoming paranoid? Or, as Cliff would say, 'was she the smell police?'

'Pardon?'

Anita had asked her something.

'Donald Button, did he ever call about taking you out?'

'Oh yes, he did once.'

A tiny fearless bird came and perched on the side of the table.

'You must meet him then,' Anita said.

'I don't know.' She didn't seem to have space in her mind for anyone but Ivor, yet every time she saw him, he seemed to be making it clearer that he was unavailable – *not now, let's not ruin what we've got.* Didn't he realise how lonely a woman can get? Yes, she had the children, but it wasn't the same, it wasn't what she needed. She'd end up like Bertie, chewing the banisters for want of company.

'It's not just about you, it's for the children. Get him on side,' Anita commanded.

'I'm not sure that's what he's after,' Clara said. 'A bit on the side maybe?' she added, which made Anita laugh because that was one bit of English slang that she did understand.

They both watched the bold little bird stick its fearless beak into the jug of milk.

When Clara got back, she saw the children had already returned from school and were entertaining someone in the parlour. Maureen had given whoever it was a slice of fruit cake – the very fruit cake Clara had been saving for Sunday.

'What?' hissed Maureen crossly in the kitchen. 'I had to offer *something.*'

It was Margot, Julian's girlfriend. Horrified, Clara puffed up her hair and quickly checked her face in her compact before daring to go into the parlour. She was red from the sun – a punishment, she supposed, for taking the afternoon off. Although she patted on plenty of powder, her nose still shone through brightly. It couldn't be helped.

'How delightful to meet you!' she lied to her guest.

Margot held out her long fingers. 'At long last.'

Now Margot was in front of her, Clara couldn't see how they were alike. They *weren't* alike. The same kind of figure maybe, almost the same colour hair perhaps, but beyond that... nothing. (It was funny that men and children couldn't see beyond that.)

Maureen took Margot's empty plate. 'Thank you, Maureen,' she said in a cloying tone. 'What a treat!'

Once Maureen had left the room, carefully shutting the door behind her, Margot said, 'What a marvellous hostess.'

'She can be,' said Clara flatly. She was wondering what the woman was doing here. God forbid Margot had come for some kind of reference for Julian? Perhaps this was something the upper classes did, to check they hadn't acquired a damp squib. It was probably a sensible idea, but what would she say? 'Julian knows how to have a good time.' Or 'Mr White has excellent taste in dogs.'

'I imagine you're wondering why I'm here?' Margot said, and Clara did a non-committal laugh and said that she was very welcome.

'I saw one of your boys running away from Farmer Buckle's shepherd's hut when it was on fire.'

Here it was. Clara tucked her hands into her armpits. She exhaled slowly. *Proceed carefully,* she told herself. This mightn't be what she feared. In fact, it most likely wasn't.

'How do you know it was one of my boys?'

'Because I saw him – up close – and I know he lives here.'

Clara stared at Margot's impassive face. Her neck was longer than Clara's, graceful and swan-like. Her cheekbones were sharp and her skin waxy. There was nothing warm about her. She wondered what she and Julian had in common. She couldn't imagine them kissing – not that she should – but, well, she couldn't.

'I'm not sure why you're telling me, then – it's a police matter.'

And a council matter.

'I'm telling you because I thought letting you know first would be the kind thing to do. Julian speaks highly of you.'

Clara decided she didn't trust this Margot. But she wouldn't lie, would she? She had no reason to – and anyway, deep down Clara *knew* she was telling the truth. Cliff *had* set fire to the shed, and now he had set fire to the shepherd's hut.

She thanked Margot for her time.

'It is a shame,' Margot said as they said their goodbyes in the hall, Clara hoping she hadn't noticed the piles of clothes waiting to be taken upstairs. 'But you must understand, we can't have this on our doorsteps.'

Cliff was trotting off after the others to a rehearsal when Clara called him back. 'No Anita's for you today, Clifford.'

His expression was mutinous.

'My name is Cliff!' he snarled. 'Get it right.'

She led him into the parlour because it would be easier to stand her ground there.

'Was it you who set fire to the shepherd's hut?'

'No, it bloody wasn't.'

Cliff wouldn't even look at her. He stared sullenly at the weaves in the carpet. *What had he done? Why did he sabotage himself?*

'And the shed in our garden – that was you too, wasn't it?' She was surprised at how certain she sounded.

Why did he insist on going down this terrible path? He sang

beautifully, didn't he? And he loved performing. It was impossible to understand why he would be so destructive. 'Can I go to the rehearsal now?'

'NO! Clifford – Cliff – the police are being called.'

'By you?'

'No. By someone who saw you.'

That was what made him lash out. He stormed out of the parlour, clattered up to his room. Maybe she shouldn't have followed him but she too was shaking with rage. 'I hate the stinking lot of you,' he yelled and then he swore at her to get out. He kicked the wardrobe door but seemed shocked to see the wood dent and cave. The next time he shouted at her to sod off, she did.

Later, Cliff came downstairs for dinner and acted with the others as though everything was normal. They were full of the rehearsal, full of the TV show. 'And if we make a good impression there, who knows what that will lead to?' said Rita in what Clara knew were Anita's words.

Tucking into his ham, Cliff joined in. He talked about his hated maths teacher and the results of a test (top of the class). He even jumped up to take his plate to the sink, where he washed it and dried it with care. Once the children had left the room, Clara tried again with him – she had this mad compulsion to get to the bottom of it.

'You've been behaving so much better lately, Cliff. I thought... I really thought you'd turned yourself round.'

'I didn't do it,' he snapped. 'Why don't you believe me?'

'Because you were seen there... Because you've been identified, that's why.' She deliberately used the language the police would use.

He didn't say anything to that. His mouth was a thin, angry line. *What was he so angry for?*

She picked up one of the shells on the windowsill and held it in her palm. Its swirl, the way it seemed to sink into itself, calmed her down. She had to be reasonable.

'I just wish you'd tell me why—'

'I didn't do it!' he howled. Clara wavered. He was so adamant.

She lit a cigarette with trembling hands. It occurred to her she might be making the most terrible mistake. Why would she take that strange woman's word over Cliff's? She should stand up for her boy. False accusations were the ugliest things. Injustice – heaped upon one who had already suffered so much – was the worst. It wasn't fair – and yet...

Just when Clara was doubting herself, doubting everything, he shut his eyes and said in a low voice, 'I can't help it, it just... it feels nice.'

'Oh, Cliff.'

CHILDREN'S REPORT 12
Clifford 'Cliff' Nelson Harvey

Date of Birth:

4 May 1938

Family Background:

Mother died when he was young, TB. His father died some time later.

He has been in four homes. The first home, there was violence among the children and the home was dissolved. We don't know what happened in the second. Third, he was thrown out for beating younger children. Fourth, asked to leave – suspected arson.

Health/Appearance:

Height and weight normal. Teeth and eyes have not been checked.

Food:

Allergic to some fruits.

Hobbies:

Singing, performing.

Other:

Due to his destructive nature and risk-taking behaviour, we can NOT recommend that Clifford is homed in a family setting or with other children or animals. On no account should he be allowed any kind of weapon, including hammers, tools, matches, alcohol, cigarettes, electrical items, etc., etc.

28

There were labels over some bits of the file and a lot of crossings-out. There were shaky additions in pen, pencil and type and someone had made quite the effort with an eraser. Clara gazed at the papers: this explained a lot.

'How could you not have shown me this before?'

Miss Cooper didn't look up but carried on with her laborious one-finger typing.

'I didn't know I had it,' she said, eyes down. 'Honestly, I had no idea.'

Miss Cooper had apparently undertaken a spring-clean in the office, although it wasn't particularly apparent. She said she had packaged up the files of adoptive parents A–Z and the adopted children A–Z and while she was unpacking them, she had found Cliff's file in between G–J, which was where it should be, but in the parents' section, where obviously it should not be.

That's what she had told Clara anyway.

'And then I wasn't sure if you'd want it, because it's so out of date.'

As Miss Cooper pulled a paper from her typewriter, it

made a ripping sound. Clara would normally have offered to help, only – she didn't want to help anymore. She was furious.

The door marked 'Head of Children's Services' was just opposite Miss Cooper's and before Clara had time to think about what she would say, she had given it a firm rap on its glass rectangle. It was a surprise that Mr Sommersby was in there, and even more of a surprise that he called out, 'Come in,' and then, when she went in, in a jovial tone enquired, 'What can I do for you today, Miss Newton?'

The story poured out of her in one long stream. Clara avoided the lost-in-the-mess file situation – it was incriminating enough without that, plus she had a feeling Mr Sommersby mightn't be interested in a catalogue of Miss Cooper's failings – she noted that he too had a teddy bear under his desk with a matching ribbon that read, 'Love from Weston-super-Mare'.

'It's important I know what I'm dealing with. Not just for my sake but for all the children at the Michael Adams Children's Home.'

She thought about the fire in the shed. *What if the house had caught alight?* She thought about the way Cliff sometimes treated poor Denny. The faces he pulled at Maureen, the sneery expression he made at her. She wouldn't keep quiet any longer. As Mr Sommersby listened, Clara felt her temper dissipate. There *was* something recuperative about letting it all out, about being heard. She felt how a tortoise might when it sticks out its head into the world after a dark period of hibernation. Sunlight helps.

At the end of it, Mr Sommersby looked quite shaken. He put his fingers together in an arch, then scratched his head.

'Sending him to you was a gamble,' he admitted.

'And it didn't pay off.'

'I'll make a note of it,' he said. 'For future reference.'

'Sending children to me *shouldn't* be a gamble,' Clara said weakly. Mr Sommersby said he agreed, 'absolutely.' He added, 'You're not wrong.'

Clara didn't know what to say now. She felt like she was banging her head against the wall. Time and time again she trusted the council, and time and time again they let her down. It was all very well them moving papers around in offices, but these were people's lives at stake. She wondered if she was expecting too much of them or if Suffolk's children's services were particularly lackadaisical or if this was replicated across the country. They were well-intentioned, she thought. And sometimes they got things very right. But my God, when they got things wrong...

'So?'

'So, we will arrange for Cliff to go somewhere else.'

At these words, relief crept over her like a blush. *It would be over soon.*

'He needs more help than I can provide, specialist help,' she admitted. It wasn't that she was a bad housemother. She must remember Cliff was a cabbage. But she was a generalist, not a horticulturist.

And if I had known that sooner, things mightn't be so painful for him now.

'There's a home for difficult boys in Hunstanton,' Mr Sommersby said. 'You would approve, I think – it's regimented but it's close to the sea, and the children are encouraged to have lots of hobbies. If they have a space, he'll be off your hands in a couple of days.'

'It's not that I want him off my—' she began furiously. *Was that what it looked like?*

'Poor phrasing,' Mr Sommersby said, back to his smooth managerial language. 'I mean he will be placed somewhere more suitable soon.'

She was still furious with herself, and with the council. It

would take some time before she would forgive them. And –
although it mightn't be fair – she wouldn't forget Miss Cooper
and all her prevarication, her procrastination and her goddam
partying. If Miss Cooper had worked harder at the, admittedly,
duller side of her job, like everyone else, then they mightn't be
in this mess. She was all about the glory, not the grind – and the
consequences were terrible.

Poor Cliff. She pulled her handbag to her, and rebuttoned
her coat. Mr Sommersby said nothing, what could he say? But
then, as she marched to the office door, he cleared his throat.

'Miss Newton, one more thing.'

Perhaps he would apologise? They should *all* apologise.
Would she accept an apology though? Clara knew she was
being ridiculous – of course she would! If anything, she would
end up apologising back. Louder. She excelled at sorrys.

Mr Sommersby had sprung back to being his commanding
self. 'I wanted to ask something, Miss Newton.'

'Yes?'

'It's about the event at the Royal Festival Hall.'

No, not an apology. Here it comes... She braced herself.
Finally, he was going to put his foot down. The children
shouldn't be out and about. Not in London. Orphans don't
perform. Orphans stay at home. Not safe. Not appropriate.

Mr Sommersby yanked at his shirt collar. The fan behind
his cabinet changed speed suddenly.

'Any chance of a ticket?'

29

There was no point drawing it out. Ripping off the plaster makes it sting less, so Clara told Cliff as soon as she got home. He stared at the ground like the ground was his enemy. He still had pockmarks on his forehead like tiny holes from an airgun. She remembered he'd only been at the Home a few days when he'd succumbed to chickenpox. She had put cold flannels on his forehead throughout the night. He had been delirious and kept saying something about a rope.

'I won't be able to do the Royal Festival Hall then?'

'No, you won't,' she said firmly. Even if it seemed brutal, it was kinder than lying to him.

'But I will still be able to do the TV recording, won't I? *The Great British Songbook?*'

'Oh, Clifford... Cliff, sorry.'

He said ever since he'd first seen a television set he had wanted to be on it. He said someone had told him as a joke that they had to shrink people to get inside but even that hadn't put him off. He dreamed of being beamed into people's homes. You couldn't say he didn't have a home of his own if he was in *all* the homes.

Clara said she would see what she could do. The television recording was only two days away, and she knew the council moved slowly – but on the other hand, what message would this send?

'Please, Miss Newton, please. It's the very last thing I'll ask of you.'

~

A Rolls-Royce – an actual Rolls-Royce – driven by a stern man in peaked cap and leather gloves picked them up and took them all the way to west London. The children were beside themselves. Denny managed not to wet himself – he had got used to being in cars again. And the children and Anita sang most of the way there.

'Why won't you join in?' Anita kept saying to Clara, who pointedly ignored her.

She had spent the day before at the police station with Clifford and she was not in the mood for this.

There were over fifty dressing rooms in the studios. And it was so airy and white, you felt like you made it dirty just by being there. A young man with a lot of teeth showed them around, showed them the place to hang their coats. It was unfussy, simple, modern. The outside was a wall of glass – 'full of natural light,' said Anita, who knew these things, 'excellent.'

'And then you go on – sing – and then it will cut away from you to the advertisements,' said the young man, who had a surprisingly loud voice. It boomed against the walls. Anita looked at him approvingly. Projection was another thing she found excellent. Clara decided he must be older than he looked. Well, he must be – he looked younger than Maureen!

Clara tried to look at the children through a stranger's eyes, as though she'd never seen them before – and she thought they *did* look 'wholesome', whatever that meant. Even

Cliff did, although she could hardly bring herself to look at him anymore. She felt like she was betraying him. In the same way as a poorly child taken to the doctor would miraculously recover once they were in front of Dr Cardew, Cliff's behaviour over the last couple of days had been beyond reproach. Even the interrogating police officer said, 'Butter wouldn't melt in this one's mouth.' Was she betraying him? She didn't know. Should she let him stay? *Was* she betraying him? She didn't know. Should she let him stay? As the days had gone by, she grew more rather than less conflicted about it.

Anita would have probably wanted to kill her if she hadn't let Cliff come today.

The boys were in their matching checked shorts, but they now had hats and bow ties. The girls were dressed in their checked dresses, Maureen had styled her's and Peg's hair while Rita had her typically severe plaits and Evelyn's hair was in its usual pretty curls with ribbon. All the girls now had little navy capes with fur trims, which Clara disliked – it was nearly summer, for goodness' sake; there was no sense in turning them out like they were yodelling in snowy mountains. Plus, they reminded her of the awful capes the children used to wear when she first arrived at the orphanage. But Anita couldn't resist tweaking, improving and changing or 'nit-picking', as Rita called it. The arguments they'd had over which songs they were going to do! Eventually, it was agreed: they would do the same today in the studio as they had at the audition– but, Anita had warned, there would be a big shake-up for the Royal Festival Hall.

Donald Button wasn't presenting *The Great British Songbook* – it was a young woman Clara didn't know called Cynthia Wilson, with jet-black hair that curled up at the ends, and an older man, Hugh Burke, whose name made the children cackle.

'Is he a berk?' Rita kept whispering.

'Don't be rude,' snapped Clara, but she was wondering something similar.

It wasn't just natural light, there were lights on pulleys and winches and great tracks up in the air and cords and leads on the floor, and chalk markings drawn on it like a crime scene. It was like an industrial complex – all fitted out for the manufacture of entertainment. No wonder they call it an industry, thought Clara. She could see the audience, although she couldn't make out any individuals, just a sea of eager faces, laughing.

The young man led them down a corridor to Make-up. Delighted, Maureen grabbed the chair in front of the mirror and a girl instantly started dabbing at her nose and cheeks.

'Next.' The young girl – now this one really could have been no older than Maureen – were they running some child labour camp here? – held out a sponge: 'It's nothing personal, it's the lights, you see.'

'Oh no, I don't—' Clara said but she was too late, she was already puffed. 'I'm not part of it,' she went on.

'Aren't you?' the girl said. She dabbed the children one by one, making them giggle and squeal. 'Shame. You should go on. The audience would love you. You're pretty, but not beautiful. Homely rather than sexy. That's ideal.'

Homely! thought Clara furiously. The make-up girl's eyelashes fluttered.

'I've been telling her that,' said Anita, who had entered into the serene mode Clara had come to expect before performances. She put her arm round Clara. 'Hear that? The audience would love you!'

When the make-up girl came to Cliff, she paused, lowered her eyelashes. Clara didn't know how it happened, but within seconds, he had taken hold of her wrist, and once they'd dabbed the sponge on his face in unison they dabbed hers, then both laughed.

Cynthia Wilson greeted them, and Clara realised that she did recognise her after all: she'd been featured in *Good House-keeping* once. In the interview, she had come across as quite ambitious, a bit intimidating – 'to succeed, women need to work five times as hard as men', Clara remembered – but in real life she was lovely. She said the children were wonderful, which helped win Clara over too.

They sang the same piece as they had done for the audition, and if anything, it was even smoother. Clara watched admiringly as Rita played the piano and her voice rang out clear and strong. Peg was fiery on the drums, Maureen and Evelyn's harmonies were charming and Cliff and Denny's doo-wops and finger-clicking made the show.

Then Cynthia Wilson bustled on, and went straight up to Peg. Clara winced. *Why did they always approach Peg?*

'So unusual to see a young lady on the drums!'

Peg nodded eagerly.

Cynthia tried again. 'What's your name?'

Peg dropped her sticks with a clatter.

'She doesn't speak,' Rita explained, after what felt like hours. She looked directly into the nearest camera. 'My name is Rita Ann Withers.'

'Do you like being part of this wonderful group?' Cynthia persisted.

'I love it,' she said. 'Mama.'

Cynthia laughed. She was ever-so-professional. 'We are so pleased to have you here tonight – do you want to give a little wave to the people at home?'

They all waved. Even Maureen. Even Cliff, who raised an eyebrow then blew kisses too.

Now it was Hugh Burke's turn. 'That was the Children of Shilling Grange Orphanage singing for their supper. And you can find them at the Royal Festival Hall on...'

'The twenty-ninth of May,' Cynthia told him, in an indulgent, oh-he's-so-funny tone that surely must have been draining for her. He *was* a berk. And she *was* doing five times more work than him.

Offstage, the children gathered around Clara. 'Were they okay?' Clara asked the toothy young man.

'They were a-may-zing!' he shrieked. 'Better than I could ever have imagined!'

Out of the corner of her eye, Clara saw the make-up girl use her eyebrow pencil to write down a telephone number on a strip of paper and then pass it to Cliff.

~

The journey home felt very long. The novelty of being in the fancy car had worn off. Peg felt ill and clutched her stomach, weeping, and they had to stop twice for Denny to pee in the roadside bushes. Clara thought Cliff was only pretending to fall asleep but then he started snoring. Once they had arrived home, Clara sent the children into the house but asked Cliff and Anita to wait behind: Anita needed to know what was going on.

'What is it, Clara?' she asked impatiently. 'I want to see Howard before bedtime.'

'Cliff has something to tell you,' Clara prompted.

'What is it, Clifford?' Anita asked and Clifford didn't correct her. Clara realised that Cliff didn't mind being called Clifford by Anita – it was just when Clara did it that he got antsy.

Cliff shuffled forward. 'I've really enjoyed being part of the Shilling Grange group,' he said. Talking had never been a problem for Cliff. 'I want to say thank you for the opportunity...'

Anita swayed on her heels uneasily. 'There's no need. Anyway' – she looked from him to Clara – 'we've still got lots more to achieve together. The Royal Fe—'

''Fraid not,' Cliff said fluently. 'I'm at the end of the road here. I'm moving from the Home.'

Anita covered her mouth with her hand. 'You're being adopted?' She looked disbelievingly at Clara.

'Uh, not quite...' muttered Clara.

'They're sending me to another home,' Clifford explained. 'Quite far from here.'

'Why?' a bewildered Anita asked.

Clara swallowed but Cliff was ready with the answers: 'That's what they do...You get settled somewhere and then, boom, you're off.'

'Oh no, Clifford, that's terrible. Clara, isn't there anything we can do?'

'It's all decided,' Cliff said. Clara couldn't say anything, her throat seemed to have closed up. 'I'm going tomorrow.'

Anita did not often look sad, but she did then. Then she tightened her expression and became resolute. 'My dear boy,' she said sorrowfully. Then she did something quite unexpected. She took off her coat and gave it to Clara to hold, and then her cardigan. She rolled up the sleeve of her blouse. Clara realised suddenly that Anita never wore short sleeves, not even in summer. Blue numbers were printed into her arm.

'See this,' she said, pointing to it.

Cliff stared; Clara did too.

'In the concentration camps, they tried to treat me like dirt,' she said. She touched the tattoo like she could still hardly believe it was there. Clara looked from her to Cliff. He was still as a statue and his usual sneer had vanished. 'They treated me like I was nothing more than a number. But I am not dirt, I am much more than a number – and so are you, Clifford. Don't let them cower you. Remember, you are much better than those who try to grind you down. You are a born performer – you have a rare talent.'

And then, she put her arm round Cliff and hugged him, her arm steely around his back.

❧

But Miss Cooper came only an hour or so later that evening. Cliff would have to go today, not tomorrow. When Clara said they weren't ready yet, Miss Cooper pouted and said, 'Never mind, I'll wait,' and went outside to smoke in her shiny car.

Clara was glad she'd had the foresight to pack Cliff's bag. After she brought it downstairs, she made them both a cup of tea, shutting the other children out of the kitchen. He hovered by her trying to help, his dark eyes unreadable. She wasn't going to hurry his last few minutes.

'What happened with your parents, Cliff?'

'My mum went to hospital and didn't come out. They didn't tell me she was dead. I found out from a neighbour about a month later. I was waiting for her every night at the bus stop, see – I guess she took pity on me.'

'Oh, Clifford,' she whispered then apologised. 'Sorry, I mean, Cliff.'

'I don't really mind what you call me,' he admitted ruefully. 'It just... it was nice to have some control.'

Clara accepted a cigarette – she usually insisted he smoked outside – and they sat there in a smoky fug. She thought, *this must be what it's like the day before an execution.* She wondered if she should at least try and put a stop to it. It had worked with the Australia plan last year, hadn't it? Tell the council it was all a big mistake, insist – but then she remembered Rita darting into the shed when it was up in flames, and Denny vomiting, and the many visits to the school. The recovered file and the interview with the police. She couldn't change her mind.

'Dad hanged himself,' he said quietly. 'I had a detention, and I came home later than usual and there he was. I got my knife out and I cut him down, he was so heavy, he smacked on the ground, like this...'

Cliff got up to demonstrate as Clara stared at him, astonished. 'Cliff...'

He collapsed onto the floor, then lay there, head down. Clara didn't dare move. Then he rolled onto his back.

'I think about it often. Perhaps if I'd come straight home that day, maybe he'd still be alive?'

'You weren't to know,' Clara said quietly.

Cliff got up and took his chair and cigarette again.

'There are other ways to feel powerful. Ways that don't hurt other people or destroy things.'

It was strange but now her anger and disbelief had subsided, she felt closer to Cliff than she ever had before. She wondered what went through his head when he sparked the match, when it caught. Was he destined to always do bad things?

'You've got to choose. We all mess things up sometimes, but you can keep messing things up or you can learn from your mistakes and try to be a better person.'

At that moment, Miss Cooper sounded her horn. *She could bloody wait*, thought Clara. Clara had asked her for help, had she not? She had asked to see Cliff's files; she had reported everything – almost everything – and the council had done nothing.

No one is completely bad; he had been failed and she had failed him.

If she had known what she was dealing with from the start, would things have turned out differently?

She'd never know.

When Cliff left, the children didn't crowd to the door like they usually would when a child was leaving, but stayed rooted in their various positions: Peg drawing Miss Fisher, Rita playing piano, Maureen flicking through a magazine, and Denny playing with marbles that Cliff had given him. Clara felt terrible for Cliff but she didn't force them to come.

~

A quiet night. Clara served up a watery lentil soup. The only sound was spoons hitting bowls. The children instinctively understood that it was not a night for playing up.

Clara had failed but here was something to learn from this. She had failed but the world had not stopped turning. Failed, but then it was not her test to pass: it was his. She could only bring the horse to water, she could not make it drink. It was up to Cliff now. She had tried with him. Maybe not hard enough, maybe too late, but there was only so much one person could do.

When Clara was a child, she had played patience endlessly. She developed cheats that were not cheats, that were still challenges. She developed shortcuts. She used to wish she had someone to play with.

She looked up at the children – only four of them now, and Denny might be gone soon too, if that nibble turned into a bite.

'Anyone want a few rounds of Newmarket?'

~

The next morning, she saw Ivor picking up his milk. He called out, 'good morning,' put the bottles inside and then came back out to speak to her. Around the garden wall were purple and white crocuses in bloom, a heartening display. The sun seemed to pick Ivor out, and he shaded his eyes to speak to her.

'Tell me if it's not my business, but what happened with Clifford?'

Clara still felt so hurt by Ivor. He didn't want them to become closer because he had to focus on his Patricia and because it would *ruin* everything? What nonsense! It must be something else. But that morning, as usual, his expression and his words disarmed her. She wasn't going to tell him about Cliff, but then she wanted to. He was always one to confide in. Keeping her eye on the flowers, she told him in a low voice about the fire – both fires, and when she looked up, she saw he was listening with his whole face, and then she grew scared about what he'd say. He had been a boy at the Home. He knew what it was like to be orphaned, underestimated, accused. Ivor would empathise with Cliff wholeheartedly. Ivor knew that sending the boy away was an admission of defeat. She might as well have come out with a white flag. But he squeezed her arm and said, 'I know you did your best, Clara.'

Suddenly she was reminded that Ivor was on her side and she wished she didn't forget it so often – that they both didn't. And then Patricia toddled out to her – walking, proper walking, although she stooped to steady herself on the ground once or twice – and the beautiful moment became a different moment. She said admiringly, 'Well, look at that!'

He raised his eyebrows and laughed, 'I'm in trouble now, aren't I?'

She was just about to go back into the Home, when he said, 'Oh, Clara, I thought I'd make you a dress.' He didn't look at her – he was watching Patricia. 'For the concert. At the Royal Festival Hall?'

'No – I'm not... I'm not going on the stage; I don't know what Anita said to you.'

He laughed. 'I know that. But it's a big occasion, isn't it? Something like this doesn't happen often.'

'I know what it is.' It was annoying enough when Anita went on about it; doubly so when Ivor did.

'And I've never made you a dress before, have I?'

'No...' Clara considered. He had made her a beautiful quilt once. And cushion covers and tablecloths but nothing as personal as a dress. She remembered the blue one she had tried on in British Home Stores. The one that had looked so pretty on the hanger yet had given her so much trouble in the changing room. A dress that Ivor made wouldn't do that.

Patricia plonked herself among the crocuses.

'Whoopsy daisy,' said Ivor. He had got very accomplished at scooping her up. He looked at Clara. 'Well?'

'Oh, all right...'

Why did his face have to be so lovely? It was such a trick the way some men's features were just right. The effect he had on her was unfair. She felt it disadvantaged her somehow. He kissed Patricia's pink cheek and tickled under her chin, then smiled at Clara.

'Will you need to... measure me?' she asked. The thought of having Ivor so close to her made her blush.

He wasn't even looking at her when he said, 'No, I've got a pretty good idea of your...' The pause made it sound even worse. '...Shape?'

'Fine.'

'Fine.'

As she waved them goodbye, Patricia was pulling Ivor's hair and he was laughing and exclaiming, 'Ow!'

Clara couldn't stop smiling – all day long as she went about her chores. Smiling and thinking. A dress? If that wasn't a declaration of intent, she didn't know what was. Maybe Ivor was finally changing his mind about her. Maybe he understood that if they did get together, nothing precious would be ruined – far from it. It would be wonderful. If he had been blowing cold, he was certainly blowing warmer now.

～

Dr Cardew had tried his best to order a television set, but he was too late. Everyone and their brother wanted one, and there was a waiting list of three entire months in some places. Undaunted, however, he continued his search and on Sunday evening, he rat-a-tatted on the door of the Home.

'Wrap up warm – we're going out!'

Clara was mystified, and there was clearing up to do – but she rallied the children and they poured into the back of Dr Cardew's car, with baby Howard squirming on Anita's lap in the front. Baby Howard was two months older than Patricia but he did not walk yet and this was causing Anita palpitations. Clara knew that because she kept saying, 'It doesn't matter,' and 'I really don't mind at all...'

Peering at Clara, Anita said suspiciously, 'You look different...'

And Clara did feel different since that conversation with Ivor. The world felt alive with possibilities. But she didn't say that, she just said, 'Oh, it's been a nice calm weekend – no big incidents!' as Anita blinked at her.

Clara didn't like to think about it, but it was true that things at the Home were just that little bit easier without Clifford, not just number-wise (although five was certainly easier to negotiate than six) but also not having to face his sneers, his unpredictability or his wrath all the time.

When Dr Cardew said they had to stop at the petrol station, Maureen stared into her lap and Clara prayed with all her might that Joe wouldn't be there, toiling away in his little shed; and thank goodness, he wasn't – an older man served them. Then they were properly away and they sang, 'Ging Gang Goolie', and Anita said, 'You'd never believe they put you lot on the television! If I close my eyes, I would think it was feeding time at the zoo!'

'We're here!' Dr Cardew parked up outside Eddie's electrical store. He had even brought a stool for Anita to sit on, which she did, elegantly. Dr Cardew was like that, he thought of everything. Howard was drooling. Evelyn was holding his teddy up for him.

There were about eight TV sets in the window and four of them were switched on. Some of them had built-in mahogany cabinets, other were standalone. Clara focused on the largest one, to her right. The picture was grey and smoggy at first; it took a while to get used to. She'd seen a television before, and had been disappointed at its picture – it wasn't half as clear as the cinema, and it didn't seem as professional as the cinema either.

The children were mesmerised. And then it was *The Great British Songbook* and there were Hugh Burke and Cynthia Wilson's faces.

Clara had her eyes on the Cliff on the screen. He was singing along and clicking his fingers, swinging his head. He was the epitome of the slick young man. She remembered thinking at the time that he wouldn't look out of place in a film. A musical with lots of tap dancing on tables. What she hadn't seen then was that tears had been streaming down his cheeks.

On the way home, Rita complained it was the fastest two minutes she had ever experienced.

'Blink and you'd have missed it.'

'It was better than nothing though,' said Maureen magnanimous since the camera had loved her.

Denny had his arm round Peg and they were both falling asleep.

'I can't believe you didn't fight the council,' Anita said when everyone was quiet. Something about the way she said it suggested to Clara that she had been mulling this over for a while.

'How do you mean?' Clara asked cautiously.

'Clifford. It's a disgrace they've sent him away. It's not right. If you ask me, it's a huge mistake.'

Clara glared at her. 'And what *has* it got to do with you exactly?' she asked icily, but Anita was impervious. She went on: 'The council move children around like dogs – worse than dogs. It's inhuman. Poor Clifford.'

'Anita!' Clara had to stop her. 'It wasn't only the council – I asked him to go too.'

'What?' Anita's mouth dropped open wide.

'It wasn't working. He's gone to a special home where they will be able to look after him better than I could.'

'You actually agreed to this?' The shock in Anita's voice was painful but Clara would not be shamed, she would not.

'Yes, I did. For the children's sake, for all of them.'

'Anita,' warned Dr Cardew from the driver's seat and Anita bit her lip and whatever she was about to come out with then, she didn't say. The rest of the journey passed in silence.

Peter telephoned. It had only been three weeks since his last call and Clara's hopes rose. Perhaps he still cared about them all?

One of the guys he shared with, Tony—

'The one who always locks himself out?'

'That's him. His uncle loves all new things, and he got a television and...'

Peter had watched it! Clara's heart was full.

'They were brilliant,' he said. 'I'm so very proud of you all.'

'And I'm proud of you too,' Clara said. She couldn't help it. He laughed.

. . .

That night, Clara was woken up by the sound of someone clattering about. First, she thought it was Denny sleepwalking but she quickly realised that the sound was coming from the street. The air was so quiet that the noise – of a bicycle being clunkily unlocked, then dropped, she thought, then righted – felt incredibly loud. She hurried to the window.

Cliff, she thought. *Cliff's run away. He's come back.*

Her heart was in her boots. What if he set fire to something again? She parted the curtains, pressed her nose against the cold pane to peer out.

Mrs Harrington was wheeling her bicycle away from Ivor's workshop. She was in a state of... what was it? *Disarray.* Clara had never seen her so dishevelled. Her auburn hair was completely loose, down to her shoulders, that beautiful deep red against the white of her blouse. And her clothes were equally informative. It looked like she'd put them on in haste; they were all skew-whiff, as though she'd buttoned up everything wrong.

Clara stared at her. *It couldn't be, could it? And where on earth was baby Leslie?*

And she understood then – Ivor had lied about not wanting to be with her because of Patricia. How had she believed that? She was a fool. Here was the evidence. Ivor didn't want her – not because he felt useless or because she was useless; not because what they had was 'too precious'. None of that was true – it was because of Mrs Harrington. He was having an affair.

30

A few days later, Clara went to meet Donald Button, at a bar just across from Charing Cross station. As he walked across to her with his arms outstretched it was as though she was his long-lost love. He was practised at meeting and greeting, she realised – and also it was definitely a wig. The children were right. She should try to notice these things more. Now, without his hat, his hair looked like a sea wave. Was it to be admired or despised that he went to such lengths to present a full head of hair?

What was she doing here? she wondered. Yet it was quite simple: she was trying to pay back Ivor. He was having an affair with an ex-childcare officer. A *married* woman with a baby. And she had thought he kept turning her down for gentlemanly reasons – well, she had been played for a fool.

'Here she is,' Donald Button said, although he was only talking to her, or maybe himself. 'She came!'

'I did,' Clara sniggered to herself. American Marilyn – Michael's mother and her friend – would love this guy. 'I wanted to tell you, the adoption show you did on the wireless last year? It made a difference. It was really powerful. It brought lots of people forward.'

'Which one was that?' he said. 'I do a lot of shows. Was it the one with the dog named Candy? Never work with children or animals!' he went on with a flourish.

'Some people *have* to work with children though,' Clara said incredulously. 'And animals.'

'You've never heard the phrase before?'

'No...'

He inhaled deeply.

She was not in show business – hers was the business of orphaned children – and what's more, she was not interested in show business either. She went on, 'So your radio show was adoption stories – with humans. Human children.'

'Was it? That's nice. Glad you enjoyed it.'

Clara didn't have the heart to say she hadn't actually listened to the whole thing. He seemed pleased and she was glad she'd told him. It was a good start.

He gripped her hands. 'It's about audience figures.'

She had been to smart places before but the bar Donald Button took her to was so glamorous even Julian would have approved. A man lit Donald Button's cigarette, and he did it almost without you noticing he'd been there. The drinks arrived in a similar way. Hers was orangey-red and came with a paper straw. The bubbles went up her nose.

As Clara sipped at it, he winked at her: 'So, tell me your news.'

'Ah!' she said, thinking there wasn't an awful lot she wanted to share with him. 'The children were very excited about being on television. Did you see it?'

'I didn't,' he said, and she saw the question had somehow displeased him. 'It's a flash in the pan.'

'What is?'

'Television. I prefer the wireless.'

'The children enjoyed it.'

'Well, exactly.' He was *definitely* annoyed. 'It's a medium for children. A lot of amateurs.'

She thought of Cynthia Wilson and Hugh Burke. Were they for children? They hadn't seemed amateurish so far as she knew.

'Anyway, Cara—'

'Clara.'

'Lots of actresses change their names.'

'I'm not an actress.'

He looked her up and down as though she were a second-hand car and he was about to squeeze her tyres. 'You could be, though. With some work. Anyone could be. In fact, often the plainer ones look better on the big screen.'

Was that supposed to be a compliment?

The bar was filling with groups and Donald Button introduced her to various men, 'his great friends,' who spoke over her head or to her breasts, and women, who ignored her or gave her weedy-grimace smiles. He put his hand on the small of her back, which made her nervous, but his cologne was nice. He had been working in Bournemouth, he said, comparing. She was stumped until she realised: 'Oh, *compèring*,' she said, 'with an E,' but he looked blank-faced, so she quickly added, 'Everyone needs a presenter.' He was thin-skinned, she thought, which was surprising for someone in the public eye. He was undeniably handsome though. *Good Housekeeping* knew their 'Men We Admire This Year'. His hair/wig might have been a disaster, but his face was chiselled, symmetrical, his ears were neat and his nose tidy; he was pleasant to look at – and he smelled good. But he wasn't Ivor.

After two more of those orangey-red drinks and no food whatsoever – he'd eaten – she said she had to get back to Lavenham. Sister Grace didn't mind if she was late, but she did. He pouted and said, 'Next time I won't let you leave so early.' She was just thinking there mightn't be a next time – this experiment had run its course – when he dug into his pockets. 'I got something for you – and the kiddies.'

It was tickets for the Festival of Britain in London.

'Can't have you missing the Skylon and the Dome of Discovery, can we?'

Clara looked at them, stunned. 'No, I can't accept these—' But Donald Button insisted and he was a man used to getting what he wanted. And while he insisted, he fiddled with his wallet and then took out a five-pound note – 'for your transport too.' Clara couldn't believe it. He winked at her and then said, 'Come here!' with his arms open, and squeezed her tight. She was still feeling amazed and uncertain – even though she didn't particularly want to – they'd have to go now, she had no excuse – and his lips were in her hair and he was mumbling something, she wasn't sure what it was, probably it was something like she would have to stay much longer next time.

31

The next afternoon, Clara walked the children home from school and then found a man and woman sitting on the doorstep of the Home. They looked like they'd been there for some time. As Clara hurried towards them, from the corner of her eye, she saw Ivor outside his workshop and she ignored him. Obviously.

The visitors said they were here to see Denny.

'Oh, I didn't know the council had arranged a meeting,' Clara began, confused.

'We telephoned yesterday. We thought the sooner the better.'

'Oh.'

No one had told her, which meant she hadn't been able to prepare Denny... How would he take it, she wondered.

Clara led them through the house to the kitchen, which fortunately didn't look too untidy. She told Denny to stay and the other children stayed too, probably hoping there would be a visitors' treat, but Clara didn't have anything to serve with the tea. The guests said that was fine. Clara apologetically made very weak black tea because she was at the end of her tea ration and had run out of milk. They said that was fine too.

The woman had blonde curled hair and was wearing a dress with a pearl necklace and little pearl earrings that swung when she spoke. She was probably in her early thirties; she seemed gentle and friendly, and she enunciated all her words very clearly, as though she were in a play. The man was balding yet good-looking, and he wore a smart suit. He too seemed kind. They were the Sweetinghams.

'We got you this,' Mr Sweetingham said to Denny, his ears were red. He looked up at Clara. 'We didn't know what else to bring.'

It was a jigsaw of a lighthouse, the one at Southwold.

'It's lovely there,' Mrs Sweetingham said. 'Maybe we could take you there one day.'

Denny shifted from one foot to the other, his golden hair flopping over his face.

Her husband patted her hand. 'Give the boy a chance,' he whispered. 'It's bound to be overwhelming for him.'

They were from the same town as Denny and his family.

'I knew your mother very well, Denny,' the woman said in her soft voice and Denny's eyes immediately filled with tears. Peg put her arm around him.

The two women had been at school together and then they were farm girls together during the war. Mrs Sweetingham said she was actually there the evening Denny's mother met Denny's father, at a dance in a church hall. 'Love at first sight,' she sighed. Denny's parents had gone to the Sweetinghams' wedding, and the Sweetinghams had gone to Denny's parents' wedding.

'It was a lovely do,' Mr Sweetingham said. 'Despite the war, the nosh was top-class.'

'I went to your christening,' Mrs Sweetingham said shyly to Denny, who had cheered up and was sitting at the table. 'But Thomas was in the RAF by then and he couldn't go. Your parents certainly knew how to throw a party!'

She looked into her lap. 'Is it all right to say that?'

And Clara looked at Denny, who was listening avidly and said, 'I think Denny likes hearing about his parents, don't you?'

The boy nodded.

The couple stayed even while Clara was serving up the children's soup and apologising there wasn't any spare. They said that was fine. After that, Clara sent the children to do their chores or to play in the parlour and she thought they'd go, but even then, they were reluctant to. Mrs Sweetingham told Clara that after the war she had worked as a window-dresser. She gave it up when she got married. 'I kept expecting babies to come along,' she said brightly. 'But they didn't.' Mr Sweetingham squeezed her arm.

Mr Sweetingham worked in a bank, a job he seemed indifferent to. They liked holidays and the seaside. They were hoping to go to the Festival of Britain, they said. At this, Clara clammed up. She hadn't told the children about the tickets yet and she felt something like a chicken sitting on her eggs. But she didn't want to go – she must have been the only person in the world who didn't want to go! – and think what else the five pounds Donald Button had given her could buy! *Interview clothes for Maureen, therapy for Peg, more music for Rita, something for Denny?*

Once the Sweetinghams were on the topic of the Festival, they wouldn't stop. Mrs Sweetingham loved design, they said, and Mr Sweetingham liked architecture.

Clara busied herself with the kettle. *Madness*, she was thinking. *A collective national insanity.* There must be something in the water for so many people to lose their cynicism and suddenly believe a festival – *a festival of all things!* – would be the answer to the nation's woes. The Sweetinghams were hoping to visit the new urban village at Peckham, they said. 'Just to get some ideas; there must be, you know, better ways to do things. That's what interests us,' they said and smiled at each other and Clara tried not to think about the way Ivor sometimes used to smile at her.

Clara felt a bit sick.

'I really must get the children to bed,' she said, even though it was early – they didn't seem capable of getting the hint. 'Do you mind awfully?' They jumped up and apologised for keeping her.

They went into the parlour, where Denny and Peg had already done most of the lighthouse jigsaw. They'd done the raging sea, the treacherous rocks, a tiny boat with tinier fishermen in oilskins, its long brick column – all they needed was that shiny light at the top.

The adults watched the children press the final jigsaw pieces into place and then Clara clapped her hands. 'Bed. Say goodbye,' she said, and Denny did something rare. He came up to Mrs Sweetingham, put his arms round her waist and hugged her. Then he did the same to Mr Sweetingham.

On the doorstep, Mrs Sweetingham still didn't stop talking. She said, 'It's so terrible, I didn't think of it at first, you know when I heard about Joan and Ron, it didn't occur to me. I assumed he'd go to relatives or something. And then one night, I heard the wireless show, and I actually heard Denny, and I thought, what would Joanie do? – and I knew then I had to try. If you say no, you say no, but at least we'll have tried.'

Miss Cooper was thrilled about the Sweetinghams. She dropped in on the Home on her way to interview some prospective parents in Norfolk, and she seemed to expect praise from Clara. Clara was determined not to praise her – she was still furious about the whole Cliff affair. In the end, Miss Cooper asked directly what she thought and Clara reluctantly admitted that she thought the Sweetinghams were very nice.

She *did* think they were nice. She had liked Mrs Sweet-ingham very much – she was the type of woman she might, in a different life, have been friends with.

Miss Cooper was looking at her. She was as stylish as ever – in neat trousers and a silky top – but she was suddenly subdued. 'I know you are angry with me,' she said.

'Oh,' said Clara.

'You'll be glad to hear I reported myself,' said Miss Cooper. 'About the Clifford file. It was my fault.'

This took the wind out of Clara's sails somewhat. She knew there wasn't an evil conspiracy against her or Clifford – so much was just incompetence. But whatever the reason, the outcome was just as horrible. Poor Cliff. The one thing that she was glad of now was that she had never hit him. But she so nearly had.

32

Ivor came over with some clothes for the children that he had mended. He was all twinkly-eyed, oblivious to her having worked out that he and Mrs Harrington were carrying on. There was no mistaking what it was: Mrs Harrington's dishevelled blouse. Her rumpled hair. The time of night. And the worst thing was – her senses had been tingling about it from day one: she should have trusted her womanly intuition from the moment Ivor said he had help for Patricia. She didn't invite him in.

'I thought I'd let you know,' he said awkwardly on the step, 'Dr Cardew is thinking about fitting a prosthetic for me. I tried one just after the war, but never really got on with it,' he went on. 'But he says they're better now, and since I've got Patricia to worry about...'

'Oh,' said Clara, surprised at this confidence. She thought that Mrs Harrington would be the one for those nowadays. 'That's good.'

'I'm lucky, I kept my elbow – some didn't.'

It was very Ivor, she thought, to look on the bright side

about losing a limb. She wasn't going to get sentimental with him now though. 'Is there anything else?'

'What?'

'Is there anything else you want to tell me?'

She tried not to picture him and Mrs Harrington passionately kissing over his worktops. Mrs Harrington's skirt pushed up, the frill of her stockings (for Mrs Harrington was no doubt the type to wear frilly stockings – her poor cuckold husband probably cheated the ration for those too)— *No.* Clara shook her head vehemently. This was probably why he was going for the prosthetic now. Mrs Harrington had probably told him it was a good idea.

Clara's new cold tone had Ivor looking quite subdued. He didn't say anything else but scratched his cheek.

'Thank you for the clothes,' she said. 'Give Mrs Harrington my love.'

'Clara?'

She was nearly crying as she slammed the front door on him. How dare he come over here with his sob stories? He disgusted her now. He knocked again and called out her name, but she went out into the back garden so she wouldn't have to hear. She would focus on Donald Button from now on.

Clara was still agitated about this interaction when she took the children out strawberry picking. Farmer Buckle always let them come in early, before the rest of the public, and charged them less than the official price.

'Ivor not with you?' he said. Although he was kind, Clara always got the impression he didn't like her much from long before Clifford had burned down his hut (which can't have helped). *No, he bloody isn't,* thought Clara, and then told herself off – Farmer Buckle wasn't the one to blame for Ivor's indiscretions – and said politely, 'Not today.'

She warned Rita, Denny, Peg and Maureen, 'only red ones,' but they knew more about fruit-picking than she did. Maureen, Peg and Rita had been doing it for years. It was lovely being out, feeling the sun on her face, and it was also the perfect place to get Ivor off her mind and to have a chat with Denny. He didn't like seated conversations but he would confide in her while doing something else.

'The council said yes to the Sweetinghams,' she told him. 'So, a few more checks and you'll be good to go.'

Denny doubled-back to show her a cluster of particularly juicy red fruit. There was something satisfying about plucking them off the plants, although some squidged in her hand if the insects had got there first. Denny still wasn't saying anything about the Sweetinghams.

Peg and Rita had run on ahead. Like being the first into fresh snow, there was something appealing about being the first to pick from a bunch: 'Only the red ones, we know,' they chanted.

'I thought you'd be pleased, Denny.' Clara persisted. 'You'll be able to go to your old school and see your old friends. It really is the best possible outcome—'

She stopped herself. Of course it wasn't the *best* possible outcome. What was she saying?

He surprised her by talking about the street the Sweetinghams lived on – he knew it – and their house with central heating.

'I bet your mum and Mrs Sweetingham had fun together,' Clara said. Her thoughts went to Judy – how lovely it was to have a friend like that.

'I feel so sad,' he said as he squatted to the lower strawberries. 'All the time. I don't want to, I try not to. But I do.'

'I know,' Clara said, she sometimes felt so useless. 'But this will pass.'

They had a strawberry picnic. Peg leaned on Denny and Denny leaned on Peg on the blanket. Rita was singing 'Daisy, Daisy,' unselfconsciously, Maureen and Denny joined in and Clara wanted to as well, but she couldn't. She just couldn't bring herself to – even a simple children's song. She hated singing in front of anyone. Instead, she clapped along with Peg.

If you breathed in, you could smell the fruit and the mud, perhaps you could smell the leaves, or the trees, or the sky even. It was lovely and earthy. The sun was peeking out from behind the grey clouds and the children sounded so happy. Things were pretty good: Maureen hadn't mentioned Joe for weeks, Rita was delighted with the upcoming performance, Peg was blossoming in her relationship with Miss Fisher and Denny, Denny would have a permanent home soon.

She sat up. Their mouths and chins were smeared berry-red.

'Let's save some,' she said.

Peg grinned. She passed Clara her paper. She was taking some for Mrs Fisher, naturally.

'Let's give some to Ivor!' suggested Rita brightly.

'No,' snapped Clara. The thought of her carefully chosen strawberries snuggled on top of one of Mrs Harrington's blooming chocolate cakes was enough to make her see red.

Two days later, Clara saw Mrs Horton out doing her shopping in town and her heart leapt. Here was a woman she could trust. After she apprised Mrs Horton of the children's stories, Clara said, smiling with the expectation of dropping a bombshell, 'You'll never guess who I went out with last week!'

'Ivor?'

'Noo,' Clara said, feeling aggrieved. 'No, that would hardly be... no. It was Donald Button. And I'm seeing him again,' she added decisively. Well, she had no choice really. She could hardly just send the tickets and the money back in the post. She was obliged.

'Donald Button?' Mrs Horton looked so mystified that for a second, Clara was seized with the desire to shake her. *You know who Donald Button is!*

'Star of stage, screen and wireless,' she added, amazed at how temperate her voice sounded.

'I know who he is,' Mrs Horton said finally. 'It's just – I thought you and Ivor were...'

'Were what?' Clara flushed.

Mrs Horton put her shopping bags down and rubbed her palms together. 'Getting on better?'

'I don't know what you mean.'

'No need to get so wound up, Clara, I just mean – you had found an equilibrium of sorts.'

An equilibrium?

'He told me to leave him alone. He told me he doesn't need me. He doesn't want to "ruin" anything precious,' Clara said contemptuously.

'Oh, you know Ivor, he says things he doesn't mean.'

'Well, how am I meant to know which things he says he means and which things he doesn't?' Clara said firmly. This reasoning was ridiculous. Was she supposed to be a mind-reader?

'He says things – but not with his words,' Mrs Horton continued as though Ivor was some kind of enigmatic puzzle in the newspaper.

'Well, he certainly said things without words this time,' Clara said self-righteously.

'How do you mean?'

'I mean, he's in a relationship with Mrs Harrington.'

Clara had turned over her trump card. But it didn't feel like a trump card, it felt miserable.

'What? How could that be?' It should have been satisfying to see how shocked Mrs Horton was at this, but somehow it made Clara feel worse. 'It seems out of character, frankly.'

'For whom? For him or her?' demanded Clara.

'For-for both of them,' stuttered Mrs Horton. 'How do you know this?'

Clara was glad to have the chance to prove her point. 'One, I saw her coming away late one night.'

'From his workshop?'

'Yes. Alone. No baby. And she looked like they had been love-making.'

They were both silent for a moment. Clara hoped Mrs Horton didn't ask what looking *like they had been love-making* looked like. She wasn't sure she would find the words. Mrs Horton didn't ask that, but she did say, 'And two?'

'She told Maureen.'

'*She told Maureen?*'

'Not in so many words, but yes.' *You have to wait for someone sometimes*: that's what she said, like a declaration in cold blood.

'And three?'

Clara frantically tried to think of her third reason. 'Three. He told me – with cake.'

At this, Mrs Horton's expression turned incredibly sceptical. Like Clara was a toddler with an overactive imagination. 'Cake?'

'Yes, cake. So that's it. I'm getting out of there – and I'm having fun with...' She was going to say 'other people' but it wasn't other people, it was one other person. It was Donald Button and she wasn't sure it was fun either – but she'd give it one more date. Everyone deserves a second chance. After all, she'd given Ivor a billion of them. And look what he'd done with them!

'And he gave me tickets to the Festival of Britain,' she added lamely. 'So, there's that too.'

Mrs Horton made a harrumphing sound as she picked up her shopping bags. 'Well,' she said primly, 'good luck.'

What Clara didn't say was that when Ruby appeared last time it was a bolt out of the blue, a painful, humiliating bolt, and she was determined never to get a shock like that again. And she had even been caught unawares that Miss Bridges and Mr Horton were carrying on too – she hadn't known until a long while after everyone else.

This time, she told herself, *I am not going to be the last one to know.*

33

Chickenpox was doing the rounds once again. This time Denny got it. He was mysteriously headachy and feverish for a few days, but it was a slight relief when the spots came, because Clara had worried he might be emotionally on the slide again. She had to cancel her second date with Donald Button – she couldn't leave a poorly child with Sister Grace. Donald Button took it well though and his reaction made her like him more. He was busy compèring, he said, and this time, she understood what he meant, and he said that as soon as she was free, she was to let him know. The telephone version of Donald Button was more amenable than the real-life version. She wondered which was the true him.

She saw Anita queueing outside the butcher's. Sawdust from the shop was spilling over onto the pavement and when Clara went over, a woman asked them to sign a petition saying, 'No more ration cuts'. Both Anita and Clara agreed to sign. Clara told Anita about Denny and Anita said she was pleased to hear it.

'You're pleased he's poorly?!'

Anita meant she had worked out if the children got chickenpox *now*, they would be better in time for their performance at the Royal Festival Hall.

'No offence meant,' she apologised.

Clara sighed. 'None taken.' For Anita every single thing – good or bad – was about the performance.

'I wish we hadn't lost Clifford,' Anita said for the hundredth time. 'He was my second best, you see – after Rita.'

'Don't let Evelyn hear you say that!' said Clara.

'Evelyn has a very sweet tone,' said Anita. 'But she is not destined to be a singer – not in the same way Clifford could be.'

It was uncomfortable how truthful Anita was.

'Cliff has some work to do on himself before that can happen, unfortunately,' Clara said. And she felt guilty. Did Anita see it as giving up on him? Because Clara knew that might be how it looked, but she was still certain that it was the right thing – the other children were important too. One couldn't take precedence over the others, it wouldn't be fair.

Anita seemed to understand Clara then because she said, 'It's much better he's in a special new place though, Clara.'

Clara was glad Anita didn't ask if she'd heard from him though. She expected she never would.

The queue moved up and the bell on the door rang.

'Come to the next rehearsal,' Anita said. Then she went in and asked for kidneys.

A couple of evenings later, Clara, Peg, Rita, Maureen and Denny walked up the road to Anita's for another rehearsal. Clara hurried them along: she didn't want to see Ivor yet but couldn't help feeling disappointed when they didn't. He was probably having a tryst with Mrs Harrington right now. Denny insisted he was better and since he wasn't contagious anymore, she thought he might as well go back. Clara had also checked if he was still okay with performing and he'd said, 'It's not my favourite thing in the world but it's not as bad as whale meat.' She realised suddenly that he hadn't been sleepwalking for a while now. Ever since Cliff had left, in fact.

'I want to do something spectacular next time we perform,' Anita said when they arrived.

And this, Clara thought, went some way to explain why she, Clara, was not a musical conductor, director, group leader or whatever it was that Anita was. The set was already good, excellent in fact; the TV show had gone down a storm – so why did Anita want to change everything around again?

'Pfft. Because this is London, Clara. This is the Royal Festival Hall!'

'Yes, I know, but—'

'We must do something marvellous,' Anita mused. 'I heard this tune the other day.' She began humming – *hmmm-hhhm*.

'That's "Shine on Harvest Moon"!' shrieked Rita.

Maureen swivelled round, then ran out of the room.

'Can we avoid that one?' Clara intervened. 'It's, um... got some personal significance.'

Anita scowled. 'Do you have a better idea?'

Clara considered. 'I did think of a poem actually, that I thought you could set to music...'

'Another Jane Taylor?'

'It's not. It's by her sister, Ann. Mr Dowsett showed it to me – I thought it was quite charming. It's called "My Mother".'

Anita pulled a face. 'A load of orphans singing about the mothers they lost. You don't think it's too much?'

'Whatever...' Clara shrugged. Anita had asked for suggestions and she'd made one, she'd done her bit. She sat herself down in an armchair and got out her knitting. Evelyn beamed at her approvingly. She had been working on this jumper for Peg on and off for six months. By the time it was ready, Peg would probably be double its size.

When she next looked up, all the children were in their positions – Rita at the piano, Peg at the drums, Denny next to her where he felt safe, Maureen, who had quietly returned, and Evelyn by them, and Anita at the front – but they all appeared to be waiting for something.

Clara didn't understand what until Anita finally came out with it: 'Oh, for goodness' sake, Clara, I thought maybe now we're one down that you could step in.'

'ME?' Clara laughed. 'Have you ever heard Stella crying for food? That's how I sound singing.'

'I'm sure you can. I can help too. You know, the children from Shilling Grange and their housemother! It's beautiful. How good would it look?'

Clara narrowed her eyes. *Dear God.* 'You want them to look like the orphans in *Oliver Twist*!'

'No, I don't,' scoffed Anita. She narrowed her eyes. 'Although you'd be a great Nancy.'

'Doesn't she get—'

'Just sing us a song, Clara, just to entertain us.' Anita had switched to pleading mode, and now the children joined in.

'Please, please,' and 'it will be fun!'

Anita murmured, 'It's important to show children that you can rise to a challenge.'

Her mother, Clara remembered, had a sweet pretty voice, but her father, like her, was uncharacteristically shy when it came to singing. She remembered the church choir. She *had* enjoyed it, hadn't she?

'All right,' she said impulsively. *What's the worst that could happen?*

Anita had already swung herself onto the piano bench. Clara pulled down her sleeves. Her heart was thumping fast as a runaway train.

'Anything you know and like,' Anita said. '"Keep the Home

Fires Burning". "We'll Meet Again"? Or how about "As Time Goes By"?'

Clara had liked Humphrey Bogart in *Casablanca*, of course – everyone did. And who could forget Ingrid Bergman walking into Rick's Cafe that first time?

Anita began to play and Clara put down her knitting.

If at first Clara felt self-conscious and foolish, within seconds it had worn off, and she felt... she felt the pleasure of it. It *was* exhilarating to let her voice out – it was something she didn't usually do, and maybe it was like a dog being allowed out for a walk after a period of confinement. She sang the words she knew well, enjoying the ups and downs of the notes, and as she did, she was back there in the church choir, with the smell of the incense, the candles, the organ. A song is just a song. The sheer joy of making those sounds, of being their source.

The children were staring at her, open-mouthed.

And, Anita played the piano beautifully, of course, like always.

Clara finished and the room felt eerily silent. Then Anita broke the silence by thumping down the piano lid and laughing.

Last month, Clara had made an apple crumble and when Anita came over, she had offered her some. Anita had taken one bite and then screwed up her face. 'Don't telephone us' – she'd announced to Clara – 'We'll telephone you!' She had been very pleased with her new English phrase, which she'd got from the American films.

'I think you mean, "Don't call us, we'll call you,"' Clara had corrected her, laughing.

'Same thing,' Anita had said haughtily.

Clara expected something like that now, but instead, Anita

removed herself from the piano bench, went and sat in her floral armchair with her palms pressed together as if she was praying.

Was she that bad?

'Clara,' Anita said gently, tapping her index fingers together. 'You have the most exquisite voice.'

The compliment flooded Clara like a dip in a warm sea. It gave her a sense of accomplishment she hadn't felt in a long time.

'It's still a no,' she said and she went back to her knitting.

A few days later, they listened to the opening ceremony of the Festival of Britain in London on the wireless. Clara pretended not to be interested at first, but soon even she was drawn in and she joined the children on the sofa and slung her arms round Denny and Peg. They smelled of strawberries and she thought, these *are* good moments. The King was speaking from St Paul's Cathedral. He did very well, she thought. She remembered when he had announced the outbreak of the war – twelve years ago now? My goodness, the world had changed since then. And her own world. And his world, she supposed too. He used to have a stutter but now his voice boomed out fluently: 'Visible sign of achievement and confidence.'

'Well,' Clara said when he'd finished, 'there we are. Up to bed. And Peg, the King didn't used to like public speaking.' She paused, unsure what message she was trying to impart. 'And uh, now he does... Although it would be good to hear him talk about something less... trivial.'

Peg was scribbling. 'Don't you like the Festival of Britain, Mama Newton?'

'It's not that I don't like it,' Clara said. She couldn't help herself. 'I just wonder if now is really the right time for a state-sponsored jamboree.'

Peg blinked at her. She wrote something else: 'I want to go there!'

Clara read the note and something buckled inside her. 'We are going to perform at the actual Royal Festival Hall – that's even better, surely?'

The children stared at each other sulkily. Rita piped up first: 'No, we want to go to the Festival as well.'

And Denny said, 'Please, please, Miss Newton. We'll love you forever!'

Maureen shrugged but her eyes were shining. 'Even if we just went to the funfair?'

Clara thought of the eight tickets quietly hatching in her safe and the five pounds spending money, all thanks to Donald Button, star of stage, screen and wireless. *Single* Donald Button with the nice face, who didn't think she was ruinous.

'Then we'll go,' she said.

34

It was windy the night before their trip to London. The wind howled at the old window frames, rattling them, and Clara could hear strange animal sounds from the garden. She thought of the trees on the line, fallen telegraph poles and upturned benches that might block their way. But in the morning, when she got up early to iron the handkerchiefs and to pair the socks, it was as calm as anything and the trains were running as normal.

Other groups and families on the train were heading to the Festival and there was a frisson of excitement among everyone. Some people were holding the Festival of Britain brochures. One family was dressed entirely in red, white and blue. Even the conductor said, 'Festival of Britain, is it?' when Clara showed him her tickets. And he said he was hoping to take his grandchildren.

Clara told the children what Mr Harris had told her about the Skylon: that the name was a combination of pylon, sky and nylon. (She didn't tell them that he'd also said that, like the British economy, it had no visible means of support.)

They merged into the great crowd marching across the

bridge from Charing Cross, Clara shouting instructions to 'stay together' and reassuring Denny, 'Yes, we'll find the lav in just a minute.'

This is all new, she told herself. This wasn't how she thought of London in recent times. She still had such strong memories of how things had looked during the war: men in uniforms everywhere, sandbags, helmets, gas masks. Even on a sunny day, it was a grey landscape. And so many of the buildings had black fronts – they just hadn't been cared for in so long. And there had been hardly any kids – most were sent away – and the few who weren't were running riot in bombed-out playgrounds.

Now, marching towards the south bank of the Thames, walking among the mums and the dads and the children, she felt that strange difference. There was another woman walking with about ten children and Clara thought, *Ah-ha, another orphanage outing*, but then she saw they were Scouts, and the next group she saw were Brownies. Another was a school group.

There were people directing the crowds, and people with placards – this way to the Festival of Britain – and a few people were waving the Union Jack or blowing little paper horns, there were fountains and little pea lights in the concrete showing the way. They'd never seen such things and there was such a party atmosphere too, it was hard to believe it was a Sunday morning.

'What's the name of this river, children?' she asked. Alex would have been able to tell you the source, the resources, the etymology of the name.

'Is it the Wye?' asked Denny sweetly. Rita suggested it was 'old man river'.

Anita, Dr Cardew, baby Howard and Evelyn met them near the entrance turnstiles. They had come down the night before and stayed in a bed and breakfast. Evelyn and Rita immediately linked arms and compared hairstyles. Anita said Howard had been tetchy all morning, but he was all smiles now.

Howard said, 'Da-da,' and Anita was irritated: 'Why doesn't he say "Mama"?' She wondered aloud if the nanny had trained him. Clara laughed, but at the look on Anita's face she stopped.

As they crossed the bridge, the Royal Festival Hall came into view in all its glory.

'I can't believe you'll be performing there,' Clara said to Peg, who took her hand and swung it wildly. 'Just next week.'

There weren't the queues they were used to for food shopping. There wasn't the drab, regimental discipline they usually had to endure everywhere they went. It felt new, it *felt* sunny – even though it wasn't particularly. The outdoor cafes and seating areas almost felt continental! And the Skylon – well, the Skylon was amazing. It was a rocket shape, elegant, quivering in the breeze. Aluminium and steel towering three hundred feet up, like something from a sci-fi film at Saturday Morning Picture Club.

Clara listened to the conversations around her; many of them variations of *How does it do it?* There were lots of foreign tourists too and although she couldn't understand the words, it was obvious how impressed they were although, as usual, there was always one who was less than impressed. One man with a group of middle-aged women was complaining, 'That's my money that paid for that!' The women smirked behind their hands and one winked at Clara: 'He thinks he's bloody Rockefeller.'

The visitors gazed upwards at the Skylon, some saw it through the eyes of their large cameras and you could hear the click, click of hundreds of photographs being born. Clara thought of Joyce – she had loved photography and would have been in her element clicking away here too. It was all so much better than she'd imagined – what had she imagined? Well, nothing like this. She had a lot to thank Donald Button for.

The boating lake on the South Bank was massive, bigger than in the pictures she'd seen, and the water was blue-black and full of pedalos. People were going around in circles, pedalling. They decided to pair up, but then Rita wanted to sit out on the side with Dr Cardew and Howard, but then Maureen wouldn't get a go in a pedalo, so Rita had to go. Before long, they were both laughing and chasing Peg and Clara.

'Don't splash,' yelped Clara, 'My hair!' but the girls ignored her.

After that, they went to the Dome of Discovery: there were four sections – Science, Outer Space, Exploration, Achievement. Victor, Bernard and Alex were coming next week. Clara could only imagine Alex's joy when he saw the Isaac Newton display. She bustled the children through, doing a rapid head-count. 'Denny, where's Denny?'

'Here!'

'Peg?' She felt a tug on her hand. 'Ah, there you are.'

Maureen was touching everything; she especially liked the display of 'Typewriting Through the Ages'. There were plenty of things that Clara would have loved to linger over that she couldn't, with the children there, and she wished guiltily for some time on her own – although she knew if she came without the children, she'd wish they were there.

In 'Achievement', a beardy man with a booming voice was explaining how an engine worked. When he'd done, he asked the children what they wanted to be when they grew up and Clara was surprised to see Denny's hand shoot up first.

'I would like to be an engineer,' Denny said in a little voice.

This was the first Clara had heard of it. The man looked pleased, and stood straighter: 'Marvellous. Then have a look at this.'

It was Frank Whittle's jet engine. Denny gasped: 'A-may-zing!'

Then the man said he could touch it, and Denny did, patting it gently. The man sought out Clara: 'What a wonderful little boy. Credit to you.'

'He *is* a good boy,' Clara replied. She couldn't say any more than that.

~

Clara had wanted to bring sandwiches, but Dr Cardew said that part of the fun was trying out the new foods on offer. He approached a stand and bought eight whole hot dogs, one for each of them. Evelyn went to help him carry them, eyes popping out of her head.

'Why is it called a hot dog?' she pondered.

'Because it's made from dog,' declared Rita, which meant Peg refused to eat it.

Anita insisted on using the stainless-steel knife and fork that she kept in her bag. Evelyn, who had always loved her food, devoured hers and Anita's and Peg's leftovers. Denny threw most of his bread at the silver-grey pigeons and then shrieked when they came close for more. All the children were afraid of getting pooped on, although Clara told them it was good luck.

Anita disagreed. 'I have never heard of that. It sounds like something superstitious people say to cheer up others' misfortunes.'

So what if it is?, Clara thought, irritated, but then she lightened up – it was hard not to here.

After lunch, they went to the funfair at Battersea Park, which was the part Maureen had been waiting for. They had timed it well, for the sun came out. The children took off their coats and made Clara carry them, which for once she didn't mind because – well, it was such a lovely day.

They took the miniature train to get their bearings past funny sculptures and models and plants. They didn't get their bearings, but it was wonderful all the same. There were men on stilts calling out greetings and women in Alpine costumes with baskets of oranges at their bosoms. Denny got caught staring at one, and everyone giggled. Clara felt so energised. It was suddenly all there in front of them – creativity, design, fun, and try as she might, she couldn't resist it! Life was not always about war, debt, austerity and struggle, there were bigger and better things out there.

The big dipper, the helter-skelter, then onto the big wheel – Dr Cardew sat next to Evelyn, Clara sat next to Maureen, Rita sat next to Peg, and Denny stayed back with Anita and Howard feeding the birds. And Clara thought how she would tell Donald Button all about it, and how could she ever thank him?

Clara had been nervous that one of the children would feel sick – didn't they always? – but the worst that happened was that they had to keep popping to the lavs. One time, Rita came out beaming: 'Soft toilet paper!' she said. They'd never had it before. 'Unbelievable!'

Then she showed Clara her satchel: she had grabbed a pile to bring home.

It had been an amazing day and the children were tired out. And slowly, as the darkness came down like a curtain, little twinkly illuminations came on and people were beginning to dance, hundreds of couples dancing, out there, in the open air by the river. Shafts of light and balls of electricity, showing the way, and Clara thought of the contrast to those years when everything was blackout and you'd be arrested for a sneaky cigarette because of its shiny tip, when the cars crawled down dark streets, and how even in your own home you had to creep around with no lights on like a criminal.

Here there was light again. Lightness. And dancing. She felt her breath catch in her throat. *Michael would have loved to see this London.* He got the dog-eared, war version, not the one he'd dreamed about – but he'd still loved it.

For a moment, she wished she were like that girl over there with the new permanent wave and the skirt; she looked so young and free, without responsibility. If she had a normal job, a nine-to-five job, she would just be coming over right now, she would be among that gaggle of girls in their sweaters and heels, pretending not to be eyeing up the gang of wet-lipped boys over there.

And if Ivor were there...

No, not Ivor. He wasn't the one she should be thinking about.

Rita grabbed her hand: 'Can we stay, Miss Newton?'

'Not today – we've got a train to catch.'

And they all trotted back to the bridge, and over and up to Charing Cross station. Dr Cardew insisted on stopping to try out candyfloss on the way. The children were in heaven, even Denny, burying their faces into puffs of pink sugar-clouds, and that had to be worth a thousand dances.

35

'We've got a new girl for you,' Miss Cooper said on the telephone.

'Oh.' Clara paused. Somehow it always gave her a shock, this passing around of people. It shouldn't – this was her job – but it did.

'I have the files!' Miss Cooper said brightly.

I should think so too, Clara thought, but she didn't say it.

Miss Cooper brought the files that afternoon, her sheepish expression doing nothing to detract from her stylish appearance. Two days later, she came over again with a little girl, a small frail thing with wobbly legs like a pony but with a big grin on her face – 'Gladys by name and glad by nature,' Miss Cooper said hopefully.

Gladys was a girl who got on with things – and people. She got on with her lunch (cauliflower cheese) and she got on with tidying away. She got on with all the children and when she started at Lavenham Primary with Peg and Denny, she got on with her lessons. She remembered her things, and she liked doing her lines. She was moved from pencil to fountain pen almost immediately in recognition of her neat handwriting.

This was quite the honour and the teacher, Miss Clifton, said she was polite and kind 'by any standards'.

Clara thought Gladys settled in rather too quickly, but when she mentioned that to Miss Cooper and then to Marilyn, who called from Buenos Aires, they both laughed, and Marilyn said, 'Don't *look* for trouble, Clara.'

Gladys formed an attachment to Stella too – which was not entirely mutual. Stella would run away from the onslaught of affection and Clara often heard Gladys shouting after the cat, 'I will tell Miss Newton on you, I WILL!'

'She said "I love you" to me within an hour,' Clara said to Mrs Horton.

'That's nice, isn't it?' Mrs Horton replied. 'I wish someone said I love you to me all the time.'

Doesn't Mr Horton?, thought Clara, but she said, 'I just think it's a little too much.'

Clara's other worry was the performance – or the *damn performance*, as she privately called it. There were only a couple of weeks to go now – and then it would be over, she thought, and normal life could resume. It felt like everything had been suctioned up into Anita's Festival of Britain show.

Naturally, on Gladys' second day, she had been summoned to performance headquarters – Anita's house.

'I don't know,' Clara had mused. 'What if she can't sing?'

'Everyone can sing!' Anita had said optimistically. Gladys, in fact, had a sweet, clear voice and once again, Anita had been thrilled to get her numbers up. 'The more the merrier,' she said. And then more sternly to Gladys, 'Make sure you attend all rehearsals, since you are a latecomer.'

'I love you,' Gladys had replied.

Anita had raised an eyebrow.

CHILDREN'S REPORT 13
Gladys Gluck

Date of Birth:

16 October 1944

Family Background:

Her father was an itinerant singer from France. Mother died in childbirth.

Health/Appearance:

Rickets have made her legs weak. Blue-eyed, dark-haired small girl.

Food:

Poor appetite. Gladys enjoys sweet things, especially custard and coconut ice.

Hobbies:

Unknown but seems enthusiastic to try most things. She loves Stella the cat.

Other:

Gladys is *very* affectionate.

36

One evening, they were having kidneys and peas at the table, Peg was weeping at her plate, and Maureen had suggested a food strike, but Gladys ate it all and then set down her knife and fork correctly. She liked to say grace before she ate, too. Clara told herself not to compare – the compare with an A – but sometimes she couldn't help herself; the others still left their cutlery at all angles like the broken hands of a clock.

'When are my brothers coming, Missus?' Gladys asked.

'What?'

'My brothers? Are they on their way?'

Clara was puzzled. 'I'm not expecting anyone else, Gladys.'

Gladys screwed up her face. 'We're supposed to be together. They promised.'

Clara felt her stomach drop. She skated upstairs to the safe and pulled out the files. Gladys' was one of the more thorough ones, but there was nothing, not a dicky bird, about any brothers.

She called Miss Cooper. She wanted to shout, *for goodness' sake*, but she kept her temper – losing it wouldn't help.

'Oh yes, there are two older brothers.'

Good Lord.

'It's not in the files.' Clara tried shaking them to see if there was a scrap of paper or a message she'd missed: there wasn't.

'Not everyone is as detailed as you, Clara,' Miss Cooper said, resentfully. She made the word detailed sound like *interfering busybody*.

'So, why aren't they all together?'

Miss Cooper went so silent that for a moment Clara supposed she'd hung up. Finally, she said in a low voice, 'I really don't know.'

'Well, could you find out, please?'

Clara hadn't seen Ivor for several days, which had helped her not think about him so much, but when she saw him in the post office, all her stupid feelings for him came flooding back. He was so – right for her, and it was hard to maintain her cool when he smiled like that, but she didn't do a bad job. *Mrs Harrington*, she reminded herself. *That's who he has chosen.* Clara was *ruinous*, Mrs Harrington was something else: voluptuous maybe.

And he was so friendly. So... oblivious. In the queue, he said he was working on her dress, and she told him he didn't need to. She didn't want to be in his debt, not now. He looked at her quizzically: 'It's not a bother.' They both kept their voices down, both understanding this was private business. He said he was worried Patricia was coming down with something, and she warned that chickenpox had been going round again. His face fell and she reassured him, 'It's fine, they all get it at some stage...'

They had reached the front of the line. The postmistress said, 'My nephew had it really badly, his whole face was scabbed up, left him disfigured for life,' which Clara thought was unhelpful.

'Damn, I can't afford for her to be ill, not now,' Ivor said as he paid for his stamps.

'There's never a good time though, is there?' Clara said. And then she remembered. 'Anyway, Mrs Harrington can look after her, can't she?' She knew that wasn't particularly helpful either but he did push her to it.

Ivor's expression was a complete blank. Once again, Clara had a vision of Mrs Harrington cycling away, without stockings, and her blouse open to her brassière. It made her feel quite nauseated and she didn't say goodbye.

Later that evening, Rita went over to Ivor's workshop with a torn pocket on her school summer dress. When she came back, all fixed and ironed, she said Patricia was covered in scabs.

'Does he want me to help?'

'He didn't say.'

The temptation to dash over there and sort everything out was powerful but Clara resisted. Ivor did not want that – he had other people/another person for that. Still, she sent Rita back with oats in a sock and a thermometer just in case – she would not lose the moral high ground.

37

Only a few more rehearsals and then they would be singing at the Royal Festival Hall! On the night they'd be performing, the Mayor of London, the American Ambassador and Princess Margaret would be in the audience! This was incredible. Despite the rumours, Margaret was still Clara's favourite royal, and she wouldn't hear a word against her. Clara imagined curt-seying in front of her and the Princess saying, 'The Michael Adams Children's Home – how extraordinary!' And then she would say something fantastically complimentary to Clara like 'I don't know how you do it,' which was always a favourite, and Clara would bat it away humbly, as she should, and say – what *would* she say? – 'It's a privilege, ma'am.' Was it ma-am to rhyme with harm or ma'am to rhyme with spam?, she wondered.

Clara did not practise her curtsey, that would be too much, but she got the children to. Rita's legs creaked when she did hers, Gladys loved it, Peg's was a thing of beauty, and Denny did a bow. His hair flopped down and he laughed. He laughed so much more recently. Maureen refused to play along, naturally.

The children were rehearsing most nights now. Gladys had dutifully memorised her part and Anita claimed her arrival was serendipity.

'I still miss Clifford though,' she said sadly.

Clara agreed she missed him too. But she didn't miss the worry or the sudden bursts of fear either. Anita didn't know the extent of Cliff's misbehaviour. Perhaps Clara had been wrong to hide it from her.

'We need to start thinking about sending Rita to a special school soon,' Anita went on. 'There's a wonderful facility in Hampshire.'

'Hampshire?' Clara laughed. 'How could she go to Hampshire every day? It's miles away. Oh...' she said.

'She could board.' Anita's fingers had flown to her collarbone. She looked as surprised as Clara. 'Rita is an exceptional pianist – she needs expert support, you must have realised this—'

'I know that!' Clara snapped. But there were no special schools nearby and the thought of Rita going to boarding school, even if it were for talented musicians, had genuinely not occurred to her. Now she thought about it. *Okay, maybe Rita could go away but not yet.* She was only eleven. Maybe when she was fifteen? Or thirteen then? For some reason, not many adopters seemed interested in coming to see Rita, and any who visited seemed to be intimidated by her talent and her commitment, and if that didn't put them off then her crying out for Mama did.

Ever since last year's near miss with the Australian homes, Clara had taken it for granted that Rita would be with her for the long term. Anita seemed about to say something else, then stopped herself.

'How are the others doing?' Clara asked, keen to change the subject.

'What Denny doesn't have in voice, he makes up for in

looks,' Anita said. 'He's coming along a treat. Peg is wonderful on the drums, Maureen is so adult nowadays... And Gladys has slotted in so well, it's like she was always with us.'

'And Evelyn?'

Anita's face softened. 'Evelyn and Howard are the two lights of my life. I wonder how I ever lived without them.'

~

In the news, British spies were defecting to the USSR and everyone was absolutely shocked. Putting out buckets of flowers in front of the shop, Mrs Garrard called Clara over to discuss it with her.

'That Guy Burgess,' she said, tweaking her roses. 'What a traitor!'

It shows how little you know someone, they said. Well, they didn't say it exactly like that, but it was what Clara thought. You could *think* you knew someone but then find out they had a lot more going on than you'd ever known. It was like being at a performance, you weren't party to all that was happening back-stage. There was a beauty in that sometimes: except when what was going on backstage was giving secrets to the Russian government.

While they were standing, chatting, Mr Garrard came out and gave Clara and Gladys a bunch of daffodils each.

'I love you!' Gladys squealed at him.

'Gladys,' scolded Clara. She had explained several times to the girl that such expressions were too much and too soon.

Gladys stuck out her lower lip. 'I adore you!' she shouted, eyeing Clara doubtfully. 'Is that better?'

~

For their next date, Donald Button wanted to meet Clara at a hotel. When she hesitated, he gave that smooth laugh, as though resistance was futile. They were speaking on the telephone, and there were obviously other people in the room with him; he kept breaking off from her to chat to them.

'Clara, it's a fine establishment.' He chortled. 'One minute – a whisky chaser. No, not you, Clara. Anyway, why not? You've nothing to be afraid of.'

Still she hesitated and still, she felt his impatience.

'Did you enjoy the Festival of Britain then? All those tickets... And you got there all right?'

'We did...' Clara curled the telephone wire around her finger. 'Okay, fine.'

One of the bars in the hotel had been blown up during the war, but the one Donald Button took Clara to the next evening, on the second floor, was the very best – 'The Krauts didn't manage to destroy this one!' he explained triumphantly, as though he personally were involved in its defence.

'Good,' Clara said, but he seemed to expect more so she added effusively, 'Excellent!'

He was more delighted with the way she looked. This time, she'd gone for Anita's 'vogue' outfit, and lots of Anita's make-up. She looked as glamorous as she ever had, she supposed, half hoping that Ivor would see her making her way up to the station and it would cause him to come to his senses. But her hopes were in vain – Ivor hadn't seen her and he certainly hadn't bowled over to declare his undying devotion. She told herself he was probably wrapped up with both his baby and his babysitter, although the thought occurred to her that she hadn't seen Mrs Harrington marching self-righteously up the high road lately. Maybe Leslie with an E had chickenpox now?

. . .

Donald Button asked her, 'What's new?' And it was awkward like he was saying, *regale me!* He had lots of exciting tales, and hers seemed paltry by comparison.

She told him about their wonderful day out at the Festival of Britain, '*thanks to you!*' but his attention wandered; he looked over her shoulder for friends or drinks. *He doesn't really care*, thought Clara. And it was silly to be surprised by this, but she was. The tickets and spending money were so generous and he came across as so sincere on the telephone and when he was in the spotlight, yet once the microphones and the audience was taken away, he didn't seem interested in the Home at all.

'I am glad to be of service,' he said finally. His fingers made a church steeple. 'I don't expect many people help these kinds of children – I'm quite exceptional in that way.'

Quite a few people did help them, actually. She thought of teachers, the doctors, and the childcare officers. And it wasn't only people whose job it was. There was Sir Alfred Munnings, the reclusive painter, who still paid for and provided transport for the children to go once a month to the cinema, a small thing that brightened their lives; she thought of Farmer Buckle, who let them into the fruit-picking fields early and cheaply, and even the Garrards, who made a point of letting the children stroke Bertie nowadays. On the whole, people were kind. Sometimes it took a while to get to know them – like Julian – and some you fell into straight away, like Mrs Horton. Mr Dowsett, who let them off their library fines, Anita and Dr Cardew, who had more than opened their house... And all the adoptive parents – like Victor or the Sweetinghams, so keen to provide a place of refuge for *these kinds of children*.

She would have told him all this only he was talking about his illustrious career (his words) and especially his co-stars, and especially, especially, the 'ladies': 'Melanie Goodyear,' he snorted, 'that was a very good year. Nancy Tomlin – a lush, absolutely.'

'Pardon?' Clara thought of lush green fields.

He put his hand to his nose and twisted: 'Sozzled. Perpetually. Bet you didn't know that?'

Clara didn't know that, nor did she particularly want to know that. Still... This was better than mooching around at home waiting for Ivor's lights to go on or off. Or was it? She wasn't sure. Donald Button – she could never think of him by only his first name – ordered her another drink, insisted she have gin too. *She* was all right to ply with alcohol, presumably, unlike Nancy Tomlin.

'Mary Campbell? You know she went away for a bit. But do you know why?'

His face was getting progressively redder and damper.

'No, why?'

'Babies – twins.'

'Remarkable,' she said. Actually, it was like talking to Mrs Garrard or the postmistress, only the people they talked about were less famous.

There were photographers in the building, but outside the bar, by the elevators, and when she and Donald Button came out, they swarmed forwards like in a circle dance, calling, 'Look this way,' and shouting, 'What's your name, love?' to her.

Clara felt herself blinded by the lights, dazzled by the noise, but it was evident that Donald Button enjoyed it. She tried to hold herself nicely, to be neither sexy nor homely. At boarding school, they used to balance books on their head – 'What is a lady without good posture?' – and she used to be one of the better ones at it.

He held on tightly to her hand, so she didn't feel physically threatened as such, but it was a weird intimidating feeling, an experience she'd never had nor imagined before. Donald Button became lively and engaged again until someone shouted, 'Is that your daughter?' and then he yelled back, in a jolly tone, 'Blooming cheek!' He clutched Clara to him and gave her a big kiss on her mouth and because he grabbed her cheek/chin, she couldn't get away. The flashes flashed.

'Donald!' she whimpered, blinking fast, but he seemed to take it to mean that she liked it.

She realised with a sudden horror that they were going up, not down, up, in the elevator, to where his room was.

'Top floor,' he said.

'I think I'd better—'

'Drinky-poo. It's a whole suite, darling.'

'Just for a...'

The lift doors opened. Clara felt she shouldn't be here; it was a mistake. He was telling the truth though, it wasn't merely a bedroom, it was a whole living space. Clara had never seen anything like this, except perhaps in photos in *Good House-keeping*. It seemed vast, far too big for just him, far too big for the two of them even. From the window she could see the Tower of London and Tower Bridge.

'Drinky-poo,' he said again.

Clara decided she had had enough. She had better stay sober. Somehow, this situation was spiralling.

'I haven't met a woman who isn't an aspiring actress.'

This seemed a strange thing to say. Clara murmured a non-committal response as he poured whisky into glasses, stirred in ice. He had *everything* here.

'That's what interests me about you, Clara: you are not like the other girls.'

Clara pondered this. He was right, she thought. She was not like anyone else. But that was because nobody was like anybody else. Mrs Horton was not like Judy was not like Miss Cooper was not like Maureen was not like Mrs Garrard was not like Anita was not like Mrs McCarthy...

He handed her a glass and gazed at her: 'You're not ambitious?'

She remembered a *Woman's Own* quiz. Her ambition was A. a happy home life. That *was* ambition, she supposed. Just not the same as his or the women he seemed to know.

'I... no, not in that way.'

'No urge to perform, no urge for a better salary?'

'Not particularly.' She did need money – for the children's shoes, for the notepads and colouring pencils, for all the extras, but for herself? No.

'Some women want to bleed me dry. Take, take, take... Not you.'

She could see, through the open door, the bed. And then there were some doors, to a bathroom presumably, and somewhere else.

'I'd better—'

He raised his finger commandingly: 'ONE drink.'

She had to now. They admired the skyline. She said just about everything she knew about the Tower of London. She remembered Alex telling her, 'When the ravens leave the Tower, the Crown will fall and Britain with it.' All she could think was that she would like to leave. Like a raven. Step off the ledge, unleash her wings, never look back.

He talked about the good old days. He put his hand on the small of her back but he had done that before, she could put up with that. She couldn't believe she had got herself into this predicament. She was the one who was supposed to be aware of things like this. She was the one who worried about other people falling into these traps – she wasn't the person to be worried about.

'Wool?' He pressed his hand harder.

'It's actually my friend's.' Clara did not know why she felt compelled to say that.

'Why don't you take off your shoes?' he said, and his voice was husky. 'Relax...'

She was weighing up her options. She was lonely, it was true. Sometimes this need to be close to someone – physically close – was as acute as hunger. And just how sometimes you can see when someone is hungry, she wondered if people could see it on her, if they could see that here was a woman who was aching to be touched. The thought made her ashamed. The desire made her embarrassed. Perhaps she gave off a scent of neediness that men like Donald Button could detect? She suddenly remembered the band member's face at Mrs Horton's wedding – he seemed to understand that – but there was also the disapproving lead singer. *Harry, was it?* It was so easy to slip from men's good books into their bad.

And if she let this go further, she would be closing the door on Ivor. But blooming Nora, he had closed the door on her often enough – slammed it, triple-locked it, put up a sign: *Keep out*.

And Donald Button wasn't any old suitor – he was, as Anita said, powerful. He could change the children's lives. *Remember those tickets?* That was something.

And she didn't want to annoy him. 'Leading men on' was virtually a criminal activity, although what it entailed, it seemed, could simply be existing as a young woman.

She might as well submit. Put it all down to the Festival of Britain.

What is so special about you? Her dad's voice.

And millions of other women before her.

This was Donald Button, star of stage, screen and wireless. The man with the cornflower-blue eyes. She obediently slipped off her shoes. Her stockings had bunched around the toes.

He kissed her.

38

Ivor left a message with Rita to say that Clara's dress was ready. Rita successfully delivered this message, although a couple of hours later, just as she was going to Anita's, she added, 'Oh, didn't I say? He said you should go over and take a look.'

It was a warm early-May evening, the day after Clara's date with Donald Button, three rehearsals away from the dress rehearsal in London. Gladys had had a headache that morning and Clara had to run up to school to fetch her, nervous in case it was chickenpox, but back at home, she had quickly recovered: 'I love you more than all the headaches in the world,' she'd said.

'Thank you, Gladys – I think,' Clara had replied.

There was a sound of grasshoppers and a backdrop of blossom. The children – including the recovered Gladys – were at Anita's, so Clara *was* free to go over and take a look...

When she arrived at the workshop, Ivor barely looked up, just handed her the dress, told her to put it on behind a velvet curtain.

She went in, wishing she was wearing better underwear. At least she had on a pretty slip, part of a bundle of five she had got at the market. She could hardly stand looking in the full-length mirror – she didn't have one in the Home, a good thing – was that really what her bottom looked like? The dress was very fitted. She was wearing Maureen's shoes – old ones that were too small for the girl – and they didn't look good. The dress warranted heels, needed them, she decided, but didn't everything? She stood on tiptoes, smoothing down the skirt and then examining the hem. The tiny even stitches were so beautiful, they almost made her emotional. It was a work of art and it did, it really did make her feel special.

When she came out, he didn't comment – that wasn't Ivor's way – but simply asked her to stand on a wooden stool. She asked if she had to. He sighed. Of course she didn't *have to*, but it would help with the fit – he thought it might be just a touch too long. She stepped up on the stool, but it wobbled and so she put some folded paper underneath and fixed it. She liked this feeling of fixing things for him, even without him noticing, especially without him noticing, for he was so defensive that fixing things was like an insult to him. She thought it was a good reminder that they would never work as a couple – how could a relationship work between someone who hated to be helped and someone who had such a compulsion for interfering?

Up she went.

'Like it?'

Well, she could be as cool as he was. 'Of course, I'd usually wear it with heels,' she said. 'It's much more colourful than I'm used to as well.'

'I think two centimetres shorter and it will be perfect.'

His hands brushed her legs. He apologised; he was concentrating hard. Clara felt she had lost the power of speech.

'Thank you,' she said faintly.

Finally, he looked up. He had safety pins in his mouth. *God, she loved that stupid face.*

∾

The date with Donald Button had not ended well. As soon as they kissed, Clara felt with utmost clarity, like a searchlight being shone into her eyes, that she did not want this. No matter how much she craved affection, this wasn't it. *His* affection wasn't it. Yet, just as she had come to this realisation, Donald Button had made a second lunge at her, as though he was playing squash, and worse, he had tried to move her face to the side with his hands.

'Cara, don't be coy,' he'd said.

'There's been a misunderstanding,' she'd said. It was like popping a balloon.

He had raised his hands. 'No misunderstanding here, just come lie down with me.' He'd half-pulled, half-led her to the bed, grabbed her hand and put it to his crotch. 'Unbutton me,' he had said. 'That's all.'

Oh God.

Still a part of her wondered if she mightn't let him get on with it – just for a quiet life? She really did not want to create a scene and she sensed that Donald Button was a man who liked scenes, who manipulated scenes, and who was not afraid of a dramatic denouement. The other part of her did not. The other part said, *no, this was not right*. The other part of her knew she was going to have to upset him.

'I need the bathroom,' she had whispered. He'd looked annoyed, and then like he didn't want her to see him looking annoyed, changed his expression to one of bemusement.

'Didn't you just go?'

'I need to fix something.' She had winked, even though her heart was pounding. She walked as calmly as she could to the door, but before she got there he called out, 'It's that way.'

She could do this. 'My bag...' she said, pointing back out to the living room. The clincher was 'I'll be right back.' Gently, she had closed the door behind her. And then she had run, run for dear life. Without her shoes. Which was why she'd been wearing a pair of Maureen's old ones all day.

'So, what happened with Mrs Harrington in the end?' Clara asked Ivor.

There was no point not being direct.

'What do you mean "what happened"?' he retorted wearily, as if he were asked that question a lot.

'I mean, one minute she's Flavour of the Month, the next, I've not seen her for a while.'

Ivor rearranged his needles. 'She was never "Flavour of the Month", Clara.'

She'd known that phrase would annoy him – it was why she'd used it.

'All right, one minute she's always here, the next she's disappeared off the face of the earth – better?'

He gave her a look that said she wasn't funny: 'All right, there was a misunderstanding.'

A spark lit inside Clara. *Don't get too excited*, she told herself. *It's probably nothing.*

'A misunderstanding?' she said, trying to sound playful.

'Yes.'

He was still working on the hem of her dress. At her back. Clara shivered. *A misunderstanding? How brilliant was that?* She closed her eyes, hoping her nerves didn't show, hoping her legs didn't look too dumpy or plain. They weren't her best feature but they weren't her worst either. 'How do you mean?' she said as though it was no big deal. (It was an enormous deal.)

Ivor was concentrating on the dress. Absently, he spoke, 'I think she's a bit... unhappy in her marriage.'

'With the ration inspector?'

'Yeah... there, done!' he said suddenly, smiling up at her. 'You shall be the belle of the ball.'

'There is no ball,' Clara said, still trying to understand what Ivor was saying. He snapped his sewing kit shut suddenly and stood up, still smiling.

'Then there should be.' He held out his arm to help her down, but she didn't take it, didn't need it. Back on solid ground, she was still curious about Mrs Harrington.

'I think her husband is in trouble with work and she was looking for an escape. I think she thought we were going somewhere I was not prepared to go.'

Must. Not. Smile.

'So, nothing happened between you?'

'Of course nothing happened between us. I told you I'm not — and anyway, she's married, Clara. I wouldn't.'

And then, like a clockwork soldier, little Patricia woke up with an almighty roar.

'There she goes,' he said affectionately, 'my master wanting her feed.'

Clara couldn't help grinning as she got changed, then ran back to the Home with the dress over her arm.

Ivor. Ivor liked her. She knew he did.

When Maureen got home from rehearsal, she said that there was going to be a bikini pageant at the Festival of Britain.

'What is a bikini?' asked Clara uncertainly and Maureen, who liked any opportunity to make Clara feel unworldly, roared with laughter.

'You don't know? It's a swimsuit with no middle.'

'A contest for bikinis?' *A sewing contest? Ivor could enter,* she thought, although the thought of him taking on more work was not a happy one.

'*Girls* in bikinis.'

Clara paused before asking, 'Is that a good idea?'

'It's what they're doing.' Maureen made a disapproving expression. 'I'll stick to the singing, thanks!'

'Good.' Clara reached out. 'You know, Maureen, you've also got to think about what you do next.'

Maureen was finishing school that summer and she was unlikely to get good grades. In fact, the teachers seemed to think she was failing most of her classes. Sewing might be one answer; baking might be another.

Maureen said she was thinking about it.

The worry about Maureen and what she was going to do in the future had never gone away. Of course, Clara would try to help her, but once Maureen was sixteen she wouldn't be under the council *or* Clara's remit. Of course, at that age, she was far too young really to be released into the world, but that was the law and the council's policy. And that would be another thing Clara would like to see changed.

Clara remembered Alex once telling her that human babies were the most dependent of mammals and she had laughed and said human teenagers were worse.

A few days later, Clara saw that a bakery and cafe in nearby Dedham was looking for staff. It wouldn't be ideal – early starts – but it was a nice place, with gold-leaf swirly writing outside, pretty booths and warm lighting inside. Clara had been in there once with Julian. She imagined bringing the children in occasionally – *Let's see where Maureen works*. Peg would love its parquet floor and Rita would be pleased there was a piano, although Clara had never seen anyone play it.

After school, Clara told Maureen about the cafe. She exaggerated its promise somewhat, but still Maureen wobbled on her feet and said, 'Ah yes, about that...'

'What?'

'I should have told you before but I've got myself a place at secretarial college,' she said.

Clara looked at her. Maureen's cheeks were flushed with a mixture of excitement, nerves and pride. She pulled out a chair and looked up at Clara.

'Aren't you going to say anything?'

'Wow,' said Clara, 'this is unexpected.'

Maureen explained that she had gone to the interview last week. Yes, she had skipped school, sorry. Yes, she had borrowed Clara's coat too – the grey woollen one she wore for best, just to make a good impression. But she had put it back and Clara never found out, did she? She said they asked her questions about her intentions and her qualities, and she told them some of the answers she had picked up from the quizzes in *Good Housekeeping*. She said she was punctual (questionable), reliable (questionable), and sincere (true). She talked about working for a prestigious law firm: Robinson, Browne and White. Her voice faltered here, perhaps at a memory of that time.

And Clara felt a sense of shame. *She* should have been the one to take Maureen to the interview, she should have lent her lipstick, stood outside the office, taken her for a currant bun when she came out. When had she not been encouraging?

But she supposed Maureen didn't want that.

'And they wrote to me yesterday,' she said, and Clara faintly recalled Maureen squirrelling away a white envelope. 'They want me to start next month.' Clara wanted to help. Wasn't that what she was for? She wondered why Maureen didn't confide in her; did she go about things the wrong way, or was it Maureen's nature to want to do it all by herself?

'Is it... free?'

'No.'

'Then how will you be able to afford it, Maureen?'

Was it something to do with her father?

Maureen winced, stared at her nails, which Clara saw were painted in the exact same shade as her own (which meant Maureen had also borrowed her nail varnish without asking).

'Sir Alfred is going to pay.'

'Sir Alfred Munnings?'

'After the trip to the cinema, he asked me what I hoped to do, and he said whatever I decided, he would support me financially for one year.'

'Oh, Maureen, this is amazing news. What an achievement.' Clara finally managed to say the right thing. 'We are definitely going to have a special dinner tonight.'

'Thank you,' said Maureen politely. She gathered her bag and went upstairs.

Later, Clara had to pop up the road and as she put her best coat on, the grey woollen one, she felt inside her pocket and there was a scrap of paper. She pulled it out and there was her own writing, writing she'd done one year ago to help Maureen with her alphabet, for her filing: *LMNOP*. Smiling, she put it back in her pocket.

∼

THE GAZETTE

Can You Hear Those Wedding Bells Star steps out with Mystery Lady.

Donald Button, star of stage, screen and wireless, who is hosting the Festival of Britain celebrations with Petula Clark, was caught in a clinch last week with a new lady-friend. The dashing blue-eyed personality has enjoyed a string of steamy romances with actresses such as Nancy Tomlin, Millie

Faraway and Annabelle Thompson, with whom he recently starred in Can You Hear Those Wedding Bells? *but he seemed very fond of this Mystery Lady.*

The bachelor, who has been married twice, has previously said that he would not rule out a lady in show business, but his ideal would be a homely young woman looking to settle down.

It is understood that the charming couple may have met at the Festival of Britain celebrations. Looks like Donald Button might have something else to celebrate soon.

Clara stared at the newspaper, dumbfounded.

A photograph of Donald Button and her – the mystery lady – on the very front page.

Of course, the photograph had captured the moment where he had knocked into her, so it looked like they were joined at the hip, couldn't put a penny between them. And he looked devastatingly tall and debonair while besides him, she looked like a tiny, scared wraith wearing too much lipstick.

She peered at the photograph again. (That was definitely not his own hair.) *Good grief.* It said underneath in small print: *Donald Button reveals his romantic side as he courts complete unknown.*

Clara angrily stuffed the newspaper in the bin and then looked out of the window at the workshop. If the paperboy had delivered Ivor his papers they might still be outside; she could take them, tell him something had happened to them.

There was nothing there yet. Ivor liked those workers' newspapers that were always on at the government to nationalise everything. He wouldn't read the gossip columns – gossip was prying, probably, in his mind – but this was the *Gazette*. The *Gazette* was supposed to offer a bit of everything.

No one mentioned it when she walked the children up to school. When she got home, the telephone rang. Her relief that it was only the twins, Billy or Barry, quickly turned to something else when one of them said, 'How is the Mystery Lady then?'

Clara tried to laugh it off: 'You know it's nonsense?'

'Didn't look like nonsense to me.' She recognised Barry, speaking in a mock-serious tone.

'What about Ivor?' That was definitely Billy. 'Don't you love him no more?'

'I...'

After that, Clara tried to call Peter, but there was no reply. She could just imagine the fun they'd be having in the office with this.

Clara panicked. She found herself hurrying up the road to Anita's.

'And Ivor will see the—' Clara would not swear '...newspaper and think I'm in a relationship with Donald Button!'

Anita was still looking startled at the early visit. Howard, in a bonnet, offered Clara his bottle.

'No, thank you, Howie. Oh, Anita, what shall I do?'

'Does it matter? I thought you and Ivor were just friends now.'

'We *are* just friends.' Clara's indignation faded slightly. 'But of course it matters – I don't want him to have the wrong idea about me.'

'I thought you said he loved the other woman.'

'I didn't say love,' Clara insisted, her face aflame. Why had she ever told Anita? She had told her after she had told Mrs Horton, hoping for a better reaction.

'You said, "having a dalliance", I remember this because I had to look it up.'

'Yes. Well...' Clara sat down, suddenly exhausted. 'What am I going to do?'

'Tell him how you feel.'

'He doesn't want to know – he definitely doesn't want me to help him.'

'Then don't *help* him,' Anita said with that glint in her eye she usually had when she was talking about the Festival, *'seduce* him.'

Clara's head was down. 'I don't know how to anymore.'

'Oh, Clara, you have lost confidence, with all the men? – Donald Button, Michael, Ivor, Julian... who am I forgetting?'

'Victor,' Clara said through gritted teeth.

'It's no surprise, so many disasters.'

'Not *that* many: anyway, this is over a number of years!'

'But still...'

Anita went into the surgery waiting room for the newspapers they laid out for the patients. When she came back, Clara gazed up at her hopefully. Perhaps she had seen a first edition of the *Gazette* and it might have subsequently changed. Maybe all the others recognised the photograph as the non-story it was.

Anita laid the newspapers across the rug. She seemed to be enjoying herself.

'You're in every single one of them,' she declared.

Clara swallowed. This wasn't a disaster, it was a catastrophe. But Anita was smiling.

'You needn't worry about this – I will sort this.' She patted the nearest newspaper. Clara glared at the photograph in the *Gazette* again. It looked utterly unambiguous – it looked like it was a done deal: Donald Button and Mystery Lady were lovers.

'What – how?'

'I have my ways,' Anita said, 'trust me.' Howard thumped

onto his bottom and began to cry. 'But you have to do the rest, eh?' she told Clara before picking up Howard.

40

Marilyn had sent a jigsaw puzzle at Christmas – of the Statue of Liberty – and Clara wanted the children to complete it so she could write in good faith and say they had done so. She sent them all into the parlour to get going with it.

There was something quiet and comfortable about doing the puzzle – although not the way Rita did it perhaps – Rita liked to force pieces in the wrong places – and it was a good way to decompress after the intensity of a day at school and the rehearsals. Gladys said she loved it but then Gladys was not the most discerning child.

The Royal Festival programme included their event on the twenty-ninth of May. It was a bright and shiny booklet full of laughing people and colour. There was also a photo of the Children of Shilling Grange Orphanage.

Clara was sending the programme to Marilyn, as promised, with a long letter of explanation and apology. What was the worst that could happen? That Marilyn would explode in fury at her son's name being missing, come over and take back control of the Home? Unlikely, but you never knew. *Hell hath no fury*, Clara remembered as she posted the envelope to the United States, half hoping that it didn't get there.

~

Clara was walking along the high road with Maureen when they saw Joe and his new wife, Janet.

He looked fine, Clara was pleased to see, happy; but then when he saw Maureen, his expression turned anguished.

Maureen held her own. They exchanged hellos and good afternoons and then walked off. Clara and Maureen gazed after them both: the girl, who was at that stage in pregnancy when she had to go slowly and waddle slightly, and Joe, who didn't look back.

'I was all right, wasn't I?' Maureen asked breathlessly. 'I didn't sound stupid?'

'Yes, love, you were more than all right.'

Maureen let Clara thread her arm through hers as they returned to the Home.

~

The Sweetinghams had news. Clara spoke to them on the telephone, Denny standing next to her nervously, fiddling with his watch.

'The council said yes?!' Clara repeated. 'Oh, I am so pleased.' She squeezed the little boy on the shoulder. 'It's a yes, Denny!'

Denny was jumping up and down and punching the air.

'We can come and collect him tomorrow!' Mrs Sweetingham said. 'I can hardly believe it.'

'Tomorrow?' Clara asked.

At this, Denny shook his head so hard that Clara was afraid

he'd do himself an injury. He tugged her sleeve: 'The show, please, we're really good now!'

Clara stroked his hair and made soothing noises. Back into the receiver, she said, 'I don't know if you are aware but Denny still has the performance in London.'

'Oh, I thought he didn't like it?' Mrs Sweetingham said.

'He didn't,' Clara admitted. 'But he seems to have changed his mind.'

Denny was now nodding his head rapidly. 'Could he perhaps stay until the thirtieth of May?' That was still only ten days – three rehearsals, one dress rehearsal and one performance – away.

If Mrs Sweetingham was disappointed, she soon picked herself up: 'Well, we've waited so long, I'm sure a couple of weeks won't make any difference. If that's what he wants...'

'It seems he does,' Clara said, feeling quite amazed about it too.

She replaced the receiver and told the agitated child, 'It's fine, Denny...!'

He ran whopping around the room: 'Yee haw!'

It was eight o'clock the same evening, but it was still light. The sky was made up of wonderful pink and red streaks, and Dr Cardew was leaning against the front door of the Home.

'Shepherd's delight!' said Clara enthusiastically.

'Wha-at? Ah, yes,' he said, 'sorry to bother you, Clara.'

He was wearing steel-framed glasses. Clara had never seen him wearing glasses before; they suited him, she thought. Of course, Anita would never let her husband wear glasses that made him anything less than handsome.

'Could you, would you come up to the hospital with me – it's Howard, he's sick.'

Baby Howard was?

'I'll call Sister Grace.'

Clara knew Howard had contracted chickenpox – Anita had telephoned her the evening of the newspaper debacle, blaming the nanny – but she'd had no idea his condition had worsened.

Thank goodness for Sister Grace. She said she would be there in twenty minutes. Maureen was home too, and offered to watch the younger ones so Clara didn't have to wait.

In the car, Dr Cardew explained that Howard had been in hospital for the last two days: 'Anita needs to rest,' he said, 'could you persuade her to go home?'

'I had no idea,' repeated Clara. She had been so busy, it felt like she had forgotten the outside world.

They found Anita in an empty corridor just outside the children's ward. It wasn't cold but she was shivering. The air felt cloyingly antiseptic and Clara could almost taste it. Dr Cardew put his arm round his wife.

'I don't know what to do,' she kept saying.

'Shhh,' he whispered into her hair, and held her so lovingly that for a moment, Clara found herself wondering – if anything awful happened to one of her children, who would whisper into her hair?

'We'll see him together and then Clara is going to take you home in a taxi. I'm staying here tonight. You need some rest, you can't look after anyone unless you look after yourself.'

∼

Evelyn opened the Cardews' front door. Anita kissed her on the forehead, but absent-mindedly, like she wasn't there. Evelyn looked mournfully after her like a kicked dog – the poor girl.

Clara told Evelyn she'd see to Anita first and then take care of her: she felt Anita needed adult company right now.

Clara made scrambled eggs and toast. She felt like a terrible cook compared to Anita, but the other woman docilely ate what was set in front of her.

Then Clara went and ran a bath: she couldn't help admiring the shiny bathroom fittings and the white enamel bathtub and the water that ran hot almost the instant you twisted the neat silver tap.

Anita was nearly falling asleep into her plate but when Clara came back into the room, she jolted back into life.

'We should never have had him, Clara,' she said. She placed her knife and fork down just so and it seemed she was saying dinner, the conversation, everything was over.

'Wha— no, don't say that.' Clara knelt on the tiled floor by Anita's chair and took her friend's hand. Anita's rings scraped against her fingers. There was a wealth of jewels there: rubies, diamonds and emeralds. But they made no difference to what Anita was going through. 'It's going to be okay,' Clara told her.

'We're being punished,' Anita continued. She wasn't talking to Clara but to herself, or someone unseen in the room perhaps. 'We should have been happy as we were. We *were* happy as we were, we went and spoiled it. Why did we ask for so much?'

'You're not being punished,' said Clara, still on her knees. God knows she had thought that enough times when her Michael had died – but it wasn't fact; it was the brain playing tricks, it was the brain searching for reasons and explanations. And karma – or getting *just deserts* – was sometimes easier to take than the idea that awful things happen randomly and arbitrarily. That sometimes good people get hurt and bad people don't. That's the way it is. Her children, the children of Shilling Grange, had all been hurt – and did they deserve it? No, never.

'My sisters died on the death march from the camp,' Anita

said softly. 'While I survived. How did I ever think I could live a good life after that? How dared I think I deserved happiness?'

It was too late for the bath, Clara decided. She led Anita upstairs, guessed which bedroom it was.

'You deserve a good life, and you deserve happiness,' Clara whispered solidly. She would never not think that.

Anita lay down on the bed, on top of the covers, without undressing, and fell asleep immediately.

And now for poor Evelyn. She was playing patience on her own and chewing her fingernails. She was just a dot in the large living room, tucked next to, almost under, the grand piano. Clara called her into the kitchen, where she devoured her scrambled eggs and some bread, and then some left-over flap-jacks Clara found. Food would always be her comfort. Tears welled up in her eyes.

'My mother would have known what to do.'

'You did everything right, Evelyn.'

Clara held her. Evelyn was now as big as her and probably twice as strong, but she was still only twelve years old, and she nestled into Clara's arms.

'I love Howard,' she said. 'I love having a baby brother. He likes me feeding him best. He always comes to me—' She was too choked up to continue.

'You delivered him, too, remember?' Clara said into her hair. In the kitchen at the Home since Howard had been in an awfully big hurry to see the world.

'I did.' Evelyn snuggled closer and Clara closed her eyes. She could have fallen asleep here, like this. After a few moments though, Evelyn lit up suddenly: 'If you have a baby, can I deliver it?'

'If I was to have a baby, yes – but that's not happening.'

Clara laughed. *Why were children so upfront about these things yet adults were not?*

'Not Ivor's baby?' she asked, and Clara felt her face burn.

'*Especially* not Ivor's,' she said, trying to sound flippant.

'Don't you love him?' Evelyn was full of questions.

'I do,' said Clara before she realised what she was saying. Horrified, she added quickly, 'but not like that.'

'How then?' said Evelyn, puzzled. And Clara thought of the complexities of romantic love and maternal love and familial love and did not know how to explain it to herself, never mind to Evelyn.

'Just as friends,' she lied.

She sent Evelyn up to her bedroom and then a few minutes later went up to tuck her in. It was a pretty and stylish room, like the rest of the house, with dark swishy curtains, a dark wooden desk, wardrobe and a dressing table and a full-length freestanding mirror. There was a toy chest with a couple of things on top of it, including Evelyn's violin – she was learning – and a recorder. On the bedside table was her knitting – she was making a hat for Howard – and the framed photograph, sun-bleached and atmospheric, Joyce had taken of Evelyn's mother last year. Miss Smith in the garden of the Home. And there was another photograph, one that Clara hadn't seen before. It must have been taken recently – in a photo studio, Clara guessed – going by its plain background and the way the subjects were positioned centrally. Evelyn was in a pretty cardigan with her hair in ribbons, holding a giggling Howard on her lap. She was beaming straight at the camera like she had just been given the best present ever.

∼

The next morning, within seconds of waking up, Clara remembered: *poor Howard.*

She would have heard if he'd turned for the worse, wouldn't she? Bad news travels fast, doesn't it? That sweet baby, with his variety of hats, his severe side-parting and his sweet toothy-pegs. *Please let him be okay. If anything happens to him, Anita will break*, she thought.

And Clara would be there for her; she would take care of her.

Just before seven, there was a knock at the door and Dr Cardew was stood there. His expression was completely different from the evening before, and right away it was obvious that things must have improved.

'He had a much better night.'

'Oh!' Overwhelmed, Clara covered her face with her hands. 'Thank God!'

'I just took Anita and Evelyn back there; I'm going home now.'

'Dr Cardew! What a relief.'

'I've been practising medicine for years...' – His voice finally cracked. He swallowed, pushed his glasses back up the bridge of his nose – 'But it's different when it's your own.'

Clara grabbed his hand between her own. 'That's natural,' she couldn't think of what else to say. 'Go and get some rest.'

It was odd for her to be giving advice to the doctor, and maybe he thought that too. He gave her a weak smile, then started walking away down the path. Even his footsteps seemed lighter, less troubled than yesterday. She saw some roses that she hadn't noticed before, nearly in bloom, by the front wall. The grass seemed to glow a more vivid green than usual.

He had a much better night.

When he was at the gate, Dr Cardew turned round.

'Anita can't do the dress rehearsal. She is awfully sorry,' he said. 'You do understand?'

'Of course,' Clara said. The concert had receded so far from her mind, it was almost out of view. And she liked it better there, in the distance, like a retreating battleship.

'But she definitely wants you to take them to London for it,' he said. 'She said, "Make sure Clara doesn't miss the dress rehearsal, it's important".'

'Oh,' said Clara, her heart sinking again. 'Okay.'

41

Their visit to the Festival had helped. Clara now knew which station they'd arrive at and how long it took. She knew where the station exit was and where the Royal Festival Hall was; which steps and slopes were the best ones to take, and where they might enter any one of those mind-boggling glass entrances on the banks of the river.

Despite it being the dress rehearsal, the children were wearing their casual clothes – Clara lived in fear of egg yolk on a dress or mud pie on a cape, so she was saving their outfits for the big day. Anita might have disapproved but she didn't have to know. Clara herself was in a shabby pre-war dress – eligible bachelors would have to lump it.

The children were in great spirits, and the truth was, even without Anita, Clifford's absence meant they *were* easier to corral. Denny was also proud to be the only boy. Anita apparently had still been making alterations to the score only days ago but even Rita approved of the changes.

'Denny's singing less,' she whispered. 'And I'm singing more.'

As they rolled up outside the Royal Festival Hall, there was a steel-drum band playing outside. A chalked board said they were 'The Trinidad All Shell Percussion Orchestra'. Evelyn's eyes lit up at the sight of them, so instead of quickly shuffling them in, Clara suggested they watch. They were early – Anita would have killed them if they were late – and this seemed a good way to kill some time.

It looked like the band were playing old dustbins, but it was wonderful music. They played 'London Is the Place for Me'. Clara was holding onto Gladys and Peg's hands. Denny was attached to Maureen and Evelyn while Rita was clutching her music. A crowd gathered around.

Without Anita and Dr Cardew to hide behind, Clara felt exposed, slightly vulnerable, but she also felt more determined. She *was* going to navigate this, by hook or by crook, for Anita's sake. So, head held high, when the band stopped, she led the children into the Royal Festival Hall, which still smelled of paint and newness, and where they were met by stewards in lanyards and name labels.

'We're the—'

'Shilling Grange orphans,' said a small woman with acne. 'I recognised you from the TV show. Congratulations.'

That *was* a good start although the children were dumbstruck, peering about them in shock.

'That's nice, isn't it?' said Clara, tapping Rita on the head. 'They are expecting us.'

'Ow!' Rita said.

The small woman looked concerned.

'She's fine,' said Clara quickly. How quickly they forgot their manners!

The Royal Festival Hall was mostly big spaces and glass and while the short lady seemed proud, all Clara could think was which of the children would walk into a door and split their lip open first. Yet when the short lady showed her the auditorium in all its glory and the people taking photos of the stage and the majestic sweep of it, and the curtains and the size and the lights, Clara changed her mind.

'It is very impressive,' she admitted. Thank God she didn't have to go on that enormous stage. Could there be anything worse?

'It's perfect,' said Rita.

Peg was writing in a flurry then she showed her notepad to Clara and Maureen. It said, 'I'm scared'.

'That's why we're rehearsing today. You can be as nervous as you like today – but not next Saturday,' Maureen said.

'Well, kind of.' Clara hadn't thought of it like that.

Even Evelyn – who until now had seemed to have copied Anita's sangfroid about 'stressful situations' said in an awestruck voice, 'This is all for us?'

Denny wasn't impressed – but that was probably because he needed the lav.

A short while after they'd arrived, as they sat waiting their turn in the large open foyer, to her surprise, Clara saw Donald Button. She knew he was working on some of the broadcasts from the Festival, but she hadn't thought he would be at the rehearsal too. But there he was, showing around a long-legged, curly-haired woman with a banner across her body. Clara thought it was the suffragette sash at first but at a second glance, she saw it said, 'Miss England'.

Donald Button either didn't see her or he ignored her, Clara wasn't sure. He and the woman found each other hilarious. How they laughed! Then she saw him put his hand on the small of the woman's back, a gesture Clara knew all too well, and steer her in the other direction – he *had* seen her.

'Is that woman really Miss England?' said Rita, noticing at the same time. 'How do you get to do that?'

'I don't know,' said Clara primly. 'And I don't care.'

'The orphans are over here!' shouted the short woman to another group of people in black uniforms and a young man jumped to attention.

'We've got ginger ale!'

'No, thank you,' Clara answered for them. They were disappearing to the lavatory enough as it was. But another lad came over with a tray and full tall glasses, and before she could say anything, the children each grabbed one. Clara decided it was time for a very quick *pep-talk*.

'Now, children, you can do this without Anita. *For* Anita.'

'Yes,' they said, like they knew this, like they'd discussed this, this was old news. Peg waved her notepaper at her: 'I'm doing it for Miss Fisher too', she read.

'That's lovely, Peg,' she told her.

The short woman was with a group of other women, all chatting animatedly and making side glances towards Clara and the children. The short woman seemed to steel herself, then peeled herself away from her colleagues.

'Did you – were you out with Donald Button last week?' she asked.

Clara lied through her teeth: 'I was not.'

The woman looked at her like she didn't believe her before she said, 'Good, because I don't know if you've heard, he is a complete octopus – hands everywhere!'

After about one hour had passed, they were told they could wait in the auditorium if they preferred.

Rita shrugged. 'Might as well.'

Now, someone was on stage, playing a grand piano. He was in an evening suit with a red bow tie (Anita would say 'gimmicky') and was playing Chopin or something. Rita stood still to listen. Clara thought it was slightly boring, although she felt ashamed at that, and when Denny said it, she gently said, 'Let's give it a chance, shall we?'

The ventriloquist Bartholomew, the one who made Peg shiver, was waiting to go on next. He came over to greet them and Nathan the dummy poked its waxy cheek with a mechanical finger: 'Can I have a kiss here, little girl?', which Clara thought was wildly inappropriate. Peg refused and Clara loudly wished him good luck, instead.

Onstage, Bartholomew and Nathan acted out some film scenes, which Maureen nodded along appreciatively to, and then he said, 'What about *Oliver!*? Everyone loves an orphan – eh, not me, can't stand them myself,' which Clara couldn't help feeling was directed at them. She tutted, not loud enough for him to hear, but loud enough that a woman near to her laughed.

And then it was the children's turn. Clara inhaled the smell of fresh furniture – it smelled like the upholstery in Ivor's workshop sometimes did. A kiss on their cheeks for luck (Peg rubbed hers off), a 'Break a leg' – 'No, don't really!' Clara had to add because Denny, in particular, was so literal and if he was told to do something, he'd quite likely try to do it.

Then they were on the stage looking like they were born to it. Peg was so content on the drums, Denny, Maureen, Evelyn and Gladys, their newest member, side by side; and Rita – the centrepiece – at the piano, rearranging her sheets of music, confident that she was the star of the show.

Clara hadn't heard Anita's new arrangement before. It began once again with a showy introduction for Rita on the piano, and then Peg joined in on the drums but it didn't go into the doo-wop bit that Clifford had done so well; instead they all were singing and all of them, even Denny, were so in tune, so melodic, tears filled Clara's eyes. She could see – no, she could just feel – it would go down well on the night. Anita, bless her, knew her stuff and the children knew how to pull at your heartstrings.

How long did it take Clara to recognise the words? Longer than it should have, she admitted afterwards.

It was Ann Taylor's poem 'My Mother'. The one Mr Dowsett had suggested that she read. Anita had set it to the most wonderful music:

> Who sat and watched my infant head,
> When sleeping in my cradle bed,
> And tears of sweet affection shed?
> My Mother.

Clara wiped away her tears. It was just so lovely – the singing, the instruments, the way they all looked. Rita was just playing a livelier piece when there was a bit of a brouhaha at the back of the hall. It was too dark and shadowy back there to see much at first, but then Clara made out that the official who had shown them in was chasing after two people. It was unexpected to see an officious-looking man like him run – don't they usually delegate? – but it was definitely him. He was going after a woman in nurse's uniform, who was charging down the centre aisle, really running, dangerously fast, and pushing a wheelchair, in which sat an older-looking woman. The older woman was plump, with long grey hair and the most extraordinary animated face, and she was shouting at the nurse, 'Go faster, don't stop!' and the official was shouting at them both: 'Stop right there!' Then, 'All right,' he yelped, changing tack, 'if you don't stop, I'll... I'll report you.'

Everyone looked up. Clara wanted to laugh; there was something about the pair of them that looked like a comedy duo. You expected to see an umbrella or a flag waving. Certainly, they were funnier than the ventriloquist or Mr and Mrs Scallywag. Rita stopped playing. Denny, Evelyn, Maureen and Gladys stopped singing. But Peg, with great timing, clattered the cymbals together and as their loud ring reverberated off the walls, she looked up, delighted with herself.

All the children were now squinting into the light, across all the people milling around.

The woman in the wheelchair and her nurse had reached the foot of the stage and were now staring up at the orphans. The official was still shouting, 'Intruders! Somebody call the police!' but with less urgency now.

Were they dangerous? Clara wondered. She didn't think it was likely.

'Mama?'

Clara wanted to grab Rita, hold her close. 'She's confused,' she would say. 'It's all too much for her... I feared it would be.'

And then Rita jumped off her piano stool and was standing up, her hand over her eyes to reduce the glare. 'It can't be!'

Then she threw her music sheets, her precious papers, up into the air.

'Rita!' called Clara. 'It's all right—'

But it was too late. Rita had thrown herself off the stage and hurled herself at the woman in the wheelchair. 'Mama, my mama, you found me!'

42

'If only she'd come a week later—'

'Clara!' Ivor exclaimed laughingly. They were drinking milky coffee in his workshop at the table by the back window. It was powdery, but Clara liked the taste. Patricia was fast asleep in her beautiful cot, both arms thrown back in surrender, her cheeks flushed. She'd had a funny phase of howling, said Ivor; he called it 'her witching hour' but he didn't seem to panic about it as much as he used to. In fact, he was looking quite sprightly – all things considered. Her chickenpox was only mild, he said, and automatically, Clara thought about poor baby Howard, who was still recovering, although he was out of hospital now, and she imagined Ivor was thinking about him too.

It was gone nine and Maureen was looking after the children at home. *What a day!* Clara couldn't get over it. She wouldn't usually leave them, but she had had to tell someone and once the exhausted children were in bed, when she saw Ivor's lights were on, she went bowling over to tell him everything that had happened. She wasn't going to wait for an invitation, she couldn't contain herself. And Ivor, who might be tetchy with her, who might be annoyed, angry, who might think she would be better off dating men who didn't care about her at all, who might think she was the hokey cokey, and with whom she had never danced, always put that behind him when it came to the children.

It *was* Rita's mother. And she had been searching for Rita for a long time. 'Years,' she said – eventually, when Rita had stopped firing questions and exclamations at her – 'it feels like centuries. Six years. Six birthdays, six Christmases, six everything you can imagine.'

This was their last-ditch attempt to find her. It was the nurse's husband who was interested in the Festival of Britain, not them. He first heard the Shilling Grange children on the wireless, then he saw the TV programme – and oddly enough, he saw a child named Rita; told his wife.

'Suffolk?' the nurse had said. 'What the heck would Rita be doing in Suffolk? She'll be in London, of course – they wouldn't put a London girl out in the sticks.'

'But she's called Rita?'

'It's a very common name,' the nurse had said, sniggering, and she told her husband, 'And by common, I mean in both senses of the word.'

Still, Rita's mother had been curious to find out about this musical Rita who lived in a Suffolk Orphanage and asked them to help her pursue it. They had tried to call the council just one week previously. Time was of the essence, and they were running out of it. But the nurse was told that Miss Cooper was the contact for Shilling Grange and Miss Cooper had shingles again. (Miss Cooper did not, so far as Clara knew, have shingles again. Miss Cooper was 'taking time off' on suspended pay because of the Cliff's-file debacle.) They had met many dead-ends over the last few years. This time it was the nurse who had a suggestion: 'Per-

haps we could see her at the Royal Festival Hall.' They looked at
the dates, that wouldn't work either: Rita's mother was going to
Switzerland for a long-awaited, very expensive operation – they
would have left the country by the 29th. But then Rita's mother
had an idea: 'There must be a dress rehearsal, no? Let's try and
get to that, then we'll see, once and for all, if it is *my* Rita.'

Clara still couldn't get over it. Rita wasn't astonished. Clara
was, the other children were, but Rita had believed it all along:
'I knew you'd come back.'

Her name was Gloria, Gloria Withers. She had told them
she had been in and out of hospitals and care homes since the
night the bomb hit their home. She had lost her memory, use of
her legs, her children – a most terrible time. Gradually, she
came to remember that there was one child who had survived –
she knew she had seen Rita alive – but by this point she was
trapped in her bed in a care home. No one believed her, or
perhaps, they believed her but didn't think there was much to
be done: 'I was useless, I was written off. They talked to me like
I was a fool. But it was my memory that was broken, not my
brains.'

Little by little, she fought back and when she could, she
commenced her search.

'Go play for me, my daughter,' Rita's mother had said after
telling them all this, and sent Rita back onstage. The officious
man said this was all most irregular, but Clara laughed and
Maureen said, 'Imagine you'd just been reunited with your
mother after six years,' and he paused, then smiled and said,
'You've got a good point.'

The rest of the rehearsal was highly charged. Rita was
playing for her mother, the rest of the children supporting her,
but tearful and emotional too, perhaps thinking of their own
hurt and their own mothers who would never return.

And when they had finished, Rita ran off the stage and back

into her mother's arms, and Clara could hear her sobbing, 'Mama.'

~

'Well, we can't possibly go ahead with the actual performance without Rita,' Clara told Ivor now. 'The group is nothing without her. It was hard enough without Clifford, but Rita really is the main event.'

'I can imagine,' Ivor mused.

'I don't want to disappoint the others but...'

Ivor got up and poured her more tea.

'So, how's the *mystery lady*?'

Clara gulped. *Here it came.*

'You know that was a load of nonsense, right?'

'Oh yes,' he said nonchalantly. 'Anita explained.'

Clara tried to keep her voice steady. 'And what exactly did she explain?'

It took some time to cajole him, Ivor never liked to talk about people behind their backs, but Clara was not going to let this go. What *on earth* had Anita said?

'Well...' said Ivor grudgingly. 'That it is an open secret that he... uh... likes to take out young women to detract from his... preferences... you know.'

Anita had told him that Donald was a homosexual and she was his cover? Clara wondered if she had ever been as red-faced as she was now. *Good grief, Anita!*

She wanted to say, 'And you actually believe this?' but then Ivor went on, 'Can't say I blame him. The way they hound men like him is nothing short of disgusting. The law should be changed.'

Ivor was so kind. Clara nearly sobbed. She looked at him again and it just seemed an incredible thing that he was in her life, this handsome, serious sometimes, funny sometimes man.

Bone-stubborn and stupidly obstinate, fiercely independent – and quite possibly very fond of her? *He must be, why else would he let her ramble on so?*

She held her cup, smiling to herself. He even made quite a good cup of tea, if slightly weak.

'I remembered you didn't have a handkerchief.' *Thank goodness Ivor had moved the conversation on.* 'I embroidered these for you.'

'A dress *and* handkerchiefs... you spoil me, Ivor.'

She opened it out. In each of the corners was written one word: CAN.

'Can?' She looked up at him, not understanding.

'Your initials.' He said the words slowly, like melting things: 'Clara Agnes Newton.'

'I never thought of that,' she said, staring at the exquisite threadwork, navy stitches on white: CAN.

'Well, it seemed a nice message.'

She nodded at him. She'd gone red again. 'It is – thank you.'

But now someone was knocking on the door. It was Anita; now that Howard was settled, she was *desperate* to find out what had happened at the dress rehearsal without her. Clara led her back to the Home to talk, beaming over her shoulder at Ivor: CAN. CAN. CAN. CAN.

'We have to pull out of the show.'

'I'm sorry,' Clara said. She had thought about how hard this might be for all the children, but she hadn't really thought about Anita. Now, though, her friend's face was a picture of disappointment.

'To be honest,' Clara went on, 'I've never really understood why it is so important to you.'

Clara had enjoyed their day out at the Festival of Britain enormously – absolutely, she had seen the positive effect it had on Peg and Rita, and especially Denny, she couldn't deny it – but they were *children*. Many things excited and inspired them. And she had enjoyed the event at the Hippodrome too. But why was Anita so invested in it all?

Anita clutched her knees. She seemed to be full of emotion. 'We need to celebrate coming out of the darkness.'

'I suppose...'

'Look to the future. It's a marker, everything has a season.'

Clara thought of her season's failures and the successes. She remembered Mr Dowsett talking about it in the same way. She hadn't really believed it. She regarded Anita. Her face was pale, but she was red around the throat, as though someone had slapped her with a ruler.

'When Dr Cardew first found me – in the camp, he said come back to England with me. I didn't want to, but I came. And how grey and drab everything was here at first! I wondered where the sun was. All I saw was the poverty, the rationing, the ugliness. I was so unhappy. I wanted to leave and so I went back to Poland to look for my family. No one was there. No one was left. My neighbours looked away and wouldn't speak to me. There was nothing. It was grey and drab and poverty there too – but there was something else there for me – something much worse.

'So then, when I no longer was being pulled backward, I was free to fall in love – fall in love with London and then Lavenham. I gave it a chance like it had given me a chance. I've always felt welcomed here. This is my place to call home. And now, I want to give something back. You could call it a thank you. Also, I have Evelyn and Howard – and for both of them, my children, I want us to look to the future – to be international, to enjoy the arts and the science, and not be stuck in the past with its fascist ideologies and dictators.'

Clara nodded.

'To be part of something bigger than ourselves.'

She understood this.

~

The following day, Mrs Horton came round with a delightfully plump fruit cake. As she made tea, Clara went over the events of the dress rehearsal once more: Rita's face, the clash of the cymbals, and the officious little man who relented...

'It's wonderful for Rita, of course,' she said, 'but it means no pianist, and it will be impossible for the children to continue.'

Raisins scattered across the cake plate as Mrs Horton cut two slices. Stella sloped in and sat under the table – she had a nose for a story. Rita was staying in London with her mother. They were flying out to Geneva in just a couple of days' time: Rita, her mother and the nurse. On the telephone, Rita told Clara that she had never been happier.

'Mr Horton plays piano. Quite well. Grade six back in the day.'

'A man of many hidden talents.'

'They're not that hidden,' retorted Mrs Horton primly at this perceived slight on her husband. 'If you know where to look. If you *bother* to look.'

'I know that,' said Clara appeasingly. She still appreciated Mr Horton taking Clifford to bowls that time – he hadn't had to.

'Mr Horton is not exactly one of the children of Shilling Grange though, is he?'

'They won't mind one adult.'

'But the whole point of it was Rita.'

'Originally maybe, but now the point is *everyone*. What about Peg, Maureen, Evelyn, Denny and little Gladys? How will they feel if their opportunity to perform is snatched away from them? They've been looking forward to it too. I'm sure

Anita will be able to rearrange the piece, she's so talented like that.'

Clara wondered. 'I'm concerned it's not what the organisers asked for... Isn't it a bit like fielding a different football team?' she said.

'Football clubs field different teams all the time,' said Mrs Horton.

'Oh, do they?' Clara asked, embarrassed. She probably should have listened to Billy and Barry's football talk more. 'I didn't realise that. It's not what they'll be expecting though – you think that won't matter?'

'Nothing ever is,' said Mrs Horton. She was smiling soppily, possibly at the thought of her new husband. 'Sometimes it can be better. Anyway, Clara, I'll see what we can do.'

She definitely seemed to be talking about something else.

In Clara's dream that night, Peg stepped forward and sang in Rita's place. She could sing! And after that, she began to speak. She spoke to everyone, and she spoke beautifully too, articulating all her words like she was on the wireless She was reciting, *She sells seashells on the seashore...* when Clara woke up.

Clara was confused momentarily over whether it was a dream or reality. Maybe it was true. Or maybe it was a premonition! Maybe things had changed. Perhaps the little girl had finally acquired her voice. Just as Denny seemed to have fewer issues once Cliff had left, maybe Peg too was about to emerge from under Rita's shadow?

In the kitchen that morning, Clara watched Peg closely as she nonchalantly ate her porridge and buttered her toast. She communicated clearly with Maureen, Gladys and Denny not with words but in her usual mixture of nods, smiles, mimes and scribbles on her notepad and Clara felt deflated suddenly. The dream was ridiculous; Peg couldn't possibly sing, she couldn't even say, 'pass the sugar'. Then the doorbell went, and Miss Fisher was there, saying she was taking Peg to see the bees in Farmer Buckle's field – didn't Clara remember? Peg ran out and threw herself into Miss Fisher's arms and then Peg pretended she was a bee and ran around the hall with her arms flapping, and Miss Fisher shyly made buzzing noises. This was a game they had. And Clara was glad – *curse her silly imagination!* She should remember: *Peg was perfect just as she was.*

Clara didn't have the time to go to the Jane Taylor Society meeting. There was so much to do in the house – you took just one day off and you spent the next two catching up. And Clara never enjoyed the meetings as much without Anita, who was still, naturally, preoccupied with baby Howard and his recovery. But Clara wanted to support Mr Dowsett –and she always enjoyed the refreshments. And the Jane Taylor Society was one of those groups with a decreasing membership that depended on everyone who could attend attending. Shrinking numbers would be its death knell – Clara didn't want that on her conscience as well as everything else.

In the library, she browsed the latest bestsellers: *The Day of the Triffids*, which she did not fancy, and *The Catcher in the Rye*, which she did – one day she hoped she would have time to get all the way through an entire novel again – and then took a seat. The chairs at the back were all taken and she was forced to the front row – a position she would never usually take, a hangover from her schooldays. Mr Dowsett, however, looked up gratefully from his music stand.

'No Mrs Cardew today? How's the baby?'

News travelled fast in Lavenham.

'Howard's doing much better,' Clara told him and was

rewarded with his toothy smile. The postmistress ran in late and grabbed the seat next to Clara. Her handbag was bulging and Clara grinned, always reassured to see someone even less organised than her.

Mr Dowsett wanted to talk about mortality. He became earnest all of a sudden and Clara wondered if his illness had returned; he'd had a health scare the previous year He talked a little more about how Jane Taylor never lived to see how popular her nursery rhyme 'Twinkle, Twinkle, Little Star' became. Clara nodded – she already knew that it was the favourite of children, in many different languages, everywhere – and she thought of the pretty musical box she had given Rita one Christmas, which played the familiar tune. Rita wouldn't be able to take that to Geneva with her, but Clara would keep it safe.

Mr Dowsett said, after Jane's sister's marriage, she had gone to live in Devon with her brother Isaac, and later developed breast cancer. In her last letters she wrote that her mind was 'teeming with unfulfilled projects'. She died aged forty in 1824.

The postmistress said, 'That's terribly sad,' and lots of people murmured similar. Clara found herself welling up again. Clara's mother's death was her personal measure of whether a death was untimely or not. Her mother had died at forty-four. Anything younger than that was too young, horribly, painfully young. She felt this more and more, especially now that she was only fourteen years away from the same age. So many of the children had lost their parents young and she felt great empathy for them all.

Poor Jane, she thought, and that beautiful phrase, 'teeming with unfulfilled projects', although written some hundred and twenty years earlier, seemed still to express such a lot and be so relevant.

As she helped Mr Dowsett with the teas and coffees, she noticed his hands were trembling slightly. His beard, that threaded feat of engineering, was more dramatic than ever. And perhaps the cakes, Bakewell pudding and macaroons were more delicious than ever too.

'I love these meetings,' Clara said.

It suddenly seemed important that he should know.

Dinner that night was terrible; Clara had to acknowledge she had surpassed herself in its awfulness: spam fritters that fell apart on the fork. Whatever CAN Ivor was referring to, it wasn't CAN COOK. Clara fried her last eggs to cheer it up. They wouldn't have any for a while now, but she had to do something. Unfortunately, it didn't seem to work. Maureen, Peg, Denny and Gladys were all looking at their plates in horror, when there was a noise at the backdoor.

It was Rita. She was in brand-new clothes and full of glee, with sparkling eyes and tidy plaits.

'What are you doing here?' Clara nearly dropped her fork. 'What on earth is going on?'

Rita came around and looked in disgust at the spam/egg mess. She kissed the girls and then affectionately punched Denny's shoulder. Then she grinned at Clara.

'Did you miss me?'

'Ye-es, but... what?'

'Mama's gone ahead of me to Switzerland. I'll join her next week instead – it means I can stay for the show.'

'Wha-at?' squeaked Clara. She couldn't take this in. Also, how on earth had Rita managed to get here? Last thing Clara knew, Rita was holed up in a hotel near Heathrow.

Mrs Horton walked in after Rita, which Clara supposed answered that question. She was puffed out but also looking very pleased with herself. She cleared her throat.

'Well, Mr Horton and I have discussed it. I don't think he plays the piano quite so well as I had imagined.'

I bet, thought Clara, still shaking her head in shock – yet growing delight.

'But Rita is going to be able to perform now. And since our honeymoon in Blackpool was rather cut short, we've decided – we're going to Geneva.'

'What? You're... you're going to take Rita there?'

For one terrifying moment, Clara imagined Mrs Horton's car screeching through the Alps. Her little Ford on two wheels on the hairpin bends.

Mrs Horton looked slightly sheepish. 'The week after. If that's all right with you, of course.'

'I mean... what? how?'

'We've booked a coach. Fifty-six hours. Did you know I've never left the country before? And I've always wanted to. Dear Mr Horton was in Germany during the war but I doubt it's the same. We'll bring you back some chocolate: Alpine milk, Clara, imagine that!'

Good on you, Clara thought. A part of her wondered how she hadn't thought of it. But then it was an ambitious plan, and she seemed to have trouble with those. There was a danger in being too rooted in reality, she supposed; it was important to dream big.

'And your mama agrees, Rita?'

'She thinks it's brilliant.'

'Then how could I say no?' Clara said. 'It's the perfect plan.'

She felt tearful again and after Mrs Horton scooped up the plates with the terrible untouched fritters on them and said she *just happened* to have brought along a saucepan of stew and a fruit cake for dessert, Clara did let herself have a little weep.

Clara couldn't sleep. For weeks, the looming performance at the Royal Festival Hall had been a black cloud, then it looked as if it wasn't going to happen at all, and now with Rita's reappearance and the show going ahead after all, she just wanted it to work out. *Please, let it go well*, she prayed, *please, please...* And then there were other things to worry about too: Denny leaving and settling in Gladys, finding out about her brothers; and getting Maureen ready for secretarial college, but they would have to wait until after the performance. She couldn't cope with anything else out of the ordinary, not now.

And all the while, her feelings for Ivor were bubbling away, never far from the surface. He and Mrs Harrington were not a pair, they were not lovers, no, he liked her, Clara, he had wanted to wait but he would soon be ready – would she be ready? Had he perhaps missed the boat, had the milk gone off the boil or whatever the saying was?

It didn't take very long for her to come up with an answer to that!

She hadn't been up long the next morning when she saw the telegram boy pulling at the latch of the gate. She froze. Historically, telegrams had never brought her good news.

But this telegram boy saw her staring out of the window and gave her a jaunty wave. They never did that, did they? At the front door, she took the paper from him and tipped him a shilling. (When she did so, strangely, a sense of being a proper grown-up, a citizen of the world, came to her: ridiculous notion.)

She opened it, dimly aware that the boy had left the gate wide open.

Good Luck with Show. Stop. All well here. Swim in Sea most days. Stop. You would be proud. Stop. I not had fight for one week! Stop. Yours Cliff.

44

Former Shilling Grange Orphans, the twins, Billy and Barry, were to attend an extremely important football match (all the matches of Arsenal youth were 'extremely important') with adoptive father Uncle Stanley, so Aunt Ruth had brought along a friend with her instead. Aunt Ruth and her friend were very excited about seeing the children perform; however, the friend – in a hat piled high with fruit and a dark fur coat – said she was also here for Donald Button: 'What a star!' Clara managed not to say anything about this when she and the children met them at Charing Cross station – he was the last person she wanted to see.

'You can't keep us away,' Aunt Ruth said and the friend added eagerly, 'When I heard that Ruth knew you lot, and the boys were from there, I was so excited. "The Children of Shilling Grange Orphanage". Oh my! You're almost famous.'

Aunt Ruth blushed and rolled her eyes.

The friend was also a big fan of Bartholomew Parsons and Nathan, the ventriloquist act: 'He's not as good as you lot, but his lips don't move,' she marvelled. 'How does he do it?'

They do, thought Clara. The deception was annoying. How

did people fall for these things? She supposed the ventriloquist got away with it because of that ten-metre distance between himself and the audience. It simply didn't work in close-up; it definitely didn't work on the wireless. The idea made her chuckle and she whispered it to Maureen, who scowled at her. Mind you, Maureen didn't find anything Clara said funny.

Clara had been given two tickets for today. Dr Cardew already had one, and she had sent Peg over to Ivor with the other. Ivor had apologised but in a beautiful note: he said they would be amazing, and he knew it would be an enormous success. He also said, 'You must all come and tell me all about it afterwards,' and Clara was secretly looking forward to that – rather more than to the event itself.

Anita had taken the other ticket for Howard: 'He deserves his own seat. And Dr Cardew's knees can't take much more of him!'

Terry came with her adoptive parents. Clara hadn't seen Terry since she left the Home, over two whole years ago, and she had grown so much: if the girl hadn't rushed over for a hug, Clara wouldn't have recognised her. Dear Terry! Her hair was shorter than ever and she and her adoptive mother both had a similar playful spark in their eyes. They somehow had the same body language too. Terry had different glasses from before; these ones were blue, but like her old ones, they also had sticky tape over one hinge. After they had caught up on all each other's news, Terry said, 'I'm glad I left when I did. If I had stayed, I bet you'd have me tapping a tambourine in fancy dress!'

'I would not,' said Clara, although she did wonder if Anita would have. Probably. 'Anyway, I'm sure if anyone tried, you would have refused!'

'Too right!' Terry snorted.

The waterway was almost as busy as the walkway. There were little boats as well as the new tourist boats: 'Like they have in Paris!' Anita said, and went into a reverie about the Parisian '*Bateaux Mouches*'. The people on the boats waved at the people on land, and the children waved back at them.

All the picnic tables overlooking the river were full, and they were eating their cheese sandwiches on some concrete steps when Clara was tapped on the shoulder: 'Photograph, mystery lady!'

Clara turned round irritably, only to see ex-resident Joyce with her adoptive parents, the Woodwards.

'Well, you haven't changed!'

They hugged. Joyce was holding a very smart-looking camera with a long nose and a flash. Joyce and Evelyn were especially thrilled to see each other, although it hadn't been that long since they had – the Cardews and the Woodwards got together every few months.

'I'm going to take loads of photographs,' Joyce said. 'And try to sell them to the newspapers.'

'No, you're not, Joyce,' said Mrs Woodward mildly. 'We didn't agree that.'

Joyce raised her eyebrows as if to say, *that's what you think.*

'And how is your leg, Joyce?'

Clara knew it was ridiculous but somehow she had expected Joyce, who had problems with her legs after having had polio, to experience a magical recovery once she was adopted.

'Not the best.' Joyce wrinkled up her nose. 'But it is what it is – I've got my sticks.'

And she twirled around on them and then grasped Evelyn, who said proudly, 'You're doing really well.'

Peter hadn't been able to get the time off from work – well, Clara suspected he didn't *want* time off from work; work was Peter's everything. Nevertheless, he had telephoned and left a message with Rita, who exasperatingly but quite unsurprisingly couldn't remember what it was ('This is why we write messages down, Rita!'). But she was sure it was something like, 'You'll be brilliant – Mabel and I will see you in the summer holidays.'

Clara doubted he would take the time off work then either, but she understood.

It was what it was.

Victor, Bernard and Alex were making a day out of it too. Clara saw them waiting near one of the many entrances to the Royal Festival Hall. Victor was holding several newspapers under his arm, and reading another, and there was, Clara noted, a woman standing close to him, reading over his shoulder. Surely he hated that? Alex saw Clara first, nudged his best friend/adopted brother Bernard, and they dashed over. Both shook her hands – Alex's manners were always impeccable – and typical Alex, always with the general knowledge, started, 'I bet you don't know how the Skylon got its name!'

'I do, actually!' retorted Clara, putting her arm round him and giving him a big squeeze. Her lovely Alex, the little professor. He was *slightly* taller than he had been, but there must still have been a whole ten inches between him and Bernard.

Alex pointed to Victor and the woman: 'See them two – I was the reason they got together.'

They're together-together?

'She's a librarian,' Bernard said, screwing up his nose.

'She's always telling me to shhh,' Alex said.

'And do you?'

'What?'

'Shhh.'

'Never,' he said proudly.

A librarian was probably a good match for Victor, Clara thought. *A good fit for the house.*

The librarian was a bony, nervous-looking woman. How fondly she looked at Victor! As Clara walked over to say hello, the librarian stroked his back and said, 'Vic.' *Vic!* Clara would never have dreamed of calling serious Professor Braithwaite 'Vic'. Nor would she have *stroked* his back in public.

'Clara.' He greeted her so delightedly, it warmed her heart. 'How ever did you get them here?'

'It wasn't me, it was Anita,' she said, and he chuckled. 'Modest as ever – well, can we agree it was both of you?'

Clara ducked her head, but since Anita wasn't near enough to have heard, she conceded, 'Okay.'

'This is so impressive,' said the librarian girlfriend, who despite their otherwise good manners, nobody had yet managed to introduce. 'Vic's told me so much about you.'

'All good, I hope?'

'Some of it was good,' she said earnestly.

It was a day for coming out of the darkness indeed.

Miss Fisher had come along to support Peg, and when Peg saw her, the girl jumped into her arms. Miss Fisher wobbled but – thank goodness – she didn't fall down. It was touching to see the awkward teacher so attached to this child. When Miss Fisher had recovered, straightened her dress and resettled her necklace, she told Peg – and everyone – she had bought two tickets, one for her and one for a bagful of shells to have the seat next to her, for good luck. Victor and his new girlfriend stared at her.

And then there was Mr Harris, Clara's old boss, his wife and two tiny girls. Clara was getting much better at guessing ages and she would have put these two at about three years old.

If Clara was feeling magnanimous then she might have said that Mr Harris's wife was one of the reasons she was in Lavenham – for she was the reason Clara had lost her job; she had replaced Clara three years ago this month. But although Clara was feeling many emotions that day, magnanimity was not one that featured strongly.

The two tiny girls held hands and had shiny tap shoes and little matching coats and hairbands.

'Two children?' said Clara.

'I know!' Mr Harris said. 'And they're not babies either.' He coughed. 'But who could say no to them, eh? The children's services in London moved so quickly, we've hardly had time to draw a breath.'

He looked proudly at his daughters.

'I must say, Clara, if it wasn't for you I think we'd have been going round in circles for years. You were the one who made me think adoption was possible – and you were the one who taught me we should widen our search, so thank you.'

Eventually, they made it through the friends and onlookers – for once, Denny didn't need the lav'! – and found themselves back-stage at the Royal Festival Hall. Cornerstone of the recovery, the arts and the sciences. There was a bright future to be had. Near them, eating spam sandwiches, was a fire-eater and another man in a strange costume. Rita said he was a clown, but Maureen whispered that he was different from the others – he was 'a Pierrot'. Gladys said she loved him. 'I wish I were a clown,' she said, and Clara grinned, thinking how there were so many different kinds of people in the world and wasn't that a marvellous thing?

Perhaps Anita thought she was grinning about something else.

'I think you should perform with the children,' she said as she straightened Rita's already straight plaits. 'It would be such a coup.'

'All right,' Clara said cheerfully. 'Why not?'

Her mind teeming with unfulfilled projects.

She had a sudden feeling of exuberance. I – CAN. It was

crazy but she felt like she could do anything. All these people who had come to support them, all the love!

'What?' said Anita and Rita at the same time.

'Did you just say all right?' said Evelyn, slightly later.

'I did.' Clara grinned again. 'It's a one-off though, got it?'

Anita nodded. She too was grinning from diamond-encrusted ear to diamond-encrusted ear.

'Here,' she handed Clara the score. 'You know these bits.'

'I'd better do – I've heard them enough times. Anyway, you'll help me, won't you, Evelyn?'

'YES!' yelped Evelyn and then in a more measured voice, 'Of course, I will, Miss Newton, you can always count on me.'

Peg threw her arms round Clara's waist and headbutted her like a goat.

Over Peg's head, Clara smiled at Anita: 'It's going to be fun!'

And then Ivor was there, pushing Patricia in the pram. What the heck? Hadn't he turned down her ticket? And goodness knows how he'd managed to get backstage. Everyone was saying it was like Fort Knox. But no matter. The children jumped on him and shouted all sorts of things, and he said he had to come and wish them good luck, didn't he?

Then he turned to Clara, one eyebrow raised.

'I changed my mind!' he said apologetically.

'How did you get in here?' she asked. She felt overwhelmed suddenly. Ivor had a history of last-minute turnarounds, but this was exceptional.

'I know a man who knows a man...'

Patricia was sitting up and cooing, wearing mittens because she tended to scratch her own face. Ivor was in jacket and shirt, just a hint of braces, and looked what younger women might call dreamy. She saw other women giving him glances; there was always something eye-catching about Ivor – even the eye-catching entertainers, people who preferred being looked at themselves, looked at him. Or maybe it was because he was pushing a pram. A man with a baby was a rare sight indeed. *Good Housekeeping* said that it was unmasculine but, Clara thought, *Good Housekeeping* did not always get it right where modern relationships were concerned.

'I hear you're going onstage?'

'I am. It's a bit of a risk,' she added, thinking no one in the world understood her like Ivor did, 'but I want the children to know that they shouldn't let fear hold them back.'

'Not just the children, actually – you set a good example to me too,' he said.

Clara smiled awkwardly. She wasn't sure what he was trying to suggest, and her legs were trembly. She felt tremendously out of her depth. He made her tongue-tied suddenly. By comparison to this, the prospect of singing in the show now felt like something easy.

He leaned forward and kissed her on the cheek. It felt like his lips stayed there, his breath on her face, for longer than normal – certainly longer than necessary. Clara closed her eyes, exhaled.

'I mean, sometimes it's important to take risks,' he said. 'In fact, you get to a point where there's no other option.'

She nodded, swallowed.

'Sister Grace is coming over to the Home this evening.' She paused. *How could she say it without ambiguity but with room for him to get out of it if he wanted?* She plunged in: 'Why don't I leave her and the children to it and head over to yours?'

There was loud applause. The act before theirs was finishing. A violinist came running past.

'I thought you'd never ask,' he said, biting his lip. 'That's a yes. A yes, please.'

There was no time for nerves. When Donald Button called out, 'Children of Shilling Grange Orphanage,' in his smarmy way, the children rearranged themselves, and then walked into the spotlight: First Maureen, then Denny, Peg, Rita, Gladys and Evelyn. Clara followed them a few seconds after, determined that she and Donald Button would not be on the stage at the same time. They stood lined up in a row, and Evelyn, next to Clara, grabbed her hand.

Act like you know what you're doing. Act like you're a star.

At the sight of them, the whole audience as one went, 'Aww.'

Clara remembered the make-up artist who'd said she was pretty in a 'homely' way and thought, *well, that's her opinion, I know that I'm all right.* She was wearing the dress Ivor had made for her and now she understood what fashion could do – it was a great illusion, for she did feel different. All the care and work he'd put into it, every stitch, every fold, was like a vote of confidence or a warm hug.

Don't look at the audience, Anita had hissed at her just before they went on. When did Clara ever listen to Anita? She looked. And they looked such an amorphous blob out there, she quite liked it. Maureen had said, *focus on someone in particular,* but this sounded like a dreadful idea; why would she pick out some poor unsuspecting soul and communicate only with them?

Were the Mayor of London, the American Ambassador and Princess Margaret out there? Clara did not have time to seek them out because Rita was already on the piano and doing that exceptional thing she did that Anita called showboating: giving the audience what they came for – you had to do that a bit, and it didn't mean you were doing anything wrong or selling yourself short. It meant you were delivering on expectations, and then once you'd done that, you could do your own thing, you could get out your own message. It was a compromise, it was a bit of everything – it was making sure everyone was happy.

What a girl! Hands crossed, hands up one end of the keyboard, hands down the other end; it drove the audience wild to see such big notes coming from such a small thing. And then Peg joined in, playing the drums and grinning fit to burst, and Maureen was swaying like a girl possessed, and Denny, who would be adopted soon, and Evelyn and Gladys were shaking maracas and all were singing their little hearts out and so was Clara. If her father ever saw it, she thought, but why would he? Popular music was not his area – but if he did see it, then fine, let him see it, let him *hear* her: she wasn't a cowed child any more. She was a housemother at the Shilling Grange Orphanage.

(Or the Michael Adams Children's Home.)

Of course, Rita was the star of the day. And maybe Ann Taylor too. But mostly it was Rita. How she played so beautifully was astonishing, and a mystery. Well, Clara did know at least some of the reason – hours and hours of dedicated practice, a fantastic teacher and lots of encouragement – but there was something else there too, something so natural. It was a mixture of nurture and nature – or as Anita had once said, to Clara's bemusement, 'Her fingers really are the perfect length.'

Then it was the next bit of the medley and Maureen was smiling at Clara, even while she was singing the Mama bit...

And when they'd finished and the sky hadn't fallen in, the children all put their arms round Clara, and Clara hadn't expected that – they hadn't said they'd do that, they should have warned her! Even Peg laid her sticks on her drums and jumped up to hug her, and Clara found tears were pouring down her cheeks. She clutched Denny and her girls close and forgot the audience and the Festival of Britain – the only thing she could think of was her deep affection for them.

All her cabbages.

Maybe it was ridiculous, but Clara sensed that the day, the performance *was* a marker, it was a sign; maybe they had slipped out of the shadow of the dreary war years, and maybe they had a better future to look forward to, maybe they had more hope. Perhaps they really had turned a corner or entered a new season. Was this how the nation felt after the Napoleonic Wars? Was this why Jane Taylor was teeming with unfulfilled projects?

In the foyer, after the performance, everyone had gathered around, slapping their backs, and some children had even asked for their autographs! It was all chaos, good chaos, and Clara had tried to see Ivor, but she couldn't; and then she had spotted the Silver Cross pram. She saw Ivor pushing it. Where was he going? She covered her mouth. He was marching straight over to Donald Button. Dear Lord! What on earth was he saying? She watched him shake Donald Button's hand. Then they had all been swallowed by the crowd and she hadn't seen them again.

Oh, my days, she'd thought. What if Donald Button had said something – what if Ivor had changed his mind about her? Would he still think it was important to take risks?

Clara didn't see Ivor again, they must have travelled back on different trains. When she got to the Home, she found Stella had left a special present for her and as she cleared it up, heart racing, she marvelled at how life was: one minute you could be posing for photographs at the Royal Festival Hall, the next you could be scrabbling around for a dustpan and brush and holding a very rushed mouse funeral in the garden.

About eight o'clock that evening, when everyone was still celebrating with squash and strudel, and going over the events of the day, Clara whispered something to Sister Grace, who laughed and said, 'Bless you, my dear, go ahead.'

She had a quick wash, put on a spritz of perfume and a dab of powder. She would have to do – Ivor wasn't going to turn her away now, was he? This was their last chance, she told herself. If he said no tonight, then she would give up on him for ever more, move on... move away.

The light in Ivor's workshop was inviting as a beacon, a good sign? It pulled her in like a star. *How I wonder what you are.* Self-consciously, Clara knocked a tune on the door, jaunty but quiet. She did *not* want to wake up Patricia to howl.

She told herself she would know how he felt about her the moment she saw his face. Ivor opened the door. He was in his white shirt and braces, and dark trousers. Her heart seemed to rise up to the very edge of her chest, pushing at her ribcage. Could he hear it beating?

'Hello, Clara.'

He was smiling that adorable smile.

She stepped inside. But still she wasn't certain, still she felt unsure. Could he smell her perfume? Had she overdone it? Could he feel her longing for him? There wasn't much she could do to disguise that.

CAN, she thought. *We can.*

'Alone at last,' she said, because he hadn't said anything else yet, and she was embarrassed. It was a terrible cliché, the sort of thing Donald Button, star of stage, screen and wireless, might say, but she felt she had to say *something*. Someone had to break the ice. The silence was too encompassing, her cheeks were too red. Goodness, was it her or was it very, very warm in here?

But actually, Ivor didn't seem to feel the need to say

anything. Instead, Ivor took her into his one arm and he kissed her for a very long time. And it was every bit as wonderful as she had hoped it would be. It was more wonderful than she had ever let herself imagine. And she clutched him to her and kissed him back. Again. And again. And again.

6 June 1951

My dear Clara,

I have only just got your letter. I have been travelling – to Mexico, Argentina, Brazil and Peru. You would not believe some of the things I have seen. I have danced the tango, lost my shoes in Caracas, eaten lima beans and cassava, and I am worn out, of course, and will need to lie down in a dark room for the rest of the month, but I did it. It seems my little sojourn in the United Kingdom lit the fire for travel within me and I am now what they call a globetrotter.

Yet let me tell you, none of those beautiful places stole my heart like my dear Lavenham.

What an achievement – to have the children sing at the Royal Festival Hall! I am sure they will look back on that for the rest of their lives. I bet they sounded wonderful – and you joined in? That is simply marvellous.

Thank you so much for sending the festival programme. I am so proud of them all. Please tell them that. I have enclosed some sweets for them to share – there will be more soon.

But, Clara, there was absolutely nothing to apologise for – not a thing. It is not important to me whether they are called the Michael Adams Children's Home or the Shilling Grange Orphanage.

Wasn't it your greatest playwright who said: What's in a name? That which we call a rose/By any other name would smell as sweet? I am sorry I gave you the impression that the name was a condition or a quest of mine – it isn't. I don't care at all if everyone knows it, or no one does – it is my son's name and it is engraved on my heart.

Be well, Clara, be proud of your successes,

With love

Marilyn Adams

A LETTER FROM LIZZIE

Hello, hello,

Thank you so much for returning to the Michael Adams Children's Home – or as some of us still call it, the Shilling Grange Orphanage – and I hope you have enjoyed *An Orphan's Song*, the third book in this series. I am currently planning and plotting Book Four, so hopefully it won't be too long before you find out what is next in store for Clara and the children.

If you would like to keep up to date with my latest releases, just sign up at the following link. Your email address will never be shared and you can unsubscribe at any time:

www.bookouture.com/lizzie-page

If you enjoyed *An Orphan's Song*, do tell your friends and I would also be very grateful for your reviews too. Some writers don't read reviews, some have family save only the best ones for them, but I read them all – and I want you to know I do take on board your comments.

A couple of years ago, I came across a lovely photograph from the early 1950s of Petula Clark (a popular British singer) and the Dr Barnardo's Home Choir. They performed together and you can even listen to their charity song on the internet: 'Where did my Snowman Go?'.

I already had a very musical girl at the Home – Rita – and

her super-ambitious coach – Anita. Why shouldn't they form a group, I decided, a very exceptional group? So, it was this photograph that inspired me and helped give me the structure or shape of *An Orphan's Song*.

I know some readers love a cliff-hanger – 'a dramatic and exciting ending to an episode of a serial, leaving the audience in suspense and anxious not to miss the next episode' – and others can't bear them – for me, I'm somewhere in the middle. Of course, a dramatic and exciting ending is important, but I don't like that feeling of being left in suspense. I don't want you to feel you *have* to read Books Four or Five to get the answers you need (I want you to feel as though you want to!).

The pressure to get Ivor and Clara together was too much in Book Three. Maybe I kept them apart for too long, maybe the timing was just right, who knows? – but I could not wait any longer and finally, Clara and Ivor have taken that extra step further here.

But, dear reader, the story is not over until the fat lady sings and I have plenty of plans for Books Four and Five – life is unpredictable and so is historical fiction. Nothing is written in stone – just because Ivor and Clara have got together doesn't mean... what? I'm saying nothing!

I love to hear directly from readers too. Do feel free to get in touch on Twitter: @LizziePagewrite, Instagram or Facebook.

With much love,

Lizzie

facebook.com/LizziePage

twitter.com/LizziePagewrite

instagram.com/LizziePagewriter

AUTHOR NOTE

On 30 September 1951, less than five months after it opened, a ceremony was held to mark the end of the Festival of Britain. The thousands of people there booed that it was over. They clasped hands, sang 'Auld Lang Syne', and the next day the bull-dozers were brought in. Most everything was destroyed: the Dome of Discovery, the funfair, the Skylon – little pieces of which went on to become souvenir pocketknives.

The Royal Festival Hall, however, remains.

The Conservative government were determined to pull down everything. They saw the Festival of Britain as a socialist festival: it didn't turn out that way, but it did showcase a nation's talent and left a legacy, especially in design and technology.

I wanted to talk about the Festival of Britain in the book because 'rebirth' and 'hope' are big themes here in *An Orphan's Song*. I wanted to show the children's reaction to the Festival. It seems all the children who went were blown away by it. They had been through the drab post-war years and emerged at a time and occasion when anything seemed possible.

I love the Olympics, and football World Cups, when

nations get together and show off their humanity through sports. I wish we did a regular something that also celebrated art and culture and science and technology every four years or so – these events can feed our dreams, nourish our memories and are a gift to ourselves and future generations.

ACKNOWLEDGEMENTS

Massive thanks to all at my publisher, Bookouture. From my brilliant editor Kathryn Taussig to the 'on it' production and marketing teams, I am very grateful I am with them and for all the work they do. Big shout-out also to my fantastically eagle-eyed copy editor and proofreader: Jacqui Lewis and Jane Donovan. When I see your names in the margins, I know I'm in safe hands.

Huge thanks also to Therese Coen, my super-agent at Hardman and Swainson literary agency. She found me on the slush-pile and got me on my way – and she has the best ideas in ALL the languages.

I've loved exploring this period in history. Thank you so much to everyone who has given me research ideas, anecdotes or photographs. I've loved hearing about the Festival of Britain from you all – special mention to the good people at the Little Baddow Society (thank you, Margaret M Martin) and my coffee buddy Jenny Barton.

Big thanks also to all my family and friends. It's been a difficult couple of years for many of us – I'm grateful to have such a loving community around me both in real life and online.

To Steve, Reuben, Ernie and Miranda (and Lenny the dog), thank you. You keep me keeping on.

But the biggest thanks must go to my readers, especially the ones still reading this. ;) Thank you for joining me in the world of The Shilling Grange/Michael Adams Orphanage. You are the ones who put the fire in my belly. It means the world to me that you're still here.

CPSIA information can be obtained
at www.ICGtesting.com
Printed in the USA
BVHW041720110722
641737BV00026B/126

(The D.A.I.T. Missions Book 3)

David Elmer

For Alinka and Zosia, thank you for believing in me.

Chapter One
The School Trip

It was a fresh Friday morning in Leicester, and at the National Space Centre coaches carrying excited school children had begun arriving for their visits to the complex.

Miss Steward had brought her year 9 science group to the centre from Applewood High School. It was an end of term treat for their hard work in class on the weather balloon project, As the coach turned into the car park the children's excitement rose to a peak.

"Can we get off the bus yet Miss, please!" asked one of the children.

"My dad said we need to be at the front of the queue to get the best views" added another.

Miss Steward stood up in the aisle of the coach to speak to the class. Her Jupiter earrings swaying from side to side.

"Can I have your attention please 9C3," she paused for effect.

The children all turned to face their teacher, eyes wide and waiting for Miss to give the word.

"Our meeting point if you get lost is marked with the letter G and the coach will be leaving at 3 pm sharp to take us back to school, so please don't wait until the last minute to go to the gift shop, I am looking at you Lewis! We don't want a repeat of the London Eye incident do we!" she continued.

The class giggled and turned to Lewis who had now sunk down into his seat.

Miss steward nodded at the coach driver who flicked a switch on the dashboard to open the doors at either end of the coach.

"Please take everything you will need with you because the coach will not be staying with us. Let's go and enjoy some space science!" she added.

The class cheered as they stood up, gathered together their belongings and stepped off the coach.

Dressed in their purple Applewood blazers with purple & orange striped ties the class joined the end of a group of students from another school and walked towards the entrance to the Centre which was at the base of the very futuristic looking, transparent rocket tower. It housed two decommissioned rockets, Thor and Blue Streak who stood proudly for all to see. When they entered the building, they were welcomed by a Soyuz spacecraft hanging above their heads like an eagle hovering with its wings outstretched.

As they entered the main hall the children didn't know which direction to look in first. The black painted walls and ceiling were covered with pictures of mankind's achievements in space along with various models of past and present spacecraft. There was a space-themed restaurant called The Soyuz Lounge, space-themed gift shop, and even space-themed toilets!

Each class was greeted by a tour guide who would accompany them for the day as they explored the Space Centre.

A young blonde woman in Space Centre uniform with her hair in a ponytail walked over to the group.

"Welcome to the National Space Centre," said the woman. "My name is Jenny and I will be your guide today."

She handed each of the students a leaflet that showed the seven different zones in the Centre which were; The Rocket Tower, Into Space, Sir Patrick Moore Planetarium, Space Oddities, Orbiting Earth, Our Solar System, and The Universe. On the back of the leaflet was a map of the Space Centre just in case you got lost.

"When I raise this flashing clipboard with your class number on it, that means we are moving on to the next zone so please follow me when that happens," she added.

Miss Steward joined Jenny at the front of the group and quickly counted the children to make sure she hadn't lost anyone already.

"9C3 you are representing Applewood High School so best behavior please, Jenny please lead the way," she asked.

The class walked to the first zone looking all around them, eyes wide, trying to take everything in. There were lots of displays to look at that showed items from space missions, parts of space suits and equipment from space probes. The class was able to touch and feel some space suits and try some space food that astronauts and cosmonauts eat while they are in orbit.

In each zone, there were interactive experiments to do, lots of space artifacts, video displays that showed current missions as well as lots of space sounds and atmospheric space music.

Lewis was really excited by the whole experience because he loved everything to do with space and science. His mum and dad were both science teachers at another school and had gotten Lewis interested in space when he was a little boy.

In his bedroom, he had space wallpaper with stars and planets on it, a space duvet set with the milky way galaxy on it and space-themed curtains covered with little aliens and flying saucers. But his favorite part of the bedroom was the space display that he started when he was given a model of the NASA space shuttle for his 6th birthday.

The display was filled with homemade space pictures and models as well as posters that his parents had brought home from work.

At weekends they would watch science documentaries and science fiction programs on tv together and Lewis' mum would make space pizza. It was like normal pizza except it was cut into the shape of a space rocket and had stardust on it which was actually edible glitter.

Lewis had decided he was going to take as many photos as he could and buy something really cool from the gift shop with his pocket money to add to his display.

The class arrived in the first zone which was titled 'Into Space'.

Here the students learned about astronauts, cosmonauts and the spacesuits they wore on their journeys into space. They also had great fun exploring the mock-up of the Columbus Module from the International Space Station and pretending they were weightless.

Lewis especially enjoyed that one as he imagined he was the space station commander directing spacecraft to the various docking rings around the station! He got some strange looks from other visitors and the girls in his class who giggled at him,

"What are you doing Lewis?" said a voice in the distance.

Lewis stepped back from the controls looking a little embarrassed as he ran his fingers through his brown hair. He was so deep in his imaginary world that he had forgotten where he was.

"I was pretending to be in control of the International Space Station," he said shyly as he turned to see who had asked the question.

It was Zara Patrick from his class, she was standing there, staring at him, head tilted slightly to one side. She was the same height as Lewis with long light brown hair in French plaits and her uniform always looked neat and tidy. Zara also happened to be the coolest girl in his class and one of the most popular girls in their year.

"That's pretty cool, but wouldn't you prefer to fly a rocket into space instead?" she asked with a smile.

"I don't like going on anything fast, theme park rides, and roller coasters make me throw up everywhere," replied Lewis.

"But only a little bit, not like carrot chunks or anything," he added, trying to make it sound less yucky than it already did but failing miserably.

Luckily Zara hadn't noticed the carrot chunks reference as she was distracted by something behind them

"Looks like we are going to the next zone now," she said, pointing to Jenny their guide who was holding up the clipboard and ushering the class forward.

Lewis and Zara walked over to join the rest of the class.

"Did everyone enjoy the 'Into Space' zone?" asked Miss Steward.

"Yes, Miss" replied the class together.

She counted the children to make sure none of the class had gone missing and she spotted Lewis and Zara walking back to the group.

"Ah Zara, thank you for making sure Lewis hadn't gotten lost already," she said.

The class giggled, Lewis and Zara looked at each other and smiled, Miss Steward continued.

"Ok Jenny please lead on to the next zone," 9C3 followed their guide through the Space Centre to continue their tour in the 'Exploring the Universe' zone.

Inside the Universe zone, the class was able to watch a simulation of the Big Bang, the event that scientists believe created the building blocks for everything we see around us. They could also travel on a journey through a wormhole in a modified flight simulator that tilted them left, right, forwards and backward. The class also found out about the science involved in the 'SETI' project (Search for Extra-Terrestrial Intelligence).

Zara tried to persuade Lewis to join them on the flight simulator, but Lewis wasn't having any of it, the thought of being thrown around in a confined space made his stomach do cartwheels. Instead, he offered to look after Zara's phone and purse while she went on the simulator.

Lewis spent the time looking at some of the space facts on display instead. There were many other activities in the zone but Lewis' favorite one was the Stellarium. It was like standing in a field at night looking up at the stars but you could zoom into every star and find out information about it.

"That wormhole simulator was so good!" exclaimed Zara as she joined Lewis in the Stellarium. "But I wonder if that is exactly what it feels like to go through a wormhole, as no one has done it yet," She pondered this for a moment and then straightened her uniform and checked her hair was still in place using her pocket mirror.

"Have you found anything with a cool name yet?" she asked.

"I found one called Arcturus just now which is a double star, and I am now trying to get a closer look at Alpha Centauri," replied Lewis.

They both stared at the large display screen while Lewis tried to navigate to the star system.

"Wait a minute, what's is that!?" enquired Zara as she pointed at a white dot flying past them on the large display screen

"Let's find out!" replied Lewis as he grabbed the controls and spun their view around to bring the fast-moving white dot into view. He clicked on the object as it flew through the digital sky.

"H-2A R/B... it's an artificial satellite," said Lewis.

"Is that all? I was hoping it was a comet or something," replied Zara with a little disappointment in her voice.

Lewis shrugged, he didn't understand Zara's disappointment, after all, it was still a spacecraft flying around in space, which to him was just as cool as a comet.

"Would you like to explore Alpha Centauri with me? It's the closest star system to ours AND it has three suns!" asked Lewis, turning to Zara who was now standing at the Stellarium door trying to spot her friends.

She turned back to Lewis.

"I better go and find the Troop before they start moaning, see you in the next zone," replied Zara. Lewis nodded.

"Ok, see you later," he said and went back to his investigations.

Zara smiled at Lewis as he continued to explore the stars and then stepped out of the Stellarium.

The Troop was a dance group that Zara and her close friends Sam, Poppy & Zia had created. They would meet every weekend at the local community centre to learn new routines with their teacher. The Troop had been very successful already, winning several awards and competitions.

Zara spotted the Troop and ran over to them.

"Where have you been?" asked Poppy as she peered behind Zara to see where she had come from.

"I was in the Stellarium with Lewis, he was showing me some stars" explained Zara.

"Ooo" replied the girls in unison.

"Sam got a boys phone number from another school!" exclaimed Poppy.

"I didn't even ask, he just dropped it on the floor next to me!" giggled Sam.

"Did you get Lewis' number? What's he like? He doesn't speak much in Chemistry" enquired Zia.

"No I didn't, it's not like that, he's ok actually" replied Zara.

Miss Steward had lost track of where exactly everyone from 9C3 had gone so she set about rounding the class up, to get them ready to move to the next zone. After about 10 minutes of herding the pupils, she had everyone back with together with Jenny the tour guide, well, everyone except for Lewis.

"Has anyone seen Lewis? Zara wasn't he with you?" she asked.

"He was Miss, but not recently, actually isn't he right behind you?" answered Zara.

Miss Steward spun around to see Lewis plodding towards them with a big grin on his face.

"You're lucky we didn't leave you behind Lewis, what were you doing over there?" asked Miss Steward.

"I was exploring the universe Miss, just like you told us to" answered Lewis.

The rest of the class giggled.

"Sorry to interrupt you Miss Steward but is the class ready to move on now? There is still one more zone to visit before your time slot in the planetarium at 12 pm" explained Jenny.

"Yes, of course, Lewis please join the rest of the class," said Miss Steward.

She counted the class one more time, just to be extra sure and everyone was present. "Ok Jenny please lead the way," said Miss Steward.

Lewis joined Zara and her friends as they walked towards the next stop on their tour.

"I found a star named after you, well kind of, it has your name in it!" exclaimed Lewis proudly.

Zara smiled

"Lewis these are my friends; Poppy, Sam, and Zia," she said.

"Hi, nice to meet you," said Lewis shyly.

"Hi, Lewis" replied Poppy.

"Hello" replied Sam.

"Alright," said Zia.

"So whats this star called then?" asked Zara.

"Al Zara" announced Lewis proudly.

"Close enough," said Zara with approval.

The next zone the class would be stopping at was called 'The Planets'. Lewis was really excited about visiting this area because there was a six-wheeled Mars rover that you could control and navigate around a mock-up of the Mars surface. And as he put it to Zara "they have actual meteorites from actual space!".

The zone was split into exhibits, one for each planet in our solar system. Starting with Mercury and traveling all the way through our system to Pluto. Lewis still considered it to be a planet even though some important scientist somewhere had decided it wasn't anymore.

In each exhibit, there was a model of that particular planet, lots of interesting facts about the planet, video simulations to watch which showed how the planet evolved over time and its orbital path around the sun. Some of the exhibits also had other fun activities to do.

"Which planet are we going to look at first?" asked Zara.

"Let's start at Mercury and make our way through them all" suggested Poppy.

"Zia and Me are going to try and find that boy, we will come and find you later," said Sam before she and Zia walked off to the Saturn exhibit of the zone where they had spotted some of the students from the other school.

This left Zara, Poppy, and Lewis at the entrance to the zone. Zara turned to Lewis.

"What about you Lewis?" she asked.

"Do you mind if I join you both?" he replied.

The three of them walked over to the Mercury exhibit and started their mini-tour of the Solar System.

Above them hung a large sign with the word Mercury on it. In front of them stood a scale model of Mercury just under a meter in size.

There wasn't as much information on display about Mercury as there was for some of the other planets but Lewis and Poppy made up for that with their own knowledge.

Poppy was top of the class when it came to class science quizzes and would always be the first one to put her hand up. Although Lewis knew most of the answers too, he didn't like the attention or the pressure of having the other children turn and stare at him to see if he knew the right answer.

"Did you know the temperature during the day on Mercury is 427 degrees Celsius!" explained Poppy.

"And at night the temperature is -173" added Lewis.

"Sounds like you're not the only one that has space knowledge Poppy," said Zara as she smiled and then turned to walked towards the following exhibit.

Lewis offered Poppy a shy smile and then gestured that she lead the way.

"Let's see what you know about Earth then Lewis," said Poppy, turning back to look him over and cracking a smile.

The Earth exhibit was laid out in a similar way to the Mercury exhibit with a large sign overhead in alternating green and blue letters that spelled out the word Earth and a model of the planet at floor level with displays and information surrounding them.

Geography wasn't one of Lewis' strengths so he decided to keep a bit quieter, besides he was more interested in what was to come next in the Mars area.

The three of them walked up to the model of Earth.

"Did you know, there are 195 countries on our planet?" said Poppy, as she examined the model of Earth that was more than twice her height.

"I have only been to five of them" replied Zara as she gazed at the giant globe "I wonder how many school holidays it would take to see them all" she continued.

Lewis stepped away from the planet and walked over to one of the large tv screens. It showed a video of two astronauts doing a spacewalk outside the international space station with the Earth below them looking very big and very far away. It made his stomach turn upside down, maybe I should look at something else he thought.

He walked across the exhibit to the Earth facts display and started reading the various pieces of information there were on show. He looked at his watch to see how long they had left before the planetarium show... 30 minutes left.

Lewis was very keen to get to the Mars exhibit soon so that he could get some time on the Mars rover. He finished reading the displays and checked the time again... 20 minutes left.

Lewis went to find Zara and Poppy to see if they were ready to move on. They were having great fun taking it in turns to use the hurricane simulator. It was a circular chamber with glass sides in which you stood and powerful fans blasted you with a strong wind to simulate the high winds of a hurricane.

The girls were rolling around with laughter at how messy their hair went inside.

"Hey Lewis, you should really try this out, it makes your hair go wild!" laughed Zara her uniform all messy and clips hanging out if her hair.

"Are you ready to go to the next exhibit yet?" asked Lewis as Poppy stepped out of the simulator, with her hair in a swirl on top of her head.

"Where did you go, Lewis, I had no one to compare Earth facts with" asked Poppy as she straightened out her hair.

"Hey! I know things too!" said Zara.

Lewis shrugged.

"I wanted to look at the rest of the exhibit quickly so we have time to visit the Mars exhibit before the planetarium show" explained Lewis.

"Ok, well, we still haven't seen everything in the Earth exhibit so you can go ahead if you like and we'll catch you up?" offered Zara.

Lewis nodded.

"Yeah ok, I will see you both in a bit," he said and went off to find the entrance to the next exhibit.

"He's a bit different isn't he?" said Poppy.

"He really is, but he seems like a nice boy too, just shy that's all" replied Zara, as she watched him walk away.

"Shall we have another go in the hurricane?" asked Poppy.

"Of course! My hair can't get any worse!" replied Zara.

The Mars exhibit was one of the bigger exhibits in 'The Planets' zone at the Space Centre. There were the usual fact-filled displays about the planet and video presentations that showed its orbit around the sun but there was also the Mars Rover challenge where you had to maneuver a six-wheeled robot over a mock-up of the Mars surface and through an obstacle course to the finish line, picking up samples along the way.

At the center of the Mars exhibit, behind the model of the planet was a glass display of meteorites from Mars that had fallen to Earth from space hundreds of years ago. Lewis had already planned out in his head the order he was going to see the different parts of the exhibit.

As he entered the area, the large red Mars sign above his head, Lewis felt goosebumps of excitement. He was going to look at the fact displays, then try out the Rover challenge and then see meteorites. But first, he checked his watch.

'Only 15 minutes left, it's going to be close' he thought. He walked over to the displays and started reading the various pieces of information. But he quickly realized that he knew most of the facts on display already. 'Maybe I should miss this part out and have more time on the Rover' he thought to himself.

Lewis began to walk over to the Rover, but then he saw a long queue of students in green and black uniforms from another school waiting to use it.

Not to worry he still had time, so he walked over to the meteorite display and kept one eye on the Rover queue.

There was one rock, in particular, that was getting a lot of attention from visitors. It was called the Nakhla Martian Meteorite and it was the newest addition to the Space Centres collection. However it was also the smallest of the three rocks on display measuring 3.4cm by 1.7cm, it was even smaller than the Lewis' asthma inhaler, which reminded him to take a quick dose before continuing to admire the rocks on display.

He was amazed how these rocks had once, thousands of years ago been a part of Mars and now they were sitting in front of him, behind glass. The two other older rocks were a lot larger than the Nakhla Meteorite. One was the size of a tennis ball and the other was as big as a coffee mug.

In the reflection of the display case glass, Lewis noticed the reflection of a very tall man with a hand bar mustache wearing a black and white striped suit.

"Excuse me, boy, have you seen any students wearing green sweatshirts over here?" the man asked. Lewis grinned to himself and turned around.

"Yes, they are over there, on the rover challenge," he said pointing.

The mans face turned from concern to annoyance as he walked over to the group of students. There was a brief telling off from the man, which

Lewis assumed was their teacher, and he marched them out of the exhibit and off towards the exit.

At last, Lewis could go on the Rover Challenger he ran over and nearly tripped over the legs of one of the displays on the way.

The Mars Rover Challenge was laid out with 6 objects to investigate, on a red sandy landscape with rocks and boulders just like the environment of the Mars surface. To pilot the rover there was a joystick for navigation and a lever for speed control. There was no time limit on the challenge, Lewis just had to complete all the tasks in order so he decided to wear the headset for the full Mars experience!

Lewis got to work completing the tasks as they appeared on the display in front of him.

The first was to maneuver the rover around two rocks and press a sensor hidden behind a rock on the left. Lewis thought that this would be very easy but it still took him three goes to get the little robot lined up at the right angle.

The next challenge was to go over some rocks with the Rover without tipping over which would mean instant failure. The path between the rocks was V-shaped like a river valley with a slope either side. Lewis worked out that he needed the wheels of the Rover on each slope of the valley to keep the Rover level and stop it falling over.

He navigated the robot to the beginning of the valley and slowly pushed the speed lever forwards, too much power would be a disaster. The Rover edged forward and Lewis made slight adjustments to its direction to try and keep it level on the slope. He could hear shouting behind him and the stomping of lots feet but that didn't matter right now, he was on Mars carrying out a special mission and he had to focus.

A tall spotty student from another school barged past Lewis knocking into him. This made him lose his concentration and sent the robot crawling up one side of the valley. Now it was completely stuck almost vertically, staring at the ceiling. He tried moving the robot forward and backward but all that it did was make the Rover slide sideways until eventually, it ended up on its back.

'YOU FAILED' flashed up on the display in front of his eyes. Lewis sighed with disappointment, as he let go of the controls and picked up his rucksack.

He looked at his watch, it was 12:02, he was late for the Planetarium show, Miss Steward would not be happy. Lewis began to walk away.

"Don't you want your certificate?" asked the attendant, who was waving a sheet of red card.

Lewis did want the certificate so he walked back to the attendant.

"What is your name?" she asked.

"Its Lewis Mudd, that's Mudd with two Ds" he replied.

The attendant used a pen with silver ink to write Lewis' name on the certificate and then stamped it with the date.

"There you go, you might have gotten further if that boy hadn't interrupted you," remarked the attendant as she handed the certificate to Lewis.

"Thank you," he said nervously, turning around to walk away.

He gazed down at the certificate '1 out of 6 challenges completed' it wasn't the best result but it was a brand new certificate for his space wall at home.

He looked up to see that the planetarium staff where just about to close the doors for the next show. 'Oh no, Miss is going to be mad that I fell behind again,' Lewis thought to himself. He walked passed the model of Mars and the meteorite display as he headed towards the planetarium entrance doors.

But then he stopped, something wasn't right, what wasn't right, had he left his backpack behind? He felt behind him, the backpack was there. His brain would do this to him sometimes, it would tell him there was something wrong but let him figure out what it was. Lewis looked around him, it all looked amazing, but he wasn't looking for amazing right now.

He turned around and looked behind him at the Mars exhibit. Something looked different in the meteorite display. He walked towards the glass box that housed the rocks and noticed that the largest of the meteorites was no longer sat on its display perch but was laying at the bottom of the display case with a piece chipped off.

Lewis looked around, there was no one else nearby and the Rover challenge attendant had gone to lunch.

He walked over to the display case for a better look 'Maybe all those children stomping past it earlier had vibrated it off its stand' he thought to himself. Lewis jumped on the spot, the rock didn't move. He kicked the metal base of the glass display with his foot, nothing happened.

As he knelt down on the floor next to the display, Lewis could hear a low humming sound coming from the display. He pressed his nose against the display to get a closer look at the now damaged rock and to hear the humming better.

The glass of the display vibrated against his nose, and the humming was louder the closer he got to the meteorite. Lewis could see that where the rock had chipped, it was very shinning underneath. 'Wow, this is weird but awesome!' he thought to himself.

He placed his right hand on the glass to steady himself as he tried to get as close as possible to the rock from Mars behind the glass. Suddenly a beam of orange light hit the glass underneath the palm of Lewis' hand and began rapidly heating up the glass.

"Ouch!" exclaimed Lewis as he pulled his hand away from the hot glass. He got up off the floor and ran over to the planetarium entrance to try and find Zara while holding his burnt hand.

Chapter Two
The Agents of DAIT

As the DAIT helicopter soared through the sky over Leicestershire Special Agent Evie Bowman and Special Agent Brent Harrogate were informed of the situation by government scientists Dr. Bailey & Dr. Alexander.

The Drop Hoop transportation network was currently offline for an extended range upgrade which was why they had to fly. The hoops allowed someone to drop through at one location and arrive instantly through a hoop at another location as if you were stepping through a doorway, hence the name Drop Hoop.

The two agents had been assigned at short notice to escort the scientists to the National Space Centre, so they could investigate the report of an unstable Martian rock.

"Lewis Mudd aged 13 witnessed the incident," said Dr. Bailey as he handed Brent a tablet and then adjusted his Black square framed spectacles.

The tablet showed a photo of Lewis and his school record, Evie leaned over to read.

"Quiet, keeps himself to himself, a bright student, impressive grades," remarked Evie.

"The CCTV in the building captured the whole incident from two angles" Dr. Alexander informed them as he gestured towards the tablet.

Brent swiped left on the tablet, and both the agents examined the video footage. It showed the rock fall off its display stand without any outside interference, and Lewis approach it, kneeling to get a better look. Followed by Lewis running off holding his hand.

Evie and Brent looked at each other, this was something new they hadn't encountered before.

"How far are we?" Evie asked the pilot.

"ETA is five minutes Agent Bowman," came the reply from the pilot.

Brent handed the tablet back to Dr. Bailey. And both the agents gave their equipment one final check, they both had their standard issue DAIT agent kit with them. It consisted of a Plasma Pistol, PSM (Portable Scanner Mobile), and Radio. The scientists looked at each other and then at Evie and Brent.

"May we ask which field you both specialise in? You don't look like scientists" asked Dr. Alexander.

"And your certainly not police" added Dr. Bailey pointing at Brent's Plasma Pistol.

They were right, Evie was wearing black army issue boots, Black denim jeans, a Black shirt, and a Black leather jacket while Brent was wearing a Black suit with waist coast and a Black tie.

"We specialise in Intelligence & Technology" Brent replied.

"What's in the case?" asked Dr. Bailey pointing to the large white metal case with a DAIT insignia on one side, sitting on the floor between Evie and Brent.

"That's our support kit," said Evie as she patted the case.

The pilot of the helicopter shouted back to his passengers.

"We're approaching the Space Centre."

Below them, the swirling rooftop of the Space Centre came into view along with the Rocket Tower standing proud. Outside the centre, there was a large crowd of school students and members of the public as well as three Police cars with their blue lights flashing.

They had been told to exit the Space Centre by Staff and wait in the car park while the situation was assessed by government officials.

The helicopter settled onto the concrete of the car park in an area ringed by blue and yellow traffic cones and Police tape, which had been specially set up for their arrival.

Evie was the first to exit the helicopter followed by Brent and the two scientists carrying bags of equipment. They were met by PC Farthing as they walked toward the Space Centre entrance. Metal barriers had already been erected along the route for the safety of the public.

"We're glad you are here, this isn't something we have had to deal with before," said PC Farthing with relief in his voice.

"Is anyone still in the building?" asked Brent as the group continued walking toward the centre.

"Just the head curator and a couple of us," replied the PC.

"And the boy who witnessed the event?" enquired Evie.

"He's being seen by paramedics right now for burns to his right hand, over there," explained PC Farthing as he pointed to the ambulance at the back of the crowd.

"This is too public, we are going to need to contain this," said Evie to Brent with concern in her voice. Brent nodded.

"I'll organize a phone wipe with HQ," he said.

Lewis watched from the steps of the ambulance as the team made their way to the centre entrance they were greeted by a member of the Space Centre staff.

"Thank goodness you're here, I'm Carol Lowe the senior curator," she said.

"I'm Special Agent Bowman, this is Special Agent Harrogate and this is Dr. Bailey and Dr. Alexander" replied Evie.

Carol shook each one's hand.

"I wasn't expecting so many of you, please follow me," she said.

They entered the building and followed Carol towards the Planets zone.

"Has there been any more activity?" asked Evie,

"Nothing since we reported it to the Police" replied Carol.

It was strangely quiet in the Space Centre since all the visitors had been escorted out of the building.

Carol led Evie, Brent, and the two doctors through the centre, past the various displays to the

Planets zone. There were still school bags and clipboards dotted around the floor which had been abandoned by the school children as they quickly made their way outside.

As they neared the Mars exhibit, Police tape could be seen enclosing the whole area.

"The display case is just behind the Mars model and off to the left," said Carol as she stopped.

"Aren't you coming?" asked Brent.

"I would rather wait over here while you deal with whatever it is" answered Carol.

Evie unholstered her pistol, raised the tape over her head and entered the exhibit. Brent unholstered his pistol and followed. Carol stopped Dr. Bailey.

"Why do they have guns? Who are they?" she asked.

Dr. Bailey looked across to the agents then back at Carol and shrugged.

"IT specialists apparently," he replied.

As the agents passed the large model of Mars, Brent took his mobile scanner out of his jacket pocket and started to take readings of the surroundings.

"It's all looking normal at the moment" he reported.

They turned left and continued slowly forward through the exhibit. Suddenly Brents scanner started to bleep, slowly at first, then faster as the display case came into view.

A hole had been but through the glass display and any objects in the way of the meteorites beam. On its diagonal route out of the Space Centre and through the corrugated metal roof.

Evie walked around the damaged display, examining the contents from all angles, the rock seemed to be lifeless. Evie retrieved her scanner from her jacket and attached it to the display glass next to the meteorite. She began scanning the structure of the rock for anything unusual.

"Gentlemen, if you wouldn't mind," said Brent gesturing at the scientists to come closer and start running the tests they had been brought here for.

The doctors set their equipment bags down on the floor and started unloading the contents while Brent grabbed a nearby waist height display case and wheeled it over for the doctors to use as a worktop.

There were microscopes, precision drills & saws, carbon dating equipment, laptops, blue medical gloves, and a well-used notebook. He walked over to Evie who was kneeling on the floor in front of her scanner pressing various menu options.

"Any luck," he asked.

"I'm not able to penetrate this rock which is concerning as I can scan the interior of the other two meteorites with no problem at all. I think we will need to use both scanners in sync mode," she replied while adjusting the settings on her scanner.

She looked up at Brent who had already attached his scanner to the glass opposite Evie's and had begun to calibrate it, so it was ready to sync with hers.

"Ok mine Sync ready, I have boosted the scanning power level," he reported.

"Ok just a minute, I will raise mine to match," replied Evie as she reconfigured her scanner.

"Ok syncing… sync locked! It shouldn't take too long now," confirmed Brent.

Dr. Bailey joined the pair by the display.

"We are going to need a sample of the rock please," he asked.

"I noticed that there is a chipped piece, lying next to the meteorite, is that big enough?" answered Brent as he pointed at the fragment in the case.

The doctor crouched down and peered into the display.

"Yes that would be perfect, we should be able to do all the analysis we need with that," replied the doctor.

"Let's go and ask the curator for the key," said Brent.

He and Dr. Bailey walked out of the exhibit and over to the police tape where Carol was still standing waiting patiently, she had been joined by PC Farthing.

"Is it safe? Have you found anything?" she asked with concern.

"We are still examining the situation at the moment, could we please have the key to that display case?" replied Brent.

"Yes of course," said Carol, as she felt her pockets to find which one had the keys in it.

She pulled out a large metal hoop with keys all the way around it. Carol unclipped a small red key from the bunch of keys and handed it to Brent.

"There you go. How much longer will this take? I need to know if I can send the Staff and visitors home," she asked.

Brent handed the key to Dr. Bailey who walked back into the exhibit to join his colleague.

"This is a category 2B incident and requires lockdown until the situation has been assessed," answered Brent

"Hang on, 2B is a DAIT incident code, your DAIT Agents?" asked PC Farthing.

Understanding DAIT level codes and procedures were part of the basic training at the Police Training College but he'd never met a DAIT agent before.

"That's correct, I can understand that this isn't something you have had to deal with before but this is our standard procedure and you will all be compensated," PC Farthing nodded.

"Understood, we will arrange for food and drinks to be distributed," he said.

This was all a lot for Carol to take in and raised a lot of questions.

"Can someone explain to me what DAIT is?" she enquired.

"Department of Alien Intelligence and Technology, they always turn up when there is something out of the ordinary," answered PC Farthing.

Carols eyes opened wide, she loved space and science fiction, that's how she came to apply for the curator's job at the Space Centre in the first place.

"You mean that meteorite could've been an actual alien all this time and we didn't know?" she asked. Brent smiled.

"I'm sorry, I can't tell you anything else at the moment" he replied.

Brent turned and walked back into the exhibit leaving Carol standing there, her head still full of questions. 'Will I see an Alien? Would it be aggressive? What do I tell my husband? Will my lovely Space Centre be damaged? Will they close us down? Will we get extra funding after this?' she thought.

The sound of precision drilling could be heard coming from the area of the display case. And as Brent turned the corner he could see the doctors hard at work analyzing the rock sample and performing various chemical tests.

Evie was still running the scan on the meteorite.

"Any luck with the scan yet?" he asked.

Evie stood up off the floor and dusted herself off.

"We should have the results in the next couple of minutes," she replied. "How are they doing at the front of the Space Centre?" she asked.

"The curator is concerned about the welfare of her staff and guests, which is understandable and the Police are managing the civilians," reported Brent.

"Well we should be able to bag and tag the rock and be back at base by 4," replied Evie while looking at her watch. "The doctors were having quite a loud disagreement just now, let's see what that was all about" she added.

They walked over to the doctors who were still mumbling at each other.

"Is there a problem doctors?" enquired Evie as she looked at them both.

"Just a disagreement over the age of the meteorite," replied Dr. Alexander. "I believe the date to be 1.38 billion years old and Dr. Bailey believes the date to be 4480 years," he added.

"Clearly its 4480 years old because the test I use is always accurate," announced Dr. Bailey.

"But your testing technique is still in development and my testing technique has been tried and tested for years" interrupted Dr. Alexander.

"So which one is it?" asked Brent who was now confused.

Before either of the doctors could reply to Brents question, a blue laser beam shot out of the meteorite and began to move around the room. The four of them turned around to face the beam.

"Nobody move!" whispered Evie.

The beam began to form various hexagon shaped symbols before it stopped at one and then continued to move around the room.

"Its some kind of holographic laser scanner" offered Brent.

Evie nodded as she looked down at her watch. She was able to get a direct feed from her scanner on her watch face and the readings were going through the roof. She looked up at Brent standing next to her and gestured with her eyes that he looks down at her watch too.

The meteorites scanner stopped moving on the ground just in front of them. It then cycled through more completely unknown alien symbols before stopping at one with a large circle surrounded by smaller circles.

Dr. Alexander slowly and quietly reached inside his trouser pocket and took out his mobile phone as the scanner moved towards Evie. It scanned its way up her body spinning clockwise and then anticlockwise until it reached her pistol holster where it paused. 'Damn, it's going to think I am aggressive' Evie thought to herself, but after a brief time, the scanner continued to move up to head height where stopped again. A cluster of circles turned green and separated from the main scanner symbol, floating to the right of it.

"What's it doing?" whispered Evie.

"Fascinating" whispered Dr. Bailey as he raised his phone, ready to take a photo.

There was a flash of white light and the scanner vanished. Brent and Evie looked around them to see Dr. Bailey standing there with his phone in hand looking sheepish.

"Sorry about that, I forgot to turn the flash off," he said as he offered a nervous smile.

"Never use a camera flash when dealing with unknown alien technology, it could have made that thing aggressive," said Evie with disapproval on her face.

"Sorry about that, but at least it didn't" replied Dr. Bailey.

The room fell silent, maybe he shouldn't have said that he thought.

"No more photos, either of you" barked Evie before she turned and walked quickly over to the meteorite.

Brent shook his head.

"Never annoy Agent Bowman," he remarked.

"But I did manage to get a photo of the scanner, surely that's good?" asked Dr. Bailey as he handed his phone to Brent.

"I'm going to need to keep this, ok?" answered Brent.

"Yes, of course, lesson learned and all that," answered the doctor.

Brent walked over to show the photo to Evie.

"I can't believe you did that," said Dr. Alexander.

"As if you wouldn't, we're scientists and being curious is what we do," he replied.

"That may be so, but I would have made sure my phone flash was off" answered, Dr. Alexander.

"Dr. Bailey managed to get a photo of that holographic scanner," said Brent as Evie crouched down to check the PSM's for their scan results.

Evie said nothing, she was too focused on what she saw on screen. Brent looked again at the photo and continued "I'll run it through DAIT Central and see if there is a match."

Evie detached her PSM from the display glass and stood up.

"There is a high energy power source inside that rock," said Evie.

Brent grabbed his mobile scanner from the glass to view the results for himself. The visual scan showed the rough exterior of the rock and a smooth internal structure.

"High energy but unstable by the look of the readings while it was scanning you, what could it be powering?" he answered while uploading the photo of the holographic scan to his PSM.

"It could be anything, even a weapon, we need to proceed with caution," replied Evie.

"The structure of the rock isn't natural, it's too perfect" announced Dr. Alexander as he joined the agents. "We also believe that the rock is approximately 4499 years old, give or take a year." He added.

"So what you're saying is, that someone built it around the device inside?" asked Brent.

"That's correct, but what we cant…" Before Dr. Alexander could finish his sentence the holographic laser from the meteorite activated once more and began its scan of the room.

The Agents and the doctor froze to the spot. Dr. Bailey, who was busy packing away the analysis equipment, didn't notice the laser activate and jumped with fright when the laser appeared between his legs.

"It's following the same path as last time" whispered Evie as they watched the laser begin its scan of Dr. Bailey.

The beam scanned its way up the doctor's body and stopped at head height once again. And just like last time a cluster of circles turned green, left the main symbol cluster and hovered just to the right of it. But then the cluster of circles changed into a picture of a hand with 4 fingers and a thumb which gently pulsed.

"What should I do?" whispered Dr. Bailey.

"It wants your hand, raise it slowly," Evie instructed him.

The doctor raised his hand up to the pulsing symbol and then reached out to touch the hologram. The cluster of green circles moved towards the doctor's hand like bees around a honeypot. Then all of a sudden the cluster of circles turned red and whole hologram vanished. Evie looked down at her watch.

"That hologram was seven minutes after the last one, it must be on a loop" she informed the group. Dr. Bailey was still standing with his hand raised, he had found the whole experience a little overwhelming.

"You can relax now Doc, it's over for the time being," said Brent as he patted the pale looking doctor on the shoulder.

He checked his PSM and noticed that he had a result back from his photo search.

"It looks like the Meteorite and its cargo are definitely from Mars, some of the symbols we saw match hieroglyphs on a Martian artifact that one of our dig teams found in New Guinea," Brent reported.

Evie paused for a moment, tapping her finger on her top lip. She did this whenever she was trying to work something out. Brent hoped that it would be followed by a finger click, which always meant that she had worked something out. Sure enough, the finger click came.

"Lewis!" she exclaimed.

"I don't follow," Answered Brent.

"When Lewis interacted with the beam it was orange, and it burned him," continued Evie.

"And he was being treated by paramedics when we arrived," Added Brent.

"But we don't know HOW it burned him," she concluded.

Brent knew where she was heading on this train of thought.

"I'll go and find Lewis," said Brent as he turned and ran out of the exhibit towards the exit. They didn't have much time before the hologram would activate again.

Chapter Three
The discovery

Lewis was sitting on the steps of the ambulance, staring at his right hand. The burn had been cleaned up by the paramedics and a bandage had been wrapped around his palm. Word had quickly spread around the rest of the class about Lewis' accident. He had been joined by Miss Steward and the dance troop who had been asking him lots of question about what had happened.

"Maybe you put your hand to close to the lights in the display," suggested Zia.

"Did it say anything to you?" enquired Zara.

"You're always involved when something happens on our school trips Lewis," said Miss Steward shaking her head and smiling.

"Ok Lewis, you are all patched up, and we have all the details we need for our records." said the female paramedic as she smiled at Lewis.

She then began to close up the ambulance ready for its departure.

Brent exited the Space Centre through the front door and quickly went over to the group.

"Sorry to interrupt ladies!" he said to the girls.

"You're Lewis Mudd right?" he asked.

Lewis nodded, Brent showed Lewis his ID badge.

"I'm Mr. Dawson and I work for the Museums and Trusts, we need to ask you a few questions, please come with me. You can leave your bag here," instructed Brent.

"Where are you taking him?" asked Miss Steward looking concerned.

"Just inside the centre for a moment, I will bring him straight back if he likes he can bring a friend with him," Brent replied.

"I'll go," offered Zara.

"Is he in trouble?" asked Poppy.

"Brent didn't say anything, he just smiled as three of them turned around and walked back towards the Centre entrance.

Brent looked over his shoulder and nodded at the paramedic in the ambulance, she nodded back and started up the ambulance.

When they entered the Space Centre Lewis noticed that it felt different for him this time. He wasn't filled with excitement as he had been a few hours ago, instead this time he was actually a little scared.

"What do you need to ask me?" he asked as they quickly walked behind Brent through the exhibits. "We actually need your help" answered Brent as they walked into the Planet zone.

Lewis and Zara looked at each other 'What do they need my help for' thought Lewis.

Brent stopped when they got to the Mars Exhibit and turned around.

"Ok Lewis, my real name is Agent Brent Harrogate and I work for the Department of Alien Intelligence and Technology. What you're about to see is extremely secret and must not be passed on to anyone," he explained.

Lewis nodded, Brent pulled a small cylindrical device out of his pocket with a button at one end and showed it to Lewis.

"I am going to insert a small device under the skin on your neck," Brent explained.

Zara could see that Lewis was a little scared at the thought of having something under his skin.

"Don't worry Lewis, they know what they are doing," said Zara.

Brent put the device on Lewis' neck and pressed the button, there was a tiny ping sound.

"If you are unable to keep what you see a secret, then we will have no choice but to erase the whole day from your memory," said Brent.

Lewis' eyes opened wide, he looked over to Zara, he would forget becoming friends with her and he didn't want that.

"Ok, I'll keep it secret for my whole life," he replied.

"Ok, good lad, you'll all done, let's go," answered Brent.

He turned around and they continued into the exhibit.

"But what about Zara?" asked Lewis.

"She knows the procedure, she has already been done," replied Brent.

Lewis looked at Zara with surprise in his eyes.

"That's right Lewis, I am tagged too!" said Zara pulling down her shirt collar.

They turned the corner and arrived at the glass display.

"You just missed it, Dr. Alexander tried this time but still nothing, we have four minutes until it activates again, Lewis may be the key," said Evie.

She looked at the worried schoolboy.

"Hello Lewis, I'm Agent Bowman but you call me Evie. Can I take a look at your hand?". Lewis put his hand out, and Evie used her PSM to scan it.

"How can your phone do that? I want mine to do that!" asked Lewis looking impressed.

Evie Smiled.

"He has a hieroglyph etched underneath the skin on his palm," she called across to Brent who was talking with the two doctors.

"Lewis, we are going to need to take that bandage off, is that ok?" asked Evie.

"Um, yeah ok, I'm not in trouble am I? I didn't mean for it to happen," said a worried Lewis.

Evie shook her head.

"You're not in any trouble Lewis, in fact, you may be saving us" she replied.

She unwrapped Lewis bandaged to reveal an intricately detailed Martian symbol on his hand. It was more complex than the ones that the hologram had shown them. Evie turned to Zara "Good call on this one Zara" she said.

"Two minutes!" announced Brent as he set up his PSM on a table to record the next hologram activation.

"Zara can you go and stand over there by the scientists," said Evie pointing at the two doctors. "And Lewis can you come and stand here" she continued as she directed Lewis to stand to face the display case at a distance of about four meters.

"One minute!" Brent informed them.

"What do you want me to do? It's not going to burn me again is it?" asked a nervous Lewis.

This was all new to him and he wasn't exactly sure what was going on.

"The rock is going to activate a hologram and scan you. When it stops at head height you are going to see a hand symbol, when that happens you need to put your hand up so it can be scanned by the meteorite. Do you understand?" explained Evie.

"Ok, I think I get it," replied Lewis.

Evie went over to join the others who were watching and waiting.

After exactly seven minutes the rock activated its hologram and began its scanning cycle. It explored the contours and shapes of the surrounding area.

Lewis stood frozen to the spot, half scared, half amazed, all excited. Here he was on what began as an amazing Friday, about to interact with some sort of Alien device while being watched by special secret agents and his new friend Zara. The scanner stopped at Lewis' feet.

"Here we go" whispered Brent.

The scanner made its way slowly up Lewis' body but it didn't stop at his head, instead, it stopped at his chest and began cycling through different hieroglyphs, finally stopping at one with wavey lines and squares.

"Has Lewis got anything in his pockets?" Evie asked Zara.

"Just his asthma inhaler I think," replied Zara.

"It must be analyzing his lungs," offered Dr. Bailey.

After a while, the scanner seemed satisfied and continued to move up Lewis' body to his head.

The hologram changed into the circle's hieroglyph and Lewis watched as a small cluster of circles broke away from the hieroglyph and floated to the left forming a hand shape. He looked over to Evie, 'was this when I have to use my hand?' he thought, Evie nodded and Lewis turned back to the glyph.

'One small step for me, one giant leap for mankind' he thought to himself as he raised his hand to meet the cluster of circles.

The circles split into smaller circles and began to orbit his hand, weaving in between and around his fingers before settling on the hieroglyph burned into the palm of his hand, but then the hologram vanished again.

Evie turned to Brent and sighed.

"Well that's disappointing," she said.

"Are you ok Lewis," asked Zara as she ran over to him.

Lewis had a big smile on his face and opened his mouth to answer when suddenly the whole area was filled with a large hologram. It showed the device contained within the rock surrounded by diagnostic information in an unknown language and a tall humanoid figure standing next to the device and speaking in an unknown language.

"Now THIS is better," said Evie as she and Brent stepped forward to examine the hologram.

"We'll need to figure out what all this means," said Brent as he looked all around him at the different parts of the hologram.

It looked like they were standing in some sort of Martian control room.

"This is a huge discovery for the scientific community," said Dr. Bailey.

"I agree, we need to take this rock back to our laboratory straight away and start a full series of tests" added Dr. Alexander.

The agents looked at each other, it was time for the scientists to leave. They had fulfilled their purpose but now they had to go before they compromised the situation.

Evie turned around to face the two scientists.

"Ok gentlemen, thank you very much for all your hard work today, you will each receive a bonus in your salary. But I'm afraid we are going to have to ask you to leave now. Agent Harrogate will escort you out" she instructed and then turned back to the hologram.

"But tests need to be performed, and departments need to be notified," answered Dr. Alexander. "And those tests will be performed by our teams, thank you" replied Evie without turning her head.

"This is the most amazing thing ever isn't it?" announced Lewis excitedly.

"There are plenty more amazing things like this to see!" replied Zara.

Lewis frowned.

"How do you know these people? Did you get abducted by aliens?! Did they rescue you?!" he asked.

"Nooo silly, I have known Evie, or Agent Bowman for years, she used to teach us to dance," she said. "but as you can see she has her hands full at the moment dealing with things like this" Zara added and pointed at the hologram in front of them.

Brent helped the scientists pack away their equipment, while they mumbled under their breath about how the odd situation was, and why they had been asked to leave. He then escorted the scientists out of the building to the waiting helicopter.

"Ok gentlemen, it has been a pleasure, thank you," he said while shaking their hands.

Then as they boarded the helicopter he discreetly placed a small device on each of their backs.

"Drop these two off at the airport," he instructed pilot over the noise of the rotor blades.

Brent closed the door and stepped back so the helicopter could take off.

"How are you feeling Lewis? It can be quite overwhelming the first time you see something like this" enquired Evie as she joined the two school students by the hologram.

Evie scanned the data displayed by the hologram with her PSM before uploading it to the DAIT Central server.

"I'm great thanks, can we stay or do we have to leave too?" asked Lewis.

"You can stay with us for the moment, how is your hand?" replied Evie.

In all the excitement Lewis had completely forgotten about the burn on his hand. He looked down at his palm, and to his surprise, the burn had completely healed.

"Its, Its gone," he announced with complete surprise in his voice.

"May I take a look?" asked Evie. Lewis nodded and raised his arm so Evie could see.

She adjusted a couple of settings on her PSM and then scanned his palm. "It looks like it healed you when you interacted with it," said Evie analyzing the results from the scan. "There are some radiation traces but nothing that will kill you," she added.

"It's like it never happened," said Lewis looking a little disappointed as he rubbed the palm of his hand.

"The scientists are on their way back to the airport," reported Brent as he joined the group back at the exhibit. "And by now they should be sound asleep with no memory of the event" he added.

"Good, the last thing we need is some mouthy scientists causing panic" answered Evie as her PSM began to bleep repeated. "It's the secure line," she said, looking at her PSM. Evie pressed a button on the display to answer the call.

"How's my number one agent," said a voice on the other end of the phone.

It was Vincent Novak Commander of DAIT Base Gamma.

"She is wondering why you are calling her personally. Arent, you supposed to be giving a talk at the Alpha Centauri conference right now?" replied Evie.

"You know me if there's going to be a breakthrough discovery I like to be involved. Besides the conference is mainly for the diplomats and the one talking right now hasn't even come up for air yet!" explained Vincent.

"I'm guessing you have some answers for us," asked Evie.

"You've guessed right, indeed I do, I am now swapping to video," he replied.

Evie quickly attached her PSM device to a nearby display monitor before pressing a button on the device to switch over to video call mode.

The display showed a man in his forties with a full beard and mustache. He was sharply dressed wearing a dark grey suit, light grey shirt, and a blue paisley tie which Evie instantly recognized as she had brought it for him as a thank you gift.

"You're wearing the tie!" she said with surprise.

"I'm hoping it brings me some luck, I hate speaking at these things" Vincent replied.

He pressed some buttons on the computer at his end and three small diagrams overlayed the video display.

"Using the symbols you've recorded at the Space Centre and the hieroglyphs on the artifact from New Guinea together with our known language database, B-A-L-I-X has been able to decipher 80% of the language. It's ancient Martian." Explained Vincent.

"So what does it say?" asked Brent

"What you're dealing with here is what the Martians call a 'Mark 3 Soul Transportation Vessel', basically a lifeboat," answered Vincent.

Both the agents looked behind them at the meteorite in the display case, then at each other before turning back at Vincent.

"It's a bit small for a lifeboat boss," replied Evie.

"This is where it gets interesting," said Vincent.

He paused while he swapped some graphics around on the display.

"The Lifeboat uses a form of miniaturization technology, powered by a type of fuel cell that we have never seen before. It was one of 2111 lifeboats that were launched to save Martian lives when the atmosphere of Mars became too toxic for them," Explained Vincent.

"Where were they heading?" asked Brent.

"To the star system Talitha. It was supposed to return to its normal size after a journey of 2000 years" replied Vincent.

"How many lives are on the lifeboat sir?" asked Lewis.

He and Zara had been listening to the conversation and now curiosity had gotten the better of him.

"Ah, Lewis is it?" asked Vincent.

Lewis nodded.

"Thank you for helping my agents to access the artifact. There are six million lives currently in cryo-sleep onboard that lifeboat" he added.

"WHAT?!" came the response from the entire room.

"Vincent are you sure about that? Could the translation be wrong?" questioned Evie.

"I couldn't believe it too that's why we've run the data through B-A-L-I-X eight times already and the result is always the same" replied Vincent.

"So if it contains six million lives, how big is it when it's normal size? Are Martians the size of Ants?" asked Brent.

"Professor James has been doing some equations based on the technical information and the medical logs from the holograph," said Vincent, he paused "The Martians are roughly the same size as us which make the lifeboat about the size of Berlin" he added.

"All this doesn't explain why it's still tiny, and how it ended up on Earth, instead of leaving our solar system," questioned Evie.

"The Professor has a theory about that, he thinks that the lifeboat collided with some space debris as it left Mars which sent it off course. That collision may have also caused the vessel to malfunction which is why it hasn't returned to full size" answered Vincent. An agent entered Vincent's office and could be seen whispering in his ear, Vincent nodded and the agent left the room.

"Ok, it looks the diplomat has run out of breath and they now need me in the conference," said Vincent as he got up from his desk and picked up a folder of paperwork with the DAIT insignia on the front.

"Evie, Brent, your PSMs have been sent an upgraded to allow you to translate the glyphs yourselves, I want to be notified if anything changes," Instructed Vincent.

"You got it boss!" replied Evie while she checked her PSM for the upgrade.

"This is now a category 3B incident, anything could happen so I want all non-essential staff to leave the site. Novak Out" added Vincent before ending the call.

Evie detached her PSM from the display and turned to the two students.

"Zara and Lewis, sorry but we need to get you both back to your class and home now," she instructed.

"I'll set up a containment zone around the display," Brent informed her.

Evie nodded and then walked out of the exhibit followed by Zara and Lewis.

Brent checked the time on his watch. 'The Drop Hoops should be back online by now' he thought to himself. Brent moved the white case they had brought with them into an open space and placed his thumb on the lock. The case bleeped twice.

"Agent Harrogate requesting a Drop Hoop" Brent instructed the case. There was a couple of clicks and then the case opened itself and millions of nanobots spilled out of it and started building a Drop Hoop. While it was building, he used his PSM to request the specific equipment that he would need.

"This has been the best day ever, it's just a shame I can't talk to anyone about it" replied Lewis.

"You can talk to me about it anytime," said Zara.

"How many times have you seen stuff like this?" he asked.

"This is the third time but I can't tell you about the other two, obviously!" she replied.

Carol the curator was waiting by the Police tape for them.

"Please tell me you have good news?" she asked.

"Yes, all visitors need to leave now, but I'm afraid we still need you to stay in case we need access to other areas" explained Evie.

Carol nodded in agreement.

"My deputy also has access, will you need her too?" she said.

"Yes indeed, all staff with all area access need to stay on site," answered Evie.

"OK, well I think she is outside with the others," said Carol.

"Let's go out and find her, you can also tell the visitors the good news that they can go home now," said Evie.

"Can I quickly go to the loo?" asked Lewis.

In all the excitement he had forgotten about his bladder but now he was desperate.

"Ok Lewis, but be quick. Zara can you stay with him please," answered Evie.

Zara and Lewis walked back towards the toilets while Carol and Evie walked out of the entrance to find the deputy curator.

Outside the Space Centre, the crowd of visitors was starting to get restless. They had been standing outside for hours and now they wanted answers. PC Farthing was talking to some of the visitors when he noticed Agent Bowman and Carol the curator leave the building. He walked over to find out what was happening, he was secretly hoping that Agent Bowman was going to tell him there was alien loose in the building and she needed his help to catch it.

"What's the situation? Do you require our assistance inside?" he asked hopefully.

Evie shook her head.

"Everything is under control, but the incident is now category 3B so the visitors and all staff except the curators must leave the site," explained Evie.

"Ok, understood, we'll get these people home" he replied before climbing up onto a wall outside the Centre to address the visitors. "Ladies, Gentlemen, and children, can I have your attention, please. We have just been instructed that the Space Centre is now closed for the rest of the day. Please make your way to your vehicles" said PC Farthing to the crowd.

"What about our money, we want a refund!" barked an angry parent.

PC Farthing looked over to Carol for an answer. He could see Evie whisper something in Carol's ear before the Curator put her thumb up. PC Farthing turned back to the crowd.

"You will all receive a refund in due course" he announced before climbing down from the wall and beginning to usher visitors back to their cars and coaches.

Meanwhile, back in the Mars exhibit, the hologram was still active and displaying the same information in a loop. Brent was busy setting up a containment zone around the Martian rock. He had erected five containment posts, evenly spaced around the rock and was now using a tablet to set them up. As each one came online the light on top and halfway down started pulsing a bright Red.

Just as Brent activated the final containment post the Martian hologram flickered and then went off.

'That's odd,' thought Brent 'Maybe the strength of the containment field was interfering with the hologram.' He adjusted some settings on the tablet to lower the field strength. This made the lights on the posts change to a bright orange. The hologram flickered back to life but this time it was red and showed a scan of the human anatomy surrounded by Martian hieroglyphs that he hadn't been seen before.

Zara was still waiting outside the toilets for Lewis, she knocked on the door.

"Come on Lewis we're going to miss our bus back to school," she said loudly.

There was a moment of silence.

"I'll be out in a minute, it's taking longer than I thought" came a slightly muffled reply from Lewis.

Eating his lunch and two bags of sweets on the bus to the Space Centre hadn't been a good idea and now his stomach was getting its revenge! He left the cubicle and walked over to the sinks. As he turned on the tap and began washing his hands, Lewis started to get a tingling sensation in his fingertips.

Sometimes just before an asthma attack, he would get the same feeling. He pulled his inhaler out of his pocket, removed the cap, placed it in his mouth and squirted a dose while breathing in. As he began counting to ten, Lewis could feel the tingling sensation flow throughout his entire body. '...3...4...5...' he counted. The tingling felt more like pins and needles now and it was distracting him from counting in his head '...5...6..7' Lewis vanished leaving his clothes and inhaler to fall to the floor.

Brent grabbed his PSM and began translating the new hieroglyphs to try and work out why the display had changed. He held his scanner in front of the scan of the human anatomy and it began to translate the hieroglyphs into words :

None Martian subject acquired.
Respiratory System Degraded.
Medical Evacuation Required.

'Medical Evacuation? For who?' Brent thought to himself. He moved his scanner across to another display which showed a blueprint of the Martian vessel with two sections highlighted in red :

Fuel cell overloaded.
Ability to support crew compromised.
Approximately 3 days until Catastrophic failure.

Brent stood wide-eyed absorbing that last sentence. Whatever the Martians categorized as a catastrophic failure meant they only had three days to put a plan together so he ran out of the exhibit to find Evie.

Zara had had enough of waiting by now, they were going to be stranded in Leicester with detentions when they finally got back if Lewis didn't get a move on. She knocked on the door to the toilets one more time but there was no answer.

"Come on Lewis, we don't have time for this" she shouted through the toilet door.

But there was still no answer.

"Zara why are you still here, where is Lewis?" said Brent as he ran up to Zara.

"Lewis is in the toilets, but he won't come out and he's not answering me" she replied. Brent grabbed the toilet door handle and turned, he looked back at Zara.

"Wait here," he instructed and then opened the door.

"Lewis? Are you in here?" he shouted through the door, there was no response.

Brent opened the door completely and walked in to find Lewis' uniform Laying on the floor in a heap with his inhaler. He quickly checked all six toilet cubicles, there was no sign of the schoolboy.

"Where is Lewis? What's happened it him?" asked Zara who had ignored Brents instructions and followed him into the toilets.

"I'm not sure Zara, go and find Evie, now!" said Brent as he and took out his scanner.

Zara nodded and ran out of the toilets.

Outside the Space Centre, the carpark was almost empty apart from a handful of cars and the coach for Applewood High School. Miss Steward was talking to Evie and Carol.

"Well it was a lovely morning, its just a shame someone had to vandalize that display," she said as Zara ran up to them.

"And where have you been Zara? And where is Lewis? We've been waiting for you both so we can go home." asked Miss Steward.

"Sorry Miss, Lewis has had an accident in the toilets, I think we'll need that paramedic back here," said Zara while she tried to catch her breath.

Zara discreetly made the DAIT sign for distress with her hand, hoping that Evie would notice it.

"What kind of accident has he had Zara?" asked Miss Steward looking concerned.

Zara thought for a moment "Umm, I think he has broken something" she replied while gesturing to Evie with her eyes to look down.

"Well, let me take a look at him, I've taken a first aid course. It might be just a bruise" said Miss Steward.

Evie glanced down and noticed Zara's hand signal, something was wrong.

"Miss Steward, please take the children back to the school and we'll organize transport home for Zara and Lewis" she instructed the teacher.

"It's not school procedure to abandon students on school trips, let me come and take a look at him," asked Miss Steward as she stepped forwards.

"I'm afraid I must insist that you leave it to us" explained Evie as she stepped in front of the teacher with her hand raised to stop her moving any closer to the building.

Miss Steward looked a little puzzled by Agent Bowman's behavior "Ok, very well, I will ring the school to let them know the situation" she said and then walked over to the coach.

Evie turned to Zara.

"Ok that was close, what exactly has happened to Lewis?" she asked.

"He's gone" replied Zara.

"Gone, what do you mean gone!?" questioned Evie as they both walked quickly back into the Space Centre.

"Well, I was waiting for him outside the toilets. I knocked once and he said he would be out in a minute but he never came out and when I knocked again there was no answer. Then Brent came by and he went into the toilets and Lewis wasn't there, just his clothes and his inhaler on the floor." Explained Zara.   Carol the Curator and Jenny her deputy were waiting in Centre lobby for them. They had just dismissed the last member of staff and were wondering what they should be doing now.

"Excuse me, Agent Bowman, what do you want us to do?" she enquired as Evie and Zara walked past them.

"Please follow us," said Evie.

The four of them walked to the males toilets and stopped. Evie pulled her memory device out of her pocket "May I please see both of your necks, don't worry this is standard DAIT procedure" she asked. Carol and Jenny both looked a bit concerned.

"Its ok, I have one too," said Zara showing them her neck.

Evie tagged them both with a memory device from her dispenser.

"What you see from this point on, is highly classified, any mention of this to anyone and you will forget today ever happened," explained Evie.

Inside the toilets, Brent was just finishing his second scan sweep of the schoolboys uniform.

"What's the situation?" asked Evie.

"The lifeboat has suffered a fuel cell overload and is going to have a catastrophic failure in three days. At the same time, Lewis' was subjected to Theta radiation. There are traces of it all over his uniform, but there are no traces of Lewis' DNA anywhere," Reported Brent.

He stood up and straightened his suit.

"It sounds like the two events are definitely linked," said Evie as she knelt down to pick up Lewis' inhaler "His asthma may have triggered something on the lifeboat" she added.

"Excuse me, can I ask what exactly is going on here?" enquired Carol.

"There is an alien vessel inside the Martian meteorite that is in your display, and there is a strong possibility it is going explode in three days. We also now have a missing schoolboy," explained Evie.

Brent pulled out a bag dispenser from his pocket and tore off one bag. He then put Lewis' belongings inside and sealed it up.

"Zara can you look after these," he said handing her the bag.

"You mean we have had a real alien ship in our exhibit all this time?" asked Jenny.

"Never mind that, what was that about it exploding? Can you take it somewhere out of the way? You have three days!" enquired Carol.

"It may not be safe to move it. We could make things worse" explained Brent.

"Let's go back to the exhibit and try to get some answers" offered Evie.

The four of them walked out of the toilets and off towards the exhibit.

The meteorite was still active when they arrived, and it was displaying information about the crew onboard.

"Oh my, I have never seen anything like this," said Carol as she stepped around the hologram.

"What language is it?" asked Jenny.

"It's ancient Martian, we have been able to decipher most of it" replied Evie.

"That symbol has changed," said Brent as he pointed to a row of hieroglyphs "The others are the same but the one at the end is different" he added.

Evie used her PSM to scan the row of symbols "6...0...0...0...0...1" she announced.

"6,000,001? It was 6,000,000 earlier" said Zara.

"I think we now know where Lewis is," said Evie pointing at the rock.

"Are you saying there are over six million people inside that meteorite and your missing schoolboy is one of them? How is that even possible?" asked Carol.

"Inside that meteorite is a Martian Lifeboat vessel which was able to shrink in size. Full size it is as big as Berlin, but it shouldn't even be here, it should have left our solar system thousands of years ago" Explained Evie

"Why could it explode now?" asked Jenny.

"It would seem that when it scanned Lewis it found that he has asthma. So it took him to provide medical assistance. Unfortunately, the power source wasn't designed to run for this long or deal with an extra crew member." explained Brent.

"We need to tell Vincent the situation has changed and request assistance," said Evie.

Chapter Four
The Odd Couple

On the junction of Grafton Way and Princes Street in Ipswich stood a modern looking office building. Various companies rented offices inside and hundreds of people walked passed every day, but none of them knew that beneath the building was the DAIT headquarters.

The council chambers of DAIT headquarters were filled with visiting delegates and diplomats from the seventeen member star systems. They had all come together for the annual Alpha Centauri conference where new trade routes would be discussed, technology exchanged and laws created as part of the Centauri Alliance.

Among these were the Gralax, a hairy race from the frozen world of 'Trimera V'. The Wyloshi an amphibious race from the water world of 'Wylosha A' and the Lorkandian reptilian race from the desert world of 'Lorka III'. The Lorkandian had signed a peace treaty at last years Alpha Centauri conference, ending their 16-year war with the Gralax and the Wyloshi after the Evil Lorkandian General was killed in battle. Tensions were still high between the Gralax and Lorkandian so Vincent had made sure that extra security personnel were on duty.

The central lecture hall was a large hexagonal room with paintings on the walls of each of the member races. It doubled as a conference venue at times like these, inside a semi-circle of seats filled with diplomats listened intently as Vincent gave his speech about the new proposed Drop Hoop transport routes between the member homeworlds.

"And with the final Drop Hoop being completed at the end of year 15, this new transportation network will allow endless possibilities for trade and travel between our worlds. Ushering in a new era of prosperity that will allow us all to thrive and be happy." Vincent paused for a moment, had he forgotten something, yes he had "There will be Drop Hoop demonstrations in the main hub for those wishing to try out the technology for themselves, Thank you" he added and then left the presentation platform to applause from the delegates and diplomats.

"Excellent speech sir, very well done" remarked Zero 17 who was also clapping and had been waiting for Vincent in the chamber hallway.

"Oh shut up, Seventeen you're programmed to be nice" replied Vincent as they walked down the hall.

"Actually since the incident, my programming and my opinions are my own" Vincent turned his head and smiled but continued walking.

"How are the preparations going for the banquet?" he asked.

"There was a delay while the chefs tried to work out how to cook Gralax Barb Fish" replied the yellow android.

"Too big?" asked Vincent.

"No, too flammable sir" explained Zero 17.

They both nodded with hands on their chests as they passed a Lorkandian diplomat wear red robes in the hallway. It was the standard formal greeting for that particular species.

"Sir, Agent Bowman needs to speak to you urgently," said a frantic agent who had run down the hall to catch up with them.

Vincent checked his PSM, there were 8 missed calls from Evie. The agent continued "The Martian Vessel's fuel cell will go into catastrophic failure in three days, sir." Vincent stopped and looked behind him, the Lorkandian had gone.

"We never discuss missions openly when we have visitors on site, agent?" said Vincent.

"Sorry sir, Agent Reynolds, sir" replied the agent.

"You're new aren't you?" he asked.

"Yes sir, transferred in last week," said the agent saluting.

"Will you cut that out, and stop calling me sir, we are all agents here. Let's go to my office," said Vincent as the three of them walked quickly down the hall and turned into another long corridor.

The Lorkandian that Vincent thought was no longer there, had in actual fact been hiding out of view behind a wall listening to their conversation. His name was Dregg and he didn't agree with the peace treaty, because Dregg secretly was a member of the Lorkandian Pirate Clan. A group of foul smelling, evil, heartless thugs who sold their own families to underground Lorkandian slave mines for credits.

Dregg followed them quickly and quietly, making sure he wasn't seen. He wanted to find out more about the Martian vessel, could his brothers and sisters profit from it.

They entered the office and Vincent used his computer to make a secure video call to Evie to find out exactly what was going on. While the call was connecting he used his PSM to ask the professor to join them in his office. The call connected to show Evie with Brent and the others standing behind her.

"Agent Bowman what's going on over there?" asked Vincent.

"The lifeboat has taken Lewis. We believe this was because of his asthma and this has caused the old fuel cell to overload. It's telling us there will be a catastrophic failure in less than three days," explained Evie.

Vincent rubbed his beard and began pacing the room.

"How many people are now on site?" he asked.

"Just us five and the four Police officers outside," replied Evie.

"And is everyone tagged?" Queried Vincent.

Evie shook her head.

"The Police haven't been tagged yet," she replied.

Professor James entered the office and Vincent brought him up to speed.

"Arent there any ships available?" asked Evie.

"The soonest we could get one to you would be at least four days, so that's not an option" explained Vincent before turning back to the professor.

"Any thoughts professor?" he asked.

Professor James scratched his beard and thought for a moment.

"Unfortunately because the technology is completely unknown to us, not to mention microscopic it would impossible for us to repair it, we can't even be sure that the vessel is correctly reporting that the crew is still alive. We could place the vessel in one of our Aqua Fuel Cell transport containers which would make it easier to handle and transport. Using a Drop Hoop is out of the question because the strain on the vessels atomic structure may be too great and cause it to explode." Explained Professor James. "As we don't have any ships available to take it off-world, we could place it in one of our hazard materials capsules and then bury it in the ground somewhere away from civilians, in a desert maybe" he added.

"Would a capsule contain it?" asked Vincent concerned.

"The 60cm thick titanium walls would contain a high percentage of the explosion I believe" replied the professor confidently.

Dregg listened outside the door 'A vessel of extreme power and advanced technology, my brothers and sisters must have it' he thought to himself as he licked his eyeball with excitement. He ran down the corridor as fast as his six legs could carry him. 'I must make contact with my brothers and sisters quickly before they bury this vessel somewhere known' he decided as he entered his delegates suite.

"But Lewis is still in there and what about the others, there are millions of people on board that lifeboat, you can't do that," said Zara who was in shock at the whole suggestion of burying the vessel.

"The protection of our own species has to take priority," said Brent.

"How deep would we need to bury the vessel for it to be safe?" asked Evie.

"But that's not right, and what about Lewis, he is one of us!" shouted Zara with frustration in her voice, why weren't they listening to her.

"Zara, please go and wait outside," asked Evie.

"No, because you're not listening to me!" replied Zara tears running down her cheeks.

"We'll take her outside," offered Carol and put her arm around Zara.

"Come on, let's find you a drink and something to eat you must be hungry," she said.

"It's not fair, why won't they listen to me" cried Zara as the three of them walked off to the kitchens.

"Burying the vessel seems like our only real solution at the moment, unless you can find another way of moving the lifeboat off world that doesn't put any lives at risk. Zero 17 will help you with containment and transport of the vessel," concluded Vincent.

"Ok thank you, sir," said Evie.

"I think it may be wise to wipe this whole incident from Zara's memory given the circumstances," advised Vincent.

"She's a strong girl I don't think that will be necessary," replied Evie.

"Well, it's your call. Good luck, Novak out," said Vincent before ending the transmission.

"I'm going to speak to Zara," said Evie.

"Maybe Vincent is right about wiping this all from her memory," replied Brent.

"Can you make preparations for the vessels transport?" asked Evie.

"Yes, of course, I'll see you shortly," said Brent before walking back to the exhibit.

Evie stood in the open entrance hall for a moment and thought about what she was going to say to Zara. The thrill and excitement of encountering something new and alien had been replaced with sadness.

She walked over to the kitchens and slowly opened the door. Jenny was making Zara a large desert while Carol was sat down next to her with her arm around her.

"There you go, everything is better with ice cream," said Jenny as she placed the giant desert on the worktop in front of Zara.

"Thank you but I'm not really that hungry," said Zara.

"Well you don't have to eat it all, maybe just the chocolate bits?" replied Carol.

Zara looked up to see Evie standing in the doorway.

"What do *you* want?" she said angrily.

"Can we talk?" asked Evie.

"I don't think we need to, do we? You guys seem to have made up your minds," said Zara looking away.

Evie turned to Carol and Jenny.

"Could you please give us a moment?" she asked.

"Of course", said Carol and the two of them left the room.

Evie sat down next to Zara.

"Sometimes in life, we have to do things we don't want to because it's the right thing to do," she said.

"But it's not the right thing to do, its killing people," replied Zara while she fixed her gaze on the slowly melting desert in front of her.

"Believe me, if there was another way, where no one got hurt and no one died I would take that opinion, but right now this is the only choice we have," explained Evie.

"Have you had to do anything like this before?" asked Zara turning her head to look Evie in the eyes.

Evie shook her head.

"No this is the first time something like this has happened," she replied. "I still keep racking my brain to trying think of another way," she added.

"So if there was another you would consider it?" asked Zara wiping her eyes with a tissue.

"If it meant everyone was safe, definitely," said Evie.

"I will think of one then," said Zara.

Evie stood up and walked over to the kitchen door.

"Zero 17 should be here in a minute, do you want to come and say hi?" she asked.

Zara nodded and stood up. Carol and Jenny were waiting outside the kitchen door.

"I'm sorry I didn't eat that desert, it looked yummy though," said Zara.

"That's ok Zara," replied Jenny.

"Everything ok?" asked Carol.

Evie nodded.

"Yes, thanks for looking after her," she replied.

They arrived back at the exhibit just as Zero 17 arrived through the Drop Hoop with a thud, as he hit the floor in the crouched position. The Android stood up and surveyed the room.

"Hello Agent Harrogate, Agent Bowman, Miss Patrick, nice to see you all," said Zero 17.

Zara ran over to the Android and gave it a hug, the last time she had seen him was when they rescued her from the warehouse.

"Its good to see you too Zee," said Evie.

They walked over to the meteorite and Zero 17 examined it from several angles.

"The rock appears to be stable at the moment," he concluded.

Evie set a countdown timer on her PSM to match the countdown to a catastrophic failure that the martian hologram was displaying. And then Brent turned the containment posts off, he then carried the cylindrical fuel cell transport container over and set it down on the ground next to the glass display. He typed a code on the containers keypad and the lid opened like an iris.

"There you go buddy, all yours," said Brent patting the Android on the back.

He then stepped back and turned the containment posts back up to full power. This caused the hologram to disappear again.

"Ok everyone please move away to a safe distance," said Zero 17 as he cut a large circle in the display glass using a laser emitted from his finger.

Both the agents and Zara quickly took cover behind a nearby display of 'The History of Mars'. The android carefully lifted the thick piece of glass out of the way so he had access to the meteorite inside the display. Zero 17 reached inside the display and carefully picked up the Martian meteorite. He lowered the rock into the transport container where it floated between cushions of energy and he then pressed the red button on the keypad to close and lock the container.

"Rock secured," reported the Android.

"Great work Zee," said Evie as the three of them reappeared from behind the display.

"Evie I was thinking…" began Zara "We are launching our school weather balloon on Tuesday, couldn't we attach the rock to that?" she said.

"Unfortunately that may be too late and your balloon wouldn't travel high enough to be a safe enough distance, but it was a good idea. Keep them coming." Replied Evie.

"How long do we have to get the rock to a desert location?" asked Brent as he shut down the containment posts.

Evie looked down at the countdown on her PSM.

"Two days and 19 hours so around 4 pm on Monday" she replied.

"I have arranged for a plane at East Midlands airport which will take us to Morroco. Ground transportation will be waiting when we arrive," reported Zero 17.

"Thank you Zee, let's see if Carol has a car we can use," replied Evie.

The android picked up the transport container and they walked back to the Space Centre reception.

Carol and Jenny were sat in the gift shop discussing the very unusual events of the day when they saw the two special agents and Zara walk towards them occupied by a tall yellow being with no face carrying a flashing metal cylinder "Do you have any transport we can use," enquired Evie.

"Yes of course, but what is that?" said Carol pointing.

"Oh that's a transport container, we've put the rock inside to move it," replied Evie.

"I mean what is the yellow thing holding it?!" asked Carol as she felt her pockets for the company car keys.

"Ah, that's Zero 17, he's one of us," explained Evie.

"He looks amazing," exclaimed Jenny as she looked him up and down.

"There you go, it's easy to spot, its got the Space Centres rocket logo on the sides," said Carol as she handed the car keys to Brent.

"Thank you for your help, a cleanup team will be sent to you shortly to put things back how they were," said Brent.

"Yes thank you both of you," said, Evie, as she shook their hands.

They exited the Space Centre and walked over to the Black 4x4 Space Centre car. Brent pressed a button on the keyfob to unlock the car and they got in while Zero 17 place the container in the boot. He pressed a blue triangular button on the side of the container which made the base magnet so it stuck to the floor and didn't roll about while they drove. Evie sat next to Brent in the front passenger seat while Zara sat behind them and Zero 17 got in next to Zara.

Zara looked back at the Space Centre and waved goodbye at Carol and Jenny who were standing outside the main entrance. She continued to stare out of her window as they drove through Leicester towards the M1 motorway. No one they passed would have any idea of the cargo they were carrying.

She began to imagine how today would have been if they hadn't gone to the Space Centre in the first place. They had voted back at school for the trip they wanted to take. Each pupil had been called up alphabetically, when they got to Zara two of the trips had equal votes, her vote secured the trip to the Space Centre, and now she felt guilty about her choice as it had put Lewis' life in danger.

Evie's PSM bleeped to announce the arrival of a new message, she retrieved her PSM from her jacket pocket and began to read.

"I bet that's Vincent wanting to know how we are getting on," suggested Brent.

Confusion covered her face and she turned to Zara.

"What do you mean where are you, you're sat right there?!" she said.

"Huh? I didn't say anything" said Zara who was now confused herself.

"You just text me to ask where you are" replied Evie who was beginning to think Zara was playing a silly game.

"No I didn't," said Zara as she checked her pockets for her phone.

"Wait a minute, I haven't got my phone, Lewis still has it, he held onto it for me while I was on the simulator" she added.

"What? Brent stop the Car!" Evie ordered.

Brent pulled the car over into the nearest layby he could find and they all stared at the container. Evie renamed Zara in her contacts list to Lewis and composed a reply to the message :

Evie: We think you were taken aboard the Martian Lifeboat. What can you see?

Her phone beeped again with another two messages :

Lewis: I am in a glass tube and there are loads of other tubes. They all have people in them.

Lewis: *All the tubes have a blue light on them and I can't open mine.*

"Lewis is in some sort of stasis pod and so is the rest of the crew by the sounds of it," Evie told the others.

Everyone was silent in the car as they all tried to process the situation.

"What do you want to do?" asked Brent.

"What if we are wrong? And catastrophic failure just means that it just returns to full size," said Evie.

"Then we will be burying those people alive, but we don't know that, it's 50:50 either way" replied Brent

"Two rockets on this car, pity they aren't real," mumbled Zara.

"What do you just say Zara," asked Evie.

"I mean there are two rockets on the car, in the Space Centre logos, it's a pity they aren't real," explained Zara.

"Two rockets… that's it! Turn the car around!" ordered Evie.

Brent quickly maneuvered the car through the traffic and they headed back towards the Space Centre.

"May I remind you that our flight leaves in fifty-five minutes and twenty-eight seconds" Zero 17 informed them.

"I don't think we are taking the plane now," said Brent looking across to Evie who was typing another message on her PSM :

Evie: *Everything will be ok Lewis, I have an idea to bring you back.*

They arrived back at the Space Centre to find the DAIT cleanup crew had just arrived.

"What are you all doing back here?" asked Carol as they got out of the car.

"We don't know yet, Agent Bowman hasn't told us," replied Brent.

"Zero 17 please bring the container," instructed Evie.

The android nodded and retrieved the cargo from the boot of the car.

Evie turned to Carol.

"We are going to need your help," She asked.

"Yes, of course" replied Carol as they all quickly walked back into the Space Centre.

"I can see in those crazy wild eyes of yours that you have a plan, what is it?" asked Brent.

"Can we borrow this?" said Evie pointing at the Soyuz capsule on display in the reception area.

"Erm, yes, if it will help, but what are you going to do with it?…" said Carol who was now a bit confused.

Evie nodded and turned around.

"We are going to need that too," she said point at Blue Streak.

"Evie, that's a crazy idea," said Brent.

"Why is it, we have all this equipment here, plus our own technology, let's build our own," Explained Evie.

"Taking into account the condition of the Rocket and the Soyuz capsule you intend to use, the current possibility of successfully getting the Martian Vessel into orbit is 5.6174%," reported Zero 17.

"See, listen to the robot, its impossible," exclaimed Brent.

"Excuse me, Agent Harrogate I didn't say it was impossible, I said the possibility of success was extremely low with the components in their current state," replied the android.

"Zee, you're not helping!" said Brent.

"Zee, could you make the necessary repairs in time?" asked Evie.

"It will take approximately 42 hours, but I could have it ready to fly," reported Zero 17.

"That's cutting it a little close, Brent I need your support on this," said Evie.

"I think its crazy, but you know me, I'm with you every step of the way," he replied.

"Where are we going to launch it from, we can't do it here, we're in the middle of the city," said Brent.

"What are they all doing back?" asked Jenny who had been busy instructing the cleanup crew where the new meteorite display should go.

"They want to use our Soyuz together with Blue Streak to get the meteorite into space," explained Carol.

"That sounds amazing, but is that possible?" asked Jenny.

"We have the technology to do it, we just need a launch location," answered Brent.

"What about Bradgate Park? It isn't far from here and parts of it are far enough away from any residential areas," offered Jenny.

"That sounds ideal, but how are we going to move this odd couple over there," replied Evie.

"What about a really big Drop Hoop," offered Zara.

"Great idea Zara!" said Evie.

"We'll need a size C Drop Hoop, I'll go and let the cleanup team know what is happening and order two more Drop Hoops," said Brent as he hurried off to the exhibit.

"Zero 17 can you help Agent Harrogate get things organized?" said Evie.

The Android nodded and went off to find Brent while still carrying the container.

"What should I do," asked Zara.

"Can you somehow let Lewis parents know that he is with us and not to worry? And you better tell your mum that you're safe too," replied Evie.

"Can I borrow one of your phones and a computer?" said Zara turning to Carol.

"There are a phone and computer in my office, follow me" replied Carol.

They both walked off in the direction of the Space Centre offices.

"Anything I can do?" asked Jenny.

"Is there somewhere suitable we can control the launch from?" asked Evie.

"I know just the place, we have our very own mission control for school children to use. I will go and start getting it ready," replied Jenny before she hurried off.

Evie took her PSM out of her pocket and scrolled through her address book while walking back to the Mars exhibit. 'I better update Vincent with the new plan' she thought as she dialed the number.

"Agent Bowman, how are things looking over there, what time is your flight?" said Vincent as he got up from his table at the banquet.

Dregg watched him from across the room and then made his own excuses to leave his table so he could try and listen to Vincent's conversation.

"We are not getting on the plane now. We received a message from Lewis. He is alive and well, it seems like the rest of the crew are alive too, and still asleep," replied Evie.

"Well, that changes things, I assume you have a plan?" asked Vincent.

"There is a rocket here called Blue Streak and also a Soyuz capsule. My plan is to use those together to make a launch vehicle to get the rock into space" said Evie.

"From what I remember, that rocket was rescued off the production line by the National Museums of Liverpool and has never been tested, how do you know it'll even fire?" asked Vincent.

"Zero 17 says he can make it flight ready in time," said Evie.

"And who is going to fly this thing?" asked Vincent. Evie hadn't thought that far ahead yet, she looked around and spotted the Mars Rover Experience.

"We are going to control it remotely from the Space Centre," she said.

"And your launch site?" asked Vincent.

"Bradgate Park, just outside Leicester," replied Evie.

There was a silent pause while Vincent processed all the information that Agent Bowman had given him.

"Well it isn't normal DAIT protocol as your no doubt aware, but this isn't a normal situation is it!" said Vincent finally "You'll need some extra support if this is going to work. I'm raising this to a category 5C incident. You can have any supplies you need and as many staff as we can spare," he added.

"Thank you, sir, we won't let you down," replied Evie.

"I will try and join you myself later if I can get away, but for now I better get back to the banquet, good luck Evie," said Vincent.

"Thank you, Vincent," replied Evie before she ended the call.

Dregg had heard every word and hurried off to an empty room to record a message to his Lorkandian Pirate Clan brothers and sisters.

"The vessel is leaving earth from Bradgate Park in two cycles of their world, good profit awaits us," he said before transmitting the message and quickly walking back to the Banquet.

"Is everything ok Commander?" asked one of the delegates as Vincent returned to his seat at the banquet.

"Yes, of course, it was just my babysitter," replied Vincent.

Chapter Five
The Preparation

Over the next Two days, the National Space Centre and Bradgate Park were prepared for the impending launch of Blue Streak and its precious cargo. Over thirty DAIT personnel ranging from welders to scientists had arrived on site to prepare for the launch. The decision was made to launch at 11 am on Monday which gave them a five hours window before catastrophic failure of the lifeboats fuel cell.

On Friday evening, trucks carrying 8 feet tall metal barriers arrived at the park. DAIT personnel erected the barriers around the perimeter of the park and Police officers were stationed at the main entrances.

Mobile flood light systems and security cameras were installed and placed along the length of the barriers to make sure the park was secured. Any residents that asked what was going on were told that a promotional event was taking place.

Saturday morning saw a launch tower constructed on the far side of the park furthest from the city and any residential areas. A size C Drop Hoop was installed into the tower to enable the team to transport Blue Streak and the Soyuz module to the launch platform quickly and safely. Any local newspapers that contacted the Space Centre asking for comment, were told that there was going to be a model rocket launch to promote the Space Centre.

The mission control room in the space education building used by schools for space mission simulations was transformed with a complete equipment upgrade from DAIT. High specification computers and monitor screens filled the room, turning it into a fully functional mission control room. From here DAIT personnel would be able to control and monitor the launch.

Zero 17 worked throughout the night and day non-stop to make sure the Soyuz capsule was spaceworthy. For it to be put on display at the Space Centre, several parts had been removed to bring the weight down and mountings had been attached. A crane was used to take lift the Soyuz as it was cut from its mountings and stood upright on the Space Centre floor.

"I hope you put that back where you found it" joked Carol.

She and Jenny had been making sure their visitors from DAIT had teas, coffees, and snacks available as well as access to any areas they needed. The android used spare parts from other salvaged capsules to rebuild the missing parts of the Soyuz module. A remote control module was fitted inside the cockpit where the cosmonauts would have normally sat.

In the early hours of Sunday morning, it was now Blue Streaks turn for a refit and upgrade. Zero 17 striped the rocket's engines down completely, laying each component neatly on the floor. He then cleaned each piece and replaced any faulty ones before rebuilding the engines which now looked even better than they did before.

With the help of other DAIT personnel, and some heavy duty lifting equipment he reinstalled the twin engines in the base of the rocket.

Two indoor cranes were erected inside the rocket tower to hold Blue Streak stable while she was detached from her display mountings. A size C Drop Hoop was constructed at the base of the rocket so that the cranes could lower Blue Streak through it slowly, transporting it straight to the launch tower where the launch team was waiting to guide her safely to her launch position. Once in place, an extra fuel tank was added to the rocket to give her enough fuel to make the journey into space.

With Blue Streak now in position, it was the turn of the Soyuz capsule to be lifted through the Drop Hoop to sit on top of the waiting launch vehicle. While the position of the cranes was altered to perform this task, Evie and Brent installed the transportation container carrying the Martian vessel into the cockpit of the module. With the cranes in place, the Soyuz was slowly lifted and then lowered through the Drop Hoop and attached to the top of Blue Streak.

Brent joined Evie on the top floor of the Space Centre rocket tower as she watched Zero 17 working on the rocket at the launch site through a pair of binoculars while the sun slowly set.

"How is he doing?" asked Brent as he held out a cup of hot coffee.

"He's done an amazing job, and we still have time to spare, maybe we can launch earlier?" replied Evie.

The aroma of coffee wafted up her nose and she lowered the binoculars.

"Thanks," she said as she grabbed the paper coffee cup and began to sip.

"How long is it going to take to fuel up?" asked Brent.

"Only ten minutes, that's for the kerosene and the liquid oxygen," replied Evie as her PSM started to beep, it was Vincent.

"How are we looking over there Agent Bowman? I hear you have been emptying out our supply stores," said Vincent as he left the conference room.

"We are almost ready here, just some final adjustments and we are good to go," replied Evie.

"That's good because this whole mission is starting to gain interest from the wrong type of people" explained Vincent.

"The Lorkandian pirates are threating to take the Martian Vessel by force once it leaves our atmosphere," he added.

"How did they find out about it? They know it going into catastrophic failure right?" replied Evie.

"There was a pirate spy at the conference called Dregg, anyway, they think we are lying to them and we are intentionally withholding technology, despite me addressing the whole conference about the situation," said Vincent.

"What did the others races say?" asked Evie

"They support us one hundred percent, even the Lorkandian's. They don't agree with the ways and methods of the pirate clan," replied Vincent.

Evie sighed, things were going to get tricky she could feel it.

"Keep us up to date, we're sitting ducks here if they do try and pull something," she said finally.

"Of course, good luck," replied Vincent before he ended the call.

"What's the problem?" asked Brent

"Lorkandian pirates, that's the problem," said Evie angrily as she slammed her coffee cup down.

"When are they NOT a problem" responded Brent.

Evie's PSM beeped just as she was about to put it back in her pocket.

"It's another message from Lewis," said Evie before handing it to Brent to read :

> **Lewis:** *Hi, its Lewis again, the sleep things are starting to shut down and the crew is waking up. We are trying to communicate with each other but, I am having trouble getting them to understand me.*

"it sounds like the failure of the lifeboats systems has already started," said Brent nervously.

"Exactly," replied Evie as they both looked out of the window towards the rocket tower. "I will feel a lot more relaxed when we have launched," she added.

Evie typed a reply to Lewis on her PSM:

Evie: Thank you for the update Lewis, we are working as hard as we can to bring you home.

"Not long now, maybe you should get some sleep, it's going to be an interesting day tomorrow," suggested Brent before he went down in the lift to find somewhere in the Space Centre to get some sleep for the night.

Evie stayed on the top floor watching the sun completely disappear behind the horizon and the lights of the launch tower twinkle in the moonlight.

"Agent Bowman, they need you downstairs," said a voice in the distance. Evie opened one eye and saw a DAIT agent standing over her.

"What time is it?" she asked blinking and adjusting her eyes to the daylight.

"09:30 hours, they need you downstairs urgently, something about the launch program missing some values" replied the agent.

Evie got up off the floor where she had fallen asleep and put her jacket on which she had been using as a blanket, it was cold in the Rocket Tower, cold and empty.

"Ok let's go down and see what's the problem" she replied as she rubbed her eyes and followed the agent into the lift.

They exited the Space Centre and walked across to the education building which now housed DAIT mission control.

"Sleep well?" said Brent with a smile as Evie and the agent entered the launch control room.

"They need to do something about the carpet, it's not very comfortable to sleep on," replied Evie stretching. "What's this about the launch program missing values?" she asked.

"Every time we try to convert the guidance program from its 1960s code into modern C++ code for our computer systems, two values keep throwing up errors" replied a technician point at lines of text on his monitor.

"Hmm, how long do these values need to be?" asked Evie.

"The first one should be three digits and the second one should be five digits," answered another technician.

Evie looked at the screens for a moment, then at the handwritten notes, the technicians had made. She was no computer programmer but she when it came to maths she knew her stuff.

"Ok, what about if you swapped those two values around. Then divided the first one by two and multiply the second one by three?" suggested Evie.

"How did you work that out?" said Brent

"Just simple maths and I can do maths," replied Evie.

The technician made the changes that Evie suggested and ran the computer program again.

"That's fixed it!" said one of the technicians with surprise.

"Not bad considering I haven't had any caffeine yet," replied Evie.

She turned to Zero 17 who was had just entered the room.

"How is Blue Streak? Is everything ready?" she asked.

"All systems are fully functional and ready to go, you'll also be delighted to hear that I have recalculated the probability of success which now stands at 87.399%" reported the android.

"I definitely prefer those odds," replied Brent.

Evie looked around the room.

"Where's Zara?" she asked.

"There wasn't much for her to do here so Jenny is showing all the exhibits we have in storage" replied Carol.

Suddenly there was a loud bang outside

"What was that?" said Brent.

"It sounded like a sonic boom," said one of the technicians.

Then there was another loud bang and another. Evie, Brent and Zero 17 went outside to see what was making the noise.

"Over there shouted one of the agents who was already outside and pointing at an object in the sky. Evie still had the pair of binoculars around her neck so she raised them up to get a closer look. She recognized the markings on the side of the object straight away

"It's those damn Lorkandian pirates, they're after the lifeboat," she said, lowering the binoculars.

"There appear to be four Lorkandian Pirate hijack ships, that's a total of 48 Lorkandian Pirates," Reported Zero 17 as he scanned the sky.

"Where are they heading?" asked Brent.

"I calculate that two of them will land on the perimeter of the Space Centre and the other two will land close to the rocket tower," replied the Android as he linked himself up with a live satellite feed of the area.

Evie used her earpiece radio to contact every DAIT agent on site simultaneously.

"All agents, this is now a category 5A incident, Lorkandian pirates are incoming, repeat, Lorkandian pirates are incoming. Alpha and Omega teams, rendezvous at the Space Centre Entrance. All other teams lock down your locations, good luck, Bowman out" she ordered before turning to Zero 17. "Zee we are going to need you in tactical mode now," she said.

"Understood Agent Bowman," replied the Android, his skin turned from pale orange to scarlet red. Evie and Brent both unholstered their plasma pistols ready for action.

Alpha and Omega teams dropped what they were doing and ran to meet the agents at the entrance with their weapons drawn.

"We can't let them get to the launch tower, millions of lives are depending on us" ordered Evie "Alpha team, you're with Agent Harrogate and Zero 17. Get over to the launch site, we must protect it at all costs. Omega team, you're with me, we'll give Alpha team cover while they leave the site and then we need to protect mission control," she added.

The sound of Lorkandian battle screams and energy bolts filled the air.

"Here they come," shouted Brent.

DAIT base was now on high alert because of the situation at the Space Centre. The conference had been put on hold with delegates and diplomats being told to stay in their visitors quarters. Vincent was now wearing full combat gear as he marched down the main DAIT corridor flanked DAIT special forces personnel towards the Drop Hoop control room. Normally he wouldn't get involved in the action on the ground but with so many lives at stake, Vincent believed he had a duty. Professor James was frantically modifying the settings on each of the Drop Hoops.

"Is everything ready professor?" enquired Vincent as they entered the room.

"Yes Yes, just double checking, wouldn't want them going both to the same location because that could end up being a bit messy and we certainly don't want that," the professor explained.

Vincent tried not to look concerned by that statement.

"Right, ok, Hoop A is set for the launch tower and Hoop B is set for the Space Centre," the professor added.

Vincent turned to the troops.

"Ok people, we are going in hot, let's move out," ordered Vincent.

Omega team gave Alpha team cover fire as they ran to two of the five DAIT trucks in the car park. The sound of plasma blasts filled the air as Omega team tried to hold back the approaching Lorkandians. The pirate ran towards them with energy shields raised and energy weapons firing.

Evie took aim down the barrel of her pistol and shot one of the pirates in its claw-like feet sending it tumbling over into a heap on the ground.

Some of the Lorkandians had noticed that DAIT agents where trying to get to the trucks and broke away from the invading force to attack them. Seeing this from her location, Evie quickly moved forward from her position, she picked up an energy shield that had been dropped by the pirate she had just shot and started firing at the Lorkandians that were heading straight for Alpha team.

Brent climbed into the front of the first truck and got behind the wheel with Zero 17 in the passenger seat. He rolled down the window and shouted across to the agent who had just got into the driving seat of another truck.

"We'll go to gate B, you take gate A so we can intercept then from both sides, good luck" he ordered.

The agent nodded and they drove their trucks out of the car park in opposite directions.

One of the pirates took a running jump and grabbed hold of the side of the truck that Brent was driving. Evie tried to shoot it off the truck but she was too far away and the truck was moving all over the place.

Zero 17 opened the passenger door of the truck and started to climb out of the moving vehicle.

"Where are you going!?" exclaimed Brent

"I will be back shortly Agent Harrogate," replied Zero 17 as he shut the passenger door and climbed on the roof of the truck to confront the pirate, who was still clinging to the side of the truck.

"I'm going to have to ask you to surrender," said the Android.

"You will die artificial man" shouted the pirate angrily.

Zero 17 grabbed hold of the pirate's claws and pulled him onto the roof of the truck. The pirate punched and kicked the android which had no effect his scarlet armor. Zero 17 grabbed the Lorkandian by its shoulders and used his hands to deliver a high voltage charge through the Lorkandians body, stunning the pirate unconscious.

"I did warn you," said the android as the alien lay in a heap on the roof.

When Alpha team arrived at the rocket tower they saw that Lorkandian pirates were already climbing the rocket tower to get to the Soyuz module.

"Team lower your weapons, only intercept enemies on the ground one poorly aimed shot and you'll damage the rocket," ordered Brent.

"What are we going to do about the others then sir?" asked one of the agents.

Brent turned to Zero 17.

"Do you think you could knock them down to our level?" he asked.

"Gladly," said Zero 17 as he ran towards the base of the rocket tower.

The Lorkandian's on the ground swiped their limbs at him and shot at him but that didn't stop the android. He reached the base of the tower and began to climb. As he climbed the tower, pirates on the tower began shooting him. He managed grabbed one by its leg and threw him off the tower he then intercepted another and whacked him across the face before three more pirates jumped on Zero 17, pinning him down.

"Zero 17 is in trouble," shouted Brent but there were several Lorkandian between them and the rocket tower.

"Sir, I'm out of ammo," reported an agent to his left.

"Me too," replied an agent to his right.

"Ok Alpha team, fall back to the cover of the truck," ordered Brent.

Suddenly there was a flash of ice blue light from the bottom of the launch tower, the Drop Hoop at the base of the rocket had been activated. This was followed by the familiar sound of plasma rifles

"We've got backup!" exclaimed Brent with relief as he peered around the truck and saw DAIT special forces take the pirates completely by surprise.

"Agent Harrogate whats your situation?" said Vincent over the radio.

"Zero 17 is pinned down on the rocket tower and we are pinned down behind our truck with limited ammo. The launch team have locked themselves in the lift," explained Brent.

"You three with me, the rest of you go and assist Agent Harrogate's team," ordered Vincent before he began climbing the launch tower to help the android, follow by his small team.

The rest of the special forces team ran to help Brents Alpha team on the ground. Their plasma rifles were more effective against the Lorkandian shields so it didn't take too long to bring the situation on the ground under control.

One of the pirates that were holding Zero 17 down noticed Vincents team climbing the rocket tower and let out a loud, angry, growl. They moved away from the now broken body of the android, poised to defend their new treasure, with weapons at the ready. The pirates leaned over the edge of the rocket tower to see where exactly the special forces troops were, and began shooting their weapons at them through the gaps in the skeletal structure of the tower.

Vincent's team now had to dodge enemy fire as well as climb the tower, but they weren't far from reaching the level that the pirates had taken. The Lorkandian pirates shot one of the DAIT agents in the chest causing her to fall off the rocket tower, Vincent looked down and saw her fall, then he looked back, up at the platform. He had to get up there before it was it was too late so he tried to speed up his climb.

Back at the Space Centre, Evie and Omega team had been joined by their own Special forces back up. The Lorkandian pirates had managed to break into the centre itself and now a battle was taking place in the main lobby.

Evie crouched down behind the empty Soyuz display while she reloaded her plasma pistol before deciding to move to the reception desk. She checked her route and then made a run for it followed by two

Omega team agents. Carol and Jenny were hiding behind the desk, hands covering their ears.

"Have either of you been hit?" asked Evie.

"No, we are ok," said Carol who was shaking with fright.

Evie looked around, confused.

"Where is Zara, wasn't she with you?" she asked looking at Jenny.

"I left the storage room to check something and then those aliens appeared. She must still be in there," replied Jenny.

Evie shook her head, she wasn't happy, but there was no time to give Jenny a lecture on DAIT procedures.

"How far is the storage room from here?" She asked.

"It's behind the gift shop and off to the left behind the black and yellow doors," replied Jenny.

Evie turned to the two agents that had accompanied her.

"Stay here and defend this position, I'll go and find Zara," she ordered before creeping out from behind the reception desk and running across to the gift shop.

Evie noticed a DAIT pistol on the ground as she ran, and picked it up.

It was pitch black in the windowless storage room because the light was on a timer. Zara could hear the battle going on outside the storage room and had been trying to find the light switch or the door, but she wasn't having much luck with either.

One pirate had been watching Evie's movements and was now climbing onto the roof of the storage room. Zara could hear something on the roof but she couldn't worry about that right now, she had to find her way out. Finally, she found the round light switch and pressed just as there was a loud crashing noise behind her. She turned around to see a Lorkandian Pirate standing in front of her, panting, with drool dripping from its mouth.

"You will make a nice trophy," growled the pirate as he walked towards her with two of his claws stretched out to grab her.

Zara screamed as loud as she could in the hope that someone would hear.

"Hey, Cockroach features, BACK OFF," shouted Evie angrily looking down the barrels of her two pistols at the Lorkandians chest. The pirate turned around and roared before charging at Evie.

She didn't move, she didn't flinch, she just pulled the triggers repeatedly, firing several plasma rounds into the Lorkandians in the chest, stunning it before she jumped up and kicked him in the face causing the pirate to land in a pile against a storage shelf. Evie tucked her pistols in the back of her jeans and ran over to Zara who was shaking in the corner.

"Are you ok? Did it hurt you?" asked a concerned Evie.

"No I'm ok, it was just so scary that's all," said Zara trembling.

Evie gave Zara a quick hug before grabbing her hand. There was still a battle going on around them.

"C' mon, let's go, stay behind me ok?" she said as she pushed a button to open the door and raised one of her pistols.

Zara nodded and the door opened to reveal several DAIT agents and Lorkandian Pirates laying on the floor wounded. Evie fired her pistol at a group of Pirates that had cornered two DAIT agents, taking them completely by surprise she hit one of them in the back and the other in the arm.

Alpha team and DAIT special forces had managed to stun the pirates on the ground at the launch site, and take the surviving ones as prisoners. When Vincent's team finally managed to overwhelm the pirates holding down Zero 17 they discovered the androids red armor had turned back to its normal yellow colour and he had been damaged. There were several holes in his body, a large chunk of his right leg was missing, exposing his internal mechanics and his left arm had been torn right off but he was still active.

"Can you move?" asked Vincent.

"Yes Commander, my remaining limbs are still 80% operational," replied the android as he picked himself up off the floor.

"Is the module and the lifeboat secure still?" asked Vincent.

Zero 17 limped over to the Soyuz capsule and scanned its structure.

"Everything appears to be fine," reported the android.

"Well that's some good news, we will continue as planned," replied Vincent.

"If we can't have the device, neither can you," said an injured pirate laying on the floor.

They turned around to see who had spoken, just as the pirate raised his weapon off the ground and fired. Two blasts of energy left the Lorkandians weapon and pierced the hull of the Soyuz. The pirate then collapsed and died from his wounds. Vincent and Zero 17 surveyed the damage to the Soyuz.

"How bad is it?" asked Vincent.

"The remote guidance system is completely destroyed and the transport container has been compromised," replied the android before opening the Soyuz and climbing inside.

He opened the transport container and scanned the lifeboat.

"We do not have long, the energy readings from the Martian vessel are extremely unstable. I believe the plasma from the Lorkandians weapon may have accelerated the catastrophic failure," reported Zero 17.

Vincent sighed and scratched his head.

"Ok Zee, I wonder if Lewis can tell how things are onboard the vessel?" enquired Vincent.

"It's a distinct possibility, if he has been able to communicate with them," replied the android.

Vincent began typing a message to Lewis on his PSM.

> **Vincent:** *Hello Lewis, its Commander Novak here from DAIT, have you been able to communicate with the beings on board the lifeboat with you? What does a catastrophic failure mean to them?*

There was a pause while Lewis typed his reply…

Lewis: *Hi Commander! They have this cool thing here where I talk and it tries to figure out what I am saying.*

Lewis: *Anyway their leader has just told me that catastrophic means the ship is going to return to full size.*

Lewis: *Whatever you're doing, you better do it quickly. Because whatever hit us has made the engine really unstable, and now there are only two hours left.*

"Looks like you were right Zero 17, we have less than two hours," said Vincent before replying to Lewis.

Vincent: *Thank you for the information Lewis, we will find a solution to bring you home.*

Back at the Space Centre, mission control was empty except for Evie and Zara. Evie had just stunned one Lorkandian with her plasma pistols and kicked another one in the face sending it collapsing in a heap on the steps of the building, but it wasn't over yet.

Evie scanned the room, she didn't have time for this, the launch window was closing, although it was now a lot shorter than she thought. Above her head, she could hear something scratching on the roof.

"Zara stay near the door," she ordered.

Zara nodded and ran over to the door. Evie slowly and quietly moved to the other side of the room with both pistols raised before firing at a bulge in the ceiling. The section of the ceiling caved in along with the pirate who had been standing on it. Evie ran over and stood guns raised over the Lorkandian.

"Don't give me a reason to kill you?" she said angrily.

There was a crackle on her earpiece radio.

"Evie, are you there," said Brent.

Evie tucked one of her pistols in her jeans and held her ear.

"Go ahead," she replied.

"Evie, we have a big problem here, the remote systems on the Soyuz have been damaged. Zero 17 says the only way to launch it now is if someone flies it manually" there was a pause "we also have less than two hours until catastrophic failure," explained Brent.

"Can Zee fly it and then eject?" suggested Evie.

"We've already thought of that, he weighs too much, no offense Zee," said Vincent.

"None taken sir," replied the android.

"We are on our way back to the Space Centre, Zero 17 is going to stay here and make some repairs," explained Vincent.

"Ok we will see you shortly," replied Evie.

This was not what she wanted to hear and she knew in her head, there was only one real option.

"ha ha ha, you lose human," growled the Lorkandian still laying on the floor.

Evie grabbed her pistol by the barrel and whacked the pirate over the head, knocking it out.

"It's not over yet," she whispered.

"What are we going to do, what about Lewis, are we going to die?" asked Zara nervously.

"I have an idea Zara, come on," said Evie.

They quickly walked out of mission control and down the steps where Agent Keyworth was waiting for them.

"The Lorkandians have been contained," said the agent.

"Great work, send those Lorkandians Pirates back to DAIT base, and let their own kind deal with them," replied Evie

"Any word from Alpha team?" asked Agent Keyworth.

"The Martian vessel has been compromised and we have less than two hours," replied Evie.

"What do you need us to do?" enquired Agent Keyworth.

"We need to get mission control back up and running, it's going to be a manual launch this time," ordered Evie.

Agent Keyworth nodded and then quickly went to gather the personnel they would need. Evie and Zara entered the space centre and found the cleanup crew had already started putting things back as they were. They were joined by Carol and Jenny who had been instructing the cleanup crew where things should go.

"Zara, I am so sorry I left you in the storage room," said Jenny.

"Its ok, Evie found me," replied Zara.

"Is it over?" asked Carol.

"Mostly, the pirates have been contained, but I am afraid I need your help again," replied Evie.

"Mostly?? How can I help?" enquired Carol.

"I noticed you have something in one of your displays that would be very helpful right now," said Evie.

"Ok, show me which item it is," replied Carol.

Alpha team and the remaining DAIT special forces arrived back in the Space Centre car park with the Lorkandian pirates in restraints. The two battered trucks pulled up outside the entrance and started to unload the prisoners.

"Take them to the Drop Hoop, Lorkandian security is waiting to collect them for transport at DAIT HQ," ordered Vincent.

"What's the plan boss?" asked Brent.

"I don't know yet, has anyone seen agent Bowman?" asked Vincent.

They walked through the main entrance and saw the remains of the battle that had taken place inside

"Looks like you've had your fair share of action in here," he remarked.

"We have three casualties but no fatalities," reported Agent Keyworth who had joined them in the main hall.

"What is the condition of mission control?" asked Vincent.

"We are now bringing the systems back online," replied Agent Keyworth.

"Where is Agent Bowman?" enquired Vincent.

"She went off with the curator to get something," answered Zara.

"All key personnel to mission control" ordered Vincent over his radio before turning around and walking to the mission control building with Brent and Agent Keyworth.

Chapter Six
The Only Way

Mission control was now fully operational but they still had a serious problem to overcome, they needed a volunteer to fly Blue Streak.

"Are we sure there is no other way?" Vincent asked the gathered team of DAIT agents, scientists and technicians.

"We simply do not have enough time to build and test a new guidance system that will work with the rocket we have available," explained Professor James over video link "The only option we have is for someone to flying the rocket manually, and the vessel at the right altitude," he added.

Vincent scratched his beard, this was going to be a big ask.

"Whoever does this, may not make it back or survive the trip up there," said Vincent addressing the entire room.

The room fell silent, all that could be heard was the sound of computer hard drives. Everyone looked at each other, who was going to take that huge risk.

"I'll do it," said a voice from the other side of the room.

Everyone turned to see Evie standing there in full Soyuz cosmonaut attire with Carol standing behind her. It was a white Sokol spacesuit with blue stripes and a union jack flag on one arm. The same spacesuit that Helen Sharman had worn on her trip to the Mir space station in 1991 as the first British astronaut. Shocked whispers filled the room as Evie walked over to the huddle of scientists and technicians.

"What? That's insane, you know the risks right?" exclaimed Brent.

"We don't have time to argue or discuss this," replied Evie.

"Agent Bowman is right, there isnt enough time to find another way, and if she is willing to do this I don't see any problem," said Vincent placing his hand on her shoulder.

"You might not make it," said Brent.

"Well you can't go, you have a wife and a little girl, it cant be much harder than flying one of our own" explained Evie.

"That's settled then, launch team make preparations for launch straight away," ordered Vincent.

The room went from almost complete silence to a hive of activity as systems were recalibrated and adjustments made to compensate for Evie's weight in the Soyuz module. Brent attached Evie's PSM to the arm of her spacesuit.

"Zero 17, is Blue Streak ready for launch?" asked Vincent over the intercom.

"All systems are fully functional, and the repairs to the Soyuz hull have been completed. Do we have a pilot?" replied the android.

"Agent Bowman has volunteered, please prepare for her arrival," explained Vincent.

"You can't go, what if you don't come back?" pleaded Zara.

"You can't live your life by 'What ifs' or you'll never accomplish anything," said Evie.

"I can't lose two friends in one day," said Zara choking back tears.

"I plan to come back, believe me," replied Evie.

She turned to Carol.

"Do you mind if I use your truck again?" she asked.

"Of course," said Carol.

She reached into her pocket, pulled out the car keys and handed them to Evie.

"Thank you, for everything," said Evie.

"Thank you for opening my eyes to a world I never knew existed," replied Carol.

Evie turned to Vincent.

"You better come back in one piece agent Bowman," he said.

Evie walked out of mission control and down the steps towards the car park. She climbed into the Space Centre truck and looked in the rearview mirror. Zara and Brent were standing on the steps of mission control watching her leave.

They waited with nervous anticipation in the launch control room as Evie drove to the launch site and through the Police controlled gates.

She parked the truck right next to the launch tower where Zero 17 and the launch team were waiting for her.

"I thought it would be you that volunteered," said the android.

"How did you work that one out?" asked Evie.

"Because you never give up," replied Zero 17.

Evie entered the tower lift and ascended the launch tower to the access hatch of the Soyuz, accompanied by Zero and two of the launch team. She climbed into the capsule and sat in the makeshift cockpit seat next to the transport container. She was then strapped in by the launch team ready for departure.

"The Nanobots should hold the capsule together during the launch. If you need to abort pull this handle," explained Zero 17 pointing to a red lever.

"Aborting isn't an option but thanks Zee," replied Evie as she grabbed the android's arm.

"Good luck Agent Bowman," said Zero 17.

He then closed the access hatch and locked it shut.

Evie closed and locked her helmet, and then turned a valve on her suit to start her oxygen supply flowing.

"Space Centre to launch tower, are you ready for launch?" asked Brent over the intercom.

"Agent Bowman is secure and Blue Streak is ready for fueling," replied the launch team.

"Commence fueling" ordered Vincent.

Evie felt a clunk and then a rumble below her as the launch tower pumps loaded Blue Streak with liquid oxygen which mixed with the kerosene already loaded on board.

"Evie, are you ready?" asked Brent.

"I'm all good here, let's do this," said Evie over the intercom as she focused on the sky she could see above her head through the viewing window of the Soyuz.

"Roger that Blue Streak, you are cleared for launch here," came the reply from Vincent.

"Agent Bowman can you please navigate to the manual override on the Soyuz computer and run the program 10043," instructed one of the technicians.

Evie reached for the computer console in front of her and used the arrow keys to navigate to the right place on the screen.

She then typed 10043 on the keypad and pressed 'Run'. The dormant systems of the Soyuz came to life with beeps and flashing lights. Evie saw a stream of commands scrolls across the monitor in front of her with the final two words flashing on the middle of the screen 'Systems Engaging'.

Mission control then advised Evie to type two more commands into the Soyuz computer which transferred power supply to the onboard power cells.

"Ok Agent Bowman that's all for now, commencing countdown," explained another technician.

"Ten... Nine... Eight..." counted Brent while he watched the timer on the wall.

The rocket beneath her rumbled as the various mechanical and electrical systems came to life. Fuel valves opened, and Blue Streak began pumping liquid around its mechanical veins.

"Ignition sequence starting...Four...Three...Two... One... Ignition" a technician informed the room.

High-pressure jets of fuel were ignited as they exited the engine nozzles and the rocket growled loudly as it roared to life like an angry dinosaur awoken from its slumber. Blue Streak creaked and groaned as it climbed into the sky with its precious cargo.

"Liftoff successful," reported one the scientists.

"Tower clear" reported another, seconds later.

Cheers of success filled the room.

"Settle down people this isn't over yet," said Vincent.

"Evie how is it looking up there," he asked over the intercom.

Evie was being shaken by the vibrations of the engines as they accelerated the rocket towards its top speed.

"All systems are running as expected," came the crackly strained reply from Evie.

The transportation container ruptured as the power systems on the Martian Vessel started to fail and the process of returning to full size began. Evie watched as the vessel increased in size, to that of a rugby ball.

"The lifeboat is growing, I don't know if we are going to make it, please advise," she said over the intercom.

The scientists urgently looked at their calculations and discussed with each other possible solutions.

"As it increases, so does its weight. If it grows too much it'll be too heavy for the rocket to carry and they'll fall back to earth. We need to burn for longer to reach the target altitude," reported Professor James over the video link up.

"Evie, we need you to burn the engines longer to make sure you get enough altitude," explained Brent.

"Ok roger that, extending the burn," replied Evie.

The Earth fell away below her, as the launch timer reached T+ 60 seconds, at a speed of over 760 mph they were only 5.9 miles up with 242 miles to go. 'Are we going to make it?' Evie thought as the Soyuz capsule rattled atop Blue Streak. Suddenly a red alert light started flashing in the capsule cockpit accompanied by loud bursts from a warning buzzer.

"Ok, what just happened?" asked Evie.

"One of the engines has just shut down," said a scientist.

Evie started typing commands into the console to try and reignite the engine but none of them seemed to work.

"The computer keeps giving me an error," said Evie.

Zero 17 grabbed the radio.

"Agent Bowman, under your seat, are four coloured cables, you need to short circuit the red and the yellow one. This will manually reignite the engines even if one of them is already running," explained the android.

Evie pulled the cables under her seat as she was rattled around and rubbed them against the sharp edges of the crude seat to cut them.

"Ok, I am now connecting red and yellow," she reported.

The second engine roared back into life throwing Evie back in her seat. There were sighs of relief in mission control as they saw the engine come back to the life.

Minutes later Blue Streak broke out of the earth's atmosphere, at a speed of 2,266 mph.

"Ok Evie, prepare to deploy the lifeboat. You have 2 minutes," Explained Brent.

Evie unstrapped herself from the seat so she could grab the Martian vessel and deploy it at the right moment.

The nanobots that were holding the hull together changed their position to reveal a hole that Evie could throw the lifeboat through. When Blue Streak final ran out of fuel, she was traveling at 3,856 mph.

"Thank you, Blue Streak, I'll see you again soon," said Evie as she detached the Soyuz module from the rocket and watched it fall away behind her.

The forward momentum given to the craft by Blue Streak was just enough to allow it to travel far enough from earth for the lifeboat to return to full size safely.

"Ok, Evie, are you ready?" asked Brent over the intercom.

Evie tried to lift the lifeboat, but it was now the size of a car wheel and too heavy to move.

"That's a negative, I can't move it, it's too big and dense now," replied Evie.

Evie thought for a moment.

"I'm going to exit the craft, please send someone to pick me up," she added.

Before anyone could tell her that it was a bad idea Evie grabbed her oxygen tank and pulled herself through the hole in the craft as quickly as she could. She turned herself around, so she could watch what would happen to the Soyuz.

Evie looked at her oxygen gauge and saw that she only had 7 minutes of oxygen remaining, but she had no way of communicating that to anyone as her PSM and radio now had no signal and the only other radio was on the Soyuz that she had just jumped out of. All she could hear was the sound of her own breathing in her helmet.

As the minutes passed the Soyuz moved further and further away and the Martian vessel got bigger and bigger tearing through the sides of the Russian spacecraft and continuing to increase in size.

There was a blinding flash of light as the vessel grew to full size in the blink of an eye. The giant Martian vessel filled Evie's field of view and reminded her of a fat starfish. The hull of the ship was white with red swirling symbols in various places all over it.

She looked down at her oxygen gauge, there were only seconds left. The Gralax ambassador's ship moved in retrieve Evie from the blackness of space just as her oxygen supply ran out.

Evie woke up in the medical bay on board the ship with the Gralax captain standing over her.

"It's a pleasure to meet you, Agent Bowman, the commander speaks very highly of you," said the Gralax captain.

"Thank you for saving me, how long have I been out?" she asked.

"Twenty-five of your Earth minutes," replied the Captain.

"The Martian vessel? Lewis?" questioned Evie as she regained full consciousness.

"The crew of the vessel is alive and well, the boy you call Lewis is over there," replied the captain.

He pointed across the medical bay to another bed were Lewis was being examined. Evie got up and walked over to Lewis who was wearing a light blue outfit.

"How are you, Lewis? Who gave you the clothes?" asked Evie.

"I'm ok, just a little tired, the Martians gave them to me, am I in trouble?" asked Lewis.

"No, of course, you aren't," said Evie.

She turned to the captain.

"I would very much like to meet with the Martians before we go home," she said.

"Of course, I will arrange for you to join the next medical team that goes aboard," replied the captain.

Evie joined the Gralax medical team as they boarded the Martian vessel with supplies and equipment to tend to those with injuries & ailments. They were greeted at the airlock by a tall humanoid looking figure.

Using a translation device, the Martian began to speak.

"I am prince Ranmig of the planet you call Mars. Would one of you be the one they call Agent Bowman?" asked the tall figure.

"That's me," said Evie stepping forwards.

"I must thank you for the assistant you have given to myself and my people. We are forever in your debt," said Ranmig.

"You are very welcome, but it's just part of my job," replied Evie.

"If there is anything we can do for you, please ask," said the Martian.

Evie looked out of one of the large windows at the earth below.

"Actually there is a little something you could do for me," replied Evie.

Back at the Space Centre mission control was silent while they waited to hear any news of Evie and Lewis.

Vincent had stepped outside the mission control building to get some fresh air, he didn't like situations like these where he had no control over the outcome, it reminded him too much of the incident at DAIT Alpha.

Brent and Zara joined Vincent outside.

"Boss we have just received a transmission from the Gralax ambassador's ship, everyone is safe and well including Evie and Lewis" reported Brent.

Vincent sighed with relief.

"Well, that's another successful mission then," replied Vincent as he looked at his watch.

"We better start packing things away and getting this place..."

Before Vincent could finish his sentence two flashes of blue light appeared in front of them. It was Evie and Lewis, they had been transported back to the Space Centre from the Martian Vessel.

"Lewis! Evie!" yelled Zara with excitement.

She ran over and hugged them both.

"Welcome back Agent Bowman," said Vincent.

"It's good to be back boss," replied Evie.

After the agents had been debriefed by Vincent they volunteered to take Zara and Lewis back to Ipswich using the Space Centre truck. Lewis changed back into his uniform that Zara had been looking after but left his inhaler in the bag and chucked it in a nearby bin as they walked to the car.

"What about your inhaler?" asked Zara.

"I don't think I need it anymore," replied Lewis.

"Hey Mr. Mudd," said Vincent.

Lewis stopped and turned around.

"We'll be in contact after your exams," said Vincent.

Lewis grinned from ear to ear as he and Zara climbed into the Space Centre truck.

"Is anyone hungry?" asked Evie as they drove out of the car park.

"Can we get pizza?" asked Zara.

"What about you Lewis?" said Brent.

"I really fancy a Mars bar right now!" replied Lewis.

The whole car burst into laughter as they left the Space Centre car park.

Printed in Great Britain
by Amazon

78694567R00072